WOLF IN SHEEP'S CLOTHING

"So you must be a famous gunslick, too, right?"

Longarm chuckled and replied, "I'm too old to be a famous gunslick. You kids are welcome to the title for as long as your luck holds out. The Good Book says it's *swords* men who live by die by, but I reckon they didn't have six-guns back when they were writing the Good Book."

He finished lighting his cheroot, with his left hand, as he added in a weary tone, "I'd assure you I was only a simple working stiff if I wasn't afraid that would encourage you, the way running away from a snarly mutt might. Why don't you just go on back to your own supper and let me enjoy my own? I ain't going to say that again."

They must not have thought he meant that, or perhaps they thought the three of them could safely slap leather on a man who'd been braced for them to try, with his own drawn double-action in his lap all the time, with five rounds of .44-40 in the wheel and the hammer back . . .

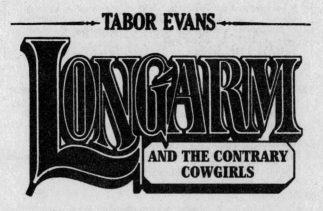

TABOR EVANS

LONGARM

AND THE CONTRARY COWGIRLS

JOVE BOOKS, NEW YORK

This is a work of fiction. Names, characters, places, and incidents either are the product of the author's imagination or are used fictitiously, and any resemblance to actual persons, living or dead, business establishments, events, or locales is entirely coincidental.

LONGARM AND THE CONTRARY COWGIRLS

A Jove Book / published by arrangement with the author

PRINTING HISTORY
Jove edition / June 2002

Copyright © 2002 by Penguin Putnam Inc.

Visit our website at
www.penguinputnam.com

ISBN: 0-515-13383-3

A JOVE BOOK®
Jove Books are published by The Berkley Publishing Group, a division of Penguin Putnam Inc., 375 Hudson Street, New York, New York 10014.
JOVE and the "J" design are trademarks belonging to Penguin Putnam Inc.

PRINTED IN THE UNITED STATES OF AMERICA

10 9 8 7 6 5 4 3 2 1

Chapter 1

The locally unknown outfit broke trail on public land along the north branch of the Wichita a hard hour's ride north of Truscott in the country of Knox, Texas, along about four of a Saturday afternoon in September.

This of itself was not contrary to usual trail herding as it was practiced by Texas riders. It was best to water and graze the herd some by daylight in unfamiliar haunts to let 'em settle down good before sundown, lest they spook after dark over nothing much. But after that the handful of strange riders pushing a modest herd of unusual cows the wrong way struck many a good old boy around Truscott as sort of contrary.

To begin with, the Double H outfit, as it called itself, seemed to be headed the wrong way at the wrong time. Texas beef was druv north to ride the rails to the eastern market by fall. It had no more business being carried southwest *to* Texas than coals had on their way to Newcastle. After that, the herd was made up of contrary cows for a market herd. Brood cows, with nary a steer but many a calf tagging along to slow the drive and make it more complexicated all the live-long-day, if not nightmarish, at many a river crossing.

The she-cows and their offspring, ever' one of 'em, were reported as black-cat-black of the longhorn persuasion, no she-cow or bull, had they had any bull along,

1

sporting near as long a rack of horns as a castrated steer, of course. But as if to make up for the lack of nutless livestock, more than half the Double H riders seemed just a tad young, even for cowboys, and sort of soft and sissy for your *schoolboys* of the *Texican* persuasion.

All of the above was the talk of Truscott by sundown as the gents bellied up to the bar in O'Hara's saloon after supper. For a couple of grubline riders had reported in after an evening visit to that Double H camp, anxious to relate their strange experiences just over the horizon to the north.

They reported they'd been offered coffee with no cake by a crusty ramrod wearing a black ten-gallon Stetson and a Schofield .45-Short. Nobody else but the she-male chuck wagon crew, a mighty contrary notion in itself, had said a word to them. The right handsome boss cook, who came with big blue eyes, ash blond hair and answered to Miss Hilda, had explained they were running low on bisquit dough after their long drive from the Cherokee reserve along the Arkansas line and that nary a scrap of grub had been left over from their early supper. But the riders sizing the outfit up had found her coffee strong enough and she'd confessed it was real Arbuckle brand when they complimented on it. Miss Hilda had seemed more willing to chew the fat than the mean-eyed ramrod in the black hat. So they'd got her to confess the black cows grazing all about were Cherokee stock. Bred from regular high-plains longhorns and black Scotch beef-stock the Civilized Tribe had brung west with 'em along that Trail of Tears they kept pissing and moaning about. That crusty ramrod had suggested they finish up their free coffee and ride before they got anything more from the friendlier Miss Hilda. But Undersheriff Lew Weaver, the law in that stretch of the county, smiled knowingly down at his beer to opine, "I reckon that explains why they seem headed the wrong way with brood stock, then. I've heard good things about them black Cherokee cows, lately. With the country coming out of Grant's Great Depression and President Hayes ending the last of them intolerable Reconstruction Acts, housewives east and west can afford to put better meat on their table with richer gravy for the grits or potatoes, north or south. So that Double H outfit ain't the only ones out to breed their beef up a grade or so without losing the thrifty ways of the original Tex-Mex longhorn. I've heard-tell them black Cherokee longhorns can get by as well on summer-cured short-grass and such water as one finds west of longitude 100° as the genuine and scrawnier North-African beef by way of Spain, then Mexico, then Texas, courtesy of Captain Ewen Cameron and his raiding rangers back in the forties."

Then Lew Weaver sipped some suds before adding in an indulgent way, "Better yet, I'd have heard-tell had anybody west of the Big Muddy stole a whole herd of coal-black cattle. So I'm expecting the rest of you gents to treat any riders from that Double H in a neighborsome way when and if they may ride into town tonight."

One of the grubline riders who'd visited the outfit's night camp piped up with, "I doubt any will. As we was leaving one of the young squirts was bitching to that crusty ramrod about that. Said he didn't have to ride picket 'til midnight and felt he rated a ride into town after so many long days in the saddle. But that ramrod told him, cold and cruel, he could have the earlier shift, advised the kid to circle slow and sing soft until midnight and then, if the kid still felt too horny to sleep, he'd be proud to take down the young rascal's jeans and fuck him unconscious, himself.

The other rider opined, "He sound like he meant it. That ramrod is one hard-cased cuss, even for a trail boss."

Down at the far end of the bar, taking no part in the conversation but listening to every word, lounged Puff Duffy, Silent Ryan and a short stocky Caddo breed they called Chief. Puff was so-called because he did most of the talking and issued the invites when the trio of troublemakers smelled blood in the water. Silent Ryan said little but naturally had to back his pard when good old Puff started a fight. Chief never said a word and found it

3

even easier to get the drop on a pilgrim willing to stand up to louder noises.

None of them said anything at the bar. They'd once made the mistake of starting up with old Lew Weaver and, having survived the older and wiser lawman's suggestion that Caddo slap leather first and save the rest of them a heap of bother, none of them ever had much to say when such a wise old bird might hear them.

They got outside and mounted up in the gathering dusk without too much further discussion. The three of them had just heard-tell there seemed to be one grown man riding herd on a dozen or so sissy boys and a good-looking chuck wagon crew. So the three of them rode, with nary a more thoughtful plan of attack in mind. It was a Saturday night, there was nothing more entertaining to be found in town with that pesky lawman and his infernal deputies on tap, and riders who made sensible plans for their futures were not inclined to wander about in search of trouble.

Riders who knew the three of them better than they knew themselves were of the opinion their three skulls, together, might have the capacity for one mad dog's brain. For like one mad dog, the three of them just added up to vicious sport with anyone they could find alone as they circled in uncertain with those coyote grins of the congenital bully breed.

They'd been gone a perilous time before Lem Hanlin from the hardware saw it was his turn to stand a round of drinks and added with a disgusted snort, "Might have known our Three Musketeers would duck on out about now. Had they stayed, the next round would have been on old Silent Ryan, our vaguely sinister young man with no visible means of support."

Another townee laughed and said, "Heard he got fired during that last roundup for shooting a pony that throwed him. Reckon he's short on pocket jingle and ashamed to say he can't afford to stand a round."

Undersheriff Lew Weaver sighed and muttered, "Curly, go see whether a wall-eyed paint, a buckskin and a chestnut are still tethered out front. It's too early for their bed-time. So what's left?"

As the younger lawman ducked out through the bat-wings someone at the bar asked what Weaver suspected of the bullies of the town.

Weaver grimaced and said, "I wouldn't worry about 'em half as much if I could be sure *what* they might be up to next. Duffy is mostly talk and Chief is just a taga-long with a mean streak. Silent Ryan calls the shots, and I warned him after that last grange dance shoot-out that they'd never sell this child another plea of self-defense, if they could prove they'd been attacked by Kiowa-Apache."

The hardware man nodded soberly and opined, "I thought that poor Mex had as much right as anyone else to 'tend that grange dance, as long as he didn't ask no white ladies to dance with him."

"It was murder, pure and simple. The Mex was alone and unarmed when Duffy invited him to a fistfight and he was dim enough to go outside with the three of 'em," declared Lew Weaver, adding, "I told your chickenshit deputy coroner what I thought of his findings after the pro forma inquest, and I warned Silent Ryan not to pull such shit no more in my county."

Curly came back to report the dangerous trio's ponies missing. So Lew Weaver muttered, "Aw, shit. I'd best ride after 'em afore they gang up on some other young cowboy. Who's riding with me?"

Curly and his two other deputies allowed they would. Nobody else in the place volunteered. Weaver knew it was mostly Silent Ryan most of 'em were afraid of. He snapped a cartwheel down beside his empty beer schooner and growled, "Let's ride, then. No saying how much of a lead they have on us by now!"

The trio of troublemakers had been well on their way before they'd been missed. So Undersheriff Weaver and his three deputies were less than half way to the Double H's night camp by the time Puff, Silent and Chief rode in. The Caddo breed's face was expressionless. Silent was trying to look innocent. Puff was grinning like a shit-eating dog as they dismounted near the night fire by the chuck wagon. There they were greeted by the Double H ramrod of renown, who declared in a fair but firm tone, "We've mostly turned in after a hard day's drive with a view to an early start at sunup. We ain't hiring and the grub's been served for the day. But you gents are welcome to water your mounts and coffee up afore you just take it on back to town."

Puff Duffy protested in a jovial tone, "Now is that any way to greet poor wayfaring strangers in the dark of the night and a long way from home? We figured we might set a spell and jaw with you-all about your contrary ways with cows. How come you ain't herding no *he*-brutes along? Are your trail hands afraid of he-brutes? Is it true what they say about your riders squatting down to piss?"

"Watch that mouth—ladies present," growled the ramrod as the blue-eyed blond they'd heard about came into the firelight with three tin cups and a pot of coffee on a tray.

She was better looking than they had been led to believe. As she moved to serve them, she calmly told Duffy, "We're herding high-grade breeding stock back to our spread on the Staked Plains. Since I see by your outfits that all three of you must be cowboys, I've no call to explain why you don't buy *steers* as *breeding* stock. We have a purebred beef-bull waiting anxious for the arrival of these Cherokee ladies."

Duffy laughed lewdly and said, "Dew Jesus and won't your fandango bull have a lot of fucking cut out for him at the end of this trail?"

The ramrod quietly said, "Carry that coffee out of earshot, Miss Hilda. Our guests just proved they ain't here for coffee, and now the three of them mean to remount and ride out by the time I count to ten if they know what's good for 'em."

None of the troublemakers appeared to be moving anywhere. Puff purred, "Why don't you tell us what's good for us, Pilgrim?"

6

The ramrod replied, "One. They call me Junior Brewster. Two. I hail from Tennessee by way of West Texas and I rid with Hood's Brigade during the war. Three. Four. Five."

"When you get to ten, feel free to take off your boots and try for twenty on your toes," suggested Puff Duffy.

By this time, naturally, Silent Ryan and the Caddo breed had spread out either way, as if to get out of the line of fire, or to trap the lone ramrod in their cross fire no matter who he might choose to draw against.

Then Junior Brewster no longer stood alone on his side of the tricky firelight. He'd been joined there by a shorter, slighter figure in a black-trimmed slate-gray charro outfit and flat-topped Spanish hat, along with a brace of double-action .38 Colt Lightnings.

Without any further ado, the second Double H rider called out in a clear contralto voice, "Six. Seven. Eight. Matt and Frieda, get on out to the herd and help Wilma hold it by the water! We're liable to have some noise over this way any minute!"

Silent Ryan gasped aloud, "Hold on! No fair! That ain't no sissy boy! That's a hard-eyed *gal* standing shameless in some old Mexican's pants!"

The target of his indignation demurely suggested, "I have the big mouth and the breed covered, Junior. Watch Smiling Boy to your left, and now it's nine, and now it's ten, God bless us every one!"

Then all hell broke loose as Herta Zimmer of the Staked Plains drew and fired both her six-guns as one to drop Duffy with a round of .38-30 over the heart, while Chief went down with another just under his own. Then Silent Ryan grabbed for the stars to wail. "Hold on! I never said nothing about fighting no crazy ladies!"

So then, as the bemused Junior Brewster drew but held his fire, the lady Silent Ryan said he hadn't come to fight shot him down like a foamy-mouthed dog whilst cows in the middle distance bawled and one of the other Double H cowgirls called out, "More riders coming in, Boss Lady!"

7

As the gun smoke cleared, with everyone's ears still ringing, the demure but deadly Herta Zimmer smiled wearily down at the three dark forms around the night fire to sigh, "Must I do everything around here myself? Couldn't you see they were looking for trouble no matter what we said or did, Junior?"

Before the mere man could answer, Herta's identical but much more properly dressed twin, Hilda, reappeared in the firelight in her gingham skirts and apron, packing a Greener ten-guage of her own as she protested, "They might have backed down. I had them covered from the dark had they failed to, and now look what you've gone and done to give our show away, *meine wutschnaubend Schwester*!"

A distant male voice called out, "Hello the camp! I'd be Undersheriff Lew Weaver and I do so hope them shots we just heard were all in fun!"

Junior Brewster called back, "Come on in, then. You just missed all the fun. Three saddle tramps started up with me just now and lost!"

Then he urgently told the twin sisters he worked for, "Let me do the talking and don't spoil my brag unless you want to see your sub-rosa move to upgrade your herd on the front pages of every newspaper west of the Big Muddy! We might be able to sell what just happened as another dim-witted showdown if I take the credit and plead self-defense. Do either of you sweet young things need to be told how any reporter worth his salt might describe a shoot-out betwixt a cowgirl and three cowboys, Indians or he-men of any description?"

Chapter 2

Six hundred miles away by rail, Deputy U.S. Marshal Custis Long of the Denver District Court enjoyed a much more pleasurable Saturday night with a York State widow woman who'd always wanted to see the wild wonders of the West. He'd assured her she had nothing to fear for her reputation when they checked into the Tremont House as one C. L. Crawford and wife. The room clerk was in on the joke, and Longarm, as he was better known to the room clerks of Denver, chose the alias because it was easy to remember. Dr. Crawford Long had come up with painless surgery just in time for a war they were giving in Longarm's teens. It would serve Reporter Crawford, of the *Denver Post*, right if talk of the town shacked him up with visiting widow women after all the bodacious lies Crawford'd printed about Denver's own answer to the late James Butler Hickok, cuss his fevered brow and careless imagination.

But the trouble with inside jokes was that other insiders tended to catch on to them. So there the two of them were, bare of ass and slugabed of a Sunday morn, on the top floor, with a Don't Disturb on the outside doorknob when, along about nine, as they were going at it dog-style, there came an imperious pounding on the hotel door. The no-longer-young-but-still-shapely widow woman was off his dick and under the bed, hissing at him like a stomped-on

9

snake as he drew his six-gun from where he'd hung it over the bedpost. He calmly hissed back, "They can't know who *you* are, sweet hips. I'm the one who got too cute downstairs with the hotel register. So hold my place whilst I find out who it is and what they want."

Padding over to the door on his bare feet with his gun in hand, and knowing from sad experience how few underpaid chambermaids could read Don't Disturbs in any lingo, he eliminated that first notion first by calling out, not unkindly, "*Quien es y que quieres? No queremos servicio de habitación, gracias.*"

A familiar male voice guffawed, "I'm not here to offer you room service, you randy cuss. Open the door and let me in."

Longarm snorted, "Not by the hair of my chinny-chin-chin. You go get your own gal, Henry!" as he realized their early morning caller was the pallid youth who played the typewriter at their office in the nearby federal building. He didn't ask how Henry had tracked him down on his day off, or who'd sent him. But Henry still said, "The boss wants you up to his house on Capitol Hill, as of two hours ago. He's building up a serious head of steam. Don't ask me why. I only work here. Just kiss her good-bye and get yourself up yonder as soon as you can or sooner. I'm headed back right now. Marshal Vail is going to cloud up and rain all over both of us if I beat you there by five minutes!"

Longarm said he was on his way and then, as he heard Henry moving off down the hall, he hunkered down by the bed to peer under it and chortle, "Come out, come out, wherever you are. It was just an old boy from the office, offering me some overtime. Were you telling me true, before he knocked, when you said you were fixing to come?"

As he helped her out from under the bed, she wryly allowed she felt hot as an oyster in an ice bucket, and when he spread her across the rumpled bedding to love her up some more, she suggested he just go ahead and enjoy himself whilst she planned lunch.

He knew that she knew, being a widow of some experience, that next to a fire hose shooting cold brine, there was nothing more cooling to a man's ardor than a suggestion he just go on and enjoy his fool self in the cold cuts of a good sport gritting her teeth, as she lay there wishing he'd just get it over with.

Hence it came to pass that Henry had only been back at the Vail house on Sherman Street a quarter hour when Longarm joined them in the kitchen, where the somewhat older, shorter, and way dumpier Marshal William Vail sat at a kitchen table wreathed in cigar smoke whilst his long-suffering old woman rustled coffee and cake for all hands.

Longarm knew better than to ask her permit to light one of his own three-for-a-nickel cheroots in self-defense. Mrs. Vail kept after old Billy about those expensive but pungent black stogies he chewed cold whenever they went out. Longarm set his coffee-brown Stetson aside and unbuttoned his tobacco tweed frock coat to let his cross-draw holster hang free as he sat astride a kitchen chair to wait, silent as a polite Arapaho, for the fuming Billy Vail to make his his point.

The older lawman might have managed to talk, drink, eat and smoke at the same time, had not his wife warned, "William, dear, for the love of Our Lord and the front of that vest . . ."

So Billy Vail set his coffee and cake aside to talk with that stogie betwixt his teeth as he demanded of his senior deputy in the tone of one who knows, "How come you never filed a report on that gunplay down along the Camp Weld road the other day?"

Henry excused himself and left the kitchen. So Longarm felt no call to ask who'd told on him as he washed some marble cake down to casually reply, "Wasn't worth no report. Wasn't no gunplay. Just had to teach some manners to a couple of country boys, Boss."

To which Billy Vail replied, "One of whom has a father who plays poker with friends in high places. Tell me about it."

Longarm shrugged and helped himself to another forkful of cake to regather and sort the facts of the matter before he explained, "It was Thursday morn. Had them papers to serve for Judge Dickerson, down Littleton way. Caught a ride aboard a southbound mail coach, served the writ afoot in town without no trouble, so I was waiting out front of the Overland in Littleton when these two sort of drunk and happy waddies came out of the saloon next door to climb aboard a surrey, whooping about the time they meant to have that afternoon up Denver way. So I naturally asked if they had room in the back for another good old boy bound for Denver. They said they did. So I got in. I wasn't looking for trouble. Just a free ride."

"You found trouble enough for the both of us," said Vail. "Go on." Longarm shrugged down more coffee and cake, thinking back, then he explained, "Things started friendly enough. We rode north for a spell, swapping lies about the action along Larimer Street of an evening. Have you ever noticed that no matter where you might belly up to the bar, you're assured you should have been there just a year or so back, when things were really wild?"

Vail snorted smoke out his nostrils like a bull fixing to charge and declared, "Things got wild enough Thursday morning on the Camp Weld road! That Collins kid's daddy wants you sent to the lunatic asylum for going so *loco en la cabeza* on his only son and heir!"

Longarm protested, "I wasn't the one acting crazy as we drove up from Littleton. I was sober. I don't know which of 'em might have been named what. They were both tedious . . . Never mind, with a lady of quality present. The one driving the team was bad enough. That one sitting up front beside him as I rode in the back was talking dirty enough to disgust a traveling salesman and I was sorry I had met up with 'em by the time we came to this nester gal of sixteen or so, walking home from Littleton with a barefoot brother of eight or less. Turned out she'd just taken him to a dentist in town to have a toothache pulled. The drunk in the left-hand seat ordered the driver to stop and the kids, dumb as me, accepted the offer of a ride on home. So they put the barefoot boy in the back

12

with me and had the gal sit up front betwixt them."

Vail growled, "*Cherchez la femme*, eh? I might have known there was a woman in the picture. Cattle King Collins says you pistol-whupped his growing boy!"

Longarm silently apologized to Henry, wherever he'd gone, as he snorted, "That raggedy nester gal was too young and innocent to call a woman. I tried to point that out when the Collins kid, I suspect, put an arm up along the seat-back and tried to kiss her. The girl said she wanted to get out, and her little brother was starting to cry, as well, when I declared that was just about enough. So they ordered me and her kid brother to get out whilst the three of them drove off across open range to have some fun."

Longarm sipped some coffee and added, "That's about all there was to the story, Boss. When they reined in to put me and the girl's little brother out, I had a better notion, and backed it up with my .44-40 and the tone one uses directing a road gang. I never had to whup neither one of 'em. The driver gave them reins to the gal as I, ah, suggested. The other did say something about his daddy being a big shot, now that I think back. But they got out and I climbed over the back of the seat with no further ado to take the reins and drive on."

He thought back, nodded, and continued, "That's about all she wrote. I drove the two nester kids on up the road to their homestead. When they invited me inside for coffee and cake I declined, polite, so's I could drive on to Denver by the time the owner of the surrey could walk back to town and raise some hue and cry. Got in without further incident around noon. Watered the team at a public trough and left 'em to be found in front of the Union Station, where I assume they must have been. So what's all the fuss about?"

The lady of the house served Longarm another slab of cake and refilled his cup as she told her husband, "I think Custis behaved as a perfect gentlemen, for once, down along the Camp Weld road."

Billy Vail grimaced; not a pretty sight with that soggy

13

length of rope smouldering so close to his lips as he replied, "I'd have done the same. But I ain't the one in dutch with the county machine. So, come Monday morning, it might be best if Sir Galahad, here, was out of town for an indefinite time."

Longarm knew Henry had told their boss where he'd caught up with him when Vail asked, knowingly, "You hadn't made important plans for the rest of the day, I hope?"

Longarm shrugged wistfully and replied, "Not *important* plans, I fear." For those last cutting remarks by a cooled-off widow woman as she dressed was nobody else's beeswax and making up with a pissed-off gal could be as much trouble and a heap less fun than starting from scratch with another.

Vail said, "*Bueno*. I sent Henry to my study to long-hand your travel orders. He'll file a copy. You'll want to burn yours once you have 'em committed to memory. With any luck you're going to get yourself killed on this mission. But we don't want to make it easy for a killer known only as the Twisted Sister."

"Are we talking about some murderous she-male?" asked Longarm with a puzzled smile.

Vail shrugged and replied, "We can't say. A dying Dutchman down to the Staked Plains wrote the name of his dry-gulcher in the dust he was bleeding his life's blood into. He writ it in High Dutch. I ain't about to try and pronounce what he scrawled, but Texas lawmen of the same persuasion translated it as Twisted Sister and there've been other whispers about the same down yonder. Some say the High-Dutch term can translate as what we might call a fairy or a queer. On the other hand, the killer could be a woman with a warped mind."

"I wish there were fewer outlaw gals," sighed Longarm, adding in a bemused tone, "You want me to head for the Staked Plains and see if I can cut the trail of a he, she or it who's prone to dry-gulching literate Dutchmen, Boss?"

Vail said, "No. I want you to hop a highballing combination Henry can tell you about down to Knox County,

14

Texas, and then buy, not hire, a mount of your own to ride up to Truscott, where they are holding a trail boss on a multiple manslaughter charge. He's innocent. We're working with Knox County and the Texas Rangers on this case. You're not to contact any local lawmen when you drift into Truscott, dressed in that faded denim outfit you fancy when you think we ain't looking. At the one hotel in Truscott fit for a lady, you'll find the Zimmer twins, Hilda and Herta, checked in to work on getting their foreman out so's they can drive on home to their own little corner of the Staked Plains, where a range war's brewing to make the recent Lincoln County War down New Mexico way seem a Sunday-go-to-meeting-on-the-green. Being it's Texas and Washington's allowed the rangers to return to full power, they can hold that arrested ramrod at least a few more days against any writ two out-of-towners, however rich, can wrangle."

He removed the stogie from his mouth long enough to wet his whistle with his own coffee before he continued, "The way we hear it, them Zimmer twins, second-generation High Dutch like most of the victims and possibly that Twisted Sister in the flesh, snuck over to the Indian Territory with a crew of other cowgirls, dressed like men, to buy and road-brand over a hundred head of prize Cherokee breeding stock to be serviced by a blue ribbon Black Angus they'd already bid high on at a sheriff's auction. Need I count the ways a saddle tramp like you might convince even one anxious cattle queen he'd once been a top hand along the Chisholm Trail?"

Longarm pointed out that the Chisholm Trail had recently been shut down.

Vail beamed and said, "My point exactsome. Hearing rumors and counter-rumors of trouble brewing on the recently thrown open Staked Plains, the rangers sent some old boys in to invesitgate, wearing a star or undercover. The ones asking officious questions as paid-up rangers got evasive answers from a tight-knit, mostly High Dutch and wide-scattered populace. As late as '77 them Staked Plains was held agin' all comers by the Quill Comanche and they call 'em the Staked Plains because they still stand high and dry above those palisade cliffs and canyon walls the Comanche used so long whilst playing tag with our cavalry. So there's many a lonesome stretch made for dry-gulching and not one of the lawmen who've rid in on the *sneak* to see if they could find out what's going on have ever rid back out. A couple have been found dead alongside the trail. Others have just vanished, as if the goblins got 'em. We're talking sort of gently rolling grasslands, crazy-quilted by sunken tree-lined canyons and draws, recently settled by mostly Texas-Dutch who come over at the same time as the Texas-Irish, without making as big a fuss about it. Some say that once you get to know them, Dutchmen can be more clannish agin' outsiders than your average Irishman."

Longarm nodded and said, "I've met up with both breeds in my day. You want me to see if I can wrangle a job with them short-handed Texas-Dutch cowgirls and see if can sort of drift into the Staked Plains with a local outfit, passing for a harmless trail hand. So what am I looking for when and if I manage?"

Billy Vail replied, simply, "If we knew, we wouldn't have to send you, would we? Might be serious. Might be no more than Wild West taproom talk. But *somebody* down yonder has been *killing* folk and it's about time we found out who and why. Hear?"

16

Chapter 3

Thanks to that pesky Reporter Crawford of the *Denver Post*, Longarm had to board that afternoon train out of Denver in violation of current civil service dress codes and packing some unusual baggage.

Those outlandish tales about him in the papers had included all too true descriptions of his usual duds and army saddle. So whilst he'd stuck with his well busted-in Stetson and low-heeled cavalry boots, he'd dressed in the hickory shirt with bandana, blue denim jeans and bolero jacket of a gent more interested in herding cows.

Breaking in new weaponry could be more risky than starting out with a new hat and boots. But heaps of riders favored the combination of a popular Colt .44-40 and Winchester '73, chambered to fire the same S&W center-fire, rounds. He still packed his six-gun cross-draw in the same familiar gun rig. His Winchester booted as handy to the off cantle of the sturdy but well-scuffed double-rig roping saddle he'd borrowed from his pals at the livery near the Union Station to tote his rump and regular saddle bags, once they all got to Texas.

That wasn't easy. Thanks to Texas choosing the wrong side in the war and getting itself reconstructed for a dozen years or more, Texas had been sort of behind the door when railroad construction contracts were being given out. So it was tougher to cover all those wide-open spaces than it might have been, and Longarm had plenty of time to read the typed and handwritten reports Henry had given him, along with a German-English dictionary he'd picked up along the way to his first leg of the trip. You changed trains some to get anywhere *particular* in Texas. "German" was the Latin term the Prussian imperialists had recently sold as the new name of a *Volk*, as they put it, who'd been calling themselves Dutch, or mayhaps *Deutsch*, since before the old-time Romans had decided they were *Germanicae*. Dutch gals Longarm had engaged in pillow talk had explained how that so-called Iron Chancellor, Von Bismarck, had worried Dutch folk, High and Low, as he'd got the Indian sign on all those smaller Dutch-speaking lands to rename them the German Empire and inspire heaps of emigration with his new income tax and military draft. As many Germans as Irish had crossed the main ocean to start over as new Americans, and some Texas Rangers said to keep that in mind as one investigated a heap of trouble brewing on the Staked Plains of late.

Plenty of Dutch, High and Low, had been in the original thirteen states, of course, along with tolerable numbers of Irishmen and most everything else, red, white or black. But the Irish potato famine and political riots of a Dutch-speaking stretch of Central Europe had dumped shiploads of less digestable furriners on the shores of an already well-settled Atlantic Coast, upsetting the "Old Families" who sometimes found themselves outnumbered in their own neighborhoods.

Rabble-rousers of the Know-Nothing party had stirred things hotter by predicting Americans of the future were more likely to have Irish or German blood than "Real American." By which they hardly meant Algonquin or Zuni, of course.

Hence some said, and you had to keep an open mind, that the Lincoln County War in New Mexico had been partly inspired by the mutual suspicions of the Irish-Catholic Murphy-Dolan faction and their not only Protestant but foreign-born rivals, Tunstall and McSween. The

18

two factions had mean-mouthed, mean-tricked and slaughtered one another for no better reasons anybody else had been able to see.

Of course, the Kid, riding for Tunstall, had been of Irish blood and there'd been Protestants riding under Dolan for Murphy. But you needed an excuse for a war before it could get confusing and out of control. Texas and the federal government, which would be stuck with the cost of sending in troops, wanted to nip trouble in the bud down on the Staked Plains.

Holing up in a compartment lest anyone read over his shoulder, the federal lawman saw how folk in and about the trail town of Sulfur Draw, deep in the heart of the newly opened Comanche hunting grounds, had moved in from hungier range in three post-war waves. Tex-Dutch Lutherans, or *lutherisch* as they put it, had horned in on Anglo-Mex nesters, followed by more Scotch-Irish Texans and, more recently, by more old-timey immigrants from Papist Austria. The Scotch-Irish found it as tough to savvy one breed as the other, and lumped them together as Dutchmen. The two breeds of Dutch only agreed to find this insulting as hell.

The earlier bunches had seemed to get along on a live-and-let-live basis. Trouble had commenced once the second bunch of Dutchfolk had claimed such grass and water as the land office had on tap.

The barn burnings and dry-gulchings had started shortly thereafter.

Nobody else seemed to know how come, or who might be most at fault. Both tight-knit immigrant factions seemed willing to do business and socialize some with their new Anglo, Mex or Indian neighbors, the Quill Comanche having been replaced by Caddo. So it was thanks to their neighbors the law knew toad squat about the feud abuilding betwixt old and new Dutch who refused to talk to one another, or the law, about why.

Longarm read some for an honest working man off a hard-scrabble West-by-God Virginia hill farm. So, knowing that folk who didn't know their history were likely to

relive it, he'd read enough history books to know few if
any religious wars had really been inspired by sincere de-
sires to get on the good side of any god. Religious or
other differences made it easier for leaders to stir folk up
for a grudge fight. But in the end the true motive was
most often land or loot on the part of one side or the other.

So somebody, down Sulfur Draw way, was out to profit
from fuzzy reports of night riding, night shooting and
mysterious fires, with nobody seeming to rightly know
what happened to that old Otto, Fritz or Franz who used
to come into town more often. A very few killings had
been reported by the county law, a Scotch-Irish sheriff
and his deputies. The ranger's surmises Longarm was
reading never said so, but he suspected their Sheriff Armstrong had won by default when neither Dutch faction
would vote for the other's candidate.

At any rate, Armstrong's riders had come upon dead
or dying Dutch from both sides and had little or no luck
pinning the deed on anybody until that one dying Dutchman, an Austrian herding sheep a good ways off on open
range, had scrawled "Twisted Sister" in the dust as he lay
dying. In point of fact he'd scrawled *Zerziehenschwester*,
which had likely taken longer, and his killer would have
erased the message with a boot heel had she ridden closer,
if it had been a she.

High-Dutch speakers Sheriff Armstrong had questioned
had translated the name, or term, having no other light to
shed on the subject. The paperbound dictionary Longarm
consulted confided that *zerziehen* could mean twisted, dis-
torted, spoiled or disappearing. But when you applied it
to *Schwester*, or sister, you were most often talking dirty
about a sex pervert, he or she. When a Dutchman implied
you were a *Warmbruder* he meant you were his warm
brother, or asshole buddy.

Longarm had bought the book with such talk in mind.
He knew from his limited Border Mex and a few Indian
dialects that cusswords, as such, were almost unique to
the English language. You could call a Mex a son of a
she-male dog and he might not like it, but Spanish had

no word with the sting of "bitch" while *mierda*, or "shit," could be used in mixed company as freely as "manure" could in English. You had to string your words together clever to cuss in Border Mex. You could say "eat shit" or "little balls of shit" to show you were not being polite. But you called a Mex a son of a whore instead of a son of a she-male dog if you were looking for a fight.

He wanted to memorize such High-Dutch notions before he got rid of all his reading material with down-home vulgarity in mind. For whilst he had no hope of passing for a recent Dutchman he might get by as third or fourth generation who'd forgot the mother tongue of his grandfolk if he still "remembered" just a few down-home phrases. He knew hardly any Irish-Americans could ask their way to the outhouse in Gaelic, but he'd yet to meet an Irishman who didn't know *Pog mo muc!* meant "kiss my pig," whilst Tex-Mex hands who'd forgot their Spanish still applied *chingado* or "fucking" to most anything they couldn't get to work right.

He saw you said *Ach, zo!* a lot and *Zum Teufel*! or "to the devil" with anything or anybody who pissed you. But as in the case of Spanish or Gaelic, as he'd been assured by Irish eyes with dirty grins, you had to use some imagination to insult a Dutchman, save for one easy insult Longarm meant to remember, since it seemed to top all others, was issued as an invite to a saber duel, and was duck-soup simple to remember.

The grammar section of the handy dictionary warned anyone unsure of the lingo to never, ever, refer to a stranger as *du*, which might translate as "thee" if English still used such delicate distinctions.

A Dutcham trying to be polite or show some respect said *Sie* for "you," polite, and referred to servants, livestock and *very* close kith and kin as *du*! So the insult was obvious. If a *du* wasn't a close pal or a member of your family, he was your kiss-my-pig inferior and what did he have to say about *that*?

The one exception to the rule was the danger of referring to any *gal* you happened to be in bed with as *du*, because that constituted a proposal of marriage. Dutch whores were referred to as *Sie* because a Dutchman only called his wife or kinswomen *du*.

There was more complexicated horseshit about plural address, formal or familiar, but Longarm had what he'd been looking for and decided not to risk pronouncing words such as *Schweinhund*, or cross betwixt a hog and a dog, as he tried to pass for an out-of-work trail hand called Kruger, Wolfgang Kruger, whose pals along the Chisholm Trail called Wolfboy. According to the little the rangers knew about the feuding faction on the Staked Plains, the Zimmer twins stuck in Truscott with that herd were English-speakers of the older Dutch Lutheran faction. Longarm didn't know enough about that particular Protestant sect to risk such a whopper. But he'd noticed in his wide travels that Protestants in general tended to gang up on Papists, and he recalled enough Sunday School from his boyhood to get by as a sort of lapsed Protestant in general.

So he worked on such notions in his head as he rode many a weary mile by rail aboard more than three lines, taking close to twenty-four hours to arrive in the county seat of Benjamin, a hard day's ride south of Truscott.

He'd gotten rid of incriminating papers before changing to that last train. It was too late in the afternoon to ride for Truscott aboard a strange mount. So he toted his roping saddle up the way to a livery owner and horse trader he'd been warned about. The late Texas sun made his heavily laden saddle even heavier, and the ponies in the back corral were huddled in the meager shade of some tall but wilted cottonwoods as the gnome in charge greeted him with an offer to marry his sister if that was the only way they could be friends.

Longarm draped the borrowed saddle over a corral rail to reply he was in the market for most anything that could carry him and his gear, adding, "I don't want to marry it. I ain't even out to work cows with it. I'm riding the grub-line a long ways from home and the poor old nag I got this far aboard gave out on me this morning and left me, as you see, afoot as well as damn near broke."

The older man asked how much he'd gotten for the carcass and hide of his foundered mount. Thinking fast on his feet, Longarm replied in a desperately casual tone, "Sold her alive but plum wore out to this nester many a dusty mile to the south. Said he was a gambling man in the market for a saddle bronc, if she ever recovers. They served me coffee and cake, at least. Barely got enough for old Nell to spend on a square meal and a flop for the night."

The horse trader shrugged and said, "I might let you have yonder roan with white stockings for thirty-nine dollars."

Longarm snorted in disbelief and replied, "That's a polite way to say forty dollars, friend. But I fail to see forty dollars worth of horseflesh in your whole remuda. I might give you ten for that swaybacked paint next to the crippled roan."

The old crook grinned boyishly, enjoying the game with a man who seemed to know his onions, and declared, "That paint is a cutting horse worth every dime of fifty dollars. Since you seem so picky about that one mismatched and darker hoof on the roan, I'll come down to nineteen dollars for her."

"Done," said Longarm, seeing it was hot as hell's hinges, and he was on an expense account. So the trader laughed, said, "Aw, you're no fun!" and they shook on it.

Longarm handed over a twenty-dollar double eagle and allowed the extra dollar was all he meant to give if they'd have the roan ready for him, there, next morning. He added, "I expect her to be watered well, fed enough for a morning's effort, and wearing this here saddle and bridle. No offense, but I mean to tote my saddle gun and possibles over to the hotel with me."

They shook on that, as well, and Longarm headed for a hotel he'd spotted across from the railroad stop. He naturally noticed the kid tagging along after him. The squirt had been seated on the steps of the livery's side door whilst he'd been dealing with the owner. It was a free country, and the kid didn't seem to be wearing any hardware a man with a Winchester cradled over his saddlebags had to be worried about.

Longarm checked into the hotel. The kid stayed out on the walk, if he hadn't gone on home. A man on the prod had to avoid leaping to conclusions about strangers just headed the same general direction along a public thoroughfare.

As his eyes adjusted to the darkness of the dinky lobby of that trail town hotel, he saw the room clerk shoving the register his way was a scrawny little sparrow who'd likely been a looker in her day, damn time's cruel teeth. She said they'd hire him a corner room on the east side, shaded from the afternoon sun, for six bits. He was too hot, bothered and hungry to argue. He asked if they had their own restaurant. She said he'd have to go next door to the Greek's and wondered aloud where their fool bellhop had gone to play with his fool self.

Longarm read the number on his key tag and said, "Never mind, Ma'am. I can find my way and I've carried by baggage this far."

She didn't seem to care. But as he turned from the desk a dimly visible figure rose from its lobby seat by a paper palm tree to say, "I'd be proud to give you a hand with your saddlebags, Longarm. You look like you've been drug through the keyhole backwards and what in blue blazes are you doing down here in Texas this afternoon?"

Chapter 4

Once he'd recognized the ranger he'd worked with on an earlier case, miles away, Longarm could only reply, "They sent me down here undercover, or they thought they had, Sergeant Culhane."

The somewhat older and nearly as tall Texan calmly replied, "In that case, you're still undercover. Miss Prudence, here, would never kiss and tell. She was just now fixing to point some suspected owlhoot riders out to me, when and if they come back to this hotel."

The once-pretty Miss Prudence sighed and said, "I swear, there's never a dull moment behind this desk. When married men who ought to be ashamed of themselves aren't checking in or out, we seem get paid assassins or . . . Not that *Longarm* I read about in the *Police Gazette* a spell back?"

Longarm modestly replied, "It was all a big fib, reprinted from Colorado headlines without a particle of truth to them, Ma'am. I've yet to shoot anybody just for shooting out some streetlamps. Those four waddies in Fort Collins had just robbed a federal post office and I asked them, nice, to rein in and surrender peaceful."

She marveled, "It was still four against one and we've never had anyone *famous* as a guest here, before!"

Longarm said, "I ain't famous, Ma'am. I'm a lawman trying to work my way into uncertain surroundings, like a worm wriggling into a rotten apple on the sneak, see?"

She assured him, "Wild horses couldn't drag your secret from these old wrinkled lips of mine!"

He gallantly replied, "Aw, you ain't so wrinkled as you are *well ripened*, Ma'am," knowing that was no way to insult any lady.

So she called him a fool, blushing fit to bust, and then Longarm and his ranger pal crawfished back in deeper shadow to talk serious a spell.

Longarm told Culhane what he thought he was up to. The ranger told him, "You're fixing to wind up dead or just as dumb as ever. I ain't on that case. But I've heard talk about that feud abuilding over to the Staked Plains. Lawmen have gone in, as lawmen, to enjoy a runaround from settlers who don't know or won't say what's going on. Lawmen who went in undercover have never come back alive. We've no idea who to blame, on either side. We've no idea who's calling the shots on either side. That rider they call the Twisted Sister, if he or she exists, could be riding for either side, or nobody at all. Half a dozen men from both Dutch factions and a couple of Scotch-Irish have been backshot by a person or persons unknown. If it wasn't for all them killings and some burned out barns and slaughtered livestock, we'd write the shithouse rumors as no more than shithouse rumors. There's nothing we can put a hand on in the way of a sensible motive."

Longarm said, "Hadn't heard about slaughtered stock. Your turn."

Culhane shrugged and said, "I told you I was on this other case. I heard-tell somebody mean as hell has taken to ripping range stock and stabled horses open with a bowie in the dark of night, leaving them alive and bawling with their guts hanging out."

"Now that does sound twisted!" Longarm decided, adding, "But farther along, as the old hymn suggests, we may know more about it. Tell me about these owlhoot riders staying in the same hotel with me this evening."

The ranger said, "They may not show. I got to wait and see. We got the tip from Miss Prudence, yonder. She reads wanted fliers as well as the *Police Gazette*. I suspect she was left at the alter by a badman, or a lawman. Seems to know the life stories of most ever' man who's ever strapped on a six-gun west of the Big Muddy. Some of her tips have panned out, though. She must have a right tidy bank account by now. The three she described to us this morning answer to a notorious trio they call the Catlin gang. Dick Catlin, his kid brother, Donald, and a squirt called Jack Frost. Last name's really Froman, but who listens? He seems to tag along to make it the usual three. Ain't it a caution how trouble comes in threes? I doubt I was certain why boys and girls were different when I learned you might not have trouble with a lone stranger, two strangers were often as not just looking for innocent fun, whilst *three*, nine times out of ten, were out looking for *trouble*."

Longarm nodded soberly and said, "Like those three Elroy Brewster Junior was arrested for shooting up Truscott way. How much longer can they hold him, seeing he never really shot a soul?"

Culhane shrugged and said, "Can't say. Had I known anything before you told me about it, I'd have never said your name in public, just now. Why do you reckon it's usually three hardy-hars you have to worry most about? I've had two old boys and four old boys pass by me without comment, many a time. But when you meet up with three there's often one wise-mouth in the bunch who just has to say something cute to you."

Longarm had noticed that, too. He suggested, "One gent playing a lone hand could be looking for most anything. Two pals riding to town together are most often looking to get laid and gals with the same events in mind tend to travel alone or in pairs. You hardly ever see three *gals* palling around together. No two women can resist saying something snotty about a mutual pal who just went to take a piss. So they feel safer with just one pal they can ask to go along to the outhouse with 'em."

The ranger nodded sagely and decided, "Makes sense. I knew that, as soon as you pointed it out. One gent might

27

meet up with one gal. Two gents might wind up with a pair of chummy gals. Three is a piss poor number for hunting gals, but handy for starting up with other men hunting alone or in pairs. Before Miss Prudence told us they'd stayed here last night, we'd got it off another branch of the grapevine that they'd been heard in the club-car of an eastbound train, making war talk about some Texas gun who needed to be taken down a peg. I should have mentioned that the Catlin Gang hails from New Mexico."

Longarm made a wry face and muttered, "I know the breed. Damned if I savvy why they think it's likely to make them one lick smarter, prettier or even richer to gun someone more famous as a gunfighter. But what the hell, we'd both be out of a job if everybody was smart as us about gunplay. I got to put this shit in my room and get some grub in my gut lest I commence to brouse this paper palm tree."

They both rose to shake on that and part friendly. Longarm went upstairs to drape his rifle boot and saddlebags over the foot of the bedstead and lock up again, his way.

His way was to shove a match stem under the bottom hinge of the freshly locked door, where nobody might notice it, picking the lock.

By the time he got back down Sergeant Culhane had rejoined Miss Prudence at the desk. He told Longarm, "My own gut's agrowl and in the off-chance those owl-hoots who never checked out proper come back to pay for another night, Miss Prudence, here, ought to be able to tell us which room they might be in, when we get back."

The elderly reader of the *Police Gazette* seemed thrilled by such an opportunity. So the two lawmen went next door, blinking in the dazzle of the afternoon sun and then blinded by the sudden plunge back into the dim light of the Greek restaurant.

So Longarm couldn't say how much he admired the waitress working for the Greeks as she assured them the blue plate special consisted of roast beef, mashed potatoes

28

and sparrow grass. Longarm said he'd have his steak rare, smothered in chili con carne with a fried egg atop it all. Sergeant Culhane allowed he'd have the same. They got to talk in circles about the cases they were on as they consumed a not-bad early supper. Then they polished off some chocolate cake with extra coffee and headed back to the hotel.

Miss Prudence allowed a teenaged cowboy had come in to hire a flop whilst they'd been eating. But she vowed she hadn't seen hide nor hair of that Catlin Gang and added it was way past checkout time.

Sergeant Culhane said, "They came in by rail, we've got other rangers watching the rail stop. They ain't left town by train. They got to stay somewheres, tonight, if they're still in town."

Longarm asked, "Who says they have to be in town? Like myself, they might have arrived by rail, planning to stay over for one night with a view to riding on at daybreak. It's none of my beeswax. But if I was staked out here in Benjamin for three strangers in town and I couldn't say where they might be in town, I'd want to check with the local liveries and town law for three mounts purchased, hired, stolen or otherwise unaccounted for."

"I wish you hadn't said that," sighed the ranger, turning on one heel to go back outside.

Longarm smiled at the room clerk to confide, "You'll know those three rascals better than me, do they ever return. So I reckon I'll just get on up to my room, now, Ma'am."

She smiled girlishly as possible and murmured, "I know why you don't want to get mixed up in another case, Mr. Longarm! You're here in Texas, undercover, to catch somebody more *serious*, aren't you?"

He chuckled and said, "When you're right, you're right, Ma'am. It's been nice talking to you."

Then he went upstairs to almost try the key in his hired door lock before he spied the match stem on the hall runner instead of under the hinge where it belonged!

Pocketing the key, Longarm drew with his right hand to gingerly try the knob as he cocked his .44-40.

The Colt Model '78 "Frontier" was double-action but fired its first shot a split second faster from the already cocked position, and sometimes a split second was all a man had to work with.

The knob twisted silently. The idjet on the other side hadn't had the wit to lock it after him. So things seemed just short of pure suicide as Longarm crouched low, shoved the door in savagely, and crabbed to one side with his ass against the inside wall as he threw down on the startled-looking kid seated on a windowsill, snapping, "Freeze solid and keep them hands where I can see 'em, Sonny! I ain't going to say that twice!"

The baby-faced cowboy in checked pants and an over-sized shirt of army blue gasped, "Jesus! Do you always enter a room like that?"

Longarm rose to his full considerable height and kicked the door shut behind him as he calmly replied, "Only when I suspect a weasel in the henhouse. Stand up and assume the position against the wallpaper with legs spread and hands flat agin' the pretty flowers."

The kid did as told, but protested, "I'm not armed. Even if I was, I'm not out to cause you any trouble."

"We'll see about that," said Longarm as he moved to pat the young stranger down with his free hand. Aiming the muzzle of his .44-40 polite but firm, he added, "I spotted you giving me the fish eye up by that livery where I bought that pony. I spotted you tailing me this far and the lady at the desk downstairs just told us how you'd checked in, to another room, I'm certain. So what's this all about and . . . How come I feel no concealed weapon but two whole tits under this floppy shirt meant for a cowboy . . . cowgirl?"

She demanded, "How long do you need to fondle that titty to make sure it ain't loaded? That roan you just paid too much for used to be mine. I had to sell her here in Benjamin for train fare home and he only offered me eight dollars for her."

Longarm stepped back to reholster his six-gun as he said, "Things are tough all over, Sis. I never suspected he was selling me a mount for *less* than he paid for it. You can lower your hands and turn around, now. Start at the beginning. What sort of a fix are you in and how do I fit in? I'd be Wolfgang Kruger, by the way. They called me Wolfboy on the Chisholm Trail. I don't mind Wolf. But I've studied on changing my handle to Walt Potter. Kruger translates as Potter in English, as you no doubt knew already?"

She said, "I'd be Florence Ralston from San Antone. They call me Flo or Friskie, and I don't speak Dutch, High or Low. That's another reason I quit the durned old Double H Monday morn to head on home where people have more sense as well as way more fun. No offense, Mr. Kruger, but when you stubborn Dutchmen ain't killing one another you seem out to *work* your fool selves to death!"

He moved to the foot of the bed to fish a bottle from among his possibles as he casually replied, "Heard the Double H had had some trouble up Truscott way. You say you quit without demanding any back pay, Miss Friskie?"

She said, "Hell, of course I got paid for the time I'd put in with that fool herd. Came close to fifty dollars and Miss Hilda was a good sport about it. Her sister, the one as shot those three saddle tramps and blamed it on poor Junior, said I'd have no choice but to go along with them if they held me to our original handshakes. I was there. I seen it all. I told the law in Truscott what really happened. But I couldn't get them to let Junior out of jail."

Longarm moved to the corner washstand and built Maryland rye and branch water highballs for them as he mused half aloud, "This Junior sounds popular with you cowgirls, Miss Friskie."

She shook her head, removing her Stetson to reveal close-cropped auburn curls as she sighed and said, "We never. Junior was forever offering to screw every rider on the crew, him being the only man. But he was just funning. He knew, just as *we* knew, that once you commence to hand out candy, you have to make sure every child at the party gets a fair share."

As he handed her her drink, Friskie sighed and said, "Don't mind saying all that celibacy in the saddle, day after day, riding astride, plays ned with a growing girls's private parts. Then, after things started to get dangerous as well as wearisome, I decided I'd had me enough of the Double H and that crazy Dutch feud over to the Staked Plains. I don't have no dogs in that fight."

That sounded reasonable. She still hadn't told him why she'd been tailing him to the point of trespass. He suggested she finish her drink so's he could pour another as she told him what in thunder she wanted from him.

As he took the empty tumbler back, Friskie moved toward the bed, unbuttoning that loose male shirt as she sighed and said, "I don't want no more, just yet. I had some red-eye earlier and you sure build a strong highball. But you don't have to get me drunk to lay *this* horny cowgirl, Wolfboy. I ain't had any in a coon's age and I have always enjoyed it better when I knew just what I was doing with a man's old organ grinder!"

Chapter 5

Longarm hesitated as long as most healthy young men of common sense might have. But by the time she'd shucked that shirt and demurely suggested he help her shuck her spurred boots, Longarm decided they'd want him to probe such a witness in depth, lest she light out angry without telling him all she knew about that Staked Plains trouble she seemed out to avoid.

Once he'd helped her get her boots off, it seemed only common courtesy to haul her jeans off, and for a gal who'd been passing for a cowboy in them mannish duds, she sure looked she-male, in a right athletic way, as she sat on the bed fumbling with his jeans in turn.

He told her he'd shuck faster if they avoided working at cross purpose. So she lay back, reached for a pillow, and fluffed it to shove under her hard horse-riding hips by the time he'd hung his six-gun on a brass bedpost and flung everything else to the four corners of the hired room.

A man surely felt welcome when a pretty little thing invited him in spread-eagle with a pillow under her rollicking rump.

He was glad she seemed well practiced in such notions. It wasn't true that if they were big enough they were old enough and she might have passed for a fourteen-year-old cherry instead of a somewhat older cowgirl hammered harder and leaner than most eighteen- or twenty-year-olds by hard riding, in or out of bed.

He believed her when she sobbed she hadn't been laid for six or eight weeks. He hadn't had any since Sunday morn and she still came ahead of him, more than once.

This took some purple passion on her part because he came sooner than usual, as most men would have. It would have been impossible as well as rude to pull out of anything that fine. But he naturally had to slow down a mite, at first, so she begged him to let her get on top and show him how it was done.

He let her. He was no fool. But as she impaled herself on his love-slicked shaft, he suggested they had a whole night ahead of them and the sun hadn't set outside as yet.

Without breaking pace Friskie husked, "We won't have until midnight, alas and goldurn it! For I've a night train to catch, coming through here around ten-thirty and I can't afford to miss her!"

He cautiously asked, "Didn't you say you got paid off and sold a personal pony before we ever . . . met up this afternoon, Miss Friskie?"

Then, because he wanted her as far offstage as possible before he went into his act in Truscott, he allowed, "I reckon I could stake you to some traveling money if that's what this is all about."

She slapped his face without missing a pussy-beat, and it hurt some to get slapped by that strong a gal.

He winced and said, "That must have been your roping arm. I'm sorry if I just offended you, Miss Friskie, but what else is left, save for your savage desire for my fair white body?"

She worked her bare feet up under her center of gravity to bounce like a cossack playing stoop tag in a sparrow grass patch as she gasped, "I'll have you know I'm a fucking lady, not a fucking whore who does this for money! I'll allow I've been looking for somebody half as good-looking as you since before I left the Double H drive. But I'm coming some more and you'll have to wait to hear my ulterior motives this afternoon!"

He rolled her over on her back to fork an elbow under either of her knees and inspire her to say "Ah!" as he spread her wide open as her lean hard thighs would stretch. So they both came, hard, and she didn't argue when he just rested in the saddle with his discharged weapon soaking in her pulsing innards.

She confided, "I was curious about who'd buy old Red, and how much that old thief would ask for her. I got more curious when I heard you say you needed a pony to ride on, and that you'd rid in from the south. I knew that meant you'd be riding on to the north, toward Truscott and my former pals with the Double H. I trailed you here to sneak you a secret message. I wasn't expecting *this*. But I confess I was sort of hoping for it!"

He thrust teasingly and replied, "You had the advantage on me. I thought you were a cowboy. Whilst we're on that subject, have you heard-tell of some Staked Plains rider called the Twisted Sister?"

She said, "Sure. That's who they say dry-gulched that sheepherder. The Luthies say she rides for the Cat Lickers. The Cat Lickers say she rides for the Luthies. I don't care. Like I said, I don't have a dog in that fight. My elders hailed from Yorkshire, way back when, and speaking American from the beginning."

He began to move in her conversationally as he said, "I follow your drift. What was the secret message you had for me?"

She asked, "Could we do it dog-style if you want to talk so much whilst you fuck me? It's tougher to talk with a man's weight on my gut."

He agreed he'd noticed dog-style was easier on everybody's wind, and, once they'd adjusted to the right pleasant change of position, Friskie explained, "The message ain't for you. It's for Miss Hilda and the other decent gals up yonder, as well as poor Junior, should they let him out of jail before he's been warned."

"Warned about what?" asked Longarm as he got a good grip on either hip bone to grind his pubis against her tailbone.

She said, "Oh, Lord, that feels so fine! Don't stop! Earlier today, before you trudged into town with your saddle and that swell hard-on, I strolled by that corral to see how poor old Red was doing. Me and old Red have been together a spell. But, as you'll find out, she's seen her best days as a roper and slowed down some."

He demanded, "Is that what you want me to convey to your former boss lady?"

She arched her spine to take him deeper as she replied, "Of course not. I want you to tell them about these three waddies who bought three other ponies, two paints and a buckskin, to ride on up to Truscott. They didn't notice me, hunkered nearby in the shade, when one of them let slip they were headed to Truscott to cut a famous gun down to size. I paid little 'tention at first. Saddle tramps are forever promising to do wonders and eat cucumbers, even when no gals are listening. Then one of them made mention of a man fast enough to take on three quick-draw artists with reps. The one I took for the leader—he sure needed a shave and a bath wouldn't kill him—said that was the whole point of the ride to Truscott. He said he meant to be known as the man who shot the man who shot Duffy, Ryan and Caddo. But it was Miss Herta Zimmer who shot them three saddle tramps last Saturday night and Junior has to be warned three more of the same are after *him*!"

Longarm whistled down at her firm young rump and kept humping as he promised to carry that message north with him. Things were going his way better than planned, not even counting such a swell time in the county seat and Friskie Ralston's hot little ass. For now he had an *excuse* to approach those Zimmer twins with his made up High-Dutch identity!

So a good time was had by all and as she rested some atop the well-warmed covers, Longarm slipped into his duds and boots with neither socks nor underwear to go downstairs and tip the rangers off that the outlaws they wanted were either in Truscott or getting close, by now.

Sergeant Culhane thanked him sincere and Miss Prudence gave him the extra hotel soap and toweling he needed to excuse his absence to Friskie Ralston. He hadn't wanted any gal prone to send warnings to old pals to suspect for one minute that he was in tight with the Texas Rangers or any other lawmen.

They didn't really need extra soap and towels, even after she'd been on top some more. And then, as all things must end, good or bad, she sighed her sated self off him. She meant to have a tub bath down the hall before she changed into fresh traveling duds in her own hired room. Then she left, sedate, to catch that train.

When he offered to tag along and give her a hand with her own saddle and possibles, Friskie laughed dirty and said, "How would it look if you were to stroll arm-in-arm through the moonlight with a pal wearing pants? I don't mean to let anyone I don't know this well guess at my gender before I'm back in San Antone, Wolf. I know this may surprise you. But I got gang-raped one time and it wasn't half as much fun as most gals imagine!"

He didn't dispute her. More than one hard-eyed trail-town whore had assured him of the same thing. So they swapped some spit and parted friendly and it seemed no time at all before he heard the clanging of a locomotive bell, tolling the funeral of a night cut short, as he lay there wide-ass awake, too late to go looking for more action and too early to go to sleep, thanks to all that enforced rest aboard all those tedious trains, with Friskie the only exercise he'd had since Sunday morning.

He'd read all the damned magazines he'd picked up along the way from Denver and it was the wrong time of the month for new issues to be on the stands if he could even find a newsstand open at this hour in a dinky Texas town.

He considered pouring himself a soothing nightcap. He decided not to take up drinking alone at this late date. Too many lawmen, leading unplanned irregular tumbleweed lives, had taken to strong drink with fatal results.

He considered going back to that livery, saddling old

37

Red, and just lighting out early for Truscott. He'd likely arrive just after sunup and ∴ then what?

"I feel for you but I just can't reach you!" he told himself, then added, "Riding a strange trail in the dark and showing up in a strange town with sleep-gummed eyes would sound dumb even if Friskie hadn't just told you that Catlin Gang is somewhere in the vicinity you've got no business riding into like a big old sleepyheaded bird!"

He trimmed his bedlamp and just lay there bare-ass and slugabed, with plenty to think about and knowing that sooner or later he'd get sleepy.

But as he lay there waiting for the sandman, a distant church bell tolled midnight and he knew, wistfully, little Friskie had to be at least fifty miles out of his love life by this time.

Then, as if to prove him wrong, there came a gentle knocking on the door and Longarm sat up, smiling uncertainly, to softly call out, "Friskie?"

The voice the replied was she-male. But it hissed back, "No, and you ought to be ashamed of yourself. But let me in, lest we wake the other guests bragging about your love life!"

He took his gun along, he was no fool, but he wasn't surprised when he cracked the door ajar, made out her mousey hair-bun by the dim hall light, and whispered, "Miss Prudence? I ain't got no love life going on in here. I could let you in and prove it to you but I ain't got no *duds* on, see?"

She shoved the door in, and, as she joined him in the dimmer light from outside, she girlishly gushed, "I like what I see, so far, and I can't wait to see it hard! I just got off duty downstairs and I've been trying not to play with myself since that horny cowgirl left you up here all alone, poor baby!"

Longarm laughed sheepishly and put his .44-40 back in its holster as he suggested, "You've been listening or even peeping through keyholes, eh? Have you got a message for me to take to Truscott, too, Miss Prudence?"

She locked the door before she turned with upraised

elbows to unpin and let fall her long mouse-colored hair. It looked brunette enough by curtain-filtered moonlight as she said, "Let's be honest and call this blackmail. I've been so exited about a famous lawman here in this very hotel with me and when you and that ranger let me in on your manhunt for that Catlin Gang I feared I'd faint from the thrill of it all!"

Not wanting her to guess at his real mission, Longarm moved to fix her a drink as he casually said, "I thought we had us an understanding that nobody else was to share our little secret, Miss Prudence."

She said, "Call me Pru and, oh, this is so exiting. Dark as it may be, I can see you're standing there stark naked. Do you find it awkward that I'm still fully dressed, Mr. Longarm?"

He said, "Not if it don't bother *you*, Miss Pru. I'm more worried about you ruining my mission than I am the state of your dress or mine!"

As he handed her the same tumbler Friskie had been drinking from, she gasped, "Oh, I'll never tell. It's wrong to kiss and tell, isn't it?"

He started to ask a dumb question. The price of her silence seemed obvious, if screwing the old bawd was more likely to buy her silence as inspire her to publish a book about their great love affair.

As she gulped half the drink, set the tumbler aside, and started to undress with the smooth skills of an older woman who'd likely been married a time or more in her day, Longarm reflected that she might just keep her word if he made up to her some, whilst a woman scorned was inclined to be mighty shrill.

But as she flopped across the bedding he'd just rumpled with a way younger gal, tittering silly as all get-out, Longarm wasn't sure he was up to the chore she was demanding of him, right out, without any shame at all, the poor old thing.

He managed not to sigh as he flopped down beside her to take her way older naked body in his arms. But after that, things commenced to to go better for the both of them. For, up close and in the dark, where all cats are gray, old Pru felt way softer than the hard-riding cowgirl he'd had earlier, and she smelled more she-male, too, thanks to that toilet water and likely more recent soap and water.

So he ran a gentle hand down her possibly wrinkled but velvety soft bare skin as they kissed, with more experience on her part. And then his questing fingers parted the moist hair betwixt her trembling and way softer thighs, and damned if he wasn't hard again and damned if it didn't feel swell to delve new surroundings with such a delighted shaft of inspiration!

Chapter 6

She took it as a compliment when it took him so long to come in spite of her gyrations and the magical effects of moonlight on bare tits of any age. He avoided looking closer when he lit a cheroot for them to share as they got their second wind.

Prudence had seemed an odd name for a self-described "silly old widow" until he got to know her better, passing the smoke back and forth as they nestled against the head of the brass bedstead, propped up on the pillows.

Pru hadn't needed the pillows under her more matronly behind as she'd tried to buck him off the bed. He'd hardly needed her confession that she'd always felt "silly" about famous gunfighters.

He didn't ask, and she didn't offer to tell whether she had or had not been giving more than occasional tips to the Texas Rangers. He knew that had she been giving anything this good to Sergeant Culhane, the ranger would have hung around downstairs until she got off desk duty. He knew the best way to assure a bedmate blabbed about slap and tickle would be to swear them to secrecy. She'd already been told he was trying to work undercover. She'd already assured him she wasn't a kiss-and-tell. Like the song said, farther along they'd know more about that. He'd warned Billy Vail back in Denver he was well-known in Texas as a lawman on an undercover mission but his boss had said it was worth a try, since nobody *else* had managed.

As if she'd been reading his mind, Pru snuggled closer to tell him, "I think it was just scandalous of that Calamity Jane to kiss and tell about her and Wild Bill Hickok up in Deadwood, don't you?"

Longarm grimaced and said, "It was more than scandalous. It was an outright lie. Jim Hickok had recently wed a bareback riding circus gal called Augusta Lake when he went looking for the marshal's job in the brand new mining camp of Deadwood and got shot from behind within days of his arrival. It was long after he was dead and buried that Calamity Jane Canary, a Deadwood drunk with no respectable means of support, declared her drab old self the one and only true love of a man she called Wild Bill. His close friends called him Jim. There's no evidence they ever met whilst he was still alive. At the most generous, he might have nodded to the town drunk in passing before he was murdered by another town drunk called Cockeyed Jack McCall."

Pru gasped, "Ooh, did you really know Wild Bill Hickok before they got him? He was such a handsome man and ever so brave!"

Longarm sighed and said, "Knew him to howdy. I reckon he was all right, as long as he was sober. Ned Buntline, the same romance writer to dub Bill Cody 'Buffalo Bill' decided to call Jim Hickok 'Wild Bill.' I've met up with Calamity Jane more often and more recent on account she's still alive and drinking on her rep as Wild Bill's one and only woman. I doubt the widow Hickok approves. In the flesh, there must be two hundred pounds of dumpy flesh that could sure use a bath under the cast-off men's clothes Calamity was wearing the last time I saw her. Her face would pass for a man's as well, and not such a good-looking gent at that. But her story is too repeatable for reporters to question why any man with a younger wife and a rep as a ladies' man would want to kiss such a drab old bawd."

The older naked woman stiffened some against him as

she asked in a desperately uncaring way just how old he thought Calamity Jane might be.

It wouldn't have been polite to guess the two of them might be about the same age. So he snuggled her closer with his free arm to reply, "Hard to say. It ain't the number of birthday candles we blow out as much as the way we spend the days and nights between. White women of quality can still seem young and lovely whilst a harder-living digger squaw the same age turns into a wrinkled hag. They say Calamity Jane was never a looker, even in her salad days as a trail-town hooker. Drinking like a fish and driving freight wagons in all sorts of weather without no face cream or regular washings doesn't do a thing for an already plain face. So she wouldn't be too kissable if she was twenty years younger. She chaws and spits as well."

He took the cheroot from his lips to kiss the part of Pru's hair as he added, "She don't look a tenth as young and pretty as you, if that's what you're asking."

She giggled and confessed, "You knew full well what I was asking and it's just not fair. A man can go a tad gray and wrinkle up some and they call him a *distinguished groom* when he weds a girl young enough to be his daughter. But they call you a dirty old woman if you bed a man twenty years your junior!"

He gallantly lied, "I doubt you have to worry about me being that much younger than you. I'll never see thirty again and you can't be more than, oh, forty or so?"

She grabbed his limp pecker and rolled half atop him as she sighed, "Bless you, my child, and put out that fucking cheroot so we can fuck some more before you turn into a pumpkin and I have to go back to my cinder-sweeping chores!"

By the time he'd snubbed the smoke, she'd kissed her way down his bare belly to prove she knew more French notions than the French tale of Cinderella. She sure blew lively tunes on the French horn and in no time at all she'd inspired him to rise to the occasion and treat her right, dog-style, missionary style and a contortion all her own involving her stroking his hair with one foot whilst she tried to shove a toe up his ass with the other.

Then she proved how prudent she was by allowing she had to get on home lest some late strollers wonder why she was leaving the premises so long after the night clerk had come on, downstairs.

When it developed she lived across town, he casually asked and felt better about that when she assured him she lived alone, save for her cat and goldfish. Horny gals who couldn't stay the night sometimes managed to get a new friend backshot by an old friend they hadn't warned him about.

Seeing the coast seemed clear, for now, Longarm locked up after old Pru and felt justified in sleeping well past sunup in bedding that smelled mighty friendly, now.

After street noises and the screaming whistle of a passing-through express train had him wide awake by eight in the morn, Longarm got his fool self cleaned up, save for a skipped shave, and dressed in fresh underwear under that faded blue denim. Soon, he was on his way, now feeling guilty about such a late start.

As he toted his saddlebags and rifle on downstairs to check out, he learned that Miss Prudence was not on duty, praise the Lord. She'd said her shift was noon to midnight. The middle-aged Irish woman who had the midnight-to-noon shift was younger with bigger tits. But Longarm had long since resigned himself that there was no way to win 'em all.

He found old Red saddled, bridled and raring to go for hours when he got to the livery. So he put himself and his baggage aboard to ride on up to Truscott, hoping his faded duds and chin stubble might make him look more cow and less like law.

Red seemed a spanky pony despite what Friskie had said about her being a tad long in the tooth. Many older horses, like many older folk, started out their days as spanky as ever. So he didn't let her lope as he warned her, "We got better than twenty miles ahead of us, old girl. Slow and steady will take us six or seven hours, but it's more likely to get us there with you still breathing sensible!"

Doing the arithmetic in his head, Longarm figured that with a now-and-then spell of trotting to make up for the hourly trail breaks, he ought to arrive in Truscott by mid-afternoon, Siesta time in Tex-Mex settlements, with nobody much out and about in the more Anglo-Tex town to the north. So with any luck, nobody would notice him at all and anyone who did might take him for a trail-weary cowboy a long way from home and anxious for some beer and gossip.

He felt he'd drawn the picture about right until, near the end of Main Street, he passed a hardware across from another corral, almost rode on, and reined in to mutter, "Of course! What in thunder was I thinking of?"

He dismounted and tethered Red to the hitchrail out front as he confided, "That's what I get from riding for the Justice Department six or eight years. It's been so long since I was *really* a top hand, I'd forgotten the most important detail!"

He went inside to ask the kindly old bird behind the counter for a forty-foot throw-rope, knowing they'd have some in stock. For whilst the outfit supplied a rider with a fresh mount for every shift, no top hand worked with anything less than a personal saddle and his own all-important throw-rope, or *lariat*, if he was prone to Tex-Mex terms. Longarm had seldom heard any working hand call his rope a *lasso*.

The hardware man asked if he favored hide or grass. Longarm said, "Grass, of course. Do you take me for a Mexican?"

As the old-timer got down a coil of Kentucky hemp with a silkbound brass honda, he soothed, "Some Anglo riders favor them snakier Spanish riatas for dally-welter roping. Easier on the stock, some say."

Getting into the mind-set of a professional provider of meat on the table Longarm growled, "They say it wrong, too. The correct way to say that is *dale vuelta*, meaning give it a turn. Mexicans riding down-home saddles with soft-wood frames learned to rope with their line belayed around a bigger saddle horn, like rope through a pulley. If it's easier on the stock to rope that way, it sure plays hell with a man's hands and that's why Three Fingered Jack was a Mexican. Like everybody else with a lick of sense, I rope tie-down with a stouter grass rope and if I break the critter's neck, and it was only born to be butchered for its beef and hide to commence with!"

The old-timer handed over the rope and rang up the sale before such a rough unshaven rider could lecture him on the tendency of dudes and townsmen to treat cattle, dogs and horses like fucking *pets*.

But as Longarm went out to fasten the coil of throw-rope to the off-swell of his borrowed stock saddle, he didn't in point of fact feel as growly about livestock as his act required.

He doubted many did. Like hangmen and grave diggers, folk who had to work with and often personally slaughter critters they'd raised from big-eyed-cute tended to seem matter-of-fact brutal about the care and feeding of the critters they worked around.

Cold hard arithmetic dictated unsentimental choices when country folk had to cope with a crippled or worn-out mount, a sick old dog no longer worth its keep, or raising food, animal or vegetable—choices as easy and inexpensive as possible to undercut the other bastard's prices on the market. Nobody with a natural heart was born wanting to be cruel to animals.

Most country kids made pets of fluffy chicks, little lambs and even calves, to say nothing of pups and kittens. But by the time they were old enough to know why boys and girls were different, they'd been served a grown chick for supper, seen Mary's little lamb or that friendly calf they rode castrated and druv with the rest of the market herd to slaughter. And, like it or not, cats and dogs got old and had to be put down by the time the kids who'd loved them had kids of their own to play with pets.

So, like unwise lovers who'd been made fools of, country kids learned to harden their eyes if not their hearts if they meant to make money off of livestock. To a professional stockman, a dude who mooned over the feelings of horses and cattle seemed as foolish as a farmer who'd worry how the wheat he was threshing felt about it.

Once he'd ridden out past the hog and truck farms betwixt the county seat and the South Branch of the Wichita, where nobody could ask why, Longarm uncoiled his spanking new throw-rope to drag most of the forty feet of hemp behind him along the wagon trace. No top hand ever dragged his rope a lick farther than he had to, of course, and he tried to keep the hemp clean with fresh waterproofing linseed oil worked in from time to time. But like a new hat or new boots, a new throw-rope stood out in a crowd. So, not wanting to say why an out-of-work drover had just bought a new throw-rope, he proceeded to beat the shit out of the one he'd just bought.

Dragging it through the shallows as he forded the South Fork did wonders. The new rope had naturally come oiled as well as stiffer than a good roper would want it. But enough water clung to the strands to pick up plenty of trail dust and for nigh three furlongs it looked as if he was dragging a long sticky length of mud. But as the mud dried, to be scraped down to the now-stained hemp by the wear and tear of the dusty wagon trace, his purchase commenced to look as if he'd had it a spell.

He drug it an hour, then broke trail where some still-green grass grew betwixt the roots of a cottonwood grove. He reined in, dismounted, and let Red graze. She'd watered on the way across the South Fork. So he stretched the right dirty throw-rope between widely spaced trees to rub clean as he could manage with bunches of drier grass from out where the sun shone brighter. He knew that visible dirt clinging to a throw-rope could occasion as much comment as a brand new one. Neither went with the rider he was trying to pass for.

Recoiling the now more broken-in throw-rope, Longarm took another leak, stretched flat in the grass to smoke the rest of his cheroot, and got back up to tell Red they'd best be on their way.

And so things went, tedious, for the next half-dozen hours under the autumn skies of North Texas, surrounded by summerkilt short-grass as far as the eye could see, which was about four miles from the back of a horse on open range this flat and treeless.

Sitting tall in the saddle Longarm naturally saw the rooftops of Truscott over an hour before they rode in, hardly acting trail worn and thirsty.

So, first things coming first, Longarm left Red and his borrowed stock saddle and bridle at the livery north of the best hotel in town, tipping the stable boy extra to make sure Red was watered and rubbed down before she was foddered, and carried his Winchester and baggage down to the hotel to bet the male desk clerk they didn't have the facilities for a hot tub bath and bed for the night.

The room clerk made sure he had the cartwheel in hand before he was willing to hand over soap, a towel and room key to such a sight.

As he started to turn away, Longarm seemed to think better of it and paused to say, "I'm here in Truscott with a message for a lady of my own breed, a Miss Hilda Zimmer or, failing that, her twin sister, Miss Herta?"

The clerk glanced down at the register as he admitted, "They're both staying here. But neither is in at the moment. When and if one or more returns I'll tell her you were asking for her, Mr. Kruger."

Chapter 7

Nobody who'd seen him so far was likely to suspect he'd come to Truscott on a flying carpet from a Turkish bath, and most cowboys got cleaned up once they'd rode in off the range for some action in town. So he left his Winchester and saddlebags in his new hired room and carried his soiled shirts and underwear down to the baths with him in a hotel pillowcase.

Once he'd enjoyed a long soak and a shave, he got dressed as best he could and carried his dirty laundry to a Chinee he'd noticed near the livery. He told them he'd pay double if they'd have it all washed and dried by sundown. The old mandarin in charge said that was hardly possible, but offered to bet a fresh shirt and a change of underwear might be fit to wear before midnight, if the weather held dry as it had been for weeks. So he went back to the hotel to see if anybody was asking about him.

The same room clerk said neither Zimmer twin had come back from wherever they'd gone. It would have sounded too smart had Longarm surmised they were either out at their cow camp, over to the jail or pestering some lawyer. He moved off through the usual lobby gloom to find himself a seat where he could watch the front desk.

As he did so, an older man sporting a gilt badge rose from his own horsehair club chair to quietly but firmly declare, "I'd be Undersheriff Lew Weaver and you'd be . . . ?"

"Kruger, Wolf Kruger," Longarm answered easily.

The older lawman nodded and waved Longarm to a seat beside the one he'd risen from, saying, "We've been expecting you, unofficial. What do you want us to do about that innocent man we're holding, and what about all the other loose cannons on deck this evening?"

Longarm said, "I reckon Knox County can hold Junior Brewster a spell as long as they don't indict him. By loose cannon, might we be talking about that Catlin Gang the rangers will have wired you about by this time?"

As they both sat down, Weaver said, "They're in town. We have held off on picking them up before we asked you about it."

Longarm asked, "How come? The rangers are the lawmen after that bunch. I was sent down here with other fish to fry."

Weaver explained, "The Catlin brothers and Jack Frost are skating around in our frying pan, making no bones about their desire to see the big bad gunslick who downed the infamous Silent Ryan, Puff Duffy and Chief, in that order of magnitude."

Longarm gravely replied, "Heard much the same brag down to the county seat. Wasn't certain they were serious. An asshole called Joe Grant was recently prone to prowl the night spots of Fort Sumner, loudly declaring he'd come all the way from Texas spoiling for a fight with that Billy the Kid he'd heard so much about."

Weaver dryly remarked, "Heard how the Kid swatted Grant like a fly with his new double-action Colt Lightning. But the Kid's an asshole as well. With a whole North American content to start over in, he's still said to be haunting New Mexico, where he's famous, in spite of the fact that his side lost that Lincoln County War. I suspect some kids never learn not to kiss and tell, or brag on gunplay that can get 'em hung. Cockeyed Jack McCall would still be alive today if he'd just shot Bill Hickok and shut up about it. The Catlin brothers brag on more

50

killings than the law could ever prove. But as soon as you say the word, we'll be proud to pick 'em up and let Texas hang the vicious half-wits!"

Longarm suggested, "Why don't we hold the thought, for now? They can't get at Elroy Brewster Junior as long as you're holding him in a patent cell and I'm hoping to use their war talk to get in good with those Zimmer twins Brewster rides for. Wouldn't have much call to pester unescorted ladies with warnings about trouble the law has already tidied up for 'em."

The undersheriff said he followed Longarm's drift and agreed to hold off until and unless the Brothers Catlin and their pal, Jack Frost, worried anyone else there in Truscott.

He added, "They sure are mean-looking bastards, should you care to point them out to them ladies. As we speak, the three of them are bellied up to the bar in O'Hara's saloon, a block north. Since you won't want to be seen in public with me, be advised Dick Catlin is growing a beard, again. He thinks nobody will recognize him, clean-shaven, after he guns somebody from behind a beard. His kid brother, Donald, is wearing a dirty red-checked shirt. Jack Frost looks cleaner in his mostly black outfit but that ain't saying much. Have I said enough for you to cut them from the herd in O'Hara's?"

Longarm asked if they were still riding two paints and a buckskin.

Weaver said, "They are. How did you know?"

Longarm said, "Heard it from another pal down in Benjamin. We've agreed how dim it is to declare war in public in advance. Reckon I ought to traipse on up to O'Hara's and look 'em over, so's I'll know who I'm meeting up with, later, in a dark alley."

As they both got back to their feet, Weaver said, "We were never told the Catlin Gang was after anybody but Junior Brewster.

Longarm said, "The evening's still young and it pays to scout out ahead before the Lakota know you might be after the same buffalo."

They shook on it, and Weaver left by a side entrance as Longarm headed for the street, past the front desk.

The room clerk called, "There you go, Mr. Kruger! Miss Hilda Zimmer just came in and I told her you'd been asking for her. She said to send you right up, directly you came by some more! You'll be wanting Room 2-F on the sunny side."

Longarm thanked him and went upstairs to find a door ajar down the dimly lit corridor, spilling a stripe of sunlight across the ratty hall runner. He suspected someone had been too country to hire a flop for the night on the *morning* side of the hotel's upper stories. Even with cross ventilation, this side of the hotel was going to stay stuffy in yonder until well after midnight.

When he got there he saw the door was marked 2-F and knocked on the jamb like a gent.

A dulcet contralto voice bade him enter, and he was glad he had when he found a straw blond vision of loveliness reclining on one of a pair of beds, in a kimono of ecru shantung. She rose as he came in, saying that she'd thought he was the ice she'd sent for.

He said, "I can see why you'd send for some on this side of a frame building on the high plains, Ma'am. Next time, book a room on the east side in summer or the west side in winter. The morning sun is cooler anytime of the year. I'd be Wolf Kruger out of Val Verde County of late and I'm here with a message from a cowgirl as used to ride with you-all."

She repeated the name and replied, "*Ich heiss Hilda Zimmer. Sprechen Sie deutsch?*"

Thanks to that dictionary and phrase book Longarm just managed to follow her drift and answer easily, "Lord, no, I barely get by in *English* if some fancy ladies are to be believed, Miss Hilda. My own folk came over from some place called Dudelsack to fight the redcoats in that revolution."

She laughed and said, "*Dudelsack* means 'bagpipe.' I'm sure you must mean Düsseldorf in Westphalia. You say you know one of our riders?"

He said, "Just in passing, Miss Hilda. Met Miss Florence Ralston down to the county seat, yesterday."

Hilda Zimmer's blue eyes blazed as she demanded, "You know where Friskie Ralston is, right now? Tell me where! For I mean to have her arrested as a common horse thief! She stole a mount from her remuda after we paid her in full for time put in, despite her breaking her compact with us!"

Longarm soothed, "No, she never, Miss Hilda. She asked me to carry her apologies as well as old Red and a warning here to you-all. She had to get to the railroad and borrowed the slowest mount in her remuda. Old Red awaits your pleasure up the street at that Acme Livery and Corral, two streets north of here."

Hilda Zimmer cooled down some to sigh, "That Friskie was ever one to leap before she looked. Lost her own personal pony early in the drive, riding full gallop across the prairie dog town. You say she had a *warning* for us?"

Longarm said, "For one of your riders called Junior. You understand Miss Florence and me passed as ships in the night and I can't say I was taking notes. But as I understand it, she told me to tell you three hard cases were gunning for this Junior because he shot someone else they admired. Miss Florence said to watch out for a beard, a dirty red shirt and a man all in black. Does that mean anything to you?"

Before she could answer they were joined by what could have been taken for her twin brother until you stared harder at the front of that sweaty cotton work shirt. A brace of .38 Lightnings rode either side of her athletic hips, hiding their womanly shape some as she took off her Stetson to let her long hair fall down, gasping, "*Gott im Himmel* it's hot in here! I just came from that lawyer's office and he says he thinks someone in high places must have it in for us."

"Do we know this rider, Sis?"

Hilda introduced "Wolf Kruger" to her twin sister, Herta, and added as if it was important, "*Er kann nicht deutsch verstehen.*"

Herta shrugged and said, "*Meinetwegen.* Our lawyer wasn't able to say who pulled strings to hold poor Junior without bail on an open-and-shut case of self-defense. But *we* know who's pulled something sneaky and we know *das katholisch schweinhund* speaks *deutsch* as well as we do."

She nodded at Longarm, fanning herself with her hat as she asked what they could do for *him*.

Her sister said, "He brought back old Red and a message from our wayward Friskie, Sis. I don't know how she could have found out, but it sounds as if the other side has sent three more hired guns to do poor Junior!"

Herta nodded knowingly and said, "*Told* you those three the other night had to be working for *Vater* Paul's bunch. We don't have to worry about anyone doing Junior before they let him out, and that lawyer has tried to get us a writ in vain. Seems there's not a judge in Knox County willing to sign him out on habeas corpus. That lawyer offered to give our retainer back. I couldn't pin him down to it but I suspect he doesn't want any more to do with such popular girls."

She put her hat back on, turned to Longarm, and said, "Let's go see about that cow pony, Mr. Kruger."

Longarm asked her to call him Wolf as she led the way out like a body used to having her own way, as well as one prone to acting upon sudden impulses. As they went downstairs, and he escorted her up the shady side of the north-south street, Longarm resisted the temptation to ask questions. He could see he'd lost some ground by not being as useful to them as a High-Dutch speaker. Neither twin had accents he could detect when they spoke English. So he figured that like heaps of second- or third-generation folk, they were more comfortable with the English they'd grown up with and fell back on old country ways when they didn't want the children to know about that castor oil or what that minister and his daughter had been up to.

As they perforce passed O'Hara's saloon he had more than the sign above the door to go by. Three wilted cow ponies, two paints and a buckskin, were tethered out front and he almost said any man who'd leave his mount at a hitchrail by the hour whilst he drank inside was a man who deserved to drink pure piss. But she was a gal and he was trying to act dumber than he really was. So it was Herta Zimmer herself who muttered, "*Verdammt Trinkerin!*" and he liked her better, seeing she seemed to feel the same way about horseflesh. He'd worked on dirty Dutch enough to know that first word meant "damned" and it was easy to guess a *Trinker* was a drinker. But since he'd confessed he spoke no Dutch, he didn't comment. They both knew hitchrails were meant for short errands, and every town in the land had livery stables and municipal corrals where any rider with a lick of common sense left a mount as he played cards or whored around.

As they approached the Acme Livery, Herta Zimmer frowned thoughtfully and said, "That's the livery where Hilda and me left our own mounts when we rode in to get our foreman out of jail! You say you have that roan with white stockings inside? How come we never saw old Red when we stabled out our own stock?"

He explained he'd just left the roan there that very afternoon and she didn't argue when, inside, they found old Red looking a tad less weary and trail-dusted, munching timothy in her shady stall.

Longarm explained to the livery crew, and the rightful owner bet a quarter none of them wanted to lead her pony out to the Double H camp along the North Fork an hour or so up the wagon trace.

When she lost, they asked Longarm about the saddle and bridle he'd left in their tack room. He started to say they could stay put, for now. Then he decided he might as well tote 'em back to his hotel, seeing he had no horse of his own to put 'em on.

Herta Zimmer didn't take the bait as he escorted her back the way they'd come with the roping saddle braced on his right hip, the bridle and reins wrapped around the horn. She didn't ask what he was doing in Truscott, nor what his plans for the future might be, and it might have sounded pushy to ask for a job just because he'd brought a stolen horse back. But he did manage to convey he'd been laid off farther south after the fall roundup. "Got left behind when they made up the market herd earlier. I suspect the ramrod was afraid I was after his job. Him and the boss were both Irish and you know how *clannish* they can be. They said they didn't want to carry me north to Dodge no more because of a little shooting scrape I was in up yonder last year. No charges were filed. But you know how some feel about *our* kind."

"What kind might that be, Mr. Kruger?" she coldly replied.

He shrugged and said, "They called me a stubborn Dutchman when I told that old Scotch-Irish tinhorn I wanted a new deck or a showdown in the Long Branch. But I reckon I'd be overstating things if I was to imply I was true-blue Dutch like you and your sister, Miss Hilda."

To which Herta Zimmer innocently replied, "That's about the size of it. What might we owe you for bringing that pony and Friskie's message up the trail to us, Mr. Kruger?"

He said, "I'm a top hand, not a paid delivery boy, Miss Herta. Like I told your Miss Florence, I was headed this way in any case and I've ever been ready and willing to do favors for . . . a pal."

The willowy ash blond in mannish garb laughed and told him, "It's safe to assume you and Friskie Ralston had gotten to be . . . pals, if you spent enough time with her for a conversation. Was she good in bed, cowboy? Lord knows she seemed *anxious* enough, ever' time we made camp near a town."

56

Chapter 8

"I'm in no position to judge Miss Florence's social graces," Longarm lied, allowing her to precede him into their hotel as he continued, "I heard your sister call her a horse thief, too. But she sent the horse back with me, along with that warning, and I'll not have her mean-mouthed when she ain't here to defend herself."

The well-armed blond mused, "Not one to kiss and tell, eh. I admire that in a man. Where do you think you're going with that saddle?"

"Upstairs, the same as yourself," he replied, quickly adding, "I am on the same floor in a more sensible room. I mean to leave my gear there to cool off even more before bedtime. By the time *your* room's as cool, the morning sun will have woke me up on that side of this building. If we never see one another again, it's been my pleasure to meet up with you ladies."

Then he turned the other way at the head of the stairs to let her call him back, or not, as she might choose. Leaving such matters up to the lady was a heap like playing a fish on the line, save for fishing being less uncertain.

When she just bade him farewell and clomped off down the hall the other way, Longarm muttered, "Up your contrary cunt, cowgirl!" and put his saddle in his hired room with his Winchester and saddlebags to await his pleasure.

Thanks to the thin balloon framing, it was a tad close

upstairs on the *shady* side of the hotel, low as the sun had sunk outside by now.

It was going on his usual suppertime after-hours at the federal building back in Denver. So figuring on two birds with one visit, he headed for O'Hara's saloon to see if he could rustle up a decent snack of soup-and-sandwich whilst he gave those three gunslicks of the Catlin Gang the once-over. Most saloons served grub, lest their customers go elsewhere with growling guts, and he figured he had the advantage on the Brothers Catlin and Jack Frost, since they'd never met before and they'd never said they were after anyone but Junior Brewster.

Those three ponies were still tethered out front, looking as if they were hoping to be put out of their misery with three merciful pistol shots, in spite of that being the shady side this late in the day. He saw they could reach a watering trough from where their thoughtless riders had tethered them, but that was still no way to treat horseflesh.

So he didn't look at the three sons of bitches seated now at a corner table with their bowls of chili and a scuttle of suds. Longarm prided himself on his poker face. But it was best not to tempt fate by locking eyes with total assholes he had nothing to say to.

He moved instead to the bar, to ask the beefy balding barkeep how you went about ordering soup and sandwiches in O'Hara's.

O'Hara, if that was him, said, "Take me advice and order some of our grand shepherd's pie with soda bread and all the apple butter you can slather on! You'll be wanting that with something to drink, of course?"

Longarm allowed he'd have a boilermaker to start, backed up by mayhaps a gallon of lager. So the barkeep directed him to another table, one empty away from the Catlin Gang, and allowed he'd be served in no time.

Longarm moved as directed and fished out a cheroot as he sat down, casually facing the doorway and the Catlin Gang without making a big deal of it. As he lit his smoke, the one in the red-checked shirt, got his feet and oozed his way, grinning, sincere as a sidewinder.

58

Three strangers in a taproom were always worth watching tight. He knew the real leader, Dick Catlin, was the one with the beard, not looking his way as he let his baby brother make the opening moves of an old familiar game. The one in black, that would be Frost, was busting a gut to keep from locking eyes with Longarm as Donald, in the dirty shirt, chuckled, "Howdy, Sir Galahad. Ain't you a long way from the Double H in the gathering dusk?"

The sunlight outside had turned sort of crimson and gold at the end of a long, hot dusty day, but Longarm found the rest of the question dumb and said so, explaining, "I don't ride for the Double H, Sonny. I take it you dubbed me Galahad becasue you noticed me earlier in the company of that Zimmer gal from that outfit?"

Donald Catlin said, "Damned A. They've hired you to take the place of that ramrod they're holding for beating three famous gunslicks to the draw. So *you* must a famous gunslick, too, right?"

Longarm chuckled and replied, "I'm too old to be a famous gunslick. You kids are welcome to the title for as long as your luck holds out. The Good Book says it's *swords* men who live by die by, but I reckon they didn't have six-guns back when they were writing the Good Book."

He finished lighting his cheroot, with his left hand, as he added in a weary tone, "I'd assure you I was only a simple working stiff if I wasn't afraid that would encourage you, the way running away from a snarly mutt might. Why don't you just go on back to your own supper and let me enjoy my own? I ain't going to say that again."

They must not have thought he meant that, or perhaps they thought that the three of them could safely slap leather on a man who'd been braced for them to try, with his own drawn double-action in his lap all the time, with five rounds of .44-40 in the wheel and the hammer back. For as the one in the dirty red-checked shirt went for his low-slung and tied-down .45 thumb buster, the two at his table rolled either way out of their chairs to aim at him cross-fire from wide-spread squats.

59

Longarm tipped the round table on its side to roll one way as he crabbed the other, aiming first at the more distant but more dangerous bearded one before he set Jack Frost on his ass with another round and fired at the one in the dirty red-checked shirt before that target could see he was blazing the wrong way.

Donald Catlin put two bullets through the hardwood top of that rolling table before 200 grains of hot lead traversed his chest from side to side, ripping his heart open as it deflated both lungs.

Through the ringing in his ears, Longarm heard a distant voice cut through the gunsmoke with, "Jasus, Mary and Joseph, and I thought it was *yourself* that would be dying at three-to-one odds. Sure, you *must* be a famous gunfighter. I'll have it known we're on your side, whoever you may be!"

Longarm said, "Aw, mush!" and then, as the smoke began to clear, Undersheriff Weaver charged in with a ten-guage Parker to demand that nobody move.

Then he saw Longarm was still on his feet, reloading, which was more than could be said for the Catlin Gang.

Jack Frost was still blowing bloody bubbles and calling for his momma near the swinging doors. Neither Catlin brother was ever going to bother anybody again. Lew Weaver said, "I was covering from the far side of the street, Mr. Kruger. I told you how them boys had been making war talk about you, remember?"

Longarm said, "I do, now."

The O'Hara, as he turned out to be, said, "I saw it all and all, Lew. Mr. Kruger, here, never made a move any Christian could be taking as a slight or threat. He was seated at that upturned table that's now in another part of this world, waiting to be served his supper, when the three of them ganged up on him for no reason at all, at all!"

Weaver dryly suggested, "Well, they were *called* a *gang*, and I've had my eye on them since they got here. Figured they might be looking for trouble. Never figured they'd be dumb enough to start up with the one and original Wolf Kruger, here."

The O'Hara asked, as if he knew, "Is *that* who we've had the honor of almost serving supper? It's a famous lawman or bounty hunter he might be, then?"

Weaver couldn't meet Longarm's eyes as he laid it on by hesitating and then declaring, "Let's just say we hold with living and letting others live, here in Truscott. As you just said, old Wolf, here, was only passing through when these fools committed suicide."

It was Longarm's turn to swallow a grin as the under-sheriff dryly asked, "You did tell me, earlier, you were only passing through this township, didn't you, Wolf?"

Longarm soberly replied, "That's about the size of it. I wasn't fibbing when I told you I wasn't after anybody here in Truscott and I sure hope you don't mean to run me in for only doing what I had to when these three piss-ants drew on me!"

Others had drifted in to stare in wonder as Lew Weaver shook his head and said, "Not hardly. Had you been the one who started it, you would have been in the clear. You just laid low the Catlin Gang this evening. They were wanted in other parts for starting up with less lethal gents. Might even be some bounty money coming to you, if only you'd be able to stick around that long."

Longarm tried to sound wistful as he holstered his six-gun to ask, "I reckon you'd as soon I moved on like I said I would, come morning?"

Old Lew Weaver knew he was doing wonders for his rep in an election year as he replied, firmly but not un-kindly, "That was the deal we made, Wolf. We shook on it, as I recall."

Longarm shrugged in resigned manner to say, "I told you I was only passing through and I wasn't lying. I reckon Truscott Township can use any bounty money on these boys to bury them proper and mayhaps paint the town hall afresh or whatever?"

Weaver nodded soberly and said, "You just let us worry about that as you ride on to where we don't have to worry about you, hear?"

Longarm glanced down at the three forms oozing blood

across the sawdust-sprinkled floor, Frost having died total by now, as he nodded and asked, "Then I'm free to go, Sheriff Weaver?"

The older play actor expansively replied, "Free as a bird, as long as I don't see you around town by this time tomorrow night!"

So Longarm left to sup somewhere's else as Undersheriff Weaver sent for help with the three cadavers, having established himself as a no-nonsense peace officer who'd just ordered the one and original Wolf Kruger to get out of town within twenty-four hours, after Wolf Kruger had just faced up to three hard-cased killers and shot them dead as turds in a milk bucket!

Longarm settled for a T-bone with home fries and mince pie with his coffee at a regular beanery before he headed back to his hotel to hole up for some serious planning.

Longarm was more famous for thinking on his feet than he was for being Wolf Kruger, whoever in blue blazes Wolf Kruger was turning out to be! So he could see how that dreadful bullshit spread by an older lawman might help as well as hurt his hopes of getting in with the Zimmer twins. Billy Vail had suggested, and Longarm had seen, how a hand riding in with a Sulfur Draw outfit under a High-Dutch name might be accepted without too much thought by the High-Dutch settlers making the rest of Texas edgy as they contested rights to that newly opened Comanche range. But getting in with the stuck-up Zimmer twins was turning out a harder row to hoe than they'd ever imagined and it was clearer, now, why other outsiders had had such poor luck over to the Staked Plains of late.

On the one hand, thanks to Lew Weaver's off-the-cuff yarn, the whole township would soon be abuzz with tales of another gunfighter of renown. Half a dozen local bullshit artists were certain to say they'd known there was trouble brewing the minute they heard Wolf Kruger was in town, for of course they knew Wolf Kruger. Didn't everybody?

On the other hand, had Weaver consulted him earlier, he'd have asked for more time to convince the Zimmer twins he might just be of some use to them. Billy Vail had assumed that since the jailed Junior Brewster wasn't a Dutchman at all, a ramrod with a Dutch name, at least, might strike them as a logical replacement for the natural man a trail crew of cowgirls needed to front for them.

But they'd barely thanked him for returning old Red and warning them about the Catlin Gang and, whilst they could still warm up with time, Lew Weaver hadn't given him that much time, Lord love his big mouth.

Longarm sat by the open window, smoking, as the sky to the east went from purple to star-spangled navy blue, with the rooftops and a distant church spire across the way flamingo red in the last rays of a sunset you couldn't see from there. Down on the street, an old coot had lit a street lamp in front of the hotel and folk were out in greater numbers to take advantage of the cool shades of a Texas evening. Somewhere a piano was marching through Mexico, and, from time to time, someone down below would pause and point up at his window.

He knew he was just a dark blob around a pinpoint of tobacco glow if they could make out that much from down yonder. The light was now at that tricky state where folk got run over by beer drays or shot in the back on a boardwalk in the mistaken belief they still saw what was going on all about them.

It was going on dark enough for lamplight and shadows to sharpen up better when there came a gentle rapping on the door to the hall. Hoping it was old Lew Weaver, so's they could rework that warning to get out of town. But seeing it was better to be safe than sorry. He had his gun out, aimed polite, as he opened the door of his darkend room to the barely lighter hallway.

It was one of the Zimmer twins. Which one was uncertain, since she was wearing a darker kimono of Turkish toweling.

As she entered, she murmured in that contralto they both spoke with, "I see you're not sure you got all of them. We have to talk. They're still holding our poor Junior Brewster and we just got a wire from down home. *Die Zerziehenschwester, ach,* I should say the Twisted Sister, has struck again and *Onkel* Klaus says we're to come on home at once, with or without a grown growly man to front for us!"

Longarm replied with some honesty, "Miss Hilda, or is it Miss Herta? You know I don't recall enough old country talk to know what you just said. Who's this Uncle Klaus and what's this twister sister of yours been up to?"

She shut the door and barred it as she said, "Not so loud. This has to be a private conversation. The *twisted* sister is no sister of ours, you silly! She might not even be a girl. Half those *katholisch*—I mean Catholic priests— are queer, and we know the Twisted Sister is working for the arch fiend who's sent six killers, so far, to do us dirty!"

As he moved to the foot of the bed to break out that bottle of Maryland rye, Longarm quietly asked, "Are you saying you suspect the Church of Rome of gunplay, ah, Ma'am?"

She said, "Of course not. I doubt the Bishop of Rome has ever heard of us. *Vater* Paul, I mean Father Paul, is the renegade priest those pushy range hogs from *Österreich*, I mean Austria, take orders from. Perhaps I'd better start from the beginning, *nicht wahr?*"

Perhaps that would be a grand notion." said Longarm, gravely.

Chapter 9

As they sat on his bed in the dark sipping highballs, Hilda Zimmer, or mayhaps it was Herta, got him up-to-date on current events on the Staked Plains of West Texas, or that's what she thought she was up to. For like many self-educated men, Longarm enjoyed reading and had an inquiring mind. So he knew she was populating Texas backwards.

You seldom read it in current history books, but after old-time Spanish-speaking settlers had taken Texas from the Indians they'd named the place for—or tried to—they'd invited the Papist Austin family to settle other English-speaking Papists, answering to the same Church of Rome, along their northeast frontier in the mistaken belief they were forming a buffer state betwixt themselves and the expanding U.S. of A. The Spanish Crown, or its underpaid colonial administration, had granted handsome tracts of bottomland between the Brazos and the Trinity, to be subdivided among the first three or four hundred families of Highland Scot, North English Papist and, of course, West Irish persuasion. When Mexico busted free of Spain back in '21 they'd confirmed the Spanish land grants, at first. But they commenced to worry when the Austins kept importing more none-Hispanic settlers, including Nominal Papists from the Germanic states betwixt the Rhine and Danube. So in spite of the way she told it, the Texas High-Dutch looking to Rome for their pie in the sky had been there first.

She had it the other way, of course, being Lutheran. Longarm felt no call to point out how the Protestant majority of Texicans had come west after the mostly Papist early Texans had revolted against Old Mexico in '36. Davy Crockett and his Tennessee Rifles had only been among the first of many an Americano welcomed as volunteers by Texicans too worried about Mexicans and Comanche to argue religion. So the original Spanish dream of a devout buffer state betwixt Old Mexico and the Gringo had turned into a nightmare, for Mexico, and a heap of the same had been sore as hell ever since.

Some Indians, the Comanche in particular, had raised even more ned about the resettlement of Texas, so aside from forming the Texas Rangers even before they declared independence from Mexico, Texicans holding on after the Alamo had welcomed a shithouse full of land-hungry High-Dutch Protestants from the northern Germanic states to come right in. So just as the Know-Nothing Party kept bitching, in no time at all, it became a toss-up in Texas whether your neighbors might be Anglo-Saxon, Irish or Dutch.

But as the Zimmer twin he was drinking with seemed bent on proving to him, neither Dutch nor Irish of opposing religious persuasions got along with one another as well as they might socialize with Anglo or Mex strangers. That was likely because folk expected *total* strangers to have odd notions, but it druv 'em wild to meet a body who talked like them, sang like them, and went to another church.

By the time he'd refilled their hotel tumblers, he'd given up trying to identify which twin he was talking to in the balmy shades of the September moonrise. He'd suspected she might not want him to be too certain, since she'd commented on how cool his room was and explained how her twin sister had ridden back out to their cow camp to try for some sleep in the open air.

When she added she'd only stayed to talk to him about

his running free after shooting the same number of gun-hands as poor Junior, he said, "My fight was in front of witnesses. The town law knew they were wanted else-where, and I was given twenty-four hours to get out of town by a lawman who must not like noise. We were talking about your own down-home situation, Ma'am."

She finished her tumbler and handed it back to him. So he rose to build her another, with good Maryland rye and mighty hard Texas well water, as she explained how the Zimmers and a dozen or more other Texas-Dutch clans had fought on the winning side in the Mexican War, the losing side in the War Betwixt the States, and barely sur-vived through reconstruction. They had to sell off land and livestock along the Brazos at a loss to get by until President Hayes was elected with the hair on his chest and the Union Army war record to end the last of those pestiferous Reconstruction Acts.

As he handed her another and sat back down beside her she said, "It was *sehr ungerecht*! We never held any *Sklaven*! It would have been stupid to put an unwilling cowboy on a horse with a gun to fight off raiders and, even if it hadn't been, Papa said it was not right to keep *Sklaven*, I mean slaves. And then the damnyankees at Chickamagua killed our Papa when we were so little and Mama had such hard times keeping the family together under Reconstruction, even with *wunderbar* friends and neighbors and then, just as we all moved to the Staked Plains together for a fresh start, Mama died and now she will never know how we've built her Double H spread up from no more than water, grass and a few head of scrub cattle!"

"Whose notion was it to register your brand as Double H instead of say Triple Z?" he quietly asked.

She answered, simply, "Mama chose the brand for our new start. She said no matter what our married names might be someday, we would always be her Hilda and Herta, *verstehen Sie*?"

He said, "Your mother must have been a lady of quality. I'm sure sorry I never had the honor. I'd have been proud to ride for such a boss lady."

It didn't work. Her daughter of either H shrugged wistfully and replied, "We've tried to do her memory proud. Could I have just a sip more of these fine *Schnapps*? I've barely recovered from the heat this afternoon and our own room across the hall is still an oven!"

"I fear we've about killed the bottle," he lied, rising again to top the little rye left in her tumbler with well-water from the ewer on the corner stand as he gently urged her to get to the part about that Twisted Sister.

There was likely enough left to get her really drunk, but gals waking up with a hangover were a pain in the ass when they *failed* to sob that they never would have if you hadn't got them drunk.

He made her continue her saga on water. She told him how her own Texas-Dutch kith and kin had moved in around Sulfur Draw in the heart of the newly opened Staked Plains, along with about as many Anglo and Anglo-Mex clans they'd gotten along with tolerable before those pestiferous Austrian Papists had commenced to horn in on them for pieces of the rapidly diminishing pie.

It was a famiiar story to Longarm. It kept happening all over a rapidly changing West, and only the details changed.

Over to Lincoln County, a mostly Irish-American faction had been led by Union vet Major Laurence Murphy, cattle barons James Dolan and John Riley, and their pal, Bill Brady, sheriff of Lincoln County.

Murphy dominated wholesale, retail and freighting in that stretch of New Mexico Territory with the blessings of the Santa Fe Ring that ran New Mexico under the Grant Administration, once Murphy's fellow Union vet and Dutchman, Emil Fritz, died early on. Dolan and Riley enjoyed beef contracts with both the Mescalero Agency and nearby Fort Stanton and, thanks to Sheriff Brady, the Old Mex community of the New Mexico county got along or got out of the way of the "Big Store," as their machine was called. This golden age had lasted nigh an Army hitch when English-born cattleman John Tunstall and Canadian lawyer Alexander McSween horned in with blessings of Scotch-Irish beef baron John Chisum to dispute control of Lincoln County with the Big Store. The resulting Lincoln County War, though written up like it had been fought betwixt France and Prussia, had lasted the first seven months of '78 and ended with Rancher Tunstall, Sheriff Brady and Lawyer McSween mudered, along with a handful of lesser lights, and the survivors on both sides scared skinny and laying low or on the run. So that was what Longarm was out to nip in the bud around Sulfur Draw, with the Zimmer twins and an Uncle Klaus Brenner they admired in the original position of the Murphy-Dolan faction and their new Dutch-speaking neighbors acting out the Tunstall-McSween roles in spite of being Papists instead of Protestants, this time.

She naturally blamed the Austrian clique led, or advised by a Father Paul Hauser, of the Jesuit Order, for everything from water-claim jumping to grasshoppers. Longarm had noticed accounts of that Lincoln County War depended a heap on the religious and party affiliation of the newspaper running the expose. A sudden thought hit him as he leafed through some old clippings in the scrapbook of his inquiring mind and he said, "Tell me some more about your innocent ramrod, Elroy Brewster Junior. Are you sure he's from Texas, not from New Mexico Territory?"

She replied, "Junior hails from Tennesee by way of Presidio County along the Rio Grande. Why do you ask? Who told you he was from Texas to begin with? You never heard it from me. I've been here all this while."

Reminding himself to watch his step with any woman who held her liquor like this one, Longarm replied in an easy tone, "I heard townsfolk jawing about that shoot-out over to your cow camp. Those Catlin brothers and Jack Frost told me they hailed from New Mexico, and they'd come to Truscott to look up your ramrod, Elroy Brewster Junior, in connection with his having shot Duffy, Ryan and that breed."

He let that sink in before he told her, "In New Mexico Territory, not all that long ago, the guns of the Tunstall-McSween faction were led by Tunstall's ramrod, another Brewster. Dick Brewster was shot in the head three days after ambushing Sheriff Brady on April Fool's day. Chased a Murphy-Dolan rider as far as the Mescalero Agency and had the misfortune of catching up with the now famous Buck Roberts, of whom little more is known. After Roberts and Brewster killed one another, the war was forty-five days old with Tunstall in his grave and that Lawyer McSween, who never packed a gun, 'pending on a teenager now known far and wide as Billy the Kid to command his remaining guns. But that's ancient history, or I thought it was until just now. But if Dick Brewster had living kin, and that New Mexico gang were sore about him gunning a Duffy and a Ryan as well as that breed . . ."

It worked. She gasped, "*Gott im Himmel*! We thought they were only bully boys looking for somebody to pick on! But now I see why they won't let our poor Junior go! We *thought* someone in high places had given orders to hold him without formal charges on what seemed such a simple affair to a lawyer who wasn't in on it! What are we to do if our foreman is in trouble with that Santa Fe Ring? We've been having enough trouble with *Vater* Paul and his Twisted Sister!"

He casually replied, "Might be nothing more than co-incidence. Them other Austrians who study brains have a name I can't recall for our habit of seeing tigers in the floral wallpaper that were never intended by the artist when he painted them roses. There's nothing in the U.S. Constitution saying two cattle outfits had no right to hire ramrods named Brewster who shot gents with Irish names on widely seperate occasions. But it may be true some-body at the county prosecution level here in Truscott has seen that same tiger in the roses and means to hold Junior until he can check that angle out."

He let her chase that ball well clear of state or federal authorities before he added, "I'd sure like to see how it all turns out. But I can't stay to watch. They've given me twenty-four hours to leave Knox County unless I want to join your Junior Brewster in the very same jail. So I was planning on an early start, come morning. I'd be on my way by the light of the moon if I wasn't waiting on laundry I left with a Chinee. I got to get somewhere I ain't as famous and find a job before my pocket-jingle runs out."

She said, "You have a job, if you'll take it. Forty-five and beans a month with a remuda of four work ponies and a Saturday-go-to-town palomino, once you get us and our herd back to Sulfur Draw. My sister and me promised Junior a bonus for getting home our nigh two hundred head of high-grade beef and the dozen other girls we're left with. If we make it with no further trouble, we're talking fifty dollars. If we have to shoot our way through anybody, we'll renegotiate. Since you say you've ridden high and low as a top hand, need I say how my sister and me feel about a foreman who'd trifle with our hired hands?"

He assured her he'd never trifled with any hired hands anywhere he had ever worked.

She laughed and suggested, "*Schon gut*, can you be ready to ride with us before dawn?"

He said, "Sure I can. If my laundry ain't dry by ten or so, that Chinee will be welcome to it. We'd best both leave calls at the desk downstairs and see about turning in afore midnight if we mean to spend tomorrow in the saddle."

She murmured, "It's still too hot in our room to even consider a flop on those hot sheets! What if I were to stay here with you until midnight, at least?"

He moved their empty tumblers to the windowsill as he honestly told her, "I ain't certain I have that much will-power, Miss Hilda, if it ain't Miss Herta. I'm a natural man, and if you ever look in the mirror you know you're a handsome woman in a loosely gathered kimono."

She let her kimono fall partways open, exposing one bare tit to the soft light from the open window as she purred in a dreamy voice, "There are limits to my own

71

willpower. You're a handsome man, and I suggest we seal our bargain with . . . a kiss?"

He took her in his arms, running one hand around to her bare back through the front of her open kimono as they kissed warm and French. But even as they flopped flat across the bedding he wasn't able to resist reminding her of what she'd just said about fooling with the help where you worked.

She fumbled with the buckle of his gun-rig as she boldly replied, "I'm *management*, not hired help, and you won't be working for me until you take charge in the morning. Do you always mount girls with a holstered six-gun, Wolf?"

He rolled away just enough to start shucking his .44-40 and all the rest as he assured her he didn't meant to take advantage of her at gunpoint. He didn't ask which twin she might be as he shucked her out of her kimono to mount her right. For he saw, now, why one or the other of the handsome Zimmer twins might find it easier to face a lover in the cold gray light of a morning after, knowing he wasn't sure whether he'd enjoyed her favors or those of somebody else entire if identical. But whichever one she was, she kept pleading with him for more "*ficken*" and, since he'd looked up the dirty Dutch words in that dictionary aboard that train, he knew just what she was asking for.

Not that he wouldn't have fucked her just as hard in any case.

Chapter 10

There was a heap to be said for riding to the moon with cowgirls. After the soft, well-mellowed flesh of that widow woman down to the county seat, the contrast of younger way-firmer sweetmeats seemed delightful and, better yet, this cowgirl was built a tad more shapely than the boyish Friskie Ralston. So Longarm was reminded once more why a tumbleweed who packed a badge and lived by the gun had no business settling down.

He'd told many a gal who'd tempted him he'd been to far too many lawmen's funerals to wish young widowhood on such a pretty little thing, and he'd partly meant it, for that was the simple truth. But it was as great a truth that no matter how far a man might roam or how many gals he might meet up with, no two were ever exactly the same, unless, of course, they were identical twins.

That inspired some posting in the saddle long after they'd come the first time as he mentally pictured what it would be like to get both this Zimmer gal and her identical twin, Hilda or Herta, in the same bed at the same time. The notion made some of the less practical positions in that scandalous Hindu book they sold under the counter seem more reasonable, seeing it would be possible, that way, to get at what seemed the same pussy two ways at once!

He didn't suggest such a ménage à trois, as you said it

in French, because he could see that whether both twins were in on this game or not, the game would be given away as soon as anyone found out they were both in on it, if they were both in on it.

It could be injurious to one's health to guess wrong if Herta Zimmer was not, since she'd proven herself quick on the draw and a straight shooter in spite of letting Junior Brewster take the blame, or credit, for gunning three men faster than your average housewife might swat three flies!

It felt closer to midnight, but somewhere a clock was tolling nine as they simmered down for a shared smoke and some needed rest. She said, *"Ach, so spât so früh?* I'd better get out to our camp and tell my sister about this before she turns in for the night!"

He passed her the smoke as he asked, "Do you always tell your twin when you meet someone nice as me, Ma'am?"

She choked on smoke, laughed and replied, "Of course not. She'd have a fit if she knew about us getting this friendly. On the trail for the next week or more I hope you'll understand this has to be a matter of lady's choice? I'll see about getting you alone, off to one side, when and if that might be possible. I don't want you making any grabs for my *Hinterteil* in front of the others, if you know what I mean!"

He knew what she meant. It was odd how gals fluent in two lingos switched from one to another whilst talking sassy. He wondered idly if she said not to grab her "ass" when laying down the same ground rules in High Dutch. But he didn't ask. Since she'd told him to behave and let her grab his ass, first, there was no pressing need to ask which twin might be which. So he snubbed out the cheroot and got a good grip on her *Hinterteil* to part with friendly, and he had to agree when she said it seemed *wunderbar* to start over afresh no matter how many times you did so in one delicious session.

She likely knew as well as he did, from sad experience, how they called those first hundred times or so the honeymoon because there *was* a limit to how many times the same two folk could get *wunderbar* before it commenced to feel like *work*. A gal who didn't want to give her name whilst fornicating hot and heavy would likely be shy about revealing past slap-and-tickle sessions. So he just silently thanked the sex maniac or maniacs who'd taught her to move so fine at such an early age. He'd met up with young widows and inexperienced whores who couldn't have held a candle to such inspired gyrations, and better yet, they seemed sincere. If she was fibbing about how many times he'd made her come, so far, she was an accomplished liar as well!

They ended up that time with her on top, examining his tonsils with her tongue as tried to twist his throbbing erection off with her warm, wet and man-hungry innards.

Then she was up up and away before he'd recovered his breath to say good night. He lay still with his weapon aimed at the ceiling until it slowly deflated. Then, figuring he'd given her time, he swung his bare feet to the braided rug and moved closer to the window in the dark of his room to see what she might be dressed like as she lit out for her cow camp, doubtless strolling innocent down the still-crowded streets.

After watching long enough to want another smoke, he decided she'd known about that side entrance downstairs, too, and murmured with a knowing smile, "Aw, you didn't think I really *gave* a hang which twin you might be. Did you, little darling?"

Then he washed up at the corner stand, got dressed, and went out, himself, to mosey first to the Truscott Western Union office whilst he still had that laundry as an excuse in case anyone asked.

There was nobody in the all-night but sleepy telegraph office. Longarm tore off a night letter form and block-lettered a progress report addressed personal to Billy Vail at his home address with no mention of his being a marshal. He brought his secret pals up on the cliques dominated or advised by Uncle Klaus Brenner and Father Paul Hauser. He suggested the new settlers affiliated with neither Dutch-speaking side were in much the same position as the New Mexico Mex and neutral Anglos in that Lincoln County dust-up. Likely wishing both sides would calm down as all concerned tried to wrest a living from marginal range and uncertain water. He explained how he'd gotten in with the Zimmer twins, leaving out the dirty parts, and said he hoped to be accepted around Sulfur Draw as a Zimmer rider of remote but likely Lutheran descent. They had agreed from the beginning there was no way he could pretend to ride for *both* sides. But at least, this way, he might get more from at least one side to tell him more than the undercover rangers had come back with, dead or alive. He felt no call to rehash the rumors of the Twisted Sister, since even night letters by wire cost more than the U.S. mail, and other lawmen would already know more than he did about those latest deadly doings. He hadn't pressed the twin he'd just been pressing against, lest he seem too eager. So farther along, as the song went, he'd doubtless know more about the latest emergency. It made no sense that a secret assassin who killed Austrian Papist sheepmen for the Lutheran faction would be scaring the liver and lights out of the ones she, he or it worked for.

On the other hand, it was widely held the Kid, riding for the side John Chisum had been backing, had run off with a heap of beef from old Chisum's Long Rail and Jingle Bob. Range wars had a way of getting out of hand that way, once you'd started 'em. The killings over to Lincoln County had gone on after the first killings of Tunstall and the men who'd killed him in February. The deaths of Sheriff Brady, Deputy Hindman and gunslicks Tom Hill and Buck or Buckshot Roberts, along with Dick Brewster on the other side, came within days of one another in April. Another showdown came on the 19th of July when scared and harmless Lawyer McSween turned over the leadership of his weaker faction to the braver but dumber Billy the Kid, who in point of fact officiated as commander of the Tunstall-McSween forces for less than twenty-four hours before he and a pair of his new followers made a break for it from the burning McSween house.

The Murphy-Dolan guns, backed by an Irish-American Colonel and his Colored Cav from Fort Stanton, spared McSween's defiant wife but shot down her husband and five others who surrendered as if they'd been mad dogs. To the Murphy-Dolan riders, and the troopers they'd been feeding, the outsiders they butchered had likely seemed mad dogs.

Since that time, of course, despite every attempt on the part of the survivors and the new territorial government to declare that the Lincoln County War officially ended, night riding, stock raiding and occasional killings had continued with nobody, officially, ordering toad squat. The sheriff who'd replaced the murdered Brady tossed his badge back lest he share the same fate. Things went that way, once folk sent away for hired guns and tried to lay them off before they'd seen enough fun and profit. They could only hope things hadn't gone that far over to the Staked Plains, yet.

Paying for the night letter from his own pocket, lest he leave a paper trail for the day shift to comment on as they tried to collect from their Denver office, Longarm drifted on up the way to discover that Chinee was still open and, better yet, had his fresh shirts and underwear ready for him.

He took his laundry back to the hotel and bet the night clerk four bits they wouldn't wake him up at quarter to four. Then he went back up, put the hotel's clean pillowcase on the pillow he'd used under that Zimmer sister's swell ass, and undressed to hit the sack, reflecting on what Mr. Thomas Edison had recently writ about the four hours of sleep a day one needed to invent a light bulb.

But Mr. Thomas Edison seldom fought and fornicated after a hard ride up from the county seat in the same day. So it felt as if he'd no sooner hit the pillow when Billy the Kid was confiding that Twisted Sister was a kissing cousin and urging him to get dressed to ride.

Somewhere that clock was striking three as Longarm reeled his late caller in to sleepily mutter, "How did you get back in without a key, little darling?"

To which the cowgirl in his arms replied, "Let go my titty. We ain't got time for that right now, Mr. Kruger."

So he woke up some more to marvel, "Do I know you, Ma'am?"

She said, "You surely seem hell bent on getting acquainted, but I never had your hand on my tit before. I'd be Wendy Delgado. I wrangle for the Double H. They sent me with a pony from your remuda to fetch you from town, knowing it was too far for you to walk and seeing the outfit will be ready to move out by the time I can get you on back with me."

Longarm let go his late caller and lit his bed lamp to see she was a sultry brunette with Anglo features, tawny hide and big brown eyes as tempting as hot chocolate. But he still asked her to step out in the hall whilst he dressed, seeing she didn't want to tear off just a quick one with him.

He hadn't lit the lamp to show off. He wanted to be sure he knew what he was doing and had everything as he dressed, gathered up his shit, and rejoined Wendy Delgado in the hall. She offered to help, but he said he had the heavily laden saddle riding about right and they went on down to tell the sleepy night man he was checking out. The night man growled, "I noticed. Who did you think woke me up?"

So Longarm tossed the key on the desk betwixt them and followed the Tex-Mex wrangler-gal out that side entrance, where two cow ponies stood tethered in the moonlight.

Knowing he had his own saddle and bridle, the wrangler gal had led his mount in with a horsehair hack. She'd chosen him a black and white pinto gelding with the chunky chest but aristocratic features of the Spanish Barb. The barb, or barbary, pony was kin to the Arab, brought to Spain by the same Moors, way back when, and favored by many a Mex vaquero for its shorter spine, missing one vertebra, which made it just a tad slower but quicker turning than the fleeter and fancier Andalusian Arab the Spanish Cav preferred for parades.

Wendy said she called the barb "Old Paint" and he saw how "Old Red" had gotten her name. As he saddled Old Paint he didn't ask Wendy how she'd wound up with an Anglo first name and a Mex last name. Things happened that way in the Southwest. Pete Maxwell, the cattle baron as owned Fort Sumner on the Pecos, was Anglo-Mex in reverse, with his mother's kin the Land Grant Spanish. But of course he got to know the spanky brunette and the outfit she rode with far better as they rode the fair piece out to the riverside camp of the Double H.

When he casually asked how come she and so many other Double H riders seemed to be cowgirls instead of cowboys, Wendy explained she and the others had signed on for a secret mission, leaving the Sulfur Draw range a few at a time in more maidenly dress to regroup at the nearest railhead and board a train for Fort Smith on the edge of the Indian Territory. She said the Zimmer twins hadn't wanted too many to know they meant to breed-up their herd with a mess of Cherokee longhorns and that Black Angus he-brute before they had a market herd of prime beef yearlings raring to go.

That made sense. She explained how come two Dutch cattle queens had been forced to recruit half their she-male riders from amongst the neutral neighbors, mostly small-holders, because hardly any proper young ladies anywhere rode astride or knew shit about herding cows.

He knew she was speaking for others aside from herself when she explained how the war and Reconstruction had left many a West Texas family shorter on boys than girls. She said two older brothers and an uncle she barely remembered had been killed in the war. Another brother who'd come home with a permanent limp and bitter memories was on the run from the law down to Old Mexico, where a gent with a Spanish name and an ill-disguised dislike for damnyankees, one word, was a tad less likely to get into fights of a Saturday night in town.

He figured much the same tale could be told by other Double H riders of the same adventuresome persuasion. He knew from many a stop for directions, cake and coffee, at many a remote homestead, that many a bored and lonesome nester gal in her teens, or even married up, had many an impractical dream to just saddle up and ride to see just what lay over that tedious horizon and whether it was true that a gal could learn to piss standing up, if she set her mind to it. So the sneaky purchasing mission by rail and astride, getting *paid*, both ways, had surely struck all those Sulfur Draw gals as a thrilling adventure and, if they were getting a tad weary of the notion by this time, what the hell, they were better than halfway home with the herd by now.

As they rode into camp under under a pearling sky a little after the time he'd set for his wake-up back in Truscott, Longarm saw they were serving breakfast around the night fire by the chuck wagon. So when Wendy offered to lead Old Paint over to the pony line for him, Longarm moseyed over to join in. That had to be Hilda Zimmer dishing out grits and gravy from the tailgate of the chuck wagon. But when she served him, she only said, "Morning, Wolf. Glad you could make it. You won't have time for seconds, and double-strength coffee will have to see you through to our next trail break, around three or four in the afternoon."

He laconically suggested he knew how you druv cows. He didn't ask if that had been her or her twin back to the hotel. He could see that, either way, she wasn't likely to give him a purely truthful answer.

Chapter 11

As Longarm was rinsing his tin plate and cup in the wreck pans of water, soapy and not-so-soapy, they were joined by Herta Zimmer in her more manly outfit and brace of six-guns. She howdied Longarm, cool, as if butter wouldn't melt in her mouth, and told her sister most of the herd seemed well rested and snuffy to go. But then she added, "Two calves and a brood cow got into that *verdammt Grunklee* along the river shallows and I thought it best to tell you before I stuck 'em."

Hilda told Longarm, "She means freshly sprouted red clover."

Before she could continue, Longarm cut in, "I know what a diet that rich can do to a critter that's been getting by on summerkilt grass, Miss Hilda. Once they're badly bloated, there's no better treatment to try than a kindly stab in the swollen paunch with a clean blade. Do you want me to do it, seeing I'm working for you-all this morning and the rest of the outfit is snuffy to go?"

Hilda handed him one of her carving knives, saying, "This blade's just been soaked in lye soap and boiling water." So he took it to follow Herta, afoot, toward the North Branch of the Wichita, where two bawling black calves and a mutely miserable cow of the same breed had been cut from the rest of the milling and restless herd.

Longarm suggested, "Why don't you and these other

ladies move 'em on out before they blow, Miss Herta? Me and these three can overtake you when and if I have 'em back on their feet. If I can't get 'em back on their feet I'll find it easier to catch up with you."

Herta yelled, "Ernestine, you heard our new ramrod! Move 'em on out while I get to my own bronc!"

Another she-male voice whooped, "Sulfur Draw and here we come, you sons of bitches!" as Longarm moseyed over to the downed cow, first, with his hopefully sterile carving knife.

It sounded like, and sort of looked and smelt like, a powerful bloody fart when you plunged a blade into the painfully swollen guts of a bloated cow. A cowgirl riding drag and close enough to notice, reined in to call, "Won't that kill her, Ramrod?"

Longarm figured she was off a barley spread until recent. So he explained without sneering, "It might. If the stab-wound mortifies. But she was fixing to die for certain unless we let all that gas out of her before she swelled worse. The bitty bugs that ferment fodder inside a cow go loco on juicy sedge or clover and blow more bubbles than the poor critter can blow out either end. So, as you just saw, it's best to let her guts deflate before they rupture."

The cowgirl protested, "That still seems a cruel way to treat a bellyache. When I et green apples as a kid, my momma made me drink baking soda and put me to bed early!"

Longarm moved toward one of the downed calves as he told her, "Your momma had more time and you were a human being. I have no bed rest to offer these critters and it's tougher to get a cow to sip baking soda. The owners don't want to see these calves grow up to be cowgirls. As grown stock they'll fetch top dollar their fourth year and be beef and shoe leather shortly after. I agree they seem to be fine stock, but they'll never sell for what it would cost to put 'em in a hospital, and this rougher and readier cure for bloat works better than half the time. So sixty-forty odds are better than total loss, and you'd best ride if you don't aim to be left behind, cowgirl!"

She spurred her bay to ride into the trail dust to the west by the first rays of sunrise as Longarm hunkered down by the first bawling calf to inform it in a conversational tone, "It might be better if you didn't look. The short sharp pang won't be nothing next to the sudden relief you'll be feeling, and your acid stomach fluids ought to cauterize the bitty hole we have to make in you, see?"

The calf just went on bawling until Longarm stabbed it, deep, to rise, soothing, "There, that didn't hurt now, did it?"

The surprised calf stopped bawling and rolled upright to look all about in wonder. By the time Longarm lanced the last calf, the first had jumped up to trot after the herd, bawling some more, but for its momma, now. He knew the bloated cow was the momma of the second calf when she got up and just stood there, chewing her cud, as she waited on her own child. So Longarm had the confounded critter up and about as Wendy Delgado rode in, leading a cordovan mare with his saddle and shit, including his Winchester, in place.

She called out, "Miss Herta said to fetch this pony back for you and give you a hand with them calves, Mr. Kruger."

He told her he only needed the pony, thanked her just the same and allowed she could call him Wolf as they followed the hopefully cured cow and her calf into the mustard-colored dust ahead.

From a bird's eye, a herd on the move was shaped like a long tear drop, running slowly in reverse with the snuffier critters forging out ahead in an ever thinning line whilst the main body needed constant driving from the drag and rear flank riders. The foreward flank and swing riders out to either side ahead were more concerned with the friskier or more independent stock as they tried to follow the course set by the point riders out front. As a rule, beef was driven slow and not too steady, with plenty of trail breaks for water and good grazing encountered along the way. Longarm figured the Zimmer twins would go for twelve or fifteen miles and call it a day, nigh any tolerable campsite they'd made by three or four so's they could settle down before night fell all around 'em on range that was new to them.

He knew this herd might move even slower with calves mixed in. For despite vaudeville songs about little dogies gitting along, you seldom saw anything but selected four-year-old beef on a regular market drive. For, like birds of a feather, beef of the same age and disposition got along best in a crowd. Breed bulls, cows in heat or with calves were a bitch to manage. But on this occasion they were pushing a smaller than usual brood of cows and some of their children *home* from the market instead of the usual way, and it hadn't been easy, according to Wendy as that calf kept trying to cut loose whilst its recovering momma forged with one of them covering either flank from the rear. Wendy said, and Longarm agreed, they'd have never in this world kept a bigger mixed herd together this far, and they still had many a mile to drive the older-and-wiser as well as the younger-and-friskier, addlepated and less surefooted calves through the uncertainties of fall weather on the high plains.

The high plains betwixt the Shining Mountains of Mister Lo, the poor Indian, and latitude 100° defined by government survey as the westward limits of unirrigated farming, stretched from parts of Old Mexico to parts of Canada, high and dry most everywhere but cool to way colder in the winters as one grazed 'em north or south. They were hot all over in summertime. How long summertime might last wasn't as easy to guess. Late wintertime in Canada could end with a Chinook or Snow Burner wind that could fill every wash with flash floods and raise the thermometers to bursting with snow still on the ground. In autumn, down the other way, you could get a Wolf Wind or what the Texicans called a Blue Norther, to freeze flesh solid as early as late August, albeit some years it stayed hot and dry past Christmas and had Texicans scanning the cloudless skies to the west for cloud one.

Longarm had noticed folk in different parts told different jokes about their weather, which was always unusual,
to hear-tell. So back East in New England, visitors were
advised that if they didn't care for the weather, they
should just set tight and wait ten minutes.

In West Texas, they told of these two old boys, spitting
and whittling on the front steps, when one of 'em glances
up to spot a cloud, way off to the west, to murmur,
"Cloudy in the west and it just might rain!"

To which his older pal replies, "I purely hope so. Not
so much for my own self as for my boys. I've done *seen*
rain in *my* day."

Longarm was hoping the weather would stay just the
way it was as he and Wendy caught up with the drag
riders, turned the cow and her calf over to them, and rode
around upwind to catch up with the head of the column.
Nobody ever rode *downwind* of even a hundred cows if
it could be avoided. The flank riders moving through all
that dust and humid body heat couldn't avoid it, of course.

As he and the boss wrangler overtook the swing riders
steering the Double H, they could see, and Longarm was
not surprised, Hilda Zimmer and her chuck wagon riders
were three furlongs on ahead, as usual. In an amusing
dime novel Longarm had recently read, published in London but set in the Dakota Territory, the chuck wagon and
other "baggage" had been bringing up the rear of a market
herd, as if it had been an army on the march. He was just
as glad Hilda Zimmer knew better. He just hated to be
served his beans and joe peppered with trail dust and powdered cow shit. He'd rid for some few bosses who thought
they were in the army. More experienced outfits sent the
wagons on ahead to call a halt for the day and put the
pots on the cow-chip coals whilst the rest of them drifted
the cows on in to the chosen night camp.

Wendy peeled off to ride with her own crew, driving
the remuda or unmounted ponies of the outfit after the
chuck wagon. Herta Zimmer and two other point riders
rode betwixt the remuda and the head of the herd, with
bandanas over their faces, albeit in truth the ponies didn't

kick up half as much dust, moving across short-grass sod.

So Longam couldn't tell whether Herta was smiling at him or not as he fell in beside her, respectsome, to her left, and told her both calves and that downed cow were back on their hooves and moving on well enough. Then he excused himself to say he had to catch up with the chuck wagon.

Herta asked how come. He said he had to return the carving knife to her sister. So Herta said, "Oh, go ahead, then. But mind that's all you try to hand my sister, Wolf Kruger!"

He reined in to soberly ask what she was talking about.

She said, "Never mind. I said go ahead. I reckon Hilda's old enough to take care of herself. But you ought to be ashamed about what you and Friskie Ralston were up to, down to the county seat!"

He trotted the cordovan ahead as he considered the ways of some women with words. He had some considering to do and a slow trot was fast enough. For most of the outfit was reining in from time to time because the natural walking gait of a horse was faster than that of a calf, even when one had the bawling veal headed in a direct line half of the time.

Seeing they had more than two hundred dusty miles to herd 'em all, Longarm was figuring on as much as two tedious weeks in the saddle, with October-and-who-knew sure to reach them before they could hope to reach Sulfur Draw. That promised from thirteen to eighteen nights of officiously sleeping alone in his or her own bedroll, no matter how hot or cold the autumn winds might blow. But the day was young and he was still working on that crack about him and Friskie Ralston as he caught up with Wendy Delgado and her two wranglers, walking their own mounts a natural three miles an hour to keep pace with the chuck wagon out ahead as both slowly widened the gap betwixt themselves and the lowing Cherokee stock. He returned Wendy's wave and rode on, chewing over that parting shot of Herta Zimmer's like a cud of stick-erbrush.

What she'd said about him and Friskie could be taken more than one way. She could have taken to brooding over second thoughts about his way with a maid if that had been her back yonder in his hotel room.

Or she could be the innocent one, worried about a man with a rep for womanizing messing with her sister, not knowing he already had. He'd thought, back in the hotel, he'd be able to tell which twin he'd enjoyed so much, more than once. But back at that first camp, the both of them had carried on as Queen Victoria would have surely approved, save for Herta wearing pants and two guns.

As he overtook the chuck wagon, he saw that, rank having its own privileges, and chuck wagons having neither springs nor thorough-braces, Hilda Zimmer was riding a cream barb, astride in her own denim jeans, as one of her chuck wagon gals drove. He waved the knife as he rode in. Hilda pointed at the wagon and told him to chuck it in the back, so he wheeled that way and did so, hoping he wasn't damaging anything as the blade rang like a bell in the mysterious depths under the canvas top. Chuck wagons had been devised by Captain Charles Goodnight of the JA Brand in the Palo Duro country of the Panhandle to the west-northwest. So the design hadn't been worked out to a T and no two of them were laid out the same way inside.

As he rode over to rein in beside the now more mannishly dressed Hilda Zimmer, Longarm said, "It does beat all how history has this habit of repeating herself. That carving knife and me just remembered Captain Charlie Goodnight. I rid with him one time, before he came back down from the north range to start his new spread in the Palo Duro."

He reminded himself once more to consider before sounding off when she asked when and where he'd ridden for Captain Goodnight if he hailed from the border lands to the south.

He easily replied, "I hail from all over, Miss Hilda. I doubt old Charlie Goodnight would recall the kid I was when I rid for him up Colorado way before the bank failings of '73. Other stockmen had crowded in around him and he'd overspent in building that fine opera house for Pueblo up yonder. So like others I could mention, Captain Goodnight and his kith and kin started over, more recent, on another stretch of Comanche hunting ground opened up for settlement by the Bureau of Land Management, if you follow my drift."

She shrugged and said, "It's no secret fortunes can be made or lost with the right combinations of water, grass and beef. We've all heard the tale of the serving wench whose boss, short on ready cash, paid her a few head of cows at a time to graze with his herd under her own brand."

Longarm nodded and soberly replied, "I was wondering where you and your twin got your inspiration to upgrade your herd. The way I heard it, when that serving wench quit, ten years later, she sold her stock and its natural increases for twenty-five thousand dollars!"

Hilda Zimmer sniffed and said, "I'd as soon you didn't worry yourself about the way my sister and me think, Wolf. I know we need you. That's why we hired you. But I'd better not hear of you *inspiring* my impulsive twin, as impulsive as poor Herta might strike you!"

Chapter 12

As they rode on, he chewed that cud long enough to decide that she had to be prick teasing whether she'd ever had his prick in her or not. So, seeing there were only two ways a man could cope with a prick-teasing woman, and seeing forcible rape was indecent, Longarm gravely assured her, "You have my word as an enlisted man and gent of the country school, I do not intend to do or say a thing to . . . ah, inspire either one of you ladies. If that ain't assurance enough, we'll say nothing more about it. It ain't too far for me to *walk* back to Truscott from here if you don't figure I've done chores enough to rate me this pony."

She smiled uncertainly and said, "Don't be silly. I just said we needed you. It's just that Herta is so inclined to leap before she looks and, well, you are a handsome devil and you did say you knew Friskie Ralston!"

He shrugged and said, "Miss Florence never called you nor your twin a soiled dove but, for the record, I make no claims to pure virginity, and, it's a known fact, few natural men would turn down worse. But as I assured the *last* gal I had back yonder, I mean to leave such matters to lady's choice until further notice. We were talking about how money can be made or lost with water, grass and beef as the wide open spaces out our way open up to new settlement."

She asked, "Has Herta been encouraging your natural interests?"

To which he truthfully replied, "Not no way a man could be *certain* of, Ma'am, and I was hired to herd cows, not to gossip like a biddie over a backyard fence!"

Then he wheeled the cordovan to lope back to where Herta and her front riders were walking their own mounts.

As he fell in beside her, Herta Zimmer shot him an arch look to ask, "So, how did it go with my sister, Wolf?"

He said, "I just offered to quit if she warned me one more time to unhand your fair white body. The offer still stands if you persist in protecting *hers*, Miss Herta. I told her as I'm telling you and . . . some other gal I met up with last night, I know better than to drool at any of you cowgirls like a moon calf by the light of broad day or in a trailside camp with no more privacy than a railroad waiting room!"

She demurely said she just wanted to get such matters settled. He said they were settled and he had to circle back and make sure the other cowgirls were paying attention to business instead of jawing about country matters like pool hall loafers.

She called him something in High Dutch that sounded dirty as he loped back, deliberate, on the downwind dusty side.

As he'd feared, the two flank riders out that way were herding too far out from the herd, allowing stock to drift ever wider over that way. He called, "Keep 'em bunched tighter! Don't ever let a critter drift far enough downwind to notice the air gets cooler and smells better as you leave more space betwixt horns. For, taken to its logical conclusion, your average cow would feel even better ranging totally free across open prairie at its own chosen pace!"

He set an example by cutting off an adventurous calf and whupping it back into the heat and dust with his new but grimy throw-rope.

He'd already formed a modest noose through the brass honda before he'd tied the other end to his horn and coiled the rest to ride just ahead of his right knee. So the tight loop, impractical to rope with unless he formed at least a yard-wide throw, made a big mace-like knot a calf just hated to be spanked with.

There was seldom if ever call to actually rope a critter on a well-managed trail drive. Wild horses got roped, sometimes in the corral, until they were gentled down and saddle broke. Unbranded and uncut calves and occasional mavericks had to be roped 'cause no critter with a lick of sense was going to come willing to be seared with hot iron and get operated on with no anesthetics. But professional stockfolk tried not to jerk beef or horseflesh around any more than they had to. For beef sold on the hoof by the pound and a busted-up pony you had to shoot was no use to anyone. What some sentimental tourists put down as cruelty to dumb animals was simply the way one raised animals, by definition dumb, at the least possible cost with the least effort on the part of hired help. The Zimmer twins were now a tad short of help, thanks to desertion and that shoot-out. But since neither of those punctured calves nor the one bloated cow had dropped out, yet, the spanky young gals were doing all right and he knew Wendy Delgado was a fair wrangler in spite of her looks.

In spite of Ned Buntline and that writer cranking out Wild West yarns in Berlin, in High Dutch, neither the self-made cattlemen nor Wall Street or European holding companies currently raising beef in the American West were in the entertainment industry, and working cows was not a blood sport for adventurous youths.

Whatever they thought they might be doing in a saddle, they'd been hired to help their outfit show a profit, and the margins of profit or loss in the beef industry were balanced on the scales of uncertainty.

The duck-soup-simple goal of management was to deliver to market—alive and healthy enough to be worth buying—the natural increase of as large a herd as you could amass and maintain on often marginal range and water. Other outfits had their own beef to offer and the meat packers' buyers played that card to pay as little as possible for the best beef available. So you were only talking pennies a head when your year's expenses came as no surprise. And you could be surprised heaps of ways, getting a five-dollar range calf to the slaughterhouse as a forty-five to sixty-dollar steer. Longarm hadn't seen fit to ask how much the Zimmer twins had paid for this herd of Cherokee stock. He knew Billy Vail would find out, sneakier.

Keeping the 'rithmetic simple as he circled the prize seed stock, Longarm guestimated that blue ribbon bull might upgrade the seventy or eighty he'd impregnate on average with seven or eight thousand dollars worth of ten-dollar calves that might sell for as much as $64,000 in four years and by then, of course that same bull would have serviced more to come.

They hadn't said, but he'd soon find out, how many head of scrub stock they'd have at their home spread ahead. He was fixing to be surprised if he didn't find they'd filed homestead claim to the usual hundred and sixty acres, strung out like an acre-wide ribbon along wet bottomland so's they and nobody else could graze the open range up and away from the water.

Another consideration that made the high plains grazing so tempting to gents as far away as Scotland and Scandinavia was that cows could be held without fencing when they had to wander more than a few hours worth for anybody else's water rights. The herds of neighbors up- and downstream would naturally mix some as they grazed. But good neighbors rounded all the stock up together and cut cows and their calves out by brands, with each outfit having indisputable rights to brand such increase as their own, unless, as rarely but sometimes did happen, a less neighborly neighbor chose to dispute the ownership of a five- or ten-dollar calf, at some risk to his own life and property.

Longarm had seen that happen, and arrested some survivors of such disputes in other parts. A heap depended on how crowded together the herds were getting as time wore on, and how neighbors felt about one another to begin with.

Over to Lincoln County in '78, John Tunstall had accused the Dolan riders of stealing his beef, Jim Dolan had pressed fatal charges against Tunstall for stealing *his* beef, and Big John Chisum had let it be known he was getting sick and tired of *everybody* stealing *his* beef!

"Why do I keep mulling over ancient history?" Longarm asked his cordovan as he nodded to a she-male drag rider and circled through the dust to move up the windward side of the plodding herd.

He hadn't been there. He'd only heard a heap about the famous and downright futile Lincoln County War. He suspected half the things one heard or read about it, this late in the game, had been edited to fit the political agenda of the newspapers rehashing the short if bloody disorder. The new governor appointed by President Hayes to tidy up had done so, with a firm but fair broom, granting amnesty to any survivors willing to quit fighting and placing draconian bounties on the heads of those who wouldn't. If the leaders of the Tunstall-McSween faction lay dead, the Big Store of Major Murphy and Jim Dolan had done little better. Major Murphy had come down with pneumonia and died in the fall of that springtime war his pals had commenced by murdering Tunstall. Dolan had gone broke the next year, defending himself in court for killing a Huston Chapman Esquire, who'd had nothing to do with the Lincoln County War. So the Big Store was now the Lincoln County courthouse and jail, seized for back taxes by the same and why did this *matter*?

Longarm pondered that hard as he rode slowly up the windward flank of the herd, nodding approval in turn to the gals riding flank on that side. It was easier to crowd cows close-packed when you rode upwind of 'em. The dust and all that moist heat blew the other way from you.

He told his cow pony, "This ain't the same situation, exactly. To begin with it was Protestant High Dutch getting along tolerable with Anglo-Mex neighbors when High-Dutch speaking Papists moved in around Sulfur

Draw to . . . do what? Both twins agree the newcomers were welcome as soap in the coffeepot, and, since then, there's been barn burnings and worse. But to what end, and why do I keep harking back to another range in other parts? All sorts of range wars have cropped up all over this land of opportunity, and some I could mention came closer to this Staked Plains feud in numbers and motivation. What are we looking for, up ahead, to remind us so much of that overblown and stupid Lincoln County War?"

He decided to settle for the stupidity, for now. The whole point of pioneering new range was to take advantage of unclaimed empty spaces, not to fight over them like cur dogs over one bone in a bone yard.

As he neared the point riders, one of them was loping her pony his way, calling, "Miss Herta wants you up ahead with the chuck wagon on the double! She's already on her own way!"

Longarm heeled the cordovan into a lope as the young cowgirl spun her roan. As they loped off together, she said she didn't know what the emergency was. One of Miss Hilda's scullery hands had loped in with bad news of some ilk, and Herta Zimmer had said to fetch Wolf.

As they passed the remuda, Wendy Delgado and her crew had the four score spare ponies grazing in place, six head to a lead. The Tex-Mex wrangler had her saddle gun out and when she said she didn't know, either, what the trouble was, he commanded, "Stay put and hold them horses tight!"

Then he and the gal who'd ridden back to fetch him forged on to join the tense discussion around the chuck wagon a quarter mile on.

Longarm guessed what was up right off as he reined in to drift on thoughtful with his own saddle gun across his saddle in front of his fly. An older man and four raggedy youths sat ratty ponies betwixt the chuck wagon team and a nigh-dry braided creek running north to the branch of the Wichita they were now well south of. Herta and the two mannishly dressed cowgirls sat their ponies in silence with their hair pinned up inside the high crowns of their

94

Texas ten gallons, the broad brims shading their faces pretty good.

So Hilda, as boss-cook in a pinafore she'd doubtless changed to sudden, was arguing with the old-timer from the box of her chuck wagon. As Longarm approached she turned to call out, "Mr. Kruger, these gentlemen dispute our right of passage across yon draw!"

The old nester grinned at Longarm like a shit-eating dog to say, "That ain't the problem, Mister. As I was just trying to explain to your cook and these young cowboys, the water still running across my land this late in the Big Dry is the problem. Since you look like a cowboy as well, I see no call to explain there's no way to herd nigh a hundred horses and even more cows across running water without them helping themselves to a heap of it! So you see how it is?"

Longarm nodded soberly and said, "I see how it is. Are we upstream or down from your home spread?"

The lean and hungry-looking old-timer waved casually at a barely visible cluster of rooftops, upstream a lot further than anyone might manage on one homestead claim, even strung along the draw like town-lots. So Longarm said, "*Bueno*. That means we won't have to drive wide to avoid mud in your dishwater this evening. That water is *running*. So even as we speak more water's flowing past than a market herd of a thousand could consume in passing. But say we accept your claim to water rights this far from home, how much were you figuring on asking for the precious liquid, friend?"

The old-timer said, "I ain't your friend, I'm Pepper Thompson and these are my four famous boys I'm sure you've heard of if you've ever been to Dodge. We're the Rocking T and this precious water is our own to hold agin' all comers, unless you'd like to share in our largess at two bits a head."

Glancing over at Herta, Longarm snapped, "Let me handle this, and let go that gun, Zimmer!" before she could draw and fire. Then, he told the older man in a calmer but no-less-firm tone. "I have a better notion. I want the five of you to dismount, slow and easy. Then, I want you to stand right where you are, polite as five wooden Indians, whilst I cover you as my outfit crosses unmolested and for free."

One of the Thompson boys laughed like hell. He looked to be about the youngest. His father, who'd managed to reach old-and-gray alive, in spite of his bullying ways, soberly replied, "You've surely been drinking something stronger than water, Ramrod. There's five of us and one of you, as I see it."

Longarm said, "Look again. I've more than five rounds in this here Winchester, with one in the chamber, and my play is being backed by a dozen or more riders."

Pepper Thompson shorted, "Shoot, can't be one of them kid cowboys old enough to shave, aside from yourself."

To which Longarm replied with an alarming grin, "You don't know how true that is. But if you think I'm bluffing, feel free to try us!"

One of his boys said, "Hot damn! Let's have us a hoedown, Dad!"

But his older and wiser father said, "Let's not and say we did. He ain't bluffing. When and if you ever reach my age, you'll have larnt to tell. For if you haven't, you'll never reach my age."

Chapter 13

So the Double H passed over Jordan, or whatever that prairie creek was called, as Longarm and his Winchester kept company with the Rocking T. It took longer than it would take to tell about it because as old Pepper Thompson had foreseen, and continued to piss and moan about, each and every critter paused to guzzle as it forded the braided stream.

Lest they mistake his good nature for weakness, Longarm told him to shut up and keep his own counsel until the cowgirls riding drag were a furlong west of the draw before he reached in his jeans with his rein hand to fish out a gold eagle of his own, saying, "I'm sure glad you-all decided to be sensible about this, seeing I'd heard of you up to Dodge. You understand I didn't want the boss to think I was a sissy. But now that we're parting friendly, I'd like to stand a round of drinks for the Rocking T."

He tossed the glittering gold to the grass near the older man's dusty boot tips. He wheeled his cordovan to lope across the creek, a difficult target, as the chief of the clan snapped, "Don't try it, Rafe! It ain't worth the risk and he *said* he was parting friendly!"

Then, and only then, he bent over to pluck the worth of two scrub calves from the stubble, explaining, "Us grown men understands one another. He called my bluff but bent enough to leave me some pride, and I'll not have him shot in the back, even if you had a hope in hell of hitting him at that range!"

So Longarm rode on at a lope to where he spied Herta Zimmer in the haze of dust stirred up by the herd ahead. She'd reined in to sit her pony with her own saddle gun across her thighs.

As Longarm rode to join her, he slid his Winchester back in its boot on the off side of his cantle to call, "War's over, Miss Herta. Better yet, I see the stock's moving on tighter after cooling off and watering up."

She put her own Winchester away with a wolfish smile to reply, "We were smart to hire you. Junior Brewster might have just dickered them down to drinking money, I fear."

Longarm replied with a poker face, "There's something to be said for bending with the wind a mite. But, as I was just telling those trash whites, two bits a head was ridiculous. Now that he's calmed down, some, Chief Quanah Parker will let you graze and water stock clean across the new Comanche reserve for two bits a head."

"I'd never pay him," she declared, as if the matter was settled.

Since they still had a far piece to go, Longarm gently but firmly replied, "Like I just said, there's something to be said for bending with the wind and you have to weigh the risks. Sometimes it can make more sense to spare Quill Indians a few plugs of tobacco or a side of beef than to chase a stampeded herd all over creation after you've *whupped* the noisy rascals. I knew a trail boss one time who was too pigheaded to let some nester kids gather the cow-chips from his herd in a wheelbarrow they'd pushed out to his bedding grounds. He lost his job as well as a whole lot of stock when some person or persons unknown set fire to the grass, upwind, in the dark of night. So I'll not fault old Junior Brewster for what he might or might not have done, back yonder. No offense, but from the way I hear-tell, Junior might have settled that unfriendly visit from Puff Duffy, Silent Ryan and that breed without anybody having to die."

She shook her head firmly and said, "I did what I had to. You would have done the same if you'd been there. Were you able to settle it without a fight when those other three came after you the other night?"

As they rode on he tried, "The Catlin gang were known killers. They were looking to build their rep with another killing, and it was three on one."

"I rest my case." She smiled, adding, "The lawyer we hired in vain for poor Junior told us Silent Ryan had killed more than once and *I* heard-tell, back in Truscott, those other three were after you for being a friend of Junior's after Junior, they thought, had shot it out with Ryan and *his* friends!"

He grudgingly conceded she might have been up against an otherwise insolvable situation, and once more caught his mind drifting over to New Mexico Territory as he recalled the Catlin gang hailing from that recent battleground along the Pecos.

Herta asked how come they were overtaking the herd's downwind flank, asking if the riding wouldn't be less hot and dusty on its upwind flank. He told her cows almost never stampeded *into* the wind whilst flank riders on the downwind side had been known to pay less attention to their jobs as they worried more about breathing or the mud in their eyes.

But as they overtook the downwind flank riders in turn, they saw the plucky cowgirls were holding the stock tight, with bandanas over their lower faces and tears streaming from their red-rimmed eyes. It was best to just go ahead and cry with dust in your eyes. Greenhorns rubbed such eyes until they learned not to, if they could still see.

Longarm and Herta Zimmer were weeping some as well by the time they got out ahead and clear of the fine alluvial not alkali dust of the high plains. You got alkali or soluble mineral salts in cactus country rather than grasslands, but Ned Buntline, writing those Wild West tales back East, didn't seem to savvy the distinction.

Plain old prairie grit was bad enough. The winds and rains of many a year had ground the silts and clays nigh as fine as baking flour, but left the sharp edges.

Through all the conversations he'd had with Herta and her sister, Hilda, since rejoining whichever one he'd screwed the night before, he was still uncertain which one that might have been. For whether smiling at him or frowning at him, neither had sent a smoke signal from even one of four big blue eyes, and if he hadn't been there he'd have said nobody had the right to talk so dirty about an innocent young thing.

But he had been there, the day was young, and so further along he'd figure out which of 'em might want some more in the dark of night.

The day's drive was uneventful from the brush with the nesters to where Hilda called a halt around three.

The high plains of northern Texas rolled like the gentle groundswells of a placid sea of grass, punctuated by timbered draws and, now and again, an isolated box elder, blackjack oak or cottonwood grove as made no sense where it had sprouted until you studied some. In spite of Freemont's describing it as "Great American Desert," the usually sunny and dry sea of grass betwixt the Rockies and Big Muddy got as much scattered rain as thriftier breeds of trees needed to get by on, once they got started. It survived long enough to sink roots to the permanent water table, way down deep. Buffalo just loved to brouse tender young box elder and cottonwood leaves, and they'd nibble bitter blackjack and chokecherry shoots above the stubble of overgrazed grass when they got hungry enough. But Mister Lo, the poor Indian, had done as much or more than Dame Nature to assure a rolling meadowland for his hunting ponies and the grazing critters he hunted on 'em by setting vast tracts of summerkilt grass aflame every fall to encourage a new crop of greenup grass whilst discouraging anything perennial.

With both Mister Lo and his buffalo herds thinned considerable, a tree seed had a fighting chance on higher windswept prairie if it managed to sprout in the lee of a buffalo skull or an already up-and-at-'em sapling. So, once established, a pioneer cottonwood in particular could develop into a spreading grove in a few summers.

The bedding ground and campsite Hilda Zimmer chose that afternoon offered the best of both possible worlds on the high plains. Nobody seemed to dispute their right to make use of a long, grassy swell sloping down to the south into a timbered draw where a steady trickle of autumn water wound through standing or fallen timber to form a pool hither and a puddle yonder. So the herd had all the water it might want all night, with the thick sticker-brush to the south as good as barbwire at discouraging adventuresome stock from straying.

The Double H riders naturally spread their rolls on the grass upstream to the west, with the remuda tethered between in a grove of juicy cottonwood brouse. Longarm noted with approval how Wendy Delgado's crew cleared some scattered wild cherry, lest some restless pony poison its fool self with a sleepy midnight snack. The scrubby wild chokecherries of the high plains were good to eat, once you'd boiled 'em in sugar-water a spell for preserves, but, like their pits, the *leaves* of most any breed of cherry contained cyanide.

The bitterness of acorns and oak leaves came from tannic acid, which wouldn't poison you because it was too bitter to swallow enough to matter.

Longarm unsaddled the cordovan, dumped everything on the grass, and started to lead it to join the other riding stock in the nearby draw.

But one of Wendy Delgado's wrangling gals, another Tex-Mex who'd turned out almost as pretty but seemed less inclined to the regular use of soap and water, headed him off with a rope hack to replace and hand back his own bridle before she led the spent pony away. As she did so, Longarm gave the cordovan a friendly pat on the rump. He had no call to pat the senorita's shaplier rump and, even if he'd been a total asshole, her's was out of easy reach.

Over to the chuck wagon they were piling dry sticks and cow-chips for the fires, dry wood being easier to get started whilst dried cow dung burned longer with less smoke. So Longarm gazed all about, spotted a grove of wind-pruned box elder atop a not-too-far rise and toted his saddle and possibles on over.

Box elder was dwarfish kin to the prouder sugar maple of the east. Thanks to growing atop a rise, the grove of half a dozen had been stunted and twisted by the winds to interlock their branches as a fluttersome bower, with the maple-shaped leaves still green where they weren't commencing to turn buckskin. He unlashed his bedroll to spread his canvas ground cloth, flannel bedding and waterproof tarp out on the greener, longer and springier orchard grass he'd hoped to find there. He placed his saddle to serve as a sort of headboard betwixt his bedding and the others camped on down the slope. Then he hung his hat on the saddle horn and sat down to light a smoke as he took a well-deserved break.

He wasn't surprised when, before he'd finished his cheroot, a familiar figure came up the slope on foot to fetch him. As she saw what he had wrought in the late afternoon shade, Wendy Delgado said, "I thought you said you were a West Texas rider. That shaded grass is surely infested with chiggers, Wolf."

He said, "I ain't as sure as you, this far north, where the fall nights will soon be frosty. But if there *are* any bugs up this way, I took the precaution of stirring larkspur lotion into the linseed oil and I used turpentine to waterproof my ground cloth and tarp. Is that why you trudged all this way, Miss Wendy?"

She said, "No. Miss Hilda wants you, over to the chuck wagon. How come *you* trudged all this way with your bedding, Wolf? Afraid some of us gals might laugh if we caught you playing with yourself after dark?"

To which he easily replied, "You strum your banjo and I'll strum mine, Miss Wendy. What did Miss Hilda want with me?"

The wrangler shrugged and said she just worked there. So Longarm put his hat back on, got up, and followed her down to the chuck wagon to find out.

Hilda Zimmer's crew had fetched water and put it on

to boil as they ground coffee, kneaded sourdough and so on. The owner and self-appointed boss-cook smiled uncertainly and said, "I thought you were headed up into those distant trees, Wolf. How come?"

He'd had time to study on his answers by then. So he knew it would sound logical when he easily replied, "General George Washington's orders, Ma'am. He started out a planter and made some awful mistakes at first. But he never forgot a mistake and toward the end he knew a thing or two about field tactics."

"George Washington told you to go off in a corner and pout?" Hilda marveled as her twin, Herta, drifted in to join them.

Longarm shook his head to calmly reply, "Not pouting, Miss Hilda. Occupying the high ground. Gentleman Johnny Burgoyne took Ticonderoga because our side had neglected to occupy a nearby hill overlooking the fort. So General Washington warned everybody not to never make that mistake again. I figured one cruel-hearted rascal up amongst them box elder with a rifle could play ned with this whole outfit from such a vantage point. So I claimed it for my very own. Is that what you wanted to talk to me about?"

She said, "No. I don't care where you bed down tonight as long as it's not with one of my riders. Ernestine Holz, riding drag, tells us one of those calves you lanced for the bloat is doing poorly. Hot, dry muzzle and drooling froth. What do you suggest?"

He shrugged and said, "It's fevered. Nothing anyone *can* do for a fevered critter that wouldn't cost more than it was worth on the hoof, if it worked. I told you earlier my rough-and-ready treatment was a tad better than letting bloated stock just die. One out of three on its last legs ain't bad."

Herta Zimmer asked if she shouldn't shoot the poor critter and get it over with.

Longarm said, "It ain't over 'til it's over, Miss Herta. If it's on its last legs, it's best to wait for it to fall down before you put it out of its misery. For whilst there's life, there's hope, and on rare occasions such fevers break. It all depends on how mortified that stab wound might be and how tough the little critter chooses to be. It may die in the night on us, saving you the price of a bullet. If it's able to get back up and stagger on, come morning, we'll just say no more about it. If it seems down for good, you can shoot it as we're leaving. Can't you wait that long?"

Herta demurely replied, with a Mona Lisa smile, "I've always been more patient than a lot of people give me credit for."

Chapter 14

It is written, though Allah be more merciful and not in the Koran, that when the Prophet was asked if it was a mortal sin, he declared that nine out of ten men jacked off and that tenth man was a liar.

But Longarm resisted temptation as the night wore on, and nobody seemed to be coming, including him, for he just knew that the minute he shot his wad way up in the middle of the air, that sneaky Zimmer twin would be crawling into that sleeping bag with him and *then* where would he be?

A million sheep over the fence later, things were stirring down the slope and he was awake with a raging erection after six or eight hours sleep, feeling frisky as all get-out.

So he got up and got dressed some more. Some other wise prophet had long-ago advised, doubtless in French, to never jack off early in the morning because you never knew who you might meet for lunch.

It was still dark, of course. Herding cows, you et hearty, saddled up and moved 'em on out before sunrise. After he'd filled the void in his middle with bisquits, bacon, tomato preserves and plenty of black coffee, Longarm rode back on the paint Wendy had chosen for him that morning to see how that ailing calf was doing.

The other punctured calf and that grown cow were

somewhere in the milling herd ahead. Ernestine Holz, a plump redhead of the High-Dutch persuasion in chinked chaps she hoped might hide her broader-than-average hips, stood by, holding the reins of her bay gelding, as she coaxed the black calf on its belly before her to rise and shine.

Longarm dismounted to hand her his reins and hunker down by the feverish calf, muttering, "You're fixing to get your calves brains displayed without chopped ice under 'em, old son."

He felt the calf's nose. It didn't seem to care. He told it, "Hot and dry. But I've felt hotter and drier and you ain't drooling all that much."

He rose, strode around to the face the critter's rump, and bent to gather up the end of its black tail in both hands before he kicked and tugged, to haul the downed calf to its feet, backwards, as it bawled like hell.

"Oh, you're hurting it!" protested the young cowgirl who seemed to favor a less disciplined approach to life. So when Longarm slapped the bawling bewildered critter's black hide with his coffee-brown Stetson to send it running after the herd, he said, "I was sure trying to, Miss Ernestine. If we hadn't been able to move it on out, we'd have had to shoot it lest it last, alone and crippled up, until the coyotes found it. I was hoping it was just feeling awful and, as you see, it was. Another day on the trail, in the steam bath of bigger brutes to all sides, ought to break its fever or put it down on the ground for good, see?"

As he took his reins from her, she dimpled and said, "My friends all call me Ernie, Mr. Kruger."

As he remounted, he told her she could call him Wolf, but she still got to ride drag until further notice. As he rode on, she answered him in High Dutch. From her tone it seemed safe to assume she'd heard their new ramrod didn't savvy the lingo.

And so the day's drive went, slowing down once an hour to graze 'em without stopping as they trended west-southwest more or less in line with the post road from Truscott to Guthrie, a county seat on the south fork of the

Wichita, say thirty miles from where Longarm had joined the outfit. He perforce oversaw setting up the afternoon camp an hour's ride out of Guthrie and rode in after supper, he said, to wet his whistle. The Zimmer twins wouldn't let any other riders keep him company and he was just as glad.

His main reason for riding to town was to wire another progress report to his "Uncle Billy" at a private address along the brow of Denver's Capitol Hill. He didn't ask whether his boss had wired him in care of their Guthrie office. He hadn't been able to say, and he still wasn't sure where they'd be camping next. You herded cows as best you could and you got there when you got there.

After he'd dropped by the Western Union, he did treat himself to a slab of ham smothered in chili con carne and some devil's food cake. Then he bellied up to the bar in a saloon catering to gents short on neckties with longer chin stubble. Nobody started up with him or offered to introduce him to their sisters. So he'd been fixing to leave anyhow when a squirt with a copper badge upped to him to say he didn't cotton to fucking cowboys packing guns in his town.

Longarm finished the last of his needled suds and set the stein down as he quietly said he was just leaving. When the squirt stuck his chest out to snap, "See that you do unless you'd like me to show you how our boot hill got started!"

It was hard not to laugh, but when a lawman was working undercover he had to put up with a reasonable amount of shit and, being it was an election year, the squirt was entitled to score a few votes with no skin off anyone's ass.

But as he led the Double H palomino show horse from the livery he'd left it in across the way, that same kid deputy caught up with him in the gathering dusk to say, "Mr. Kruger, we got to talk."

Longarm sighed and said, "Let's not push it, Sheriff, I said I was on my way back to my outfit."

The squirt said, "I didn't know who you were, back

there, when I may have got just a little out of line. A rider who'd come in from Truscott this morning just now told us how you'd shot it out with that Catlin gang in that other saloon."

Longarm shrugged and said, "They wouldn't leave me alone. As long as folk leave me alone I'm a live-and-live cuss and, like I told you inside, I was leaving anyhow. So what's got you so wide-eyed and lip-licking, now?"

The kid said, "You. Come morning it's likely to be all over Kings County that I ran the famous Wolf Kruger out of town all by myself!"

Longarm nodded in understanding and said, "I feel for you, but I just can't reach you. I don't *want* to go back inside with you to belly back up to the bar and convince everybody we're pals and you were only joshing. You made your bed as big bad *buscadero*, and so now I suggest you lie in it and practice your draw, unless you'd as soon turn in your badge and follow some less uncertain career."

The callow punk who'd bullied him almost sobbed, "Practice won't do me much good if they come after me in numbers, looking to count coup on the man who ran Wolf Kruger out of town! You just gotta help me nip such a rep in the bud. It ain't that I'm yaller, Mr. Kruger, it's just that I have yet to *have* any gunfights!"

Longarm mounted the palomino as he soothed, "Don't worry, I feel sure you'll be having your first one anytime, now. You're fixing to have one here and now if you don't get the fuck out of my way. For I have never liked bullies of any breed, and a bully who hides behind a badge and a bluff is a specimen of the breed who'd eat shit. So, like I said, run home to your momma or learn to fight if you mean to act the part of King County's Wild Town-tamer."

Then he rode off to leave the mean-mouthed kid considering the errors of his ways. Odds were the real lawmen he worked for would fire him and save his fool neck as soon as they heard what a stupid saloon brag he'd cut loose with.

Back at the night camp, Hilda Zimmer was still up and

poured him a last cup as she quietly asked, "How come you're back so early? No *Huren*, I mean fancy ladies, in so large a town?"

He poured half the cup in the night fire as he calmly replied, "I better not finish this joe lest I fail to meet up with the gal of my dreams tonight. Nobody I saw in town was as exiting."

"Oh? So what might this girl of your dreams look like, Wolf?" she asked in a mocking tone.

He confessed, "Can't say, for certain. She's a shy little thing who makes love in the dark."

"She'd better not be real! She'd better not be one of our riders!" Hilda Zimmer snapped with a flounce of her ash blond hair.

Longarm said, "I can't say whether she's real or not, Miss Hilda. But I'm sure she don't work for you or your sister."

The Zimmer twin turned away, as if she was trying not to sneeze, or bust out laughing. So Longarm bade her "*Auf Wiedersehen*" which was High Dutch for *adios*—he'd looked it up. Then, he trudged away in the dark to where he'd spread his bedding under blackjack oaks, that night.

But nobody came, not even him, and then it was time to get up and move 'em on out some more, riding a blue roan from the remuda that morning. He didn't see that fevered calf apart from the herd by the tricky early light. Since it didn't stay behind when they moved on, he figured it was still alive. Lord willing, and it was able to water and graze some, now, its odds on ever seeing the Staked Plains, now, stood around sixty-forty against the infected critter.

Acting in his capacity as Wolf Kruger, Longarm suggested to Hilda that she steer more to the southwest. When she protested they'd likely wind up crossing higher and dried range, he explained, "That's what I just said. There's more home spreads and drift fences closer to the post road and that south fork of yonder Wichita. Longhorns can last a day or more without water and we'll have druv 'em to the drainage of the White River off your Staked Plains before you lose many."

She said, "We don't want to lose *any*!" Then she asked, "What about *Cherokee* longhorns, Wolf?"

He shrugged in the saddle and said, "You and your sister knew when you set out to fetch 'em home they were a thrifty breed you could hope to raise on the Staked Plains, didn't you?"

He let that sink in and added, "We're driving this herd cross-grain and contrary to the dreams and aspirations of all the homesteaders or stockfolk in these parts. You've already had a brush with bully boys confounded by your contrary ways, Miss Hilda. After that, the way I heard it, you and your whole bunch of cowgirls meant to slip away to the Indian Territory and bring these black cows back on the Q.T. So do you really want to answer heaps of questions as we detour miles around fenced croplands or untangle your herd from others grazing nigh the headwaters of the Wichita?"

She allowed she didn't, and the next time they had to circle south of a roadside spread she kept heading that way instead of veering back to the north. So later that afternoon they broke trail for the day on wide-open range miles from anything or anybody, and the cows bitched like hell about that all through the night.

Next morning, after yet another night alone in his lonesome bedroll, Longarm scouted ahead for water. Some crowbirds rising from far-off cottonwoods put him on to a brushy draw where scattered ponds along the soggy bottom assured birds and now livestock and the camp pots and kettles of tepid water to go around.

But whilst both Hilda and Herta congratulated him for his range savvy at suppertime, neither twin, nor anybody else, came to join him in a mighty private clump of willow up the draw a ways.

So next morning they had some trouble getting the herd to move on from that watered draw. It wasn't true that cows were totally dumb animals and the independent Hispano-Moorish longhorn they'd started out as had memories to rival elephants and held grudges when they felt abused, as many a Spanish matador had discovered to his sorrow on the horns of less ornery Andalusian bulls.

But with some determination, some pistol shots and a heap of sheer she-male stubbornness, the cowgirls of the Double H got them going some more and none of 'em seemed really stressed until around noon, when Longarm rode foreward to suggest to Hilda that she rein in the chuck wagon and call it a day.

As he passed the remuda at a lope aboard a buckskin barb, Longarm saw the chuck wagon was already standing still atop the next rise to the southwest. As he joined Hilda Zimmer, seated on a chestnut gelding with Morgan lines, out ahead of her chuck wagon team a piece, she grimly asked, "Do you know any other swell shortcuts, Wolf?"

He followed her gaze to where a ragged-ass line of Indian ponies faced them from another rise three furlongs on out, with eight or ten Quill Indians and thrice that many dependants mounted on the same.

Hilda Zimmer quietly added, "Some of them are wearing feathers."

Longarm said, "Two of 'em are wearing hats and I don't see no paint. They look to be Arapaho."

She asked how he could tell and he said, "That fat old jasper in the cavalry hat and blouse is signing us they're Arapaho."

She marveled, "Is that what he's doing? I thought we was beating his chest like an ape trying to scare me!"

Then as Longarm stood taller in his stirrups to sign his friendly intentions with two fingers of his upraised right hand, she added in a quietly thoughtful tone, "He succeded, too!"

Longarm warned, "Let me do the talking for now. This is no time to make the wrong gesture!" as he wig-wagged his open palm to sign, "Question," followed by the scissored fingers in front of his face to sign "Talking with mouth." Then he made the sort of stiff eyeshading salute that signified white folk.

The fat, distant Indian raised one finger to say "Yes."

111

Longarm told Hilda, "He speaks English. Save time if I ride on to powwow with 'em. They look to be runaways from north of the old Cimarron. Some bands of holdouts never moved on up to their reserve in the Wind River country when the Bureau of Indian Affairs allowed they ought to."

As he signed for a powwow, they were joined by Herta and two other armed and dangerous-looking cowgirls. Herta started to ask why they were stopping, took in the view ahead, and swore, "*Ach, Donnerwetter!* Where did all those Indians come from and what do they want?"

To which Longarm could only reply, "Only one way to find out. So hold your fire unless and until you see me go down."

As he heeled his mount forward Hilda called, "Come back here and let's talk about this, Wolf!"

But he rode on, calling back, "Got to talk to *them*, Miss Hilda! I already know what *you* want, in broad daylight, leastways."

Chapter 15

Longarm met the overweight Arapaho in the cavalry hat and blouse alone, in the middle of the grassy swale as their followers covered them from either rise. Up closer, the older man's plump legs were bare and his beaded moccasins were Lakota-made. Like their Algonquin-speaking Cheyenne cousins, the Arapaho had rid with the so-called Sioux Confederacy in the Indian scares of the late sixties and early seventies, leaving them in no bargaining position with the Great White Father, later.

The older man struck a pose, allowed they called him Snake Tears and added, "I am taking my people south forever to live out of the reach of Little Big Eyes and his Blue Sleeves. They told us we had to live with our enemies, the Snakes. They call themselves Shoshoni. By any name they hate us as much as we hate them and still the B.I.A. said we had to obey their chief as our own chief if we wanted to have any flour in our coffee when the wolf winds of winter blow up there in such cruel country!"

Longarm nodded to reply, "Well, Chief Washakie and his Shoshoni rid as U.S. Cavalry scouts in the frantic summer of '76 and it just ain't true that my kind has no memory at all. It stands to reason the B.I.A. would rather deal with a chief who's never lifted a white man's hair nor broken his given word. I understand it hurts to be treated as a loser. We've just seen the last of Reconstruction here in Texas. But when *my* kind raid, rape and slaughter they generally *hang*. They never get a reservation twice the size of Delaware."

Snake Tears sobbed, "Our enemies hold the most sheltered draws and nobody lied when they named it the Wind River Country. Hear me! In our shining times, our people, the mother of all the plains nations, could have ranged north of the Platte or south of the Arkansas if we wanted to. But we did not want to. We held the just-right buffalo range you people have named Colorado or Kansas and now . . ."

Longarm cut in with, "Now the palefaces have killed all your women and raped all your buffalo and things have gone to hell in a hack. But you ain't going to like it any better farther south. Victorio and his Bronco Apache have things stirred up along the border with both the U.S. and Mex Cav out Indian hunting this fall. But far be it for me to waste my breath talking sense to a woman, a bible thumper or one of *you* birds. So what *can* I do for you?"

Snake Tears said, "We are hungry. When we heard the Snakes you call Comanche were no longer hunting down this way, we thought there would be plenty buffalo. But we have found no buffalo. None. Since we rode south of the iron tracks from sea to sea!"

Longarm nodded to observe, "South herd's about shot off. North herd ain't long for this world at the rate things are going. That was what the Comanche War of '77 was all about. The Great Sioux Wars began with Lakota helping themselves to livestock from a Mormon wagon train, a tad earlier. But to save us both a heap of haggling, I'll make you a take-it-or-leave-it offer."

Snake Tears beamed and said, "I thought you might not want to fight over just a little tobacco, flour, coffee and fresh meat!"

Longarm said, "Our young men might want to. Young men have a lot to learn about the prices of such commodities. So here's how we're going to work it out."

"Don't I have any say in how you pay tribute to us?" asked the old defeated war chief, wistfully.

Longarm sootheed, "You can tell your young men you gave the orders if you want. I don't want them near any of the young men riding with me as we ride on by you. But between us pals, I want your party to get out of the way because it's easier to keep a herd headed the way it's been going all day. After we pass, you'll find we've left you a couple of plugs of tobacco, a sack of flour, a tin of fine Arbuckle Brand coffee you'll never see at any trading post and a fine fresh-slaughtered calf."

The Indian gravely replied, "Hear me, that is not very much for a band the size of mine!"

Longarm said, "I'm riding with as many or more guns. *Texas* guns the Comanche never once whupped at anything like even odds. They ain't too likely to approve my generous offer. They're as likely to want to make a fight of it. You know how young men are."

"Two calves?" asked the Indian with an obvious appetite.

Longarm was tempted. But they only had that one lanced critter who was likely to die any minute in any case. So he stuck to his guns with, "One fine fat calf bred by Cherokee with a fine black robe a buffalo would have been proud to wear. You'll find the tobacco, the flour and the coffee on the grass beside it, once we move on. If you all move in before we leave, all bets are off and many of your young men—many—will die before the sun goes down, whether you win or not."

"Why do you have to kill the calf for us?" asked the Indian, adding with a frown, "Do you think we are children who do not know how to kill anything we want to kill?"

Longarm shrugged and asked, "How were you fixing to cut one calf out of the herd for a running target without causing us a stampede? That might have been fun, hunting buffalo, but it ain't the way to butcher beef. Do we have a deal or do you want to see if you can shop for the tobacco, flour, coffee and carcass the hard way, with both sides just whooping and shooting like wild . . . assholes?"

Snake Tears said they had a deal. They didn't shake on it. Honest Indians gave their word and kept it, with or without further ado. A dishonest Indian, or white man, broke his word whether he'd sworn on a stack of Bibles and signed his name in blood or not.

When he got back to the worried Zimmer twins, he told them what he and Snake Tears had agreed on, adding, "I know the trade tobacco, the one sack of flour and a whole tin of coffee are worth more than that dying calf. But had he held out for livestock with a fighting chance, you'd have lost more money in the end. The other calf I lanced will sell for fifty or sixty bucks in the sweet bye and bye, whilst the cow ought to drop half a dozen more in as many years."

The Zimmer sisters agreed he'd done well. Even the ferocious Herta failed to suggest a shoot-out with an Arapaho band might be more fun. So as Snake Tears and his own riders north along their rise the Double H moved on across it to the southwest, leaving the feverish fresh meat and other luxuries in their wake to be enjoyed that evening as old Snake Tears counted coup once more around his own night fire.

Longarm didn't suggest that to any of the Texas cowgirls. He knew white folk could be just as wrongheaded when it came to telling how they'd saved the day during the war or chased a famous bully out of town. He'd never quite fathomed why. For it seemed as dumb for a man to warn everyone he was dangerous as it was for a woman to warn men she was smart.

They drove farther that afternoon, partly to camp well clear of those Indians, and partly in hopes of finding more water before they settled the thirsty herd against the coming sundown. But that night was spent on wide-ass open prairie with the remuda and their riders getting by on bagwater and the cows chewing their cuds for comfort.

Longarm, having assumed by now the one Zimmer Twin didn't care to risk getting caught, or hadn't enjoyed that romp at the hotel as much as he had, spread his roll off a ways atop a higher rise with a bird's-eye view of the night camp and bedded-down herd. Being the thirsty herd would be more restless than usual, he'd detailed extra night riders to circle slow and sing low. It was true cowboys, and cowgirls, sang songs to the cattle, albeit never the wahoo noises of the vaudeville cowboys with their rope tricks and wooly chaps. Cows were inclined to spook at strange noises in the dark. It doubtless came from the simple fact that lions and wolves hunted by night and cows had run wild long before cowboys had been invented.

But once they were used to riders who druv 'em and pestered 'em but never bit 'em on the rump in the dark, cows seemed to cotton to the notion that was a harmless horse with a human being on top of it as it circled out yonder after sundown. So, neither lions nor wolves at all inclined to sing soft and low, night riders did, as much to keep themselves awake as to lull the cattle.

Hence, as he lay there under the stars atop that rise, Longarm was lulled some, himself, by a distant soprano voice softly but sweetly singing some High-Dutch *Volkslied* that meant as much to Longarm as it did to the cows down yonder. The tune was pretty in a sad and restful way. So he shut his eyes to just let the lullaby wash over him and, thanks to a long day in the saddle, he was almost but not quite asleep when he heard a less restful noise, closer, and rolled on his gut with his .44-40 in hand to softly but firmly call out, "*Quien es?*" which was as close to High Dutch as he felt up to.

A familiar she-male voice whispered back, "Not so loud! We don't want the others to know!"

It would have been dumb to ask what a she-male night crawler might not want others to know. So he made room for her under the top tarp as he put his six-gun back in its rolled-up gun-rig.

He felt no call to apologize for turning in bare-ass, since he was sure she wouldn't mind. He saw he'd been right about that when she slithered in beside him naked as a jay to wrap her arms and horsewoman's thighs around

117

him, sobbing, "*Ach, Lieber*, I've been waiting so long for this!"

He couldn't answer as he entered her with her tongue halfway down his throat. When they did come up for air it would have sounded silly to say that hadn't been his fault as he pounded her to glory with her firm rider's butt on the ground cloth padded by firm prairie sod. So he just treated her to some saved-up ammunition and when he came in her she moaned, "Ooooh, that feels so dirty! We're going to leave spots on your bedding and it serves you right for holding out on me so long!"

To which he could only reply, without missing a stroke, "I thought that was the way you said it had to be, back in Truscott, Ma'am. I agreed with you it might be best if you decided where and when and I'll not have it said I wasn't willing our first night out on this drive!"

She told him to just shut up and *ficken* her, so, not needing a translation, he tossed the tarp off, spread her lean thighs as wide as he could, and hammered another into her as she responded like a honeymooner who hadn't noticed any bad habits yet. So there was a lot to be said for starting from scratch after a cooler spell.

After they'd come again, she said she felt more than cool atop that rise with the night breezes playing over their sweaty bare hides. So he hauled the covers back up to cuddle against his saddle with her as they shared a cheroot, whoever she might be.

As they did so Herta, or Hilda, sighed, "That was lovely and I want to do it again before I have to sneak back to my own bedroll. Was it as *schön* for you, *mein Schatz*?"

He snuggled her closer and confessed, "Better than I remembered it from our first time."

So she rolled half atop him to grab hold his sated shaft as she half sobbed, "I'm so happy, Wolf! Did you really mean that? Do you really want me, more, tonight?"

He kissed her and ran a palm down her spine to return the favor as he honestly replied, "Sure I do. To begin with, I ain't been getting any lately, and, after that, the screwing always tends to get better as new lovers get to be old pals."

He felt no call to comment on how things tended to go downhill from that swell peak in the proceedings betwixt the first fumbling with unfamiliar tools and the first time you noticed it was turning into a steady job under a demanding boss. He suspected that being way more demanding than most women, this cattle-raising Zimmer twin, be it one or the other, had been over that same peak more than once. Some old boy or boys had surely taught her to screw like a mink.

As if she'd been reading his mind, the twin in his bedroll with him said, "I'm sorry if I left you feeling lonely so long, too. But . . . as we agreed that first night, we can't take this chance too often. So let's go on behaving the same in front of the others and maybe we'll be able to get away with this a few more times without getting caught in the act, *verstehen*?"

Longarm searched his memory of that dictionary to reply, "Not entire, *meine Puppe*. You and your sister *own* the Double H, and all your riders are beholden to you-all. What could any of 'em do if they found out you had natural feelings, fire you?"

She sighed and said, "They could *talk*. After we got back to Sulfur Draw. I'm not worried about them *watching*, out here on open range, but Sulfur Draw is a small, tight, spiteful neighborhood and my sister and I have already lived down malicious rumors started by those Holy Mary *Österreichisch Huren*!"

He thought back, and asked if she'd just called some Austrian ladies of the Holy Name Society a bunch of whores. She snuggled closer to purr, as his High Dutch seemed to be coming back to him, and added, "Soon we should understand one another better, *nicht wahr*?"

As he thoughtfully fingered the mole on her tailbone, Longarm was in point of fact commencing to understand her better than she might have intended. For he'd run the same hand down the crack of that same ass, or thought he had, back at that hotel in Truscott, and he had marveled at the time how flawless her ass had felt.

So unless a gal could grow a mole that size in less than a week, he had his hand on the ass of another twin entire and, being there were only two of the same, it was all he could do to keep from laughing like a jackass as the penny dropped.

He still didn't know whether this was Herta or Hilda he'd just now laid and was fixing to lay some more. It didn't matter as much, now that he knew he'd laid *both* of them and understood the game such a loving and sharing set of sisters had doubtless played before, bless their warm natures and cautious ways.

But he never let on he knew as he rolled back in this one's love saddle to ride over the moon with her and soberly agree it might be best if her sister never found out.

Chapter 16

Most men enjoyed a zim-zam-thank-you-Ma'am as often as possible whilst most women preferred widely spaced but protracted orgies. So the twins took alternate turns every third of fourth night as the otherwise tedious drive averaged fifteen miles a day for many a day until, at last, they'd made it to Sulfur Draw in the heart of the Staked Plains.

The vast so-called tableland rose a tad higher to the west, where its *estacado* or staked palisade ran north and south in line with the lower Pecos Valley more than two hundred miles. So such rain as fell drained mostly east-ways across the New Mexico-Texas line to bust out of canyon mouths a hundred miles off, where less dramatic but dramatic enough palisaded bluffs loomed above the already high High Plains of Texas.

Sulfur Draw, named for the rotten-egg smell of its standing water in hot weather, ran many a mile from nor'west to sou'east mid rises north or south. But the *town* of Sulfur Draw was little more than one main street running north and south away from the stickerbrush and braided streambed down the lower center of the draw it was named for.

Longarm wasn't surprised to learn the home spread of the Double H was up the draw a good two miles from the church and market town they drove past on higher ground.

Other riders from miles around still came to watch as Longarm and the cowgirls he was overseeing spread new stock like jelly over peanut butter on the already well-stocked Double H range along the slope and up over the rim of Sulfur Draw to the north. Some of the earlier brown, calico or even black Tex-Mex longhorns on the scene made swishy-tailed and dust-pawing displays as some of the new girls in town huffed and puffed right back at them. But that prize Black Angus bull was penned up where he could do no harm at the moment, and things settled down after the first hour or so.

By then the cowgirls who'd helped drive the Cherokee stock all the way from the Indian Territory had joined in with the permanent hands of the home spread, a smaller handful of male Texicans and breeds, to enjoy a set-down homecoming meal in the mess hall, prepared by the old Chinee who'd been with the twins since they were little, and he'd been cooking for their momma.

None of the cowgirls hired for the drive seemed as surprised as Longarm when Hilda Zimmer proceeded to pay them off after supper for a job well done. When he studied on it, of course, he saw hardly any outfit kept that many hands on a permanent payroll betwixt drives or roundups. Most outfits only kept a few top hands and some dollar-a-day hired hands expected to handle any chore as might come up, from hunting strays or riding fences to swamping stables or digging post holes. "They handed me a shovel," was the top hand's laconic way of saying he'd been laid off. Sometimes this was true. Gently informing a top hand you only had call for a chore boy was a graceful way to get him to quit.

Knowing it was only a question of time before they'd just have to let Junior Brewster out of the jail, over to Knox County, Longarm as Wolf Kruger was braced for one or more of the twins to inform him his own services were no longer needed, seeing they'd made it all the way, he'd screwed the both of 'em more than once, and there was that Holy Name Society down the draw to study on.

But later that night, as the last of their temporary help,

Wendy Delgado, left with her back pay and a wistful smile at Longarm, old Hilda Zimmer led Longarm to a small private shed apart from the main house or 'dobe bunkhouse, to tell him it was where their foreman got to bunk when they weren't out on the trail.

Since neither twin ever let on she'd sucked his cock when he was in a position to know which one he was talking to, Longarm addressed her in the respectful tone she desired as he asked, "Have you and your sister considered how this might go down with your regular ramrod, Junior Brewster, Miss Hilda?"

He could see they hadn't when she frowned thoughtfully and asked him, "Don't you think they're going to keep him in jail for killing those three Truscott riders, Wolf?"

Longarm shook his head to say, "I'm sure at least one of your other riders must have told you who really shot Puff Duffy, Silent Ryan and that Caddo, Ma'am. I know they told *me* and, even if Junior *had* shot 'em, they were known killers and any court-appointed lawyer halfways sober would surely get him off on self-defense."

She said, "We've been wondering and wondering about that. Herta thinks somebody had it in for Junior. Why do you imagine they've been holding him so long if they don't really mean to try him for what . . . somebody did to those three bully boys?"

Longarm lied, "Can't say, Ma'am. I'm not a lawyer. My point is that he'll likely get out, in time, and so what's he likely to say when he comes home to find me . . . sleeping in his bed?"

She said she and her sister would study in that and suggested that meanwhile he make himself at home and get some rest. So, seeing it had been a longer day than most, and the one without the mole on her tailbone had been ferocious as hell that last night on the trail, he tried to do just that, wondering whether the one with the mole would be by later and sort of wishing they'd drop the bullshit and come at him all at once, at least once.

He wasn't sure he'd care for that as a steady diet. For,

like that *Kama Sutra* book they sold under the counter with a plain brown cover, the slap-and-tickle a man might dream up when he wasn't getting any could be downright fatiguing when his dirty daydreams came true.

As he undressed and stretched out on the real brass bedstead, not a bunk, in Junior's quarters, Longarm reflected he'd forgotten how swell it felt to have a feather mattress under his tired bones for a change. Somewhere somebody was strumming a High-Dutch tune on a Spanish guitar as crickets kept time from the brushy banks of the nearby stinky old creek down the center of the draw. So Longarm trimmed the oil lamp to sleep the sleep of the just, or try to.

Then somebody was tapping on the nearby window shutters. So he got back up, armed himself and moved over to the jalousies to ask what the raven bird out yonder might want.

A familiar voice whispered back, "It's Ernestine Holz. Open these blinds and let me in. They may be watching the front door!"

He opened the jalousies, declaring, "This sure sounds interesting, drag rider. Who might be watching yonder door from where?"

As he helped her pudgy form over the sill, the redhead confided in a breathless tone, "The side veranda door of the main house fronts yon entrance to this foreman's shed. *Gott im Himmel*, are you standing in front of me with no clothes on?"

He shrugged his bare shoulders to reply, "It was your notion to come calling on me at this hour, Miss Ernestine. If people don't like me they can leave me alone. If you ain't going, stay and tell me what this is all about, hear?"

She said, "I just overheard Hilda and Herta stewing about you and Junior Brewster. It's a good thing for you I speak *Hochdeutsch*. Hilda wants to fire you. Herta wants to keep you. She says you have more *Ruckgrat* than Junior. Hilda says she is not so sure and they just got a wire saying Junior is out of jail and on his way home!"

Longarm whistled softly, calculated mentally, and decided, "I've a day or more to decide how I want to play the tune. I never met old Junior Brewster. So I can't quite picture how he's liable to take my replacing him as foreman, here."

As he moved from the window to put his .44-40 back in its holster on a bedpost, the plump redhead tagged along in the tricky light to tell him, "I can. He had me riding drag and the two of them backed him, damn their *schlimme* hides, because I wouldn't join the three of them in a *Zuber*."

Longarm didn't ask if she was some sort of poor relation to those horny twins. They didn't have time for idle speculation. Cutting to the bone, he asked her, "How many of you other cowgirls figured I'd been taking Junior's place more ways than one, Miss Ernestine?"

She said, "Every one of us. Didn't you think lonesome cowgirls a long way from home with just their own fingers for company paid any attention to the only thing in pants for miles? None of us dared, of course. Lest we wind up walking home without references. I thought I said you could call me Ernie?"

Since she was standing so close it seemed only natural to reach out and reel her in to hide his frontal nudity in the soft denim betwixt the upper wings of her chinked leather chaps. From the way Ernie thrust her pelvis forward, she aimed to help him hide his dawning erection from view. So he kissed her, then kissed her some more before he said, "Since you put her that way, I reckon my best bet would be a dignified resignation, come morning. No sense to bother nobody about quitting at this hour, right?"

Ernie skimmered her Stetson across the room to reach back and unbuckle her chaps as he helped out with the buttons down the front of her mannish shirt and, Lord have mercy if her big bare breasts weren't a delightful novelty after taking turns with the leaner and more muscular Zimmer sisters.

Thanks to both Hilda and Herta, along with the work-hardened Friskie Ralston, earlier, Ernestine Holz didn't remind Longarm too much of the stenographer gal they called Miss Bubbles up to that Denver federal building, albeit, like the blond Miss Bubbles, the redheaded drag rider he lowered to the mattress and mounted without one pillow under her heroic rump, seemed to be composed of globes of firm lard under a smooth hairless hide underlaid with marshmallow.

She demanded "*Ach!* What are you *doing* to me?" as he plunged his old organ grinder in to meet the upward thrusts of her way wider hips and, since it was too stupid a question to answer, he didn't try and she seemed to like it, a heap, as he gave her the load he'd been saving up two nights for Hilda, Herta or both.

But as them head doctors had put down in cold print, no man was ever more sane than he felt right after a warm meal and a hot fuck. So as they shared a second-wind smoke Longarm worried aloud how a stranger to Sulfur Draw might get another job in such a tight-knit neck of the woods.

Draping a plump thigh over his as she steered his free hand down to the damp red thatch in her soft lap, Ernestine soothed. "You're not a stranger around here, Wolf. The other girls all liked you and by now they'll have said so all up and down the draw at many another spread. On the trail you were firm but fair and you knew your oats. None of us were sore about you fucking the Zimmer sisters. Everyone fucks the Zimmer sisters. They just don't want anybody to *say* anything about it, see?"

He softly strummed her banjo for her as he mused, "I hope you're right. Somebody told me other hands had drifted into this new range in search of work, only to be frozen out, or worse."

She spread her legs wider as she demurely replied, "That was not the same at all. *Those* strangers were Texas Rangers, working undercover to investigate tax records and so forth. All of us know you're a real top hand who was *asked* to work for a Sulfur Draw outfit, not a sneak who came pussyfooting in on us and . . . Do you think we

126

could do it again if I got it hard for you with some *säu-gen*?"

He allowed it might be worth a try and *säugen* turned out to be just what it sounded like, as Ernie rolled to her hands and knees betwixt his spread thighs to go down yonder like an unweaned calf.

So that's how things were when all of a sudden the door flew open to spill yardlight from outside across him and mostly Ernestine's broad bare behind, as she knelt there with her red head in his lap.

So Longarm could only say, "Howdy, Miss Hilda, or is it Miss Herta?"

Whoever it was raged, "You're fired! Both of you! You'll both find your back-pay in the tack room when you go to pick up your saddles and other possibles. I'll be going back to my own quarters, now, and I'll expect both of you to be off the premises when my sister and me have breakfast in the morning!"

Longarm didn't ask how she'd let her sister in on their own little secret. As she slammed the door shut to storm off in the night, Ernie started blowing him again. So he said, "I'm sorry about this, honey. Do you reckon it might be best to stop and study on what we might want to do, now?"

The redhead raised her moist lips just far enough to huskily reply. "I know what I want to do. I want to fuck some more. You just heard her say we had until morning and a girl can worry about finding a *job* most *any* old time!"

Chapter 17

Once he'd calmed her down a mite, it developed that Ernie knew of kith or kin who didn't think much of the Zimmer twins and would surely shelter them both for a spell, albeit not in the same bunk, Ernie feared.

The only problem was their getting there, down the draw on the far side of the town, since neither of them owned a pony of their own and whichever twin had just fired them hadn't sounded like she'd want to loan them any Double H stock.

As they got dressed, Longarm said not to stew about it before they got on out to the tack room to see what might be seen.

Once they had, they found envelopes thumbtacked to the swells of both their saddles. So after they made certain they hadn't been shortchanged Longarm said, "She must have been suffering *honest* indignation, bless her peculiar approach to romance. So as long as she seems to have turned in for the night, why don't we just borrow a couple of ponies and ride down to that dairy spread to see if they have room for us?"

The redhead blanched as she demanded, "*Gott im Himmel*! Are you suggesting we help ourselves to horses that don't *belong* to us?"

He said, "Ain't *suggesting* it. I ain't about to haul you and two loaded saddles half that far in the dark through country I don't know that well! Would *you* charge anyone you'd just fired as a horse thief if they sent your horses back to you, never asked how come you'd fired 'em, and never raised more . . . personal questions?"

Ernie said she could only speak for herself. But she didn't want to walk six or eight miles in spurred high heels any more than he did. So they rode out grinning like a pair of apple-swiping kids—on that cream personal mount of Hilda's and Herta's prize-cutting horse, a paint.

Along the way they agreed on their stories and swapped some spit in the dark before reining in at a kissing cousin's spread a mile to the east of the town. They'd circled said town through the trees on the far side of the draw lest anyone ask what she was doing at that hour with a rider who was still a stranger to most of the local folk.

Ernie's cousin, Lilo, was married up to a Mex of the Papist persuasion. That was how come Ernie thought their dairy spread would be a good place to lie low a spell. Lilo's own High-Dutch kin were Lutheran whilst the new Austrian Papists in those parts didn't think too much of Mexicans, or yet another redhead who'd marry up with the same.

Lilo's hombre was called Bob instead of Roberto, making him Bob Ramos. As luck would have it, they were night owls, or still awake at any rate, when Lilo opened the door to their 'dobe in her nightgown. Bob joined them in the kitchen a spell later, buttoning up his fresh shirt. Bob and Longarm, as Wolf Kruger, got to stare bemused at one another across the kitchen table as the two gals jawed a mile a minute in High Dutch. Bob Ramos seemed relieved to hear Wolf Kruger didn't savvy such girl talk, neither. Longarm felt no call to try his fair Border Mex on the agreeable young Mex. Old Bob's English was swell and a man who bragged needless about his smart ass was a fool.

As she dealt out coffee and cake, Lilo Ramos née Holz told her hombre the yarn Longarm and Ernie had agreed upon, saying one of the Zimmer twins had laid them off sudden upon receiving news that their foreman was headed home from jail.

Bob Ramos proved how folktales spread up and down Sulfur Draw when he said, "I can see why they wouldn't want two ramrods competing for a chance to ram 'em both. *Querida*, but for why did they fire your poor cousin, here?"

Lilo said, "She made the mistake of saying it wasn't fair when they they paid Wolf off and told him to git, without offering to loan him a ride to town."

The Mex dairy man frowned thoughtfully and asked, "Where did those two *caballos* in our corral just come from, then?"

Lilo said, "That's another thing Ernie wants us to help her out with. If one of our hands led those Double H ponies home on his own mount, they might not raise as big a stink."

Bob Ramos looked dubious and decided, "They might or they might not. *Quien sabe*? I can't ask one of our *muchachos* to risk it. I'll run them as far as the Double H cattle guard in the *muy* small hours and haze them on in without disturbing such *mujeres contrariosas!*"

So that was settled, and, as they coffeed and caked, the dairy owners asked questions and made suggestions about their plans for the future. Ernie's future didn't shape up too complicated.

Longarm wasn't the first lawman who'd noticed folk tended to suspect sneaky chess moves when the name of the game was checkers. A chance remark from the older cousin Lilo gave away how Ernestine Holz had grown up tomboy enough to ride astride without ever learning to rope, cut or even mill before she'd signed up as a High-Dutch-speaking cowgirl. So whether they'd asked her to play slap-and-tickle with 'em or not, the Zimmer twins had doubtless assigned her to riding drag because that was all she was good for on a cow pony. So her chances on another such job were no better than marrying up with a good provider, and as Lilo said, that had being a half-ass cowgirl beat.

In the meanwhile she could make more waiting tables or behind many a counter in many a shop, once she'd spent some time with them to find some she-male duds to wear and ask around town for a sensible job.

They explained to Longarm that having left the employ of the Double H under a cloud, he'd do better, in spite of his name, looking for a job with some Tex-Mex or Anglo outfit. Bob said, "I can't afford to pay my own help a dollar a day, and you did say your were a top hand, Wolf."

When Longarm asked how many such outfits there might be in a mostly High-Dutch-speaking community, the Tex-Mex conceded, "Not many. Aside from the Lazy Sevens and Clover Bar, one Gulf Coast Creole. The other is Irish. The bigger ranchos are all Dutch. You may have a time getting hired by anyone else with your Dutch surname, Wolf. Everyone has got *muy agrio* on you Dutchmen since this night riding and barn burning started. If I were in your boots, with a name like your own, I would approach either *Padre* Paul or Uncle Klaus and tell him the same story you told us about being laid off unjustly by the Double H. You will not get a job with either Dutch faction unless one or the other acts as your *patron, comprende?*"

Longarm said, "Not entire. Who are these birds who say who works or dosen't work in these parts?"

Ramos explained *Padre*, Father or *Vater* Paul Hauser was the priest those Austrian newcomers confessed to and took advice from. Longarm wasn't surprised to hear a Papist Mex say the Jesuit seemed like a regular gent, for a Dutchman.

Uncle Klaus or *Onkel* Klaus Brenner had been one of the founders of the nearby town of Sulfur Draw. He rented buildings he'd put up to the tradesmen and professionals of all descriptions a town so far from anywheres else required. Longarm knew the type, but didn't say so. Mr. Karl Marx, over to London Town, said all such adventure investors were sons of bitches. He was only right three-fourths of the time. You had to keep an open mind about land speculators and mushroom growers. Ramos said the

131

earlier arrivals, Anglo, Dutch or Mex, still held most of the better bottomland and water rights. But the newer Austrian faction seemed more organized with more *dinero* backing the slicker moves they tended to make.

His wife gave away how much Ernie had told her in High Dutch by deciding, "Those gunfighters you and Junior Brewster shot between you in Truscott couldn't have been working for the same faction as *Onkel* Klaus. It's commonly known, at least in *Hochdeutsch*, Klaus Brenner loaned the Zimmer twins the money to upgrade their herd with Black Angus and Cherokee stock."

"*Ay, chihuahua* might be a smart time for to change sides, no?" asked her hombre with a knowing wink.

Longarm didn't say so, but he'd heard the Kid had ridden for the Murphy-Dolan faction before the Tunstall-McSween side had made him a better offer, just west of the Pecos on the far side of the state line. He said, "I'd best study some before I ask anybody for a job. Got me such pocket jingle as I'll need to spit and whittle in town for some time to come as the town makes up its mind about me, and vice versa."

So Lilo put him and her kid cousin to bed, in separate rooms, Lord love her, whilst old Bob ducked out to carry the Double H stock home before the twins found out they were missing.

Longarm was sleeping the sleep of the just exhausted in a small 'dobe-walled guestroom when someone shook him awake and, smelling she-male sweat, he reached out languidly to reel her in. But before he could get in real trouble she snapped, "Stop that, Wolf. This is serious! Bob hasn't come home yet, and it's almost milking time!"

He sat up and covered his bare frame more modestly as he replied, "Morning, Miss Lilo. Are you sure he didn't stop off somewheres along the way, seeing he was up so late and had to rise and shine by three in any case?"

She asked, "Where would a man who loved his wife stop off at such an hour? Sulfur Draw isn't New Orleans or even Dodge. Even the whorehouse closes after midnight and Bob would never in this world go *there*!"

Longarm suggested she duck outside and let him dress. As she moved toward the door, he added, "Save time if you rustled up another pony for me to ride after Bob. I can saddle it myself."

But when he got out to their stable yard he found a sleepy-eyed *muchacho* holding the reins of a gelding bearing his borrowed roping saddle. The moon had set, but the lamplight spilling out the kitchen door outlined Lilo through her nightgown in a manner to suggest Bob Ramos would have to be a fool to waste his hard earned *dinero* in whorehouses.

Of course, he reasoned as he rode for town, many a man was a mortal fool when it came to dining out on forbidden delights, and there was always an all-night card game to consider.

As he rode through the very late night, he spied other lamplit doors and windows and somewhere in the night a woman was scolding like a shrew in High Dutch. So it was likely later than it looked by starlight.

City folk who chided country folk for going to sleep with their livestock had no idea how early livestock *got up*. Dairy cows had to be milked twice a day, at three to four P.M. and three to four A.M. If you were too lazy to get up at such an ungodly hour you had no beeswax milking cows. They dried up on you when you failed to milk twice a day. And city ordinances against keeping chickens in the fancier parts of most cities derived from the sleeping habits of Vanderbilts, Astors and Stanfords, who raised hell when they woke up before dawn to the dulcet crows of a rooster raising hell outside their window.

Out in the county, where it couldn't be helped, most folk turned in early to get a good night's sleep before they had to get up to tend to their stock. But Bob Ramos was Mex and Mexicans weren't like most folk when it came to being night owls. Things *did* stay open all night in Old Mexico or even closer to the border.

So Longarm rode in slow, with his eyes and both ears open to, sure enough, hear a door slam hither and a voice raised yon as he got his first serious look at the town in

the dark. For coming up the draw by daylight they'd circled the Double H herd past the town.

From what he could see by the few puddles of lamplight up and down the one main street, it seemed a typical
specimen of Remote, with one or two at the most of the
seriously needed needs of a West Texas town. You
couldn't make out many of the shop signs. Somewhere in
the night somebody strong was hammering steel. He
couldn't say whether it was an all-night forge or an early
riser making repairs. Now and again a dog barked as he
rode past. He didn't care. Dogs were not allowed to run
loose at night where men rode armed on easily spooked
ponies.

Attracted by the sound of voices from a puddle of light
up the ways, Longarm rode close to a quartet of ponies
hitched along a rail out front, hitched the bay gelding to
the same, and strode over to join the animated conversation in the doorway of the local law, as things turned out.

There were three times as many men as horses in the
vicinity as a voice of reason cautioned, "Let's not get our
bowels in an uproar, boys. They've sent for Sheriff Armstrong and he'll know what to do."

A less-reasonable voice insisted, "Aw, you're no fun!
I say string the greaser up right now, before the sissy
sheriff lets him jaw with a lawyer and that fucking Papist
priest!"

"Got some Mex inside?" asked Longarm casually as he
drifted in to join the bunch, as if he belonged there.

An old-timer barely glanced his way to reply, "Yep.
Horse thief name of Ramos. Stole some Double H stock
earlier tonight and they caught him red-ass-handed with
it on the road. Said he was on his way to return the ponies.
Ain't that a bitch? When since the dawn of creation have
you ever heard of a fucking Mexican horse thief bringing
back a horse he just *stole*?"

Longarm swallowed the green taste in his mouth and
elbowed his way inside, or tried to. One deputy was seated
just inside the door with a double-twelve-gauge across his
knees as another presided over the desk in the middle of

134

the front office. The one by the door said, "Nobody sees the prisoner until the sheriff gets here, and who in blue blazes are you, stranger?"

Longarm said, "They call me Wolf Kruger. I ride for the Double H. Or I did until recent. You got the wrong man locked up this morning."

From the gloom of his patent cell Bob Ramos called out, "Wolf! Don't do it! I told them nothing, and right now we both need a lawyer. So go get a lawyer. While you still have the chance!"

Longarm called back, "Your Lilo's worried, and I told her I'd try and get you home to her and your cows, Bob. Simmer down and let me do the talking, here."

Addressing the obvious senior at the desk, Longarm asked if it was safe to assume someone had ridden in from the Double H earlier to raise holy hell about missing two saddle broncs.

When the deputy at the desk said that was about the size of it, Longarm said, "I helped myself to a cream and led a paint to pack my possibles as I left the Double H after they laid me off this evening. It was that or walk. I mayhaps should have asked permit, but the twins who owned the stock had turned in for the night. So I never. When I met up with Bob Ramos, yonder, I asked him to return the Double H stock to its rightful owners. You'd know best what happened after that. But, as you see, it was all an innocent mistake."

Both deputies rose. The one with the shotgun aimed it impolite as the one standing behind the desk dryly remarked, "Can't say just how *innocent* it was, but it sure was a *mistake*, Pilgrim. So now you fucking horse thieves are *both* under arrest!"

Chapter 18

After they'd disarmed him and even helped themselves to his three-for-a-nickel cheroots, they frog-marched Longarm into the same patent cell with Bob Ramos, who groaned, "I told you so!"

A patent cell was so-called because it was a patented mail-order kit of prefabricated boilerplates and barred grills you could rivet together to form a box way harder to bust out of than your average mud, brick or timber-enclosed drunk tank. Longarm hadn't argued with them for more than one good reason.

To begin with, he was working undercover. So he wasn't supposed to ask for professional courtesies. After that, he and Bob Ramos were in the power of that most unpredictable of all dangerously armed youths, the invincibly ignorant deputies of an uncertainly legitimate sheriff.

Longarm had the advantage on all of them in knowing the West Texas county they'd recently filed corporation papers on was still unproven homestead tracts and unincorperated as a county until Austin damn well got around to it. So whether the recent election of a contract drover hitherto known as Pink Armstrong had been fair or not, Longarm and Bob Ramos were technically at the mercy of a locally approved lynch mob.

Longarm knew that wasn't such an unusual situation in

some parts of a rapidly expanding republic. He'd heard how, out in that new Arizona Territory, a popular Tombstone livery service owner named Behan was running for sheriff of spanking new Cochise County against one of the saloon-keeping Earp brothers, with rival papers predicting dire results should the totally inexperienced opposition win. Fussy landed gentry in other lands pointed to the wild American West as a fine example of the dangers of Democracy, and Longarm was willing to grant they had a point, provided they could come up with any fairer way to populate a continent. He never said it to Bob Ramos, naturally, but neither the Royal French, Spanish Mission nor more recent Mexican experiments in revolving governments had settled half as many folk on half as many acres worth shit.

Letting folk vote, hoping they voted honest and proclaiming martial law when it got too noisy, was as good a way as human beings, by definition imperfect, were likely to come up with in spite of Herr Bismarck, Mr. Marx and all those other utopian twits who kept saying the U.S. of A. was never going to work.

Longarm sat on the bottom bunk, pining for a smoke, as Bob Ramos paced back and forth, bitching about his unmilked cows. Longarm knew no dairyman wanted to hear his infernal cows could likely last a day without his tender care, so he never suggested that.

It only seemed a million years. The sun hadn't risen when Sheriff Armstrong stomped in, rubbing his sleep-gummed face, to have a look at the fucking horse thieves. As he came closer to the bars, Longarm got up to see if he could get Bob off, at least.

Pink Armstrong, likely so-called because his mustache and sideburns were somewhere betwixt blond and rusty, was one of those burly gents who got thick-bodied but solid, like a Comanche, as they aged. He had to be about forty-five by this time. He didn't smile, but he didn't glare mean at them as he peered into the dimly lit patent cell, had a closer look, and demanded, "Bob Ramos, what the fuck are you doing in my jail on a charge of horse theft! Have you gone out of your mind entire?"

Ramos said, "Was all a mistake."

Before he could say too much, Longarm cut in with, "I'm the guilty party, sort of, Sheriff. I asked Bob Ramos to carry two ponies I'd sort of borrowed back to their rightful owner. He had nothing to do with the taking of either. He wasn't there. He's pure as the driven snow!"

Pink Armstrong growled, "Shit, I knew that. Bob's daddy and me rid with Goodnight and Loving back when we and the world were younger. My kids drink Bob's milk regular. He's clean, for a Mex, and you never see cow shit or hairs when you pour."

He turned to call, "Lefty, get the keys and let Bob out so's he can make his morning run to our creamery!"

As he turned back to them, Longarm asked, "What about me? I can explain how I just had to ride and pack on borrowed stock when I was laid off too far west of town to walk and carry."

The unincorporated sheriff said, not unkindly, "You can explain it to the judge, next time he rides this circuit, stranger. Like I said, I rid with old Bob's daddy, years ago, but I've never seen *you* before, and Miss Hilda Zimmer did press formal charges."

As the deputy let Ramos out, the older lawman relented enough to say, "Since you were man enough to own up and get this innocent greaser off the hook, you can have your smokes and small change back for now. Our circuit judge is due in any day now. So just sit tight and we'll try to make you comfortable 'til they decide what's to be done with you."

Longarm started to raise another point. But Pink Armstrong raised a hand for silence and growled, "Don't push it, cowboy. Unless you're deaf, you just heard me say it's for others to decide. I just work here. You shouldn't help yourself to horses you never had no bill of sale for if you ain't up to explaining to the judge."

So as they locked the cell door in his face and Bob Ramos said he'd see about getting him a lawyer, come business hours there in town. Longarm accepted the smokes, matches and some small change for the candy-butcher who'd be coming by from time to time and sat back down to sweat it out. Being in jail wasn't much more tedious than being on picket guard or staked out along the owlhoot trail. It only hurt when you kept looking at your watch, and they'd put his in a drawer with his guns and wallet.

He refrained from lighting up at that hour and lay down to see if he could catch some shut-eye. He must have felt more tired than he'd expected. For the next he knew they were rattling his cage, and when he sat up it was broad-ass day outside.

A little bald gnome who looked like an undertaker for the wee people was standing there with a briefcase, derby hat in hand. So it might have seemed awkward to shove a glad hand through the bars at him when he introduced himself as Lawyer Halpmann of the Texas Bar. When Longarm asked what Bob Ramos had told him about the case, and asked how much this was likely to cost, Lawyer Halpmann explained he hadn't been sent by any pals Longarm knew. The runty attorney had been sent by a client who wanted to talk to Longarm. He said the papers had been served, and the door was unlocked, if Longarm would care to cut the idle chatter and follow him outside.

So Longarm did, picking up his wallet, watch, derringer and gun-rig, complete with extra rounds of .44-40 for his Colt Frontier revolver from the new day shift along the way.

Outside in the dazzle of a September morn in West Texas, the gnomish lawyer waved his derby up the street toward the bluffs beyond, then he put his hat back on and together they made it to the last but not least business block at the north end of Main Street. The bottom floor of the one big building seemed a sort of grange hall, albeit the High-Dutch sign above its imposing front entrance declared it a *Tanzsaal* if he he was reading the old-timey Gothic lettering right. He asked the lawyer if that meant something like "dance hall." Halpmann said it did and they had to go up the outside steps to the top floor, now. So they did.

The outside of the establishment had struck Longarm as sort of barnlike and bleak, with the Texas sun already chalking fresh-painted red vertical siding. But once they were inside, upstairs, it seemed as if they'd been whisked to a New Orleans parlor house, an expensive one, by magic carpet. The plush hall carpeting they strode along felt like grass beneath his army boots, and there was just no saying where such uncertain underpinning might lead a confounded visitor.

The lawyer led Longarm into a majestic office, where a beefy bullet-headed man who shaved his scalp as well as his jowels presided behind an acre of mahogany desk. Photographs on the paneled walls all about showed the same portly Dutchman smiling the same way as he posed with everybody from army officers and Indian chiefs to a damned fine wax dummy if it wasn't old Sam Grant in the flesh.

As the lawyer sent to fetch him vanished like a spooked crawdad, the big shot who'd sent for him waved Longarm to an easy chair upholstered in red plush velvet—to hell with expenses—and confided, "They call me *Onkel* Klaus. You may have heard of me, seeing you rode for a time with the Zimmer twins?"

Longarm nodded soberly and replied, "I have. You'd be the head of one of the Dutch factions in and about Sulfur Draw."

Klaus Brenner looked pained and shoved a cigar humidor Longarm's way across the vast expanse as he modestly replied, "Not the *head*, Mr. Kruger. Like you, I barely speak the lingo and I only *advise* greener settlers of any kith or kin who care to listen. For example, I warned those Zimmer twins they'd be wasting expensive sperm if they served scrub longhorns with that prize bull they'd come by. I loaned them a few dollars more for the expedition you just took part in."

Longarm helped himself to a fancy Tampa Claro as he

140

nodded and said, "I follow your drift. Why did you tell Miss Hilda to drop the charges?"

Onkel Klaus said, "You don't follow my drift at all. As I just told you, Wolf, I don't *tell* anyone to do anything. I only offer well-informed *advice*."

As Longarm lit up, Brenner leaned back to observe, "To offer my well-informed advice I have to stay well informed. Before you say you did or you didn't, more than one of those cowgirls the Zimmer twins drove back with think you did. So I suggested, and little Hilda had to agree, she didn't want it suggested at a public hearing that she might have fired you, and then charged you with horse theft because of jealous feelings."

He sighed and added, "I never advised them to hire those extra cowgirls, by the way. I stood ready to provide them with . . . let's say casual help I know of, more qualified by far than those tomboys you just rode with. As I was just telling the Zimmer twins this very morn, that shoot-out Junior Brewster had in Truscott might have been avoided if those bully boys had ridden in to find a regular outfit backing Junior's play."

Longarm blew a thoughtful smoke ring and casually asked, "Is that how you were informed about the shoot-out with Puff Duffy, Silent Ryan and the breed called Caddo? I wasn't there."

Onkel Klaus smiled thinly and replied, "Let's say I have no call to doubt things happened as they were reported to the law. Junior is out and on his way home with no harm done, as things now stand. So my advice was to let things stand and let sleeping dogs lie, however you mean *lie*. You'll find I'm a sort of mellow old fart, as long as you take my advice."

Longarm quietly asked, "What do you advise I do next, seeing you got me out of jail and that's one I owe you."

The big frog in the little puddle of the Staked Plains beamed across the desk at Longarm to say, "I'll let you know if ever I should think of something, Wolf. I've been told you're a top hand and one hell of a gunfighter. Top hands aren't that hard to find if you're willing to pay forty a month and found. Good gunfighters are hard to come by for love or money."

Longarm said, "I thought you said you didn't want me saying whether I was working for love or money, coming west with the Double H."

Onkel Klaus laughed knowingly and replied, "So I did and so let's forget that gossip. The tale told about you shooting it out with that Catlin Gang has you moving like spit on a hot stove and punching all their tickets faster than a woodpecker could peck!"

Longarm modestly replied, "This here Frontier Colt fires double-action. But it sounded slower than a woodpecker, to me, at the time."

The older man said, "It always does. I've been there and found I was moving way too slow, through air as thick as glue. The one who gets his gun muzzle up through the glue and manages to somehow *aim* with his heart pounding like a trip hammer and every fiber of his being all atingle is generally the one who lives."

Longarm shrugged and muttered, "Some old boys must enjoy swimming in glue. I've often wondered what it felt like to the ones I beat by an eyeblink or less. Are you asking me if I'm a gun for hire?"

"I like to be well informed," *Onkel* Klaus replied.

Longarm had a drag on the fine cigar, let it trickle out his nostrils, and said, "I'm an out-of-work cowboy a long way from home and like the song says, when people don't like me they can leave me alone. I've yet to kill a man for the bounty on his head or to please any paying customer. But if the truth be known, the Catlin brothers and Jack Frost weren't the first ones who ever pushed me too far. Like I said, some old boys must enjoy those split seconds of slowed-down time, or mebbe it's just something about my face."

"How many notches might you have in your gun, Wolf?" asked the man who claimed to know about such matters.

Longarm said, "Nobody but a pool-hall punk keeps score. How many gals have you kissed and do you count

142

the ones who recover from their wounds the same as you count the totally dead?"

"Your modesty becomes you," *Onkel* Klaus decided, as he glanced at his own gold-washed repeater watch, then added, "I know more than one stock spread in these parts who might be able to use a top hand who's good with a gun and isn't afraid to use it. What were your plans here in the Staked Plains, Wolf, now that you've been laid off by the Double H?"

Longarm said, "Ain't sure. Just got out of jail after being fired in the middle of nowhere. If I had a lick of sense I'd head on home to Val Verde County before my pocket jingle runs out. But I might just stay over a day or more to study the lay of the land up this way. Might you be suggesting some other course of action?"

Onkel Klaus smiled thinly and replied, "Maybe we'd best both study on the lay of the land, Wolf. Why don't you just make yourself at home whilst we both make up our minds what happens next."

Chapter 19

They'd let Bob Ramos lead his own pony home with him, but kept Longarm's saddle and such in the tack room of the sheriff department's stable. He decided to rustle up new quarters before he asked for his shit.

The nearest thing to a hotel in such an out-of-the-way town was the coaching inn kept there by the short-run stage outfit that ran from the bigger town of La Mesa to Fort Sumner to the west, crossing the Staked Plains in the process. Their manager in Sulfur Draw offered Longarm a job riding shotgun. He modestly allowed he was only in the market for a room at the moment. So they hired him a clean small room up under roof tiles with a double bed. Folk traveling overland by coach were inclined to scrimp on the price of private rooms. So he had to pay double, fifty cents a night.

He draped his heavily laden saddle over the foot of the bed, with the Winchester leaned against the wall in the narrow space betwixt the head of the bed and a lamp table.

Then he locked up with a match stem wedged under a botton hinge and went down to explore Sulfur Draw by daylight.

Nothing he saw at first surprised him all that much. Some older buildings near the east-west wagon trace running in line with the watercourse down the center of the draw were 'dobe. Most newer ones were of hauled in frame lumber. Nobody built log cabins with crooked cottonwood or the chinaberry trees that had somehow escaped from gardens to run wild through the canyons of the Staked Plains.

Ambling south along Main Street, he soon saw the small town had the usual supply of business establishments and an oversupply of churches for any possible population figures.

Two Roman Catholic churches rose about midway down to the smelly watercourse. A white frame Lutheran church with a copper-sheathed spire stood on higher ground. A smaller Methodist meetinghouse of plainer design stared across Main Street at the likely older 'dobe church favored by the local Tex-Mex settlers. Sabbaths in Sulfur Draw might or might not be as restful as their common Prince of Peace had preached on that mountain.

Most of the signs above the doors of other establishments on both sides of the two long city blocks of the business district were in plain English, with some few in Spanish and twice that many in the old-timey lettering Dutch folk called *Blockschrift*. It was tougher to read than the "Olde English" of your average "Ye Olde Tea Shoppe." It had tall letters as looked to be *F*s but read as *S* in High Dutch, if he'd read that dictionary right on the train.

After you knew that, it wasn't hard to decide a *Delikatessen* had to be just what it sounded like and everybody knew what a *cantina* was.

They had twice as many canteens or saloons as churches. An open-to-the-street smithy repaired all implements when it wasn't shoeing horses or shrinking new steel rims on wagon wheels. There was a gunsmith and ammunition outlet with a doctor's office above it. A dentist was open for business, painless, he claimed, over a *Billardspielhalle* or poolroom run by a gent named Gerber. Longarm didn't have to translate this too hard. A couple of teenaged kids came to the doorway with pool sticks in their hands to comment about him in High Dutch as he passed by. He didn't need a translation to guess

145

what they were saying. They reminded him of that verse in "Riley's Daughter" where the poor outcast sings,

> "As I go walking down the street,
> The paple from their doorsteps holler.
> There goes that Protestant son of a
>   bitch,
> The one who shagged the Riley's
>   daughter!"

A stranger in a small town had to expect such suspicions, striding by a small-town poolroom. He didn't let it fluster him. The more they gassed about him, the less a stranger he might seem.

Knowing he was being watched, and not having much for an out-of-work rider named Wolf Kruger to send by telegraph wire, Longarm stode past the Western Union office under a Spanish lingo newspaper office. The bank beyond called itself the Drover's Savings and Loan in regular old English, as did the feed store and livery stable beyond.

Serious buildings gave way to corrals and shacks along the east-west wagon trace at the bottom of the slope. He'd ridden it both ways in the dark. By day, he could see narrow trails leading off through the stickerbrush and dotted lines of swampy pools along the bottom of the draw. He saw chimney smoke above the autumn leaves to the south. He'd already figured there'd be as many or more homestead claims filed on that side of the sometimes serious streambed. Hither and yon, a sunflower wind mill, mostly F.O.B. Chicago, loomed above the closer-in treetops. Close to town you'd lay out your claim in forty-acre plots string-beaned back from the east-west traffic as far as it took to fence your government issue quarter-section. Within an easy wagon drive to a city and closer to a small town, you raised pigs, chickens, dairy goats or cows along with garden truck you could sell fresh in season. Farther east or west, Longarm knew, the stud and cattle operations such as the Double H would reverse directions to front as far as possible on the watered draw, cutting off the same from the free grass of the open range behind the barn.

He didn't care. His stomach kept reminding him they hadn't had any breakfast that morning. So he retraced his steps up Main Street to find a Tex-Mex *cafetín* where a pleasingly plump *mestiza* smiled across the counter at him to ask in perfect English what she could do for him. He didn't think it would be polite to tell her what he really needed after a night in jail. So he said he'd have tamales smothered in chili con carne not trusting any Mex short-order cook to rustle him up a rare steak you could cut with anything less than a hacksaw.

Considering they'd invented the western cattle industry, Spanish-speaking folk held conservative views on *eating* cows. Left to their druthers, they preferred pigs and chickens, in that order, and any Mex could tell you goat meat was more tender than your average longhorn.

Before beef-eating Anglo-Americans noticed all that beef on the hoof down Mexico way and helped themselves to some, the rancheros of old and new Mexico had raised cows for their superior hides and tallow. Cordovan leather and castile soap were only two of the products made from Spanish hide and tallow. They'd served the leftover meat to the servants and such. Poor folk lined up for free cuts of beef out behind the *Plaza de los Toros* in most Spanish-speaking towns after a Sunday afternoon of bullfighting. The beef in both his tamales and with the chili beans would be ground and simmered softer than your average Mexican steak.

As the old geezer at the grill prepared his order, the counter gal lounged on her plump elbows closer to the open breezeway to the street. So Longarm knew the un-shaven hatchet-faced vaquero who'd just come in was talking to her when he growled, "*Quien es el chulo gringo?*" so Longarm felt no pressing need to inform them he spoke some Border Mex.

The waitress warned, "*No degas fregadas,*" which was only fair. But it was the old geezer at the grill who de-clared in Spanish as he filled Longarm's bowl, "To begin with he helps us pay the rent by ordering food instead of flirting with Rosalinda. But in truth this one is more than a customer. He is not a, as you say, a gringo pimp. He is a man of sympathy and he is much a *man*! Last night, when one of our own was arrested by *los tiros* as a horse thief, this one came forward to take the blame and tell them they had the wrong man!"

The vaquero laughed and decided, "Nobody who steals horse can be all bad. But what is he doing here instead of there in their *carcel* after he admitted he was a horse thief, eh?"

As Longarm accepted his order with a silent nod and dug in, the gal who'd handed it to him told the Mex, "I heard them talking about that when I delivered some nachos earlier this morning. They wanted for to hold him until the circuit judge came around from Sulfur Springs next week. But *Tio* Klaus, *el patron de los Alemanes* told them for to let him out."

It was all Longarm could do not to ask for his coffee with his grub in Spanish as the vaquero made the sign of the cross and said, "Some day my big mouth is going to be the end of me! You know what he has to be if he rides for *Tio* Klaus, don't you?"

The old man at the grill opined, "If he is a *buscadero* he has no quarrel with *La Raza*. Roberto Ramos is one of *us*, not one of *them* and as long as this one seems to be a friend of Roberto Ramos I will not have him insulted as he eats my cooking."

He added, "Rosalinda, serve his coffee now. Haven't I told you they need their coffee with their chili for to wash it down?"

The vaquero must have only dropped by to flirt with Rosalinda. For he suddenly and silently slipped away, mayhaps wondering just how much Spanish a gringo who packed a gun for a living in Texas might or might not savvy.

Once he'd filled the void without asking Rosalinda's hand in marriage, Longarm bit his tongue to keep from asking, "*La cuenta, por favor*," instead of, "The check, please." For a man who played dumb never knew what he was fixing to find out next.

Discussion of his relations with the Ramos clan reminded Longarm of some other questions before the house that morning. So he went on back to his hired room, found nobody had busted in whilst he'd been out, and removed the saddlebags and bedroll to tote just the saddle, bridle and saddle gun down Main Street to that livery.

In their front office he discovered what Wendy Delgado did for a living when she wasn't wrangling on trail drives. She looked more like a regular gal in a mint-and-white gingham frock that favored her dusky complexion and big brown eyes. As she rose from her writing desk, smiling brightly up at him, Longarm said, "I was set to argue about the livery nag I need for today, Miss Wendy. Seeing you work here, I'll let you pick one for me. Ain't going far. Won't have to rope or even cut unless this afternoon turns out a big surprise!"

She dimpled and told him she'd be proud to fix him up. As he followed her out back, he was sure she'd meant that innocent, Lord love her firm little rump and the way she moved it under that summerweight gingham.

As she and an uglier Mex stable hand offered Longarm his choice of three bay and a gray Wendy said she'd heard-tell how Longarm and Bob Ramos had run afoul of the law the night before. He tried to brush that aside. But Wendy insisted with a frown, "How come the Double H charged you two with horse theft if *Tio* Klaus thinks so highly of you, Wolf?"

Longarm shrugged and said, "Reckon Miss Hilda Zimmer acted hasty."

The Tex-Mex gal smiled like Miss Mona Lisa and allowed she'd heard both the Zimmer twins were inclined to be hasty.

Longarm said that seemed the size of it as he and the hand got the gray ready to carry him out to the Ramos spread. The pretty Tex-Mex brunette could have meant her remark more ways than dirty.

The gray gelding they'd offered proved a fine mount

149

for a livery nag. In no time at all he reined it down from a mile-eating trot in the dooryard of the dairy spread.

Bob Ramos came out to greet him with a friendly grin and invited him right in for tequila and to hell with the coffee and cake.

As they sprinkled salt on the backs of their hands at his kitchen table with the pint of hundred-proof cactus juice and a dish of lemon slices betwixt them, Bob said Lilo and cousin Ernie had caught the morning coach-run for La Mesa.

Not wanting to tell tales out of school, albeit being a woman, Ernie had surely told Lilo exactly how long his dick was, Longarm muttered a desperately casual "How come?" before he sucked on a lemon slice, had a swig of tequila and licked the back of his hand before a gasp of pain could escape him.

The Tex-Mex said, "Is not true Lilo makes me do the dishes. But we both know she has a better head for figures and, of course, the English tongue Anglo bankers and lawyers speak."

He put some tequila of his own away and added, "We have spoken of leaving this *chingado* draw before, and last night was the, how you say, last straw! *Tio* Sam can have this quarter-section back for to shove up his *culo!* Our stock can be driven or ride with our implements and furnishings in the few extra wagons we can hire if we can not borrow any from the friends we still have around here! Lubbock is a bigger market for our milk, butter and eggs to begin with. Was stupid of me for to file a claim in the middle of a *campo de batalia!* In truth I was blinded by my feelings for the redheaded daughter of a *ranchero protestanto* but now that my Lilo has come to her senses about such matters she agrees this is no place for reasonable people. She was most *altero* for to hear about *La Hermana Vuelta* struck so near, against one of *my* kind, less than a month ago!"

Longarm asked for a translation, even though he knew the Spanish term, *vuelta* agreed with the High Dutch in describing the Twisted Sister as twisted in a queer peculiar way. Plain old twisted like a dish rag would have been *torcero*.

Once the Tex-Mex had set him straight about the Twisted Sister, Longarm said, "Now that you mention it, I did hear the Zimmer twins talking about something the mysterious whatever had done whilst they were over by Truscott. Wasn't my beeswax, so I didn't ask for details."

As Longarm sucked another lemon slice, Ramos said, "The details were *loco en la cabeza*! Poor old Pablo Herrerra, a harmless old *cabrero* who lived alone in a brushwood *jacal* among *los alamos* came home from the *cantina* in town for to find six poor goats hanging by their horns from tree branches, still alive, with their *tripas*, I mean guts, hanging to the dirt. The Twisted Sister had, of course, burned Herrerra's *jacal* with everything else he owned. A few mornings later the old man was just not there, as if he had been spirited away in darkness by those, how you say, *Kobolds*, my Lilo was afraid of, growing up."

"Or like an A-rab folding his tent to steal away in the night." Longarm suggested, adding, "A bitter old loner with nothing left to hold him but the IOU's he might have written could have decided to get it on down the road. What made everybody say it was the work of this Twisted Sister if nobody caught her in the act?"

Ramos said, "Nobody ever catches her in the act. But who else would it have been? Is true we have some, how you say, trash along Sulfur Draw and many cut fences or steal stock when they think they can get away with it. But nobody else has ever been so *malicioso* as *La Hermana Vuelta*. Was Lilo's people who found out who was acting so *loco en la cabeza* and named her. They say it another way. You would have to ask some *Alemano* for why they call her the Twisted Sister."

So Longarm, starting to feel the tequila, and seeing Bob Ramos had been at it long enough to slur his second lingo, allowed he'd head back to town to do just that.

Chapter 20

As they were unsaddling the gray back at that livery, the sultry Wendy Delgado shyly asked if he'd heard about the Conferternity Dance that evening. When he allowed he hadn't, she allowed a swain who'd asked her to 'tend it with him had asked less than three days before the dance, the poor sap.

Longarm smiled down at her smouldering brown eyes to say, "Just my luck I hadn't heard there was to be such a dance. No decent gal would ever accept an invite the very day of the event, right?"

She said, "Oh, I don't know, seeing you're a stranger in town. It's not as if I had to worry you'd asked somebody prettier, first, and settled for me."

"I don't know any other gals in town well enough to ask," Longarm replied, which was the simple truth when you studied on it. So she told him it might be easier to meet right there after suppertime and stroll down the way to the rectory hall of Sankt Josef's in the cool of the evening.

Longarm smiled uncertainly and said, "Hold on, Miss Wendy, we're talking about a dance at that Austrian Papist church down the way?"

She said, "Not in the church, silly. Their Conferternity Society meets in a sort of barn behind the quarters of Father Paul. My own folk 'tend Santa Rosas most of the

152

time, of course, but Father Paul and *Padre* Alejandro agree members of the Santa Fe should know one another, and so we all attend the Conferternity affairs at the new Austrian church."

He said, "That sounds reasonable, to me, but were those Lutheran Zimmer twins aware of your *Santa Fe* whilst you were wrangling for 'em way back when?"

Wendy said, "I suppose so. It never came up. I didn't ask them how they said their own prayers, and, to tell you the truth, I've never been one for praying all that much. None of us younger girls worry as much about the hereafter as the poor old shawly ladies you see mumbling their beads in the gathering dusk as the sun goes down on yet another of their days."

Longarm grimaced and said, "I've noticed old *gents* seem to get more holy or more horny-acting as their days grow shorter. But this day, we have to share figures to drag on forever before I can squire you on down to that dance, Miss Wendy!"

She blushed under her dusky cheeks, and they shook on it before he asked if he could leave his saddle and bridle in their tack room.

When she allowed he sure could, he bade her *auf Wiedersehen* as Wolf Kruger and told them that was who he was when he dropped by the Drover's Savings and Loan to jaw with a prune-faced loan officer.

Not wanting to show his badge and ID, Longarm fibbed about some daydreams involving a cattle spread of his own, down the draw a piece.

The banker stared at his faded denims in ill-disguised dismissal to declare, "A quarter-section claim with all-year water and perhaps five thousand dollars in cash or credit gives a would-be cattle baron a better chance than a snowball in hell. How much of that do you have to work with?"

Longarm said, "Mebbe five hundred if I sent home for more. I just got paid off for a cattle drive and had some pocket jingle left when I did."

The banker sneered, "Five hundred dollars would buy

you a seed herd of a hundred scrub calves if you never spent any of it on tobacco and beans for the four years it would take to see a modest profit on a hundred scrub steers. Then there's the land office filing fees and you were fixing to sleep under a roof for the five years it takes to prove a claim, weren't you?"

Longarm smiled sheepishly and confessed, "I reckon I'd need more like eight or ten grand to get started."

Before the banker could ask what security he had to put up, Longarm added, "I could borrow that much secured by the land and stock, once I had 'em, right?"

The banker's face got even prunier as he sniffed, "How? You have to *own* land and livestock before you can hope to borrow against either. I frankly frown on loaning money on anything mortal as a range cow, and, even if we were willing, you don't *own* any range cows. Before you ask if we'd loan you the money to buy the collateral, you're being silly, Mr. Kruger. As for borrowing against an unproven homestead claim, that's only slightly less silly. President Lincoln's already over-generous terms only grant you free title to your hundred and sixty acres after you've improved and occupied it for five years. In sum, it is not yours to sell or borrow on until such time as you can show us your deed from the Bureau of Land Management. I'm sorry, but you're wasting both our time, Mr. Kruger."

Longarm offered a three-for-a-nickel cheroot as he wistfully said, "Reckon I am. Reckon you have this conversation often, with other dreamers, don't you?"

The banker's prune face softened a tad as he refused the smoke with a wave of his hand and said, not unkindly, "If daydreams were horses, nobody would walk. I'd like to own my own bank, someday, too. Nobody enjoys working for the kindest boss, and you don't get too many of those, these days, in or out of the saddle."

When Longarm went on sitting there, he asked, awkwardly, "Was there anything else you wanted to know?"

Longarm chose his words as he nodded and said, "Mebbe. I've heard more than one small holder has pulled up stakes and left these parts without proving his claim or trying to sell his squat. Would an old boy looking to pick up some cheap land be able to pick up a deserted quarter section hither and yon for say the owner's back taxes or bad debts?"

The banker shook his head and firmly declared, "No. Not unless the land had been owned fee simple with a property deed one could transfer to the new owner. I've heard about night riders running off some Mex squatters and gunning that Dutch sheepman a spell back. None of that made any sense if the motive was land or money."

"What do you reckon the motive was, then?" Longarm asked.

The banker shrugged and said, "I gave up trying to figure the way cowboys think the first time one of them made me dance with a six-gun in Fort Worth. I was in uniform at the time. A generation of growing boys lost out on formal education as the armies of both causes taught them to get there first and shoot before asking questions. Reconstruction didn't do a thing for the social graces of the riders on the losing side and now, just as we've seen the last of Reconstruction, those Dutchmen up and down the draw, no offense, have started their own war over God knows what!"

Longarm rose as he suggested, "God, Himself, the way I've heard-tell. He's likely the only one who could tell me just what the feud is really about. I'll take your word there's no way to grab an unproven land claim just by running the claimants out of the country."

He lit a cheroot of his own as he stepped back out in the glare of what was turning into early afternoon. Aiming to become a familiar face around town in as many parts of the same as possible, Longarm ordered a late noon dinner at a fancier Anglo restaurant with tablecloths and moseyed up to a saloon not far from *Onkel* Klaus's big red dance hall.

Nobody seemed to care after someone asked the barkeep in High Dutch how come he was serving the shitface, and the barkeep replied he was "*in Ordnung*," which

155

was easy enough to follow in context. So Longarm knew they'd been paying attention when Lawyer Halpmann had carried him up those outside steps across the way.

The saloon was called *Der Rinderhirt*, which was High Dutch for a cowboy, as Longarm recalled. After that it looked much like any other Texas saloon, save for some old-timey Dutch beer steins along the top of the back bar and a framed photograph of von Bismarck staring at you stern from a back wall.

Rinderhirts had named a whole *town* for old Bismarck up to the Dakota Territory. Other Dutch-Americans Longarm knew described Prussia's new Iron Chancellor as a baby-butchering cocksucker. The cock in question belonging to that old Prussian kaiser, which was how they said "caesar," and they said his grandson, Prince Willy, scared the shit out of von Bismarck with his imperial ambitions.

Despite the saloon's name and interior decorations, he noticed all the other *Rinderhirts* were jawing in English as they shared tolerable free cold cuts and mighty fine beer. So Longarm didn't have to make excuses when a sort of weasel wearing batwing chaps and a dust-gray Stetson too big for his ferretlike face bellied up beside him to observe, "I'd be Jake Wohl off the Lazy Diamond. They tell me you brushed with Pink Armstrong last night. I reckon *Onkel* Klaus set *him* straight about you, eh?"

Longarm truthfully replied, "Can't say what Mr. Brenner said to Sheriff Armstrong. I wasn't there. But, what the hell, I'm out and you can call me Wolf, Wolf Kruger, if you'll let me buy the next round."

So they shook on that. Then Wohl asked if it was true he'd shot it out with some Irishmen pestering the Zimmer twins along the trail.

Longarm noticed others were listening as he modestly explained, "I understand it was their ramrod, Junior Brewster, who had it out with them Irish bully boys. You have that confused with my brush with some other toughs entire. I was fighting for me, not the Zimmer gals."

Another voice in the crowd horned in, "Yeah, but then

you hired on with the Double H, and did a fair job with some other toughs along the way, I heard-tell."

Longarm shrugged and asked, "What can I tell you? Drop a jar of olives on one side of town and it turns into a smashed-up wagonload of watermelons by the time word gets to the other. I'm just an old boy getting by as best I can, and looking for another job, now that I've been laid off by the Double H."

Jake Wohl asked, slithery, "Didn't *Onkel* Klaus have any openings for you when he got you out of jail this morning?"

Had it only been that morning? Longarm laughed and said, "I told him, as I'm telling you-all, a man needs a day or so to consider his options before he marries up or hires on."

He tried to buy drinks for himself and the ones he was talking to but the barkeep said it was on the house. Longarm was starting to see how they respected men they thought *Onkel* Klaus might be backing.

The conversation shifted to the dance the "Cat Lickers" would be giving that evening. When someone asked Longarm if he'd heard about it, he allowed he'd asked a pretty little Cat Licker to attend the Conferternity Dance with him.

It got mighty quiet in *Der Rinderhirt* for a spell.

Finally somebody quietly asked, "You ain't a Cat Licker, are you?"

Longarm easily replied, "I'm a natural man a long way from home and I'd like to get laid some more before I die. Might any of you gents know any warm-natured *Lutheran* lassies I could carry to that big red dance hall across the way on such short notice?"

Most of them laughed. Jake Wohl said, "I reckon any old port in a storm is more fun than your own fist. But if I were you, Wolf, I'd carry your warm-natured Cat Licker somewhere's else tonight. Heard some of the boys might *shivaree* the sons of bitches after dark."

Shivaree was not a High-Dutch term. It was likely Irish to begin with and, as used west of the Big Muddy, it signified the asshole behavior of what amounted to just short of a lynch mob. In its original form, it seemed confined to sending newlyweds off on their honeymoon with the bride too shook-up to notice she was being fucked. When *night riders* shivareed someone they weren't good pals with, it could end up mighty messy.

Sipping some suds, Longarm quietly asked whether anybody had asked *Onkel* Klaus for advice on the matter before they risked an head-on confrontation with Sheriff Armstrong and his deputies. When someone suggested *Onkel* Klaus might just say no and spoil their fun, Longarm, said, "You'd be a better judge than a stranger like me, but they do say those Truscott riders killed at the Double H camp might have only started out to have some fun with what they took for a sissy outfit. Seems to me even one of them Austrian or Tex-Mex Papists down the way might put somebody on the ground if he thought he was drawing with the law on his side."

A teenager snorted and guffawed, "Let 'em try and let her buck! Any fucking Cat Licker draws on *this* child, and he's sure to catch a round of .45-Short betwixt his eyes!"

Longarm nodded but asked, "Then what? How do you mean to explain a win to the judge and jury with the sheriff allowing the loser had a perfect *right* to draw on *you*? In the eyes of the law, the one who *starts* the fight is in the wrong, no matter who wins. Pick a fight with a man and kill him and you'll hang for it at least half the time. Pick a fight with a man and he kills you, he gets off on self-defense and spends the rest of his life bragging on what an asshole you were. You call picking a fight without just cause *fun*?"

Jake Wohl sniffed, "What if we said we *had* just cause, Wolf? Who says them Cat Lickers get to have a big dance smack in the center of *our town*?"

Longarm shrugged and said, "The town, of course. I'm sure the town council, the sheriff, even *Onkel* Klaus, if he wanted to put his back into it, could get them to call off that dance tonight. But unless they do, I mean to 'tend it in the hopes of enjoying more innocent fun. Do any of you boys ride by ashooting, make sure you don't kill me if you ever want me to speak to any of you again!"

They all laughed and most sounded sincere. So Longarm changed the subject to the more important topic of the Twisted Sister.

They all agreed that was about what you called the mysterious rider, in any lingo. After that, nobody seemed to know how come. The Twisted Sister was just the mysterious force said to be behind most of the deviltry in those parts, even though a bunch of local riders had just suggested busting up a church dance with wild whoops and gunfire.

Later on, after an early supper at yet another place, Longarm went up to his hired room and changed into a clean white shirt and some newer jeans before he went down to the livery to find Wendy waiting in a crisp white blouse and flamenco skirt with a silk rose pinned to her hip and a mantilla of filmy Spanish lace draped over the high ivory comb in her pinned-up hair.

He told her she looked pretty as a picture and suggested they go somewheres else, explaining he'd heard there might be trouble at the dance that night.

Wendy Delgado demurely replied, "We heard that, too. I have a .36 Navy Conversion strapped to the inside of my thigh under the folds of this skirt. Did you think I was dressed so out-of-fashion because I didn't know any better?"

Chapter 21

The barn-like but plank-floored meeting hall of the Conferternity, or Get Together Society, had been fixed up festive for the dance with Japanese paper lanterns, wreaths of broom corn, crepe streamers and so on. You had to pay to get in but Wendy said they'd be drawing for a handsome door prize, later. They'd been neither the first nor the last to arrive, so the floor was a quarter crowded and the music hadn't started yet. Wendy introduced him around the floor to gals she knew of mostly Dutch or Mex persuasion. Albeit there were some few Tex-Anglo Papists in town, unless, like him, they just wanted to dance that evening.

Father Paul Hauser S.J. was almost as tall but darker and heavier-set than Longarm, with bushy black brows as met in the middle. He had a firm handshake and a friendly smile, but he still looked more like you expected a construction hand to look than a sky pilot. He said he'd heard about Wolf Kruger, didn't ask why he hadn't been to mass as yet and allowed they were glad he'd come to their dance.

The part-time musicians were setting up on a dais down to one end. A counter ran along one wall, piled with refreshments and both the cold cuts favored by Dutchfolk and the nachos Mexicans nibbled. The wall directly across provided benches for wallflowers to perch on as they waited to be asked to dance. Some poor little things were already in position, sitting up alert as birds on a wire and not missing all that much. All of 'em had their eyes on the fronts of their skulls and their ears to either side, as far as Longarm could see. But he didn't see any he was dying to dance with. So he stuck tight with Wendy lest someone else ask her.

A fussy old Dutchman with a walrus mustache came up to them to say Longarm had to check his gun-rig as well as his hat if he meant to 'tend their dance. But before Longarm could answer a firm but not excited voice cut through the crowd like a gentle jerk on the coach reins, in High Dutch, and the old Dutchman said to forget what he'd just said. So Longarm turned to nod his thanks at Father Paul.

Then the band struck up and it took Longarm a spell to recognize "*La Paloma*" as played by an oom-pa-pa Dutch band. Wendy Delgado had to laugh, too. But she said she thought it was sweet of them to try.

Some of the folk assembled might not have known the steps had they had someone there to call a square dance in Tex-Mex. So the first couple out on the floor did the two-step, and Wendy allowed that was good enough for her and, once they got going, she complimented her escort for his fancy stepping.

He said, "Mush, Miss Wendy. When you got feet as big as mine, you have to learn to pick 'em up and put 'em down with some care!"

She laughed and snuggled closer, the way two-stepping allowed, to the consternation of some stricter sects, and he was just as glad he'd never messed with her out on the trail whilst she'd been in denim and leather with no powder and perfume. For now that she felt and smelled so much more womanly, he was looking forward to closer snuggles by far.

So after they'd danced around the floor to another Spanish tune played oom-pa-pa, Longarm set her down with the wallflowers to rustle them up some drinks from across the way. Father Paul was standing by the punch bowls, and when Longarm asked how much they were asking, the priest told him his money was no good there that evening.

Longarm smiled uncertainly and said, "I have the jingle to pay my own way, Father."

The beetle-browed Jesuit said, "No, you don't. We heard about your conversation in *Der Rinderhirt* this afternoon, Mr. Kruger. Are you sure you're not one of our boys, on the run from a Jezzie parochial school? The reasoned arguments you raised against trying to break up this dance this evening had a decidedly Jesuit ring to them!"

Longarm laughed and said, "Logic is logic, Father. So I'll take that as a compliment. I've been told by others of your faith how your Society of Jesus led the Counter-Reformation with sweet reason after that Spanish Inquisition didn't seem to be getting anywheres with, ah, cruder arguments."

The Jesuit smiled thinly and replied, "The vandalism and public executions ordered by Cromwell made little impression on the Irish, either. Let's agree it's a balmy autumn night, the music is grand, and anything you see on these refreshment stands is free."

So Longarm told the young gal presiding on the far side he'd sure like two glasses of her apple cider.

But before he could get away with them Father Paul asked if it was true Bob and Lilo Ramos were pulling up stakes for good.

Longarm cocked a brow to observe, "You don't miss much up or down Sulfur Draw, do you, Father? As your altar boy or verger likely told you, I found old Bob alone and blue this morning and did nothing to discourage him from leaving. For like he said, and as anyone can see, this feud betwixt you opposing Dutch factions can't be as important to a sensible Tex-Mex with nothing to gain no matter which side wins. I just got here. So it's none of my beeswax, but if you'd care to hear a prediction, neither side stands to win half as much as it's sure to lose unless you-all cease and desist this foolishness!"

162

The priest sighed and said, "My words from the pulpit and up in the office of that Protestant octopus, Klaus Brenner! Have you ever found yourself talking with someone, only to find they'd gone into another room and hadn't been listening to a word you've just said?"

Longarm gently suggested, "*Onkel* Klaus seems to feel your parish horned in on him and his and, no offense, Father, I've heard you mentioned by name as the one stirring up trouble."

The priest snorted in disbelief and suggested, "Confession is said to be good for the soul, so have it your way— the Twisted Sister is a demented Catholic nun we sent away to Rome for! That's why she attacks so many people on our side. She's all twisted up!"

Longarm shrugged and set the glasses down as he replied, "Like I said, I just got here. I've yet to have it explained to me why *anybody* would blame random unwitnessed attacks on one rider and ... if it *is* only one rider, who in thunder decided to name a lunatic nobody's ever seen as a twisted anything!"

Father Paul frowned thoughtfully and said, "I've asked that same question and gotten no better answer, Mr. Kruger. Try as I might, I've been unable to trace the origin of the term to anyone who first called her anything. Our Mexican friends say it another way, but they agree *they* heard some mysterious madwoman or perhaps a *Schmetterling* was behind those vicious random attacks all up and down the draw!"

Longarm said he'd forgotten what a *Schmetterling* was. When the Dutch priest said Mexicans called such confused souls *mariposos* or boy butterflies, Longarm recalled a Twisted Sister could be most any old gender, to a Dutchman, as long as he, she or it was ... twisted. When he asked Father Paul if the original meaning might have been just all twisted up like *loco* as all get-out the Jesuit said, "I suppose so. I have yet to talk to anyone who's actually *seen* the Twisted Sister!"

Longarm muttered half to himself, "Deadwood Joaquin Lightfoot, the mysterious midnight rider."

Father Paul asked what he was talking about, observing he'd never heard of any such outlaw as Deadwood Joaquin Lightfoot.

Longarm said, "That on account there was never no such rider all in one, or even seperate. Human nature forbids acceptance of 'We just don't know!' as the final answer. So folktales are spun together out of shadows and night noises with one know-it-all adding this detail and a second know-it-all another, until things that went bump in the night wind up with names and romanticated life stories nobody ever lived at all. Deadwood Dick ain't nobody real. He was made up by this dime-novel writer, Ed Wheeler, for a book published in London, England, but so far I've met up with three gents claiming to be the one and original Deadwood Dick. One's an old Englishman with a drinking problem, who was born in London Town, leastways. Another's a ranch hand of color who claims he got the name by winning the big Deadwood rodeo of 1876, an event that never took place in a spanking new mining camp laid out in buffalo country late that very year. The third Deadwood Dick who asked me to buy him a drink was named Richard, and he was begging drinks in Deadwood. So I reckon he thought he was on to something."

The priest sighed and asked, "What about those other names you've hung on your own mystery rider, Mr. Kruger?"

Longarm said, "You can start fights in the California Mother Lode country, saying there never was no such thing as a Robin Hood of the gold fields named Joaquin Murieta, holding up stagecoaches because mean '49ers jumped his claim, abused his woman and lashed him with a drover's bullwhip."

The priest said, "Just a minute! I believe I've *read* that story!"

Longarm shrugged and said, "So have I, Father. Fortyniners who were out yonder say that after more than one stagecoach had been held up by one or more road agents dressed Mex, and after more than one Californee Mex had been roughed up and told he'd better talk or else, one or more came up with mebbe it had been Joaquin Murieta, or Sulky Jack, as you'd say it in English. Nobody in those parts had ever been named Murieta. Nobody's ever been able to find out where and when anybody jumped such a claim, raped such a wife or lashed any man that hard with a bullwhip without killing him."

The priest insisted, "But I read how a posse caught up with Joaquin Murieta and brought his head back in a jar of spirits to claim the reward!"

Longarm said, "Californios I've talked to tell it different. That's what you call Spanish-speaking folk who grew up out yonder, Californios. They say the reward posted on Sulky Jack got some vaqueros out hunting wild horses near Tule Lake murdered. The so-called posse was led by a drunken wife-beating Texan who 'scribed his fool self as Captain Love of the Texas Rangers. If he was ever a Texas Ranger he had no authority to shoot Mexicans in California. But suffice it to say he killed *some* Mexicans he described as Joaquin Murieta and the hitherto unheard of Three Finger Jack. They still have the preserved head and a hand missing two fingers on display at a penny arcade out Frisco way. To be fair, the *Mexicans* argue about who the vaqueros who died down by Tule Lake might have been. Nobody can just say they don't know. So details keep piling up."

He saw Wendy Delgado threading her way toward them through the dancers, with a puzzled frown on her face, and quickly added, "Captain Lightfoot came into being to explain the first stagecoach robberies in New England, back around the turn of the century. One of 'em was caught and lynched in Massachusetts and the holdups stopped for a spell. So everyone knew they'd caught the one and only Captain Lightfoot who'd already been a famous highwayman in Ireland, or mayhaps Scotland, if it hadn't been England. All that's known for certain is that an Irish immigrant named Mike Martin stole a horse near

Springfield, got strung up to a tree a short time later, followed by the publication of *The Confessions of Captain Lightfoot* dictated by the horse thief as he was waiting to be hung from the nearest tree."

As Wendy joined them he added, "You know how fast Irishmen have been known to talk, and the book sure makes good bedtime reading."

Wendy smiled up at the priest to demurely suggest, "If you don't mean to dance with Wolf, yourself, Father, I'd like to give in a whirl!"

The two men laughed, and, as Longarm handed Wendy some cider to cool her down, the Jesuit said he was sorry, but thanked Longarm for offering him some interesting options on that Twisted Sister.

As he moved away, Wendy put her half-drained cider glass down and sighed, "I might have known the two of you were talking about another girl. What has *La Hermana Vuelta* got that I don't have, Wolf?"

He took her in his arms to two-step her out on the floor as he told her, "Nothing, even if she turns out to be pretty. You don't know who first started the story of a mysterious night rider by that name, do you, Miss Wendy?"

She frowned thoughtfully before she decided, "Now that you mention it, no. First I knew about her was when somebody said they had another way of saying *La Hermana Vuelta* in High Dutch. How come you care so much, Wolf? You're not a lawman, are you?"

He told her to perish the thought as they circled the floor with the other dancers. One of the nice things about the two-step that made it so popular was that you got to jaw with your partner as if you were already in bed together. So while he perforce lied like a rug about himself herding cows all over creation, he figured Wendy was likely telling him true about growing up Anglo-Mex in other parts and moving out to the Staked Plains a year or so back with her Irish husband.

When Longarm cautiously asked whether she expected her Irish husband to show up for the last dance, she explained he'd been killed by dry lightning hunting strays on the higher range to the south, leaving her to prove their claim as best she could, and accounting for her willingness to work as a wrangler, livery manager or whatever. Longarm said he was sorry to hear about her husband, but in truth he was just as glad to hear she lived alone, now, down the draw this side of the Ramos place but across the creek through the tanglewood. When Longarm asked if she'd meant to ride home after the dance, she told him her place wasn't too far for them to walk. So that saved him the awkwardness of offering to walk her home, later, and did those Dutchmen mean to oom-pa-pa forever, for Gawd's sake?

But in point of fact, the Conferternity Dance that night was to end way earlier than scheduled. For Longarm and Wendy had just put away some Vienna sausage wrapped in tortillas and washed down by sangria from another punch bowl when, just as they were fixing to two-step some more, the music was interrupted, considerable, by a fusillade of gunfire just outside and close in!

As Father Paul raised his big hands and stentorian voice for one and all to stay calm, Longarm told Wendy to get behind the refreshments and hold herself set to duck until he could get back to her.

Then he made for a nearby side door and drew his .44-40 on the way out. He circled round for the source of other noises that still seemed to be coming from Main Street, off across the grounds of the Papist church holdings. As he got closer he saw torchlights and a wild bunch of townsmen gathered around something on the dust and powdered horse shit in the center of Main Street. So he holstered his six-gun as he drifted in, noting others from the dance had beaten him there after running out the front door of the dance hall like saps.

Recognizing one of the hands he'd been drinking with that afternoon at *Der Rinderhirt*, Longarm asked what was up.

The cowboy snarled, "You're asking who was shot

down! One of our own, this time! Axel Schroder off the Lazy Diamond! Dead as a turd in a milk bucket! Shot in the back by that Twisted Sister, smack in front of that Cat Licking church!"

Chapter 22

Elbowing his way through the crowd, Longarm saw they'd rolled the dead hand over so's he could smile lifeless up at them. Longarm wasn't able to cut him from the crowd who'd been in *Der Rinderhirt*, earlier. He recognized one of the two gents hunkered down to either side of the body as a deputy he'd seen up to that jailhouse. Then Sheriff Pink Armstrong bulled through to the puddle of torchlight from the other direction to state soberly down and grumble, "Aw, shit, is he dead?"

The deputy new to Longarm glanced up to reply, "Never knew what hit him, Pink. The bullets failed to come out his front side, but he was stitched up the back as if by a sewing machine. Me and Wes, here, both heard the rapid fire and, man, we're talking *rapid*!"

"Sounded like a Gatling gun," his sidekick, the one Longarm had seen before, confirmed before adding, "We were patrolling down this way on foot, like you told us. We met poor Schroder, here, just down the way. We asked him why he was hanging around this neck of the woods after business hours, and he said he was just listening to that Dutch dance music from across the way."

The first deputy said, "We advised him, as per your instructions, to either pay his way in to 'tend the dance or get it on up the road and stay out of trouble. We thought he'd done so. He must have circled back as we patrolled further south. We hadn't gone far when we heard the shots and, like Wes said, they came quick as a kid running a stick along a picket fence!"

"How could even a lunatic·like the Twisted Sister fire so fast?" asked a dubious voice from the crowd, and Longarm saw it was *Onkel* Klaus Brenner from up the way, smoking another fancy cigar under the brim of a Stetson Boss model or ten-gallon hat.

Longarm said, "It wasn't one gun firing that fast. It was two guns. Different calibers or different powder loads. It's for your coroner to say which. But I'd guestimate this Lazy Diamond hand was shot in the back by two or more sneaks."

Pink Armstrong glanced up to growl, "Were you there, Kruger?"

Longarm said, "Nope. Heard the shots from inside, with the music playing. That's how come I can only say for certain it sounded like two different guns."

Armstrong dryly asked if Longarm was some sort of lawman and once again the undercover lawman had to pull in his horns by lamely replying, "Hell, anybody who know which end of a gun the bullets fly out of can tell one gun from two!"

"Let him talk, Pink," said *Onkel* Klaus, aiming his cigar Longarm's way as he asked, "As an expert gunslick, Kruger, would you concede our *Zerziehenschwester* could have shot this poor Lutheran with a gun in each hand?"

Someone in the crowd muttered, "That's right! I have heard the crazy bitch packs a gun on each hip!"

Longarm muttered, "Doubtless under that black cloak as she rides her big black stallion through the moonlight."

Then he raised his voice to tell *Onkel* Klaus, "If we're talking about *possible*, your Twisted Sister could be an Eskimo on stilts with a Colt dragoon in one fist and a .32 whore pistol in the other. But most two-gun men I've met up with loaded both guns from the same gun belt with the same sort of rounds. Would you care to fumble for the right bullets, reloading hasty in a tense situation, *Onkel* Klaus?"

Brenner conceded, "I would not. So maybe there *were* two of them, this time, and what's that shit about an Eskimo on stilts?"

Longarm said, "As sensible a description as a night-riding pervert nobody seems to have been acting queer with, no matter how she, he or it may be built. I just got here. But nobody I've talked to, yet, has ever seen or talked direct to anybody who's ever laid eyes on this so-called Twisted Sister. So what if there's no such person?"

Above the collective gasp, Pink Armstrong demanded, "Are you saying nobody at all shot this poor boy in the back just now, you asshole?"

Longarm shook his head and replied, "Flattery will get you nowhere. Neither will hunting high and low for a mental picture that might not fit for shit, Sheriff! It's plain as day this old boy and others have been attacked by a *person*, or mayhaps *persons* unknown. Out California way, as we speak, the Wells Fargo stages are being held up monotonous by a mysterious spooky rider they call Black Bart, described as seven feet tall and backed by a gang of Mexicans, or make that Miwok Indians, unless they're ferocious frustrated mining men like their leader. I have no idea who Black Bart might be, what he looks like when he ain't suited up head to toe in white linen, despite his pen name, or where he'll be sipping cider, innocent, when they finally catch up with him. But when they do, I'll bet you they discover Black Bart's just a mortal man who dosen't stand out in a crowd when he's not dressed up to stop a stagecoach."

Pink Armstrong frowned thoughtfully as *Onkel* Klaus conceded the Twisted Sister might have a faithful companion they hadn't known about before. Longarm refrained from suggesting two fairies might be shooting lone riders who refused to get queer with them. He feared he'd already opined too much for a stranger who didn't want to be suspected as an undercover lawman. Pink Armstrong and his deputies were paid to suspect strangers, and for all he knew, the very gunslicks who'd just assassinated Axel Schroder off the Lazy Diamond could be standing

171

in that very crowd as the last place any posse would be trying to cut their trail out of town!

Without excusing himself, Longarm as Wolf Kruger slowly crawfished back through the crowd to where he could bust loose and go back to see if Wendy was still there.

She was, albeit by the front door with Father Paul instead of on the floor behind the refreshments. As he joined them, Longarm tersely told them what had happened out front. Before he could advise it, the burly priest decided the dance had just ended and declared so, loud and clear, directing his flock to leave by the side doors and avoid the stirred-up largely Protestant crowd out front. When he saw he was getting no back talk he turned wearily back to Longarm and Wendy to say, "You know who they're going to blame for that troublemaking Protestant's death, don't you?"

Longarm said, "Mayhaps not for certain, this time. Other victims have been your own kind, or neutrals on neither side. So I just now pointed out the killers, plural, could really be most anybody from these parts. As soon as you study on it, as I hope I've got at least some of them studying, now, it's way more likely them night riders have been two-facers with a place to be and visible means of support than funny-looking lunatics hiding out between raids . . . where? On the wide open plains to north and south, or under some willows nobody knows about down here in Sulfur Draw?"

Father Paul nodded soberly and said, "William of Ockham's razor! A basic tenet of Jesuit Reasoning, and why didn't *I* think of that?"

Longarm gently suggested, "Too close to the forest to see the trees, most likely. I started out with the advantage of being a stranger who couldn't pronounce Twisted Sister in High Dutch."

Wendy Delgado was tugging on his sleeve so he excused the both of them, and led her off into the darkness as she asked him who on earth William of Ockham might be.

172

As they followed a dark alley south toward the eastwest wagon trace Longarm told her, "William of Ockham was a monk or something as lived and taught in the Old English town of Ockham back in them dark ages. He allowed things might not be as dark if folk applied more simple logic to things going bump in the night. They recall his system of peeling away nonsense a slice at a time as Ockham's razor because that was how it worked. This lawman I know calls it a process of eliminating."

"Who's the lawman you know?" she asked.

He said, "We were talking about William of Ockham. When, say, somebody allowed they'd heard a werewolf howling in the graveyard about the time wheat rust started breaking out in the fields all about, old William suggested slicing that notion apart with his razor and most anyone with a lick of sense could see a plain old wolf howling most anywhere near the village made as much sense as a *were*wolf nobody had laid eyes on howling from a graveyard, just to be spooky."

Wendy said that made sense to her.

Longarm said, "The next slice of the razor cuts most any sort of critter howling anything from anywhere as the source of wheat rust. I doubt William of Ockham could have known *all* about wheat rust before a microscope had been invented, but you didn't need a microscope to see wheat rust was a sickness that struck the same fields over and over in wet weather whether wolves howled or not."

She took his arm and snuggled closer as they strode in step. She said, "I'm starting to see what you mean. I've been sort of using that razor on you, trying to fathom what sort of a man you are, and not having much luck."

He chuckled and replied, "I'm just a knock-around saddle bum as soon as you slice away the more wonderous things I might be."

She said, "Maybe. I suppose you've been whittling on *this* girl with Bill Ockham's fool razor?"

When he suggested everybody with common sense used much the same logic, no matter what they called it, she teased, "Tell me what you and old Bill have whittled *me* down to, then?"

She'd asked for it. So as they walked through the moonlight with his gun hand free, he told her, "I'd already noticed you were a handsome gal as well as good with horses before you told me you were a widow woman with an unproven claim, an ambitious nature and that little old chip on your pretty shoulder."

"What chip are you talking about?" she demanded, adding, "I've never stuck out my lower lip at you, have I?"

He gently replied, "Not at me. Likely not at anybody who treats you with respect. But when a Tex-Mex widow woman reverts to a maiden name, a sensible man just meeting up with her has to wonder why."

"Why do you imagine I prefer to be known as Wendy Delgado instead of Widow Malone?" she softly demanded.

He easily replied, "Still slicing, but I do keep coming back to a quarter-breed gal I met up Denver way, one time."

"Oh, have you been to Denver, too?" she thrilled.

He quicky assured her, "Herding beef with Captain Goodnight more than once but a long time ago. This Denver gal I'm speaking of was the daughter of a snow-white mining man and a pretty Ute breed raised white by her *own* dad. So the modestly well-off result, who owned her own rooming house near the Denver stock yards, could have passed for a white gal of swarthy complexion had she wanted to."

"But she didn't want to," the Tex-Mex Wendy cut in as if she knew.

Longarm said, "Oh, she might have *wanted* to. She might have *tried* to, now and again. But some folk being as they are, from time to time I suppose someone just had to ask her if she was Jewish or mayhaps I-talian. So she found it easier to just say no, she was a blankety blank Quill Indian, and she saved some asking by calling herself Miss Many Ponies, which was sort of silly in a way because Quill Indians don't pass down family names, or didn't, until recent."

Wendy Delgado said, "I know just how the poor girl felt. Was she pretty? Did you make love to her, Wolf?"

Longarm didn't like to lie outright. So he said, "Like I said, it was a long time ago and how would you like it if, someday in another place and time, I was to tell some other gal I'd made love to you?"

She didn't answer for six or eight paces. When she did she'd decided, "I find it easy to picture you with some other woman, some other time and place. But aren't we taking a little bit much for granted, here and now, Wolf Kruger?"

He said, "Nope. Apply Ockham's razor to what I just said and you'll see I never implied I was *fixing* to make love to anybody. I only asked *if* it would be fair to say I had, whether I had or not, see?"

She walked along silently a spell before she decided, "Father Paul would call that line of argument *sophistry* if his Sunday school up this way teaches the same as our old one, down home. It's nice to hear you're not a kiss and tell, or so you say. But our Sunday school taught us girls more than praying. The nuns warned us about sophistry or the slick ways of a man with a maid and I do believe you only told that tale about another *mestiza* to assure me, without bragging, that you have no prejudice against halfway attractive women of mixed blood, that you tend to remember us tender and that you don't kiss and tell."

Longarm didn't argue. Life was too short to squander precious moments of it trying to change a woman's mind, once it had set in cooled-down cast iron.

They got to the east-west wagon trace and turned east. But before they'd walked a furlong, Wendy let go his arm and decided, "I can find my way from here, thanks. I'd invite you in for a nightcap if I lived alone. But my yard dog and house cat might not understand."

Life was too short to argue with a woman brushing you off as one awful mistake, too. So he gallantly ticked his hat brim to her in the moonlight and thanked her for a swell evening as she turned on one heel to march off down the tree-shaded wagon trace.

He stared wistfully after her just long enough to tell his fool self to cut that out. Then he shrugged, turned on his own heel and headed the other way. Another night alone in a more comfortable bed for a change wasn't likely to occasion serious injury. So he started walking.

He hadn't walked half a furlong when he heard running footsteps on the grit behind him and spun into some deeper shade with his six-gun in hand. But when she called his name, he saw it was Wendy Delgado all hot and bothered about something. So he holstered the .44-40 and stepped back into view as Wendy sobbed, "Oh, there you are, thank heavens! I thought I'd lost you! I thought I'd spoiled things again with my big mouth and Spanish pride!"

As he took her in his arms in the middle of the moonlit wagon trace, Longarm didn't say anything. Skating with a woman on ice that thin, it was best for the man to let her do all the talking.

Chapter 23

Once he'd walked her all the way home, swapping spit without saying all that much along the way, Wendy never offered that nightcap. Neither her yard dog nor house cat seemed to have anything to say as she hauled him back to her bedroom through her unlit frame house. They proceeded to shuck one another's duds off by in stripes of moonlight through the jalousies. Wendy reminded him of a mighty shapely zebra as she beat him down to the mattress of her four-poster and rolled over, wide, in welcome. She gasped; *he* had a lovely body, too. He allowed he'd seldom met up with a zebra-striped cowgirl built so fine.

She said he was a gallant liar but he believed her when she sobbed she'd forgotten how swell it felt when he entered her tight warm innards with a mighty love-hungry organ grinder of his own. He didn't want to hear about other swains she'd sent home with their tails betwixt their legs since her man had died, so he didn't ask. A good time was had by all. After they'd both come, more than once, Wendy rolled out of bed to stride off zebra-striped and bare-ass to fetch that liquor she'd mentioned earlier.

When she returned with a pitcher of water and a fifth of potato whiskey, he forgave her for giving her cherry to a fucking Irishman indeed. For whiskey-and-water highballs were less complicated to put away than tequila with lemon, salt and so on.

As they worked on their second winds, before they got down and dirty as old pals, now, Longarm asked polite questions about the spread he could barely picture from what he'd seen of it, so far.

She said their fenced acres lay fallow and she'd sold off the stock including that dog and cat he'd been wondering about because day jobs in town or contracting for a drive or roundup payed better than a woman working alone could wring out of a hundred and sixty acres. She said she was just hanging on to prove her claim and get free title so's she could sell out and move on. She explained moving far away from her own kith and kin had been her man's ambition, not her own. So she'd been lonely enough without the worry anyone dwelling alone along the draw was commencing to feel about that Twisted Sister or, have it his way, person or persons unknown.

Trying not to sound like a lawman questioning a bareass witness with one arm around her, Longarm casually asked Wendy if anyone had offered to buy her out.

She sipped her drink thoughtfully and replied, "I haven't said I was ready to pull out and why should anyone offer if I did? I can't sell this claim and nobody will be able to buy it before I have my proven deed from the land office. Is that what you suspect the twisted whatever is up to, a land grab?"

Longarm sipped his own highball, she'd mixed it just right, and had to confess, "It's a caution how easy it is to see patterns in the wallpaper. I was just now chiding Pink Armstrong for picturing a sinister figure that might be no more real than them *Kobold* goblins the Dutch folk scare their fool selves with. But if the troublemakers in these parts ain't acting out of religious conviction, race hatreds or land greed, what's left?"

She suggested, "*Practice?* How do you know she, or they, have no racial or religious motives? That Ku Klux Klan night rides for reasons like so, no?"

He said, "No. As wrongheaded as the Klan may be, it lets everyone know what it's trying to establish when it assassinates a carpetbagger or burns out a colored church. The point of a terrorist is to scare folk into letting him have his own way. None of the random acts I've heard-tell of out this way have taken place before or after the warning threats or demands the Klan and other such night riders issue. Up to now, this self-appointed goblin or goblins along Sulfur Draw have hit members of all local factions and complexions, rich or poor, maliciously mischievous or downright murderous. I ain't certain I buy one mastermind or one bunch behind it all. Disemboweling goats and burning shacks is one dirty trick. Shooting a man in the back, a lot, is another!"

She drained her glass and set it aside to take the limp matter in hand as she languidly chided, "Is that how you apply Ockham's razor to the deadly doings of *La Hermana Vuelta*, or perhaps Billy the Kid?"

He laughed and said, "Don't you *dare* mention *that* notion to a living soul in Texas, girl! Until they shot him and made him stop, Lawyer Alex McSween had the Kid and them other Tunstall-McSween riders convinced they were special deputies appointed by a lawyer, at least. The Murphy-Dolan gun hands who murdered Tunstall and McSween were just as certain they were deputy sheriffs, and they may have had a point. Before the Tunstall-McSween riders murdered *him*, Sheriff Bill Brady had been appointed sheriff, if not elected, with a little help from his friends in higher places."

Wendy didn't answer. She couldn't talk with her mouth so full and Longarm lost the thread of that Lincoln County War of another time and place as he perforce paid more attention to what they were doing, in direct violation of the Texas statutes dealing with public or private morals.

So Wendy waited 'til they were going at it dog-style, half an hour later, before she languidly asked how he figured that Lincoln County War had anything at all to do with current events along Sulfur Draw.

Smiling down at her zebra-striped rump as their bumps and grinds moved her cute little asshole in and out of the moonlight, Longarm explained, "It don't. It can't. The leaders on both sides were killed or ruined by their six months of feuding and fussing. The two most dangerous guns still alive, the Kid and Jim Dolan, are still gunning for one another or laying low entire. Nobody else seems to know which. But I find myself coming back again and again to that almost pointless penny-ante Lincoln County War and I sure wish I knew *why*."

She arched her spine to purr, "Oooh, yesss! *Chinge me mucho y chinge me feroz!*" So he did, even though he wasn't supposed to speak Spanish, either.

The lonely but particular young widow woman didn't ask how Longarm knew just what she wanted. Most any mortal man she'd been shoving her fine rump at would have given her his all as ferocious as he could.

The next thing they knew they were on the braided rag rug, with her on top, bare heels planted to either side of his bare hips as she went up and down like a delighted kid on a merry-go-round she'd been pining to ride for many a day.

Then, having climaxed joyously that way and hauling him back up on her rumpled bedding to try for another with him on top, Wendy Delgado was suddenly bawling fit to bust.

Longarm didn't ask her what was wrong. He suspected he knew, since she was hardly the first widow woman he'd ever consoled. He kept on, moving in her with an elbow hooked under either of her wide spread knees until he had her bawling and bumping up to meet him at the same time, and it hardly seemed fair for her to call him a beast as she was coming with him again. But he wasn't as surprised as resigned, having forded that same river of tears before in his time.

When she quietly said he was getting too heavy for her, Longarm just rolled over and asked in a conversational tone if he had time for a smoke whilst he gathered his wits and recovered his breath.

She murmured in a soft, sad voice, "I'm sorry, Wolf. I know I'm not being fair to you. You were willing to let me go on alone and then . . . something came over me and

I reckon I went *loco en la cabeza* for just just a little while. I know you don't understand, but . . ."

"I understand," he cut in, sitting up to swing his bare feet to that rug as he continued, "Just-a-little-while sure beats never-in-this-world and you said you'd been alone out here a spell."

"Don't make me sound like a sex-mad *puta*!" she sobbed.

He gently replied, "I know what a *puta* is and you ain't no sex-mad *puta* because to be such a commercial-minded gal, you have to be cold-blooded and uncaring about such matters. If it matters to you how I'll remember you in days to come, when we just nod in passing on the street, Miss Wendy, I'll think of you as a lady of quality who got a mite warmed up at a dance, satisfied the itch as best she could with an understanding improvement on her fingers or an ear of corn and . . ."

"An ear of corn? Are you serious?" Wendy cut in incredulously.

Longarm soberly replied, "I've never had occasion to try any ears of corn up private parts I don't have, Ma'am. But I have it on the authority of more than one farm gal that a buttered-up ear of corn, not cooked, of course, has a candle or even a Vienna sausage beat by miles. They told me that the size and rippled surface makes up some for the fact it ain't attached to nobody you can talk to, see?"

She laughed like hell, but when he started to roll back in bed with her she said, more calmly now, "Please don't, Wolf. You know I wouldn't be able to resist, but I still think it's better to quit before this . . . walk home from a dance gets us in any deeper. I have my reputation to consider and . . ."

"I got my breath back. I ain't got time for a smoke, no offense," Longarm cut in as he rose from the bed to gather his shit from all over the floor. As he dressed in the stripes of moonlight, Wendy dryly observed she could see he was used to quick exits. He didn't answer. She was commencing to piss him off a mite. He'd just *said* he followed her drift, but being a woman, unlike most men, she seemed to feel the situation called for one of those drawing room conversations in a French bedroom farce. Gals were good at such talk. A man had to be a sissified dude to pull it off without sounding snide or sore and, in his day, in such last acts, Longarm had learned no exit line had ever beaten just closing the door softly after you as you left.

He knew he'd scored a point when something slammed and busted against her bedroom door as he shut it on the way out. That had happened more than once before as well. It was the way women got from reading infernal romance novels, he suspected.

Walking back to town seemed to take way longer than coming out so far in the moonlight had. Once he got there he had to walk the length of Main Street to the coaching inn he'd planned on staying at in the first place. When he asked the night clerk how come they'd built the stage stop so far from the east-west wagon trace, the night clerk said he only worked there and added, "There's a lady here to see you, Mr. Kruger. I told her she could wait for you in our waiting room."

Longarm said that sounded fair and ambled through an archway to find Herta Zimmer seated on a waiting room bench, judging by the *charro* riding outfit and two guns she'd worn into town. When she saw Longarm she rose to her feet, saying, "It was Hilda's idea to fire you, Wolf! I had nothing to do with it, and now Hilda's sorry she lost her temper, too!"

As she moved closer to put her hands on him for the first time with the lights on, Longarm soberly replied, "Well, she likely felt she had good reason. I've never had too much control of my own natural feelings, Miss Herta."

She laughed in spite of herself and said, "Hilda said she caught Ernestine Holz sucking you off!"

Then she demurely added, looking away with her hands on his sleeves, "I suppose she felt that was . . . all right, *our* privilege alone."

"*Alone* would be a contradiction in terms for hot-tempered twins, Miss Herta. But what's done is done, and nobody got hurt."

She said, "You're wrong, Wolf. We just heard about Axel Schroder, and we're hurting for a gun hand as good as you!"

He said, "Aw, shucks, I thought you admired me for my mind."

Herta soberly replied, "That, too, and you're swell in a bedroll as well. So what say you ride back out to the Double H with me and let naughty Hilda and me . . . make it up to you?"

Longarm shook his head to say, not unkindly, "No offense and thanks for the offer, Miss Herta. But as I was saying earlier this evening to another pal, I'd as soon we just be friends for now. I've hired a room here, as you must know, and there's no saying how long I may be here in Sulfur Draw, getting the feel of things before I decide to go or stay."

She pleaded, "You've finer quarters and plenty to feel up out at the Double H, Wolf! We're scared and, more than that, we both agree no man we've ever played our little tricks on has been half so fine a playmate! Won't you ride with me tonight, both ways, darling? Hoping you would, I led that palomino you like into town for you!"

He gently but firmly took hold her upper arms to hold her back as he said, "That's a swell pony and Lord knows I enjoyed your game of puss, pussy, who's-got-the-pussy as well as any mortal man would have. But I *know* what's going on out to the Double H, 'til that other ramrod arrives, leastways. I'm more curious about what's going on here in town than I aim in having it out with a doubtless ticked-off Junior Brewster. So I won't even ask whether you and your twin played your cute little games on *him!*"

She said, "Don't be *schlimm*, Wolf. Hilda and I agree there's not room enough for both of you in one . . . position. So since you are twice the man in bed, and I had to deal with those gunslicks in Truscott all by myself, you're the obvious choice and that's that."

But Longarm said, "No, I ain't. I learned long ago not

to go back after I'd been discharged by an army, fired by an outfit or told by a woman to never darken her door no more. On those few occasions I've bent them rules, I've regretted it sincere. So thanks, but no thanks, Miss Herta. It's been nice talking to you, but I've had a hard day, and I'd as soon go on up to bed, now."

She purred, "Let me go with you, Wolf. Let's just tear off a fast fuck, and see if you still feel the same about our offer."

But he shook his head and insisted, "Let's not and say we did."

She blanched and stammered, "You can't mean that, Wolf! You know what I have to offer you, between these very legs and how could you ever refuse?"

To which he truthfully replied, without explaining why, "It ain't as tough as you might imagine, Ma'am."

But of course, once she'd flounced out, red-faced and slapping her leg with a riding quirt, Longarm naturally sighed and softly muttered, "Shit, now I'll never rightly know which twin had that mole in the crack of her ass!"

Chapter 24

Longarm woke the next morning with a mild piss-erection and the refreshing sense of freedom a man only feels right after he's left or been left by a woman and hasn't had time to get really hard up.

He broke fast at that Mex *cafetín*, and Rosalinda acted as if she'd been missing him. It felt swell to feel for certain that she was too fat for him no matter what.

As she served him, the obese but clean-smelling *mestiza* asked if he'd heard about the killing just down the street the night before.

He said he'd heard something about it but hadn't been keeping track. Rosalinda said the coroner who rode circuit like their judge to serve such a big unincorporated county had declared Axel Schroder's cause of death a Murder Most Foul by a person or persons unknown pumping .45-Shorts and .44-Longs into him at short range, with the lead from both guns scored with knife cuts to expand inside and tear things up instead of punching on through. When he asked how she knew so much she confided some deputies who'd been to the hearing had ordered *huevos rancheros* a few minutes earlier. She said they'd said the High-Dutch Protestants were all het up about that. He had to agree it was bad enough to shoot a man in the back without using expanding dum-dum bullets invented in British India by somebody mighty mean on one side or the other, near a Hindu town called Dumdum. Rosalinda couldn't say whether they were sure the Papist faction had been ahint the killing or not. Last she'd heard, they were still arguing abut that over to that big red *Tanzsaal* run by *Onkel* Klaus.

Once he'd et, wanting to know where he might saddle up and ride but not feeling up to another awkward conversation with a recent lover, Longarm ambled up to *Der Rinderhirt* to find they'd opened for business, and it served him right for sleeping later than usual.

He ordered a lager and as the barkeep served it, he asked how come the nearby coaching inn, stage stop and that livery Wendy worked at were so far upslope from the east-west wagon trace passing on through Sulfur Draw.

The barkeep blinked and replied, "Hell, how should I know? Why should I care? Why should *you* care, Mr. Kruger?"

It felt comfortable to be so well-known in town, now. As Wolf Kruger, Longarm said, "Just wondering, is all. Like to sit with my back to the wall in strange surroundings, too. Makes me jumpy when I notice things out of place."

One of the deputies who'd been down by that crime scene the night before came over from his corner table to belly up beside Longarm as he observed with a puzzled frown, "That stage stop ain't out of place, pard. Coach runs through every day, running east or west on alternate days. Stops for a fresh team and any passengers to get on, off, or take a crap not far from where you bedded down last night."

Longarm said, "I know that. Still wondering why. If I was running a stage line, I'd have things set up down along the wagon trace. I'd have that livery down yonder, too."

The deputy laughed, "Lucky you ain't running neither, then. Saves everyone else a heap of walking. Wasn't you talking to Pink Armstrong and Wes over the body of Axel Schroder last night, down in front of the Cat Licker church?"

Longarm nodded and said, "I was. They call me Wolf Kruger and you'd be . . . ?"

"Cooper, Ike Cooper," the deputy declared, and, as they shook, Longarm reflected on both names. Neither Wesley nor Isaac were first names a Dutch Lutheran family would be inclined to pick. John Wesley had been an Anglican, not a Lutheran, who'd gone on to found the Methodist persuasion. Calvinist fundamentalist were as inclined as Jewish folk to name their babies after Old Testament prophets such as Isaac. Hence, like their boss, Pink Armstrong, they didn't work as full members of either High-Dutch faction, no matter where they might drink.

Longarm decided as long as *he* found *Der Rinderhirt* a tolerable saloon, it was a free country.

Remembering his own true reasons for coming there that morning he asked nobody in particular where a man might buy a saddle bronc in or about their fair city.

Ike Cooper suggested the livery Wendy worked at. Longarm said he didn't want to *hire* a mount. He wanted one for his very own.

The barkeep said, "I always wanted a pony, growing up, but take my advice and just hire one. A horse is more trouble to care for than six dogs and you only need one a few hours now and again for casual errands on horseback."

Longarm said, "Don't need a pony for casual errands. Mean to do some serious riding. With winter coming on I got to think about my moving on or wrangling a good steady job. So I'd better ask here, and I'd better ask yonder, and I doubt any of the small holders in *walking* distance are in the market for a top hand."

The barkeep suggested, "Why don't you try at the *Sulfur Star* before you go galloping off on your own?"

Longarm started to say he hadn't heard-tell of such a local brand, and then he recalled that was the name on the window of a newspaper office he'd passed more than once, across from the *cafetín* where old Rosalinda seemed to like him. The barkeep explained the *Star* came out once a week, carrying classified ads as well a local gossip.

Longarm didn't need to be told they'd likely have want ads placed by anyone seriously in the market for hired help, or for that matter, anxious to sell a horse. But the barkeep told him anyway.

Longarm nursed his suds long enough to keep from seeming anxious, and then he allowed, like a slow thinker, they might let him know what they were set to publish in days to come. He added, "By jimmies, that could give a man an edge on the competition! Reckon I ought to go see."

Ike Cooper said, "Old man Slade will never let you read next week's edition. Why should he take the time out from his drinking? He can't charge you more than double and his rag only sells for a nickel."

Longarm almost asked how bad a drinking problem they might be talking about. He decided it was smarter to find out for his own self. So he put down his empty stein and *auffed* all their *Wiedersehens* as he headed for the door. Behind him, Deputy Cooper was asking the Dutch barkeep if that meant *adios*. Longarm was just as surprised to learn he'd just said something more like *hasta luego* or "until later." He hadn't thought Cooper was a Dutch name.

A bell above the door of the editorial and printing office of the *Sulfur Star* fetched a little brown-haired gal in a denim artist's smock out from the back. She had a smudge of printer's ink on her pert nose and she wasn't pretty until she smiled. Once she had, Longarm had her down as one of those schoolmarmish little things a man who wanted to marry up and settle down was in the market for. Her breed of she-male tended to look around thirty when they were sixteen, and not much older when they were sixty. But unless a man was in it for the long haul, a face and build like hers didn't offer a thrilling one-night stand.

She dimpled across the front counter at him to say the owner, Wilbur Slade, was out working on a news story. She introduced herself as his assistant editor, type sticker, press operator and doubtless maid of all work. When he told her what he'd come for, she allowed that having stuck the want ads her own self, she could assure him nobody was hiring, but a couple of owners within an easy livery ride or a long walk had riding stock for sale.

Before he could ask, she said she'd fetch the copy and turned on one heel to swirl that smock and duck in the back.

Moments later she'd spread four handwritten slips of yellow foolscap across the counter before him. As he reached for a stub pencil in the breast pocket of his denim jacket, Robin said, "Keep them. I've stuck the ads already, Mr. Kruger."

Then she shyly added, "It *is* Mr. Kruger, isn't it?"

Longarm smiled down at her to remark, "You noticed, huh?"

She said, "We'll be running a feature on you in our next issue. We don't see many famous . . . cowboys here in Sulfur Draw, and one of the other girls pointed you out to me at the Papist ball last night. You were with that Tex-Mex widow woman, so you naturally wouldn't remember *me* in my less dramatic party frock."

"Saints preserve us, I failed to recognize you dressed so different and, no offense, smeared with printer's ink," Longarm lied.

The little brown-haired gal in the shapeless smock flustered and gathered up the slips to offer in bunch as she replied, "Aw, mush, you're just saying that! I don't suppose you'll be 'tending the ball at Uncle Klaus's big red barn this evening, you being a Papist and all?"

He knew he was on safe ground as he asked, "Where did you get that notion?" knowing "Papist" was not what folk who called themselves Roman Catholics were inclined to use.

Robin said, "I thought you might be, seeing you were squiring that Tex-Mex widow woman and talking to that priest so much."

He said, "Wendy Delgado and I are just friends and Father Paul was throwing the shindig, so who else was I supposed to thank for letting me in and what's *your* excuse, Miss Robin?"

She smiled up sheepishly to confess, "I just like to dance, is all. Wasn't that awful, about that Protestant boy being shot in the back right outside that Papist church whilst the night was still so young?"

He said, "It was. The lady I was escorting allowed it was time to leave before Father Paul called it a night inside. Might the *Sulfur Star* be running the story as a case of religious frenzy?"

She said, "Oh, heavens no! Wilbur interviewed Sheriff Armstrong about the shooting late last night and Sheriff Armstrong said he'd decided Axel Schroder might have been shot in the back by more than one villain he was on nodding terms with. Sheriff Armstrong said he just couldn't see any total strangers or masked riders laying for a man along Main Street with a church dance in progress near the scene of the crime."

Longarm dryly said he was glad to see their local sheriff was a man who paid attention to such small details. When he asked how much he owed her for the advanced want ads, she laughed and suggested he buy a copy of their next edition whether he'd found a horse that suited him or not.

As he was fixing to leave, she wistfully asked if he'd be taking that same Tex-Mex widow woman to the *Tanzsaal* up the street that night.

Longarm truthfully replied, "Not hardly. To begin with, I doubt she'd feel welcome as you or me. After that, like I said, we're no more than friends, and it's tough to keep it at that once you commence to squire the same gal to one dance after the other."

Robin said, "Oh, I got the impression last night, watching the two of you with the other girls, she'd be *more* than a friend of yours for the taking. A woman can tell when another woman has . . . feelings for a man."

Longarm heaved a fake sigh and muttered, "*Now* they tell me! She was pretty, too. But betwixt us gals, Miss Robin, that ship has sailed if there was ever anything more

190

serious than a pleasant evening planned by either of us."

"Then you'll be going to that other dance, tonight alone?" Robin Jones tried.

It didn't work. Longarm shrugged and said, "Ain't sure I'll be there. If I decide to go, and you decide to go, we'll likey run into each other up there, later."

She said, "Later, I'll save one for you 'til I know whether you want to or not."

Longarm left, feeling somewhat torn. For on the one hand, a newspaper gal could be just the one to ask a heap of questions about the recent history of Sulfur Draw. But on the other, as in the case of jacking off in the morning before you knew who you might meet for lunch, showing up at a dance with a mousy little drab on one's arm and one's name all over her dance card sounded like a dumb move for a stranger out to meet as many of the locals as possible, at a High-Dutch dance where the Zimmer twins would hardly be the only blonds on the dance floor!

He was in the market for something bigger and blonder to take his mind off Wendy Delgado's sultry brunette face and tawny tits and ass and, after that, he didn't want to have to worry about *any* other gals before he got the lay of the land and found out whether Herta Zimmer waltzed with those guns on.

Out on the plank walk the sun was higher and hotter in spite of the season. The weather was like that betwixt the Big Muddy and the Continental Divide. Subject to heat waves at Christmas or frost in late summer, with too little or too much rain, depending on which might hurt the most.

As he stuffed the slips in a pocket to read later, Pink Armstrong hailed him from across the way, then crossed to the sunny side to join him, saying, "I've been looking for you, Kruger. You're in deep shit, and I'd as soon you left town before sundown!"

Longarm frowned and asked, "What in thunder have I ever done to you, Sheriff?"

Armstrong said, "Nothing. I like you. You have a head I could use on your shoulders and I'd offer you a job as a senior deputy if that was possible. But it ain't possible. They elected me to serve as a peace officer, not a disturber of the peace, and that's why I want you to get out of Sulfur Draw. They told me you didn't have a mount. I can give you one, free, from our own remuda."

"That's mighty generous," Longarm replied with a thin smile before asking, "You mind telling me what the fuck this is all about?"

The sheriff said, "Junior Brewster's what it's all about. He just blew in after spending some time in the Knox County Jail for gunning three men. Now he says he aims to gun you, on sight, for reasons best known to himself. When I tried to talk reason to him and asked what his beef was, he said you knew and he knew and nobody else had to know. So do *you* know what in thunder might be eating that poor boy?"

Longarm grimaced and said, "If I do, he's right and it's betwixt the two of us. But I thank you for the warning because to tell the truth, I've never laid eyes on Junior Brewster and I could have been in a fix before I knew it. I'll see if I can have somebody point him out at a safe distance. You reckon he'll be at that dance at the big red *Tanzsaal* this evening?"

Sheriff Armstrong snapped, "Of course he will, with a heap of pals to back his play, and that's why you don't want to show your face in the *Tanzsaal* tonight!"

Longarm quietly replied, "Got to. Told a lady I might see her there, and I've always tried to be a man of my word."

Chapter 25

By that evening, Longarm had bought a tolerable chestnut mare with a white blaze off a nester on the edge of town who said he needed money to move on. They told Longarm, as Wolf Kruger, he could stable his pony with spare coaching stock out back and offered him that job as a shotgun messenger again.

He said he'd think about it, but had a dance to go to that evening.

He wasn't feeling as brave and foolish as he knew he sounded. Had he been left to his druthers, he'd have just moved on to let old Junior simmer down as he made up with the Zimmer twins. But he knew Billy Vail expected him to stay put near Sulfur Draw, now that he'd wormed his way in so discreet.

Not wanting his hands full at the dance after sundown, Longarm went to that *cafetín* to line his stomach with plenty of tamales, frijoles and such ahead of time.

The plump Rosalinda waited until they were alone in the back for the moment before she leaned across the counter to confide, "We have to find some place for to hide you, tonight, *Señor Lobo*. Is all over town that an *hombre muy malo* who has already killed three others has said he is going to kill *you*, next!"

Longarm didn't want anyone to know he savvied more Spanish than Dutch, so he made her explain how *lobo* meant "wolf" in Spanish before he allowed he'd like another slice of tuna pie with his last mug of coffee. When a Tex-Mex said *tuna* he or she meant juicy red cactus fruit, not fish.

As she served him, Rosalinda suggested Junior Brewster would most likely get himself fired up at that *baile protestante* they'd soon be having just up the way that night. She intimated all sorts of dreadful affairs emanated from that big red *Tanzsaal*. So, seeing he had time to kill, Longarm told her the tale of the two big gray Gothic piles atop Capitol Hill in Denver.

He'd heard it from an Irish lady who, new to Denver, had asked the way to the big Roman Catholic cathedral she'd been told she'd find near the state house atop Capitol Hill. So some boys pointed it out to her and she went on in, marveling at how grand and Gothic they had it fixed up, that far west of Goth country. She slid in with all the regular-looking folk she found herself amidst, and when the services started, the only thing unusual, to a lady of her faith raised back in Ireland, was the natural-looking priest offering the mass she knew by heart in English instead of Latin.

Rosalinda said Mexican priests said the mass in Latin, even though Spanish was a tad different, and it wasn't always easy to follow the words in Church Latin.

He nodded and said, "This Irish lady knew her services forward and backwards in English, Latin or Gaelic. So she didn't get too confused 'til near the end, when the standing and kneeling and crossings and so on got tough for a stranger in town to follow. So that's when a neighborly lay usher took her aside to discreetly ask her if she was certain she had the right church."

"Didn't she?" gasped Rosalinda.

He smiled and said, "Not hardly. The neighborly usher assured her it happened all the time. She was in the big Anglican Episcopalian pile on the *south* side of the Capitol Grounds instead of the one she'd aimed for to the *north* of the same."

"*Ay, que desconcierto!*" she laughed, "What did *la pobrecita* do when everyone laughed at her?"

Longarm said, "Nobody did. The usher offered to walk her across to the other church, unless she wanted to stay for the end of the services, of course. So she stayed, figuring that since she didn't see all that much difference, she'd spent enough time in church for one Sabbath, and a week later, kneeling in the church across the way with folk of her own faith, she still found herself wondering why folk back where she'd come from held regular riots over such differences as she'd been able to make out."

Washing down his pie, he conceded, "Of course, some extremely holy parishes do seem more excitable. But I doubt I'll see any holy rolling or hear any speaking in tongues at that *Tanzsaal*, tonight."

She warned, "You may not see or hear *anything* if that *hombre muy malo* sees you first, *Señor Lobo!*"

He knew her words made perfect sense.

But he paid up and moved it on out in any case. A man who rode for the law had to set perfect sense to one side, now and again. Hoping you'd see the other son of a bitch first went with the job.

Out on Main Street, the light was getting too tricky to see a thing too clearly as the lowering sun painted everything purple and gold under a cloudless lavender sky. As Longarm stepped into his last stop before that big red *Tanzsaal*, the old gunsmith behind the glass counter said they'd just been fixing to close.

"I know," said Longarm as he peeled off his denim jacket to explain, "I planned this visit with that in mind. I'm in the market for a whore pistol. Double-action Harrington Richardson .32 with a snub barrel ought to do me and I'll need a shoulder holster and a box of .32-20s as well."

The gunsmith smiled thinly and said, "Glad you could make it. For business has been slow this afternoon. I can fix you up as you want for less than one week's wages, Mr. Kruger, but what's wrong with that .44-40 Colt Frontier you seem to be packing already?"

Longarm said, "Since you know who I am, and you sell guns for a living, I'll take that as idle chatter and you don't have to wrap nothing up. I'll put it on and wear it home."

So as he approached that *Tanzsaal* near the end of Main Street in the gathering dusk Longarm was still packing his six-gun openly on his left hip with the snub-nosed .32 riding closer to his heart in its concealed shoulder holster. He'd broken open the paper box of ammunition to distribute the fifty rounds in various pockets, loose.

Longarm was just as glad when he got to the front door of the big red *Tanzsaal*. Wes Wade and a deputy Longarm hadn't met before were in the doorway with a bookish Dutchman in a business suit. As Longarm joined them, Wade said, "Evening, Kruger. We're here to back this old boy who's asking everybody to check his guns at the desk inside. But Pink don't want to let you inside, with or without your side arm."

Longarm asked, "Is Brewster inside, then?"

When Wade said, "Not yet," Longarm beamed, patted the holster of his .44-40 and said, "*Bueno*. I'll just wait out here with you boys and seeing I can't go in, I don't have to check this six-gun, do I."

He'd issued that as statement rather than a question. Wade still said he'd find out and ducked inside as Longarm asked the other two whether they thought it might cloud up by morning.

The other deputy said he surely hoped not. Then Wes came back out to say, "You can go on in, then, but you'll have to hand that .44-40 over to the Dutchman at the desk as you buy your ticket to the dance.

When Longarm asked who'd changed the standing order, Wes Wade said, soft and low, "Don't press your luck, cowboy."

So Longarm went on in and if the upstairs office had reminded him of a New Orleans whorehouse, the cavernous ballroom he was entering now transported him to somewhere in the Black Forest he'd studied on in illustrated travel books at the Denver Public Library.

Longarm idly wondered how many great halls along the River Rhine sported rows of elk antlers on high with impractical long-stemmed pipes nobody had ever smoked, knight's tin helmets and sculptured antique fowling pieces stuck up all over the dark-stained pine paneling. Longarm had heard-tell how Dutch gunsmiths had first come up with the notion of rifle guns and brought their art with 'em to the Pennsylvania Dutch towns.

The band wasn't set up yet. The refreshments were fancier and set up along a regular counter along a back wall. Longarm took off his gun-rig and swapped it along with two bits for a purple stamp mark on the back of his gun hand that would allow him to go in or out if he had to take a shit before his evening was over inside.

Longarm threaded his way through the thin crowd of early arrivals and found a corner where he could cover the doorway with his back protected. Nobody else was smoking, so he held that thought.

He hadn't been standing there long before little Robin Jones of the *Sulfur Star* caught up with him. She looked prettier with her face washed and that shapeless smock exchanged for a party dress of yellow taffeta that set her brown hair off nice. If she'd picked it out her own self, she knew her oats about working with what one had. The well-tailored bodice allowed for a not-to-subtle display of her petite but mighty shapely figure.

Robin said, "There you are! We seem to be early!"

He smiled down at her to say, "There you are, too. Could I get you some punch or soda pop, Miss Robin?"

She wrinkled her pert nose and said, "Not at this hour. I try to hold out as long as I can, lest I wind up having to wee wee just as someone was about to ask me to dance!"

Longarm smiled knowingly but didn't grab the ball and run with it.

Ladies who played by the rules of Queen Victoria never mentioned such matters whilst squatting over the chamber pot unless they were fixing to ask outright or unless they were prick-teasing, and farther along, as the old song suggested, would be time enough to find out.

He said, "If I don't ask you to dance when the music starts, it won't mean I don't like your swell outfit, Miss Robin. I hope it ain't all that obvious but I'm sort of holed up in this corner and I wouldn't care to swing any partner at all betwixt me and any of the three ways in and out I've made out, so far."

She nodded soberly and said, "There's another door behind those curtains along the back of the bandstand. I come here often. We heard that ramrod from the Double H was looking for a showdown with you. Do you think it wise to wait for him in such a public place, with your gun checked at the door?"

Longarm said, "He'll have to check his own side arm if he comes in the front way. I'm hoping we can talk sweet reason if we meet without six-guns clouding out judgment. Who told you he was gunning for me, Miss Robin?"

She said, "One of the sheriff's deputies. Ike Cooper, I think. The sheriff says neither one of you had best have it out where he can hear it, and suggests the winner ride far and fast if he doesn't want to be run in for murder in the first degree. Our Pink Armstrong just doesn't seem to understand the code of the West."

Longarm grimaced and said, "That makes two of us. I've never met many, off the pages of dime novels, that followed it. May I take it you and Mr. Slade of the *Sulfur Star* don't believe there's some natural law against shooting a man in the back or laying for him from ambush with a scoped rifle?"

She sighed wearily and said, "Happens all the time. More so around Sulfur Draw, of late!"

He didn't want her to think he didn't admire the cupcakes she had to offer under that yellow taffeta, so he chose his words with care before he said, "I've been hoping to meet up with someone who had the whole history of this trouble betwixt Dutchmen old and new laid out in their head in chronologic order, Miss Robin. When I ask if you were here when things started I don't mean to imply you look like an old-timer to me, but . . . ."

"I'm a hag of going-on-thirty," she cut in with a laugh, adding, "Of course I was here before those Austrians. Less than three years ago, this was still Comanche country. Wilbur and me hauled his print shop's innards up from San Antone in a Conestoga and moved into one of Klaus Brenner's new buildings before the paint was dry!"

Longarm said, "Heard *Onkel* Klaus went in for such notions. Mebbe you could tell me, then, why they built the stage stop and livery so far from the eastwest wagon trace?"

She said, "That's easy as pie. Both were far closer to the road west when they were first built . . . Land's sakes, where has all the time flown?"

"You mean they've *moved* that eastwest wagon trace along the bottom of the draw, Miss Robin?" he cut in.

She said, "Of course. It ran drier and more sensibly on higher ground before higher ground got so valuable as this town mushroomed. The new road flooded this spring. It'll probably flood every spring. But there you have it, and wagons have to roll through *some* way, see?"

He said he was commencing to. He felt no call to lecture *her* on how *sudden* things kept happening out this way since he'd first come out from West-by-God Virginia after the war with the same restless nature driving most everyone else, it seemed. In his six or eight years with the Justice Department, he'd seen towns sprout, wither and die within the lifespan of your average chicken.

As if she'd read his mind, Robin volunteered, "Wilbur says all this nonsense between the *Onkel* Klaus and *Vater* Paul factions remind him of that short and snappy Lincoln County War that Governor Wallace just tidied up in the New Mexico Territory."

Longarm said, "I thought the same thing, at first. I wasn't there, but from what I heard there's some differences and . . . I dunno, I get the feeling there's a real *important* difference that might *mean* something if only I could put my finger on it!"

199

She suggested, "Well, there's that sinister Twisted Sister, said to night ride against both sides . . ."

He made a wry face and said, "That ain't it. Billy the Kid and Jim Dolan were both said to ride for and agin' both sides and, after that the so-called Twisted Sister may be no more than a ghost story made up by . . . I wonder who?"

A mousy little gal in a party dress she'd borrowed from somebody way bigger timidly approached them to stammer, "Are you Wolf Kruger, sir?"

Robin Jones only sounded half-mocking as she replied, "He is and I saw him first, Iris Jane!"

Iris Jane said, "Pooh, I'm here with my own swain. I only have a message for him, is all."

Then she turned to Longarm to add, "There's someone outside in the street who wants to talk to you, Mr. Kruger. He asked me if I'd come in and ask if you'd come out."

"Don't go, Wolf!" Robin gasped as she saw Longarm move away from the pine paneling at his back.

He said, "Stay here. Keep Iris Jane with you. I don't want to go but I got to go. Didn't you just hear her say he'd called me out?"

Chapter 26

Longarm had figured his new two-dollar pissoliver a match for anything Junior Brewster might smuggle in under his own duds. But seeing he'd been invited outside, Longarm stopped at the desk to redeem and strap on his more serious .44-40. Then he took a deep breath and stepped out and to one side as he called out, "What's your pleasure, you son of a bitch!"

But it was the sheriff and two of his deputies standing there in the lamplight from above the entrance. Pink Armstrong said, "Hold your fire. He ain't here. We were just wondering what *you* might have to say about that, Kruger."

Longarm let go that breath with a bang and wheezed, "Jesus H. Christ, don't ever do that again, Pink! Last time a pretty little thing was sent in to call me out from a dance was in El Paso, all involved but me were Border Mex and my ears were ringing half the night by the time it was over!"

The sheriff said, "I don't want no more gunplay here in Sulfur Draw and I'll not *have* no more gunplay here in Sulfur Draw! I told my fucking deputies neither one of you would 'tend the dance inside this evening but good help's getting hard to find!"

Wes Wade protested, "Hell, Pink, Uncle Klaus said to let this one in without his gun."

Armstong snapped, "That fucking Dutchman ain't the law here in Sulfur Draw! *I* am the law here in Sulfur Draw. But what's done is done, and the question before the house is where in the fuck is old Junior Brewster right now?"

Longarm said, "Don't look at me. I was talking to a pretty lady when you sent another in to scare the shit out of me!"

Ike Cooper said, "I told you he was over by *Der Rinderhirt* around sundown, making war talk and not too sober, Pink. I told him that even if he could *take* a man with this one's rep, you'd bust his ass for premeditation. That's what the charge is when you tell everybody you mean to clean a man's plow before you do so, right?"

Armstrong said, "Damned A. A formal invite to a duel is bad enough. All too many gunslicks pining for a reputation tell everyone but the intended victim they're at feud, and then shoot him when he's least expecting it."

He turned to Longarm to demand, "Has Elroy Brewster Junior ever issued you an engraved invite to an affair of honor, Wolf?"

Longarm replied, "Not hardly. As a matter of fact I've never laid eyes on the gent. What does he look like?"

Others had drifted out from the dance by now as Armstrong declared, "Something like you, Wolf. Tall, lean and poker-faced when he's on the prod. You may have a few inches on him and his mustache ain't as heroic. But let me and my boys worry about what he looks like because I don't want you throwing down on him, and that's an order!"

It wouldn't have been diplomatic to point out he didn't work for the local sheriff, so Longarm soberly replied, "I never throw down on nobody unless I have to, Pink. I want it distinctly understood by one and all here assembled that I've declared no feud against any man I don't even know. And be it further resolved I've never once slighted him or knowingly done shit to offend him. So should any of you see him before I do, tell him for me I

202

ain't after any job or other privileges he may feel he's fighting for!"

Then he turned to Ike Cooper to ask, "You say he was getting his fool self likkered up in *Der Rinderhirt* saloon, Ike?"

The deputy said, "He ain't there now. I just looked. I don't know where he might be at this hour. Let's hope he's gone on home to the Double H for now."

"Or left town with his tail between his legs," suggested a voice from the doorway.

It was *Onkel* Klaus, the burly Dutchman who added, "I've been listening. You boys are making a mountain out of a molehill. I've known Junior Brewster since he first signed on with the Zimmer twins last summer. I told them then he talked too tough for any man who'd ever seen the elephant. We all know, off-the-record, he didn't have the hair on his chest to fight those bullies in Truscott he's taken credit for. So try her my way. Say he just rode in to hear how Wolf, here, had, ah, taken his place with the Zimmer twins. Then say he danced his war dance before he'd fully considered who he was trying to run out of town."

Another townsman in the growing crowd laughed and said, "I follow your drift, *Onkel* Klaus! Once it's been announced that somebody is fixing to die unless someone leaves town, someone dies, or someone leaves town!"

Wes Wade asked Pink Armstrong if he wanted them to see if they could cut fresh sign along that wagon trace.

The sheriff growled, "Don't *you* talk like an asshole, too! Even if you could cut sign in the dark on a well-traveled road, we have nothing to charge nobody with. There's no law against running yourself out of town, Wes!"

Everyone but Longarm laughed. He couldn't help feeling a tad sorry for Brewster whether that was the answer or not and, after that, he could still be in trouble if that wasn't the answer.

He asked, "Can I go back inside, now? Like I said, I

was talking to a pretty lady when you called me out here like a border *buscadero.*"

Pink Armstrong smiled indulgently and said, "Go ahead. I'll still have my boys keep an eye on this doorway, just in case."

So Longarm went back inside, brushing past the desk with his gun hand out to expose the stamped pass and made it into the swirl before anyone could demand his .44-40.

As he found Robin Jones, easy, in that yellow dress, she glanced down to remark, "I see you're armed and dangerous again. You won, of course. So how come we heard no shots?"

He confided, "Wasn't him. You heard no shots because he's left town ahead of me, I hope, or he's laying for me somewhere in the dark, I hope not."

She gasped, "How awful! What are we to do, Wolf?"

He smiled thinly and replied, "*We* don't have to do toad squat, Miss Robin. I asked you to stay out of it, and where did Iris Jane go?"

Robin said, "She's dancing out on the floor with a rider off the Lazy Diamond. This is a *dance*, you see. But I'm with you, now, and I know how to get out of here and over to my place without anyone else having to know!"

He started to say he had his own hired room at the coaching inn. He saw how easy it would be for Junior Brewster to find that out from Herta Zimmer. He couldn't help asking Robin if she was in the habit of sneaking dance partners out of the *Tanzsaal* on the Q.T.

She said, "Don't be snide. I'm trying to make nice-nice. Do you want my help or not?"

He warned, "It ain't your fight," then added, "I sure could use a safer place to hole up than a hired room everyone knows about."

She said, "Let's wait until the band takes its next rest break. I told you about that door behind the curtains, and who looks hard at a deserted bandstand when they're sizing one another up for later?"

So that was how they busted out the back way into an

a dark alley running in line with Main Street north and south. They didn't speak and tried to walk soft along the dry cinder paving until they were well clear of the bright lights and festivities at the north end of town. Then Robin opened a back gate to lead him around a shit house and through a weedy back garth, murmuring, "Here we are. I have my key out. My quarters are at the top of these stairs."

He followed her up the outside backstairs to the second-story level. As she led him into a small but tastefully furnished flat, she suggested he make himself to home whilst she rustled up some refreshments. So Longarm took off his hat, hesitated about his .44-40 and decided the shoulder-holstered .32 would save him from Robin Jones if she attacked him from her kitchen.

Hanging his hat on the same coat rack with his six-gun, Longarm drifted over to the lace-curtained window of the unlit parlor to gaze out and down at Main Street, more brightly lit down yonder than up there by coal-oil street lamps. Trying to place where he was with the help of shop signs across the way, he saw they were close to the street-level layout of the *Sulfur Star*. It figured a newspaper gal who worked there would live somewheres close. She said she'd been in town from the beginning.

She came out to join him in another denim smock, bearing a tray as she asked what he was doing on his fool feet after she'd told him to make his fool self at home.

They sat down together on her horsehair sofa. She spread what she'd brought across the rosewood coffee table before them. He'd been braced for the usual coffee and cake. Robin had rustled up two kinds of cheese, mild and sharp, with some sardines on soda crackers and a bottle of red wine she said came all the way from California.

She asked him to open it for them, and when he did, it was a dry dago red that went swell with cheese and even the fish, if it *was* a red wine. Had it not, he'd have still felt no call to brag about that society gal who'd lectured him on which breed of wine went with what. The same society gal had insisted dog-style was right vulgar.

As they nibbled and talked, the newspaper gal who'd stuck the type for many an incident of the smouldering feud bewixt opposing High-Dutch-speaking factions drew a clearer picture than anyone had been about to offer him before.

It seemed that, as in the case of that other nasty flare-up over to the New Mexico Territory, whatever was going on had only been going on a few months. Robin told him Klaus Brenner and a handful of his own kind had been there from the beginning, along with regular Anglo and Tex-Mex pioneers staking claims in old Comanche hunting grounds. She said other Dutchmen had followed in greater numbers, attracted by Brenner's mushroom market town, a high water table and the good grass all around. She said everyone had seemed to feel the-more-the-merrier at first. There hadn't been any trouble when Father Paul's congregation had moved in the summer before and some earlier Mex and Irish nesters had seemed pleased as punch, in fact.

Pressing more wine on him, Robin continued, "Late last fall, not quite a full year ago, somebody cut a fence and stampeded range cows across forty acres of winter wheat. You plant winter wheat in the fall as crazy as that sounds, you see."

Longarm said, "I know them Rooshin immigrants taught our own kind how you manage to raise wheat out this way. So somebody drove a stampede across a crop drilled in to get an early start under the ground and shoot up green and sassy with the spring rains when the soil's too muddy to plow. What I'd like to know was which side was that first victim on?"

Robin thought and said, "Neither. The homesteaders who lost their first crop to mean mischief were Swedes. The range stock belonged to the Irish Clover Bar and the stampede cost *them* money, too."

He studied on that, sipping dago red, and then Robin told him the next victim had been an Austrian Papist, shot off his pony by a dry-gulcher, with a Lutheran stable and all the ponies in it going up in flames a few midnights later. She said it had been back and forth ever since, with more mischief and near misses than killings, albeit the eight or nine killings, so far, hardly qualified as kid stuff.

He asked how that stuff about a mysterious Twisted Sister had been started. She said, "Until that poor breed sheepherder wrote the name in Dutch as he lay dying, Wilbur and me thought the rumors had been based on a poor wayfaring stranger of an effeminate nature and a fast draw."

Longarm said, "Hold on. You're getting ahead of me. I was told a *Dutch* sheepherder wrote down 'Twisted Sister' in High Dutch as he lay dying!"

She poured more wine in both their glasses as she shook her head to reply, "His name was Pedro Navajo. He liked to be called Pete and he did belong to that Conferternity Society started by Father Paul. So he must have heard what his Dutch pals called that sinister sissy and when they met up out on the range . . ."

Longarm warned, "You're getting ahead of me some more. Leaving aside how likely it would be for a dying breed sheepherder to be fluent in High Dutch, you haven't explained who he might have had in mind, yet!"

She said, "The Twisted Sister, or so they called him, came through last winter by coach, bound for that new silver strike called Tombstone and working his way west with a deck of cards, he said. Have some more wine."

"Tell me a story." Longarm insisted.

She said, "We ran it in the *Sulfur Star* as a humorous item. I never saw the poor thing, myself, but it seems he walked mincy, had long blond curls and made up his face like a scarlet woman. So naturally the boys who will be boys tried to rawhide him when he offered to deal nickel-ante blackjack."

Longarm grimaced and said, "I get the picture. They called him a *Zerziehenschwester* and worse. Then they tried to make him dance for them, right?"

She shrugged and said, "Someone did sugest it. Then he found himself staring down the awesome muzzle of a

Le Mat revolver the sissy boy had materialized from thin air. So they decided to leave him be, and he left on the next coach, or some said he had. Others were as certain he was lurking about Sulfur Draw with hard feelings for the entire population. Somebody who reminded Pedro Navajo of that sort of rider must have inspired the dying breed to leave that message, right?"

Longarm said, "Unless some killer who could spell such a bodacious name in High Dutch meant to drag a red herring across his own trail and, no thanks, Miss Robin. I've had enough wine for now, unless you want to see me drunk."

She purred, "I've been trying to get us *both* drunk, Wolf. What sort of a girl would bed a man on his first visit to her quarters if they weren't both a teeny-weeny bit tipsy?"

He took the bottle from her, set it aside, and reeled her in for a howdy kiss as he answered, "Trust me on this. I know from experience. It's way more fun to go to bed, any fool time, with everybody sober enough to know just what they're doing!"

Chapter 27

Longarm was not surprised to discover Robin had nothing on under that loose artist's smock she'd changed into. He idly wondered if she stuck type at the nearby *Sulfur Star* with nothing on under her work duds. That wouldn't have surprised him, either, now that he was getting to know her better.

Since she'd been feeling him up at the same time, she took her tongue out of his mouth to sweetly ask, "Wolf, dear, did you know you carry a concealed weapon?"

He said, "Life is full of little surprises, and I'd like to keep that ace in the hole a secret, Miss Robin."

She kissed him some more, swore they'd never hear it from her and asked her to call her something less formal and for heaven's sake take her into her bedroom.

So he called her kitten and swept her up in his arms to carry her, laughing all the way, to an even bigger four poster than the one the way different Wendy Delgado had fucked him in, in other ways entire.

After that, Robin Jones made up for her somewhat plainer face and chunkier build by using nigh every square foot of that big and firm mattress bucking under him like an inverted bronco as she moaned and groaned he was hurting her so good with the biggest old thing she had ever dreamed of. It seemed neither the time nor place to tell her she was full of shit because Longarm had gone skinny-dipping with other boys in his time and *she'd* been the one who'd known how to sneak a man out of that ballroom and up her backstairs.

They both came fast, more than once, as most like-minded and halfway sober consenting adults might have. As she teased his bare butt with her nails, Robin purred, "That was lovely. Can we do it again?"

He kissed her, sincerely, and told her, "You can bet the farm on it, as soon as I get my second wind. But what say we share a smoke and simmer back down from the stars, first? I'm sure I had a shirt with a pocket full of cheroots on when we first came in here."

She didn't argue as he sat up to bend over and rummage through the duds on the floor for the smokes and some waterproof Mex matches. But she was enough of a newspaper woman to dryly note he'd remained calm enough to hang that shoulder holster on a drawer knob of her bed lamp table.

As he rolled back in bed with her, Longarm confessed, "Had to. No way to hang a gun on a bedpost holding a canopy so close to your ceiling."

As he lay back beside her to light up, she asked if he was expecting somebody he might have to shoot.

To which he could only reply, "I hope not. It's none of my beeswax how many others in town saw me talking earlier with such a friendly gal."

Her voice chilled ten degrees or more as she quietly asked if by any chance he had her down as the local punching board.

Taking a drag and passing the cheroot to her, he soothed, "If you are, I'm no better than you, sweet lips. By now you know me well enough, in the biblical sense, to be privy to my own horny nature. Ain't we awful?"

She coughed on the cheroot, passed it back and said, "You *smoke* like a he-man, too. I know some say it's wrong for a girl to have such a . . . warm nature. I was brought up by hard-shell Baptist parents who tried to raise me right, and I never lost my cherry before my wedding night."

210

"When might that have been?" Longarm cut in.

She patted his limp member reassuringly and said, "Ages ago, and I still curse my loving parents when I consider how many boys I said no to before I married an older man with a future and found out what I'd been saving up for, all that while, between these thighs!"

He knew what was coming next. But he listened patiently as she sighed and said, "It was just my luck my man with a future was so much closer to the future than I was when I married him. For it seemed I'd no sooner learned how grand it felt to fuck and fuck some more when I found myself married to a nice old man who apologized for his lack of self-control when we went at it twice in the same week!"

Longarm had heard the same sad story from many a gay divorcée. You met more of those out west, where folk were allowed to start fresh with a new deck and few considering it polite to ask about the past.

Blowing a smoke ring, Longarm mused aloud, "That effeminate but well-armed gambling man likely went on out to Tombstone to explain he was the illegitimate son of Oberon, the king of the fairies, and so all that gossip about twisted sisters can be pared away from the core with Ockham's razor. A murderous night rider would hardly sign his own name at the scene of his crime, either."

Robin marveled, "My God, you want to talk about that range war at a time like *this*?"

He snuggled her closer with his free arm to soothe, "Got to talk about something unless we aim to fuck some more or go to sleep, and I just now figured out the vital difference betwixt these troubles along Sulfur Draw and that more famous fight just across the Pecos."

She sighed, "I was just about to suggest we fuck some more, but get it off your chest, dear. What's so different about this feud and that Lincoln County War?"

He said, "The balance of power. In Lincoln County, the same as here, you had the established Big Store faction resenting newcomers horning in on already marginal range and limited business opportunity. After that, from

211

the beginning, the balance of power was with the older Murphy-Dolan faction. Most everyone else in the county but the hard core of the Tunstall-McSween faction were neutral or with the county, territorial and federal officials backing Major Murphy and Jim Dolan!"

"Was that fair?" she asked, interested despite what she was doing to his old organ grinder with her skilled little hand.

Longarm said, "Fair or not, Lawyer McSween should have thrown in the towel the day after lawfully deputized county riders murdered his partner, Tunstall, in cold blood. Anybody with a lick of sense could see they meant it sincere, and when McSween, being a lawyer, tried to have the killers arrested, the judges appointed by the Santa Fe Ring just laughed at him. He deputized some of Tunstall's riders to track down and pay back members of the posse-cum-lynch mob riding for the Murphy-Dolan faction. They killed some fair, and they killed some dirty, and, in the end, the U.S. Army eating Murphy-Dolan beef sided with yet more pet lawmen serving McSween with legal briefs and bullets. So that was that, and then was then. But here along Sulfur Draw, such government and law as there seems to be seems to be *neutral*, allowing the two sides to slug it out with both sides claiming to be on the defensive! So tell me about your county machinery, honey."

She shrugged a smooth bare shoulder against his rib cage to tell him, "There isn't any. Most of us just got here, and the incorporation papers are still being processed in Austin, if they haven't been lost. We've elected a nominal county supervisor and his board, who haven't taken their seats yet because they've nothing to legislate until we have an incorporated county out this way. The circuit judge who rides over from Sulfur *Springs* now and again is an ad hoc courtesy from a neighboring governing body in being. Wilbur says that anyone who really wanted to appeal an arrest up this way would have good grounds if he had a good lawyer."

Longarm nodded, took another drag, and said, "You

don't need to be an educated newspaper editor to see that. What does your boss say about your so-called Sheriff Armstrong, then?"

She said, "Oh, he seems to be what Wilbur calls de facto lawful as long as no other jurisdiction claims seniority. We did hold an informal but fair election as legal as a union election, and Pink, having held a cavalry commission in Hood's Texas Brigade one time and being neither breed of Dutchman, won. So why do you ask so many nitty picky details, Wolfie? One would think you were a newspaper reporter or a lawman, for heaven's sake!"

He said, "Just like to cover all bets after someone says he's out to shoot me on sight. I heard-tell *real* newspaper men and undercover lawmen have met up with hard times in thse parts, too?"

She shrugged again and said, "Rumors, like all that guff about a night-riding sissy gunning for both sides. I hadn't heard any newspaper men had met foul play. More than one has naturally dropped by the office, downstairs, asking about a range war they've heard so much about. We've told them the little we know. Some left acting as if we held something back on them. As to undercover lawmen, we've heard of rangers with *badges* asking about missing pals in these parts. We'd have run the stories in the *Star* if anyone around here had actually reported a dead ranger or anyone more important than a saddle bum."

Longarm started to ask another question, saw she hadn't answered one about the *Sulfur Star* all the way, and quietly asked if he was correct in assuming she'd just said they were in bed upstairs in the same building.

She answered innocently, "Of course? Didn't you know that, lover boy? We naturally moved in over the store, dosen't everyone?"

A big gray cat got up and turned around in Longarm's gut before it sat back down, kneading its claws on his stomach lining, as he hopefully asked, "*We*? You mean

213

you and Wilbur Slade both have flats up here above your newpaper layout?"

She laughed lightly and said, "Silly, this is a two-story building. Wilbur and me are married up. Have been for years. Everyone in town knows that and . . . where are you going, dear?"

Longarm said, "Somewhere safer for a child my age. I'm allowed to shoot an assassin in my own room at the coaching inn. But they'll bust my ass for surving a gun-fight with any married man under his own roof who just caught me in bed with his own wife!"

She purred, "Silly, Wilbur's in La Mesa on business and I don't expect him back for days!"

As she saw he was still hauling on his socks she insisted, "Even if he did come home tonight, you've nothing to worry about. Wilbur understands my needs, now. After I left him, years ago, for failing to give me all the loving I needed, he begged and pleaded for me to come back and so, one night after I'd taken pity on him and gave him some for old time's sake, I agreed to come back to him if he'd let me have my own fun on the side."

Longarm muttered, "I've heard-tell of such deals. Must surely beat working in a laundry, or a parlor house, for that matter!"

"Don't be snide. I'll have you know I'm a respectable married woman with an . . . understanding husband. I'd never cheat on Wilbur behind his back. I've always been honest with him. I told him from the first that I was fond of him, but needed more from a bigger cock. And he said he was sorry and pleaded with me to forgive him. So I did, and we have quite a good marriage, however odd some may find our understanding. I'm happy, since I get more affection than one man seems able to manage, and Wilbur gets all the affection he can *take*. So come back to bed and give me more affection, you big silly! You have nothing to worry about, and we haven't begun to get really down and dirty yet!"

Longarm buttoned his shirt and strapped on his shoulder holster as he murmured, "Yes, we have," without go-

214

ing in to how dirty she'd just made him feel. For slap-and-tickle betwixt free agents was one thing; poaching in a married man's bed was another. The poor suckers already had a hard enough row to hoe!

So though she joshed and cajoled and explained she hadn't meant to trick him when she'd given her maiden name downstairs, Longarm left as somewhere in the night a clock was striking eleven, and he figured what the hell. If Junior Brewster had been serious he'd have been by the coaching inn before eleven.

Longarm still moved down the back steps and along the alley sneaky, never knowing when or if he might have been spotted with a cheating wife by a knowing gossip.

So whoever was coming down the alley the other way never noticed Longarm as he crawfished betwixt a carriage house and an arched back gate. The cuss was afoot, dressed townsman, packing a big bunch of what smelled like roses, jet-black in the moonlight.

After it was safe for Longarm to move on, he heard another back gate open and shut, farther down. As he forged on, Longarm wondered, then shook his head and decided, "Not hardly. The timing would be too neat for Ned Buntline to use in one of his tall tales."

Then he added with a chuckle, "But, by jimmies, if that *was* old Wilbur getting home sooner than expected, he sure owes me for the warmed up welcome he's fixing to get for them roses!"

Chapter 28

As he indulged his used and abused body in a hot tub soak at the carriage house, after midnight, he wryly informed the head of his old organ grinder, peeking up at him from the soapy water, "You ought to be ashamed of yourself, pard. Thanks to you I can't go back to that newspaper office, the Double H or Wendy Delgado's and I still have questions for all concerned!"

Then he remembered he'd left out the Ramos spread and sighed, "Oh, well, might be just as well to fish fresh waters. For had anyone we talked to earlier had anything else they wanted us to know, they'd have doubtless told you. Billy Vail told us before we left Denver it would be a bodacious clockwork puzzle with the wheels within the bigger wheels running contrary. So that's how come nothing down this way fits any other pattern or makes any sort of sense. We're missing the key that winds all this contrary clockwork!"

His old organ grinder offered no answer. It had had a rough night.

As he got out and dried it off, Longarm muttered, "A lot of help *you* are! We've been weeks in the field and had lots of fun, but we ain't found out a thing Billy Vail didn't know when he sent us out in the field to begin with!"

By the time he'd bolted his bedroom door and turned

with a six-gun hanging on both sides of the headboard he'd realized that strictly speaking that hadn't been true. Thanks to Billy Vail's process of eliminating and Ockham's razor, he now knew some possible mysteries might not be so mysterious.

Next morning, as Rosalinda was serving him *huevos rancheros* at the *cafetín*, Pink Armstrong joined him at the counter to announce, "Junior Brewster's cut and run. I just spoke with Herta Zimmer, and she says he never came home from town last night."

As Rosalinda poured for both of them, the sheriff added, "He's nowheres to be found *in* town. So you called his bluff, and you won, you ornery cuss."

He told Rosalinda he didn't need any grub before he turned back to Longarm and said, "That offer I made you was meant serious. Good help is getting harder to find by the minute, and one of my kid deputies just quit on me!"

"Anyone I know?" asked Longarm as the plump waitress slid his hot sauce for his Mex-style eggs across the counter to him.

Pink Armstrong shook his head and said, "Ain't been on duty since you've been in town, Kruger. He was with Ike and Wes when they found that dead sheepherder up on the higher range, and it must have unsettled the boy. He took to drinking, shortly after, and this morning we got his letter of resignation, posted from Sulfur Springs to the south. Said I wasn't paying enough for such a spooky job."

Longarm poured hot sauce over his *huevos rancheros* to where dumpy Rosalinda murmured, "*Ay, que heroico!*" before he asked the sheriff the name of the missing deputy.

Armstrong said they'd called him Lefty Boyle because he was a southpaw who's folk had escaped to Texas from the Irish potato famine.

Longarm asked how deputies named Boyle, Cooper or Wade had been able to read *Zerziehenschwester* written in dust by a dying hand.

217

Pink Armstrong snorted, "They couldn't, of course. None of them were dying Dutchmen!"

Longarm washed down a forkful of sassy eggs and quietly objected, "Neither was that sheepherder, unless somebody has the story all messed up. Way I hear-tell, he was a breed called Pedro or Pete Navajo. Likely left over from that civilizing effort over on the Pecos a few years back. Cross betwixt a hungry Navajo gal and one of our own, Anglo or Mex, would likely grow up speaking Nadéné and English or Spanish, not High Dutch, if you see what I mean."

Armstrong said, "I see what you mean. Wes, or maybe Ike or maybe Lefty copied down what the dying man had scribbled in the sand. We asked a Dutchman to translate, and when he said the victim had tried to write 'Twisted Sister' and almost made it, we put that down in our officious report."

Longarm chewed thoughtfully and decided, "I can't come up with a thing in English or Spanish that would look like *Zerziehenschwester* to the excited or uneducated eye. Some Nadéné or Navajo words have heaps of Zs and run on mighty long. Take a literate Navajo to say for sure. I don't suppose you have many of them along Sulfur Draw?"

The sheriff laughed incredulously and said, "You're loco but I do admire your imagination, and I'm in the market for a deputy who tends to back his gun hand with a brain, and Lord knows you know how to use a gun."

He sipped some coffee, chuckled and added, "Like I just now told Herta Zimmer, that big-talking ramrod of theirs is likely riding his pony at a full gallop this very minute!"

Longarm shrugged modestly and said, "I'd as soon not mean-mouth a man I never met. But I'm glad he chose the better part of valor once he'd left us both no better choice."

Armstrong observed, "I dunno, *you* could have run as easy, with less reason to stay. Junior left behind a good job and the respect of a heap of folk in these parts. What

218

would it have cost a stranger like you, had you been the one who backed down?"

"My respect for myself," Longarm answered easily, as the famous gunfighting Wolf Kruger. He wasn't ready to admit he'd *had* no choice Who in the matter. Others along Sulfur Draw who might have or might not have known Junior Brewster had known he'd never really shot Duffy, Ryan or that breed, whilst the man he was trying to bluff had certainly dropped all three of the Catlin Gang with no help from a contrary cowgirl.

Armstrong repeated his job offer. Longarm as Wolf Kruger allowed he'd as soon herd cows and meant to ride out across the range to see if any cattle outfits were hiring.

Armstrong said the Double H seemed to be missing a foreman.

Longarm smiled thinly to reply, "Rode in here with that outfit. Got laid off by that outfit. Met a man who'd returned to a nagging wife one time. He told me to never go back once you've gotten away clear."

Armstrong chuckled and said, "Heard Miss Hilda has bossy ways about her. If you want a job with either Dutch faction, you'd best clear it with Uncle Klaus or Father Paul and just go where they send you. If you don't want to ride for either side, or me, you might want to try the Clover Bar, which is owned by Irish who don't 'tend mass at Saint Josef's down the street, or ask at the Lazy Seven, owned by Creole French of the same persuasion, albeit, like them Black Irish on the Clover Bar, at odds with that Cat Licking Dutch priest for reasons I just can't say."

Longarm thanked him for the suggestions and after Armstrong had left, he thanked Rosalinda and asked what he owed her.

She said two bits would do her and added, "I know for why those *rancheros católico* do not attend *La Iglesia San Jose* anymore. Is *porqué* they do not wish for to be shot in the back by the other side. Is a saying in Old *Méjico* that when the bulls fight the grasshoppers get out of the way if they wish for to live. They will not hire you or any other *desconocido*, I mean stranger, they cannot be sure of with both those *facciónes alemanes* sending away for more *buscaderos* for to trample grasshoppers, *comprende*?"

Like most lawmen, Longarm knew how folk who hadn't had Englsh as their first lingo tended to talk more confusing as they got exited. He considered questioning her in Spanish. But she wasn't supposed to knew he wasn't a Dutch-American cowboy, and he doubted she knew who was behind any killings to begin with. So he left with a smile, saying he meant to give the Clover Bar a try.

"Soñar no cuesta nada," she wisfully sighed after him, which was Border Mex for dreams cost nothing. He wasn't certain who's dream the fat gal had been talking about. Robin had allowed it was kind to screw charity cases. He'd done so himself, now and again. But he wasn't sure whether throwing a quick one into old Rosalinda would be charity or cruelty in the end. Growing up so fat with a name that meant "pretty as a rose" could likely leave a poor bucket of lard confused.

He mounted his new chestnut mare out back of the stage stop and made for that Clover Bar, down the draw to the east. He passed both the Ramos place and looked for signs of life on Wendy's side of the tanglewood as he rode by, hoping she was at work and not peering weepy-eyed through the fluttering autumn leaves at him.

As he'd noticed before, spreads with the wagon trace betwixt them and the watercourse resorted to cleaner and steadier windmill water, since the water table lay high along the bottomlands. Outfits on the far side of the some-times stream pumped windmill water for human consumption but had more direct access to the braided stream through the tanglewood for their grazing stock, who'd have no call to cross the draw nor be tempted to stray out of reach of water across the higher range outside the draw. To the south, in this case. He'd already noticed the Double H lay north of the wagon trace and pumped long watering troughs in back of the home spread, on higher ground, for their stock grazing out that way. He rode the better part of an hour or more than three miles past the Ramos farm before he saw a crossing with the brand of the Clover Bar burnt into a dead cottonwood to the side of the trace.

He rode across the shallow fetlock-deep ford to follow wagon ruts through close-cropped grass to a sprawl of whitewashed frame buildings with corrugated iron roofing, the galvinized gray not showing much rust yet.

As he rode into their dooryard, a stocky older gent with a clay pipe in his mouth came out on the veranda to declare, "It's just in time for some tea you are, if you mean to pass by and all. But we're not buying and we're not hiring, to save you the trouble of asking."

Longarm allowed that in that case he wouldn't ask. The brogue who confessed to being the Gentle Geraldine himself insisted he get down, come in and have some damned tea and all and all.

Longarm did so and as he sipped mighty fine tea with butter and jam on his soda bread with the stockman and his vapidly pretty and much younger wife, he learned in passing he hadn't completely wasted his time. For it developed the man who described himself as Gentle Geraldine was a younger son of an Irish country squire named Fitzgerald who'd been paid off with a ticket to Texas and the grubstake for land of his own. Longarm had already read how the landed gents of Britain left all their land to the eldest heir. It sounded mean and it likely was, on everybody. For it forced all the great families under Queen Victoria to keep buying or grabbing more land with each and every generation.

Conan Fitzgerald of the Clover Bar was Irish enough to perform jigs on the vaudeville stage. But after that he wasn't Black, or Roman Catholic Irish. He was Orange, or Protestant Irish and *that* was why he seldom felt any call to 'tend mass at Father Paul's church in town. When asked, he explained they had no use for Dutch Lutheran services, either. So Longarm thanked them for their friendly welcome without mentioning Ockham's razor and headed back to town aboard his well-watered and rested pony, considering how in thunder he was to wire a progress report to Billy Vail and the outside world without tipping his mitt. He knew it was time to bring other lawmen up to date on the confusion he'd eliminated, some. For if someone made him vanish like those earlier undercover lawmen, someone else would have to start all over from scratch!

But of course, he assured his pony as he headed her for the ford through the tanglewood their side of the wagon trace back to town, he had no call to suspect anyone was gunning for him, now that Junior had crawfished off and away.

Longarm had chosen the somewhat long-in-the-tooth chestnut with her experience in sunshine or shadow in mind and, up to then, she'd proven a sure and steady old mare. But for reasons best known to her own kind, as they were crossing back over the sluggish water, she spooked at something in the shallows and saved his life.

For just as her unexpected balk threw Longrm forward against his saddle swells, a shot rang out to his left and the slug buzzed like a bumble bee past the nape of his neck to go on tic-tic-tic-tic through the leaves of the tanglewood!

As a result, his hat went one way, his pony went another way, and Longarm wound up flat on his ass with a mighty splash in tea-brown water!

He'd drawn on the way down, of course, and rolled over to dive behind a clump of cattails with his eyes and gun muzzle peering up the draw toward the echos of that rifle report. He knew the dry-gulcher, or in this case the wet woodser, had been laying for him upstream amid the trees and reeds. So he yelled, "I see you, you son of a bitch!"

When that didn't work he summoned all the scorn he could muster up to loudly sneer, *"Du!"* and that seemed to work better.

Longarm fired back, blind, at the sound of the gunshots that he'd inspired and rolled to another position as rifle rounds parted the juicy green reeds he'd been sprawling behind. So he was wet front and back as he returned the rifle fire with his pistol and heard someone yip like a kicked dog before the dulcet tones of crashing branches hinted at somebody running like hell up the draw through the tanglewood. So Longarm got to his feet to reload and look for that thoroughly spooked chestnut.

He called her some awful names as he floundered on over to the wagon trace to find it deserted in both directions. He was afraid she'd run all the way home, meaning the spread he'd bought her from. Spooked horses were like that when they found themselves bewildered under an empty saddle.

He heard thrashing and crashing behind him. He turned, gun in hand, to see the Gentle Geraldine and two Mex hands had mounted up to ride on the sound of those gunshots with their own saddle guns out and ready for anything.

As they reined in at easy shouting range, Longarm called, "Howdy. That was me and some person or persons unknown. Pegged a shot at me as I was fording, and, as you see, missed me. Now I sure could use the loan of a mount to get me back to town, Mr. Fitzgerald."

The Gentle Gerladine snapped, "And would you, now? Sure you'll not get one from us! Be off with yez all and take your Dutch feud with you! For it's enough of this *cuspair go tinn* I've put up with and, faith, I've a good mind to pack me bags, round up me cows and dwell somewhere they don't grow mad Dutchmen!"

Chapter 29

It was a hell of a way to walk, but Longarm had walked farther in his time, and it hadn't killed him. So he trudged on up the wagon trace with his reloaded .44-40 in hand but held polite, hoping to find a more friendly spread before that son of a bitch he hoped he'd winged doubled back for another try at a slower moving target.

But as he'd known all along, the cattle spreads this far out from town grew farther apart, and his duds had gone from soggy to damp by the time he heard rumbles and jingles from the east and turned to see the afternoon coach from La Mesa headed his way, Lord love it!

He stopped to see if he could flag it down. Before it reached him he had a better notion. For a familiar figure was coming his way from the west, leading that chestnut mare.

It was Armstrong's senior deputy, Ike Cooper, mounted on a buckskin as he led Longarm's missing mount. When he spotted Longarm, he called out, "Lose something, Kruger? I thought this looked like the pony I saw you ride down Main Street, earlier."

Since the two of them and both ponies met in the middle of the trace and since coach crews were as curious as other folk, the coach slowed down and the jehu reined in as his shotgun messenger called down to the deputy, "Evening, Ike. What all this about?"

So Longarm got to tell them all, including a passenger gal hanging out one window, and they all agreed he'd had a narrow brush with that Twisted Sister.

Longarm didn't argue that point. He mounted up and they all went on together, with the two riders trailing the coach at an easy lope all the way. For a hell of a walk was an easy ride and that was how come mankind had gone to all that trouble with taming horses to begin with.

Longarm would have been easier on his mare but Ike said he aimed to raise a hue and cry and his notion made sense. There was an outside chance he'd *dropped* somebody somewhere in that tanglewood, or winged somebody enough to have left a blood trail.

So once they got back to town to spread the news, Pink Armstrong naturally formed a posse and Longarm had to ride all the way back to the scene of his ambush on a fresh pony with a score of riders whose faces were strange or familiar to him. He reflected as they rode how familiar his own face was becoming in and about Sulfur Draw. If only somebody who knew something would *confide* in such an old pal!

All the way back where he'd been dumped on his ass in the shallows, the sluggish current had healed the muddy puddle he'd rolled on out of. At Pink Armstrong's direction, they dismounted; some younger kids were detailed to hold the horses, and everyone fanned out to beat the brush westward through the tanglewood.

A Tex-Mex with Apache eyes called Jesus spotted blood flecks on the rough bark of a streamside cottonwood and called out to come see.

As they gathered 'round, Pablo hunkered down to examine the nearby damp soil and decide. "*Un hombre* wearing spurs on foot. He fell when he was hit, got up with one dug-in spur rowel for to run on *that* way, toward the *camino*. He ran *muy pronto* for an hombre with a bullet in him. He may not be *muy herido*."

Pink Armstrong smiled boyishly to declare, "Wounded at all will be wounded enough when he has to explain what he's doing with old Wolf's bullet in him to a doctor!"

Someone asked what might happen if that Twisted Sister never went to no doctor with a minor wound, adding, "I've bled like hell after cutting my fool chin with a razor. Never went to no doctor, though."

Armstrong said, "You never larnt to read signs worth shit, neither. A grazing bullet wound don't knock a man flat and inspire him to spur the ground as he gets his wind back. You seldom go down unless the bullet stays in you. It's your meat soaking up the shock of moving metal as it knocks you down."

He beamed at Longarm to add, "He, she or its as good as in the box, thanks to you, Wolf! You were riding for me today whether you aimed to or not. The shooter you shot rides for one Dutch faction or the other, seeing the way you say it responded to that obscure insult you throwed at it. After that, whoever you winged is either fixing to get medical attention or die from an untreated bullet wound obtained under mighty unsanitary conditions!"

Another posseman marveled, "That's right! Kruger, here, set her on her ass, bleeding, in pissy mud and water draining many a mess upstream. There's cowshit, horseshit, human shit and all kind of shit in that shitty brown water!"

Longarm muttered, "Thanks, I just had a bath, last night."

Search as they might, they cut no further sign. Longarm's victim had made it far as the wagon trace, where he'd likely left his own pony tethered, to ride west, toward town, leaving no distinct trail in the well-traveled ruts of a heavily traveled route. Someone asked how Longarm could be sure the Twisted Sister had ridden west instead of east. There was always someone that green in your average posse. Before Longarm or Pink Armstrong had to answer, Ike Cooper snorted, "Kruger would have seen or at least *heard* anyone he'd winged riding past him to the east! So the son of a bitch was streaking for town and . . .

hold on, I was coming from town. How come *I* never saw anybody on the trace before I spotted a riderless pony, gathered up its reins and went looking for its rider?"

Longarm said, "He saw you first and turned off to let you pass. After that, I wish you'd all stop picturing the killer or killers in question as fantastic looking as that gun-toting but sissy-looking tinhorn who passed through these parts months ago!"

Pink Armstrong announced, "That's right, me and my pal, Wolf, here, figure the Twisted Sister might be no such thing. Any of you boys who were in Hood's Brigade must recall the latrine rumors about all sorts of unusual camp followers nobody ever seemed to have really laid their own eyes on!"

Another rider in his thirties laughed and wistfully recalled how he and his own squad pulled night picket in the hills of Tennessee and seemed to be the only ones who'd never challenged a misty form out in the dark to discover, closer in, they were facing an unarmed bare-ass naked lady who sure liked soldiers.

Another rider laughed, "Oh, I remember *her,* only she put out to the night pickets in the hills of *Georgia* and some said the next day, when they tried to backtrack her home, they only found a nearby deserted country graveyard. Never saw her, myself."

Pink Armstrong said, "There you go. Let's mount up and get on back to town. Somebody along the way might have seen something. Mayhaps a rider slumped low in the saddle or a familiar figure walking funny and trying to avoid them. Me and Wolf, here, suspect somebody we all know on sight and don't suspect may be behind all this bullshit!"

Nobody argued. They remounted and rode. When they got back to town Longarm took his saddle and bridle from the borrowed pony, toted 'em back to the coaching inn, said howdy to his spent chestnut, and went upstairs to gather some fresh duds before we went back to strip off his stiff and stinky denims, shirt and underwear before he took another tub bath.

By the time he was out on the street again, feeling disgustingly clean, things had simmered down. Another deputy he met up with at *Der Rinderhirt* said none of the logical suspects had seemed to be reeling about town with a .44-40 slug in them.

When Longarm asked who the usual suspects were, the deputy, a sort of dapper young cuss who favored mail-order sateen shirts of shiny black with white trim, said they called him Duke Winters and explained they'd questioned *Onkel* Klaus, *Vater* Paul and all their known lieutenants around the *Tanzsaal* or *Sankt Josef* down the way.

Longarm took Duke's word for it. As if he'd suspected they might be talking about him, *Onkel* Klaus Brenner came in to belly up to the bar beside them, saying, "Evening, Wolf, Duke, what's all this bullshit about one of my boys riding into town full of bullet holes?"

Duke easily replied, "It was Kruger, here, shot the son of a bitch. I was just now saying it didn't seem to have been you or any of them loafers spitting and whittling around your dance hall. How come you're so edgy about it, Uncle Klaus? You hiding some wounded game in your meat locker across the way?"

Onkel Klaus growled, "*Zum Teufel*! Pink Armstrong *looked*! If one of my riders had come in dying of a bullet wound, do I look stupid enough to put the body on *ice*?"

Duke soothed, "Not if Pink never *found* no body in your meat locker, Uncle Klaus. Pink says what we've been doing is called a process of eliminating by us old pros. We just eliminated you and yours, so why get your bowels in an uproar? We were just doing our duty and if it's any comfort, we questioned the Cat Licker priest and his own church ladies this afternoon."

Winking at Longarm, the deputy slyly added, "We got a tip that Twisted Sister sang in the choir down to Saint Joe's."

Onkel Klaus managed a mollified chuckle and bought the next round. Then it was Longarm's turn, as Wolf Kruger. But before Duke had to spring for another, Pink Armstrong came in, looking sort of pink all over as he confessed, "Well, I've searched high, and I've searched low, and most everyone in town I could think of seems present and accounted for. The cuss you winged must have holed up somewhere's else, Wolf. So let's hope the wound festers."

Nobody needed to have Duke explain, but he was young and so he felt they ought to be told, "Should an obscure nester take some time to get better, or should he die and they bury him under the chicken coop, we may never know who Kruger, here, shot it out with!"

Pink Armstrong growled, "Thanks, I never might have figured that out, and now I'd best get home to supper lest my old woman bury *me* under the chicken coop!"

That 'minded the others it was getting along about that time. Nobody invited Longarm for supper, and he didn't want to tempt fate by tempting himself with Rosalinda. So he ambled down to that fancier restaurant with table linen and ordered steak smothered in onions with mashed potatoes from a waitress he hadn't started getting to know.

As a knockaround rider who followed the Tex-Mex code of "*Todo, pero con manera*" around Tex-Mexicans, Longarm understood the first thing a man had to understand was his own weak nature if he meant to get way with most anything in moderation, or with decent manners, as the Tex-Mex adage warned.

So he knew that having the coming night alone after scrubbing his fool self fit for wedding night, anything halfway willing wearing a skirt was going to look better and better in the gathering dusk.

The fact he was even *thinking* of fat old Rosalinda warned him he'd been *considering* just what might be lurking in wait for him betwixt her elephantine thighs, and he'd already told himself that taking pity on a friendly pup who kept wagging her tail to be petted could lead to uncertain results.

As he casually eyed the retreating rump of a far shaplier Anglo gal waiting tables that evening, Longarm caught himself weighing the odds of Rosalinda being a jolly fat gal who'd learned to be a good sport about empty pillows in the cold, gray dawn or one of those lost souls who fell in everlasting love with every man who laid 'em. There was a lot of that going around in Tex-Mex circles.

He told himself not to even wonder about that, since it wasn't about to happen. The Anglo waitress locked eyes with him as she headed his way with some other diner's coffee. She served it and came puppy dogging back to Longarm, asking what he'd just been saying.

He smiled up at her to explain, "Talking to myself, Ma'am. A man gets peculiar, herding cows. I reckon I'd like some pumpkin pie for dessert."

She went to fetch it as he finished the last of his blue plate. As she cleared space and placed the pie before him, she asked what he'd been talking about. The place was nigh empty, now, and it sure beat all how waitress gals liked to talk to him when things were slow.

He said, "Since you ask, I was pondering a wager. If you were asked whether you wanted to bet on something hurting a heap against it offering mild pleasure, how would you bet, Miss . . ."

"Eliza, Eliza Davenport. My friends call me Liza and you must be talking about some bad habit you're trying to break!"

He grinned up at her to say, "You just hit the nail on the head. But decency forbids I describe my bad habits to one so young and innocent."

Liza said, "Oh, I don't know about that, and all habits are as hard to break. I lost some weight I'd been putting on in the kitchen as I snacked on nibbles of this, that and everything. I managed to break myself of the habit and lose fifteen pounds when I asked myself that very question. Whenever I caught myself reaching for a Napoleon, I'd ask myself if it hurt worse to forego a swallow of pleasure or to to look at a fat girl in my mirror, with results I hope you see."

He said, "It's hard to picture you without that swell figure, Miss Liza, but I'll take your word for it and you can call me Wolf, Wolf Kruger."

She said she'd known who he was all along, and that

they closed at nine, and she got off as soon as she'd helped them straighten up.

But before Longarm could take her up on her kind offer the front door flew in and one of the riders from that afternoon posse burst in to yell, "Pink Armstrong wants you on the double, Kruger! We got to posse-up for some serious night riding! All hell's broken loose on the range this evening! Sorry, Miss Liza, but facts is facts!"

As Longarm rose, dropping a silver dollar by his plate to cover all bets, he asked what hell they were talking about.

The rider the sheriff had sent to fetch him panted, "Over to the Double H. Miss Hilda Zimmer just rode in on a lathered pony. Somebody just shot her sister and a couple of their hands as they were driving off with half their herd!"

As Longarm chased him outside he added, "They killed that blue-ribbon bull entire. Leastways, Miss Hilda had to shoot him when she found him bawling with his guts trailing after him in the dusty straw!"

Chapter 30

It seemed the whole town was there in the flickering light as they possied-up out front of the sheriff's office. *Onkel* Klaus grabbed onto Hilda Zimmer to calm her down as she caught sight of Longarm in the lamp light and commenced to scream like a banshee in High Dutch as she pointed at him. It wasn't too hard to figure what she meant by *verdammt katholisch Zweigesichter*, since he'd gone to that Papist dance after she'd fired him. Others tried to assure her in a mishmash of Dutch and English that Wolf Kruger's recent movements could be attested to by the local law.

As they saddled up, Hilda wanted to ride back with them but her *Onkel* Klaus and a flock of clucking Dutch hens carried her off somewhere to bed her down with hot chocolate and sympathy lest she wreck her health tearing back and forth through the night all hot and bothered.

They all knew the way, and as they approached the home spread of the Double H, surviving help had lit hanging lanterns and a bonfire in the barnyard, where Herta Zimmer still lay face down in her *charro* outfit with a mud puddle starting to dry between her spread pant legs. One of the first to dismount was a druggist from town who turned her over to feel her throat, look her over, and decide, "Dead before Miss Hilda rode for town. But she died hard with a low chest wound that drowned her, slow, inside, in her own blood."

"How far could someone ride with a wound like that?" asked one of the deputies, Ike Cooper. Sheriff Armstrong said, "Use your ears more and your yap less, Ike. Miss Hilda *told us* they both ran out the back when they heard their prize bull bawling! Miss Herta was hit and Miss Hilda ran for her life. She was the only one who *rode* anywheres this evening, you fool kid!"

Longarm tried to picture such a scene and decided it wasn't all that impossible. The timing was a tad tight. To hit the Double H in that uncertain gloaming light just after sundown, the raiders would have had to move into position by broad daylight. He said so as he tagged along Armstrong on the way to the barn, where an agitated Mex kid stood waving a torch.

Armstrong said, "I'm ahead of you there by a country mile. I mean to have my deputies canvas all the spreads nearby to see if anyone recalls any strangers riding by this afternoon."

Longarm suggested, "Have them take down *any* riders riding by, Pink. Do you ride through totally strange country by day with nightfall just over the horizon?"

Armstrong smiled wearily and said, "You're right. Why take chances you don't need to and it's commencing to sink in that we ain't dealing with no masked figures in freak costumes, here. The rascals probably look as innocent as you and me, and they'd be likely to wave a howdy as they passed anyone they knew along the way."

"Be a swell way to move in tight on the men they've murdered so far," Longarm suggested. He wasn't ready to bring up those missing undercover lawmen yet. But the same notion could account for getting the drop, more than once, on an experienced Texas Ranger on the prod for just such an event!

Longarm had never seen that prize Black Angus bull he'd heard so much about. All that they'd left of it, the bastards, was a whole lot of rapidly spoiling meat. You could see where Herta had shot it in the head and . . . wait a minute!

Longarm told the sheriff, "Miss Hilda's tale won't jibe as she told it. How could Miss Herta, yonder, gun this gutted bull over here if they shot her coming out her back door?"

Armstrong replied, "Hell, I was with you in town at the time! After you've served as one of my deputies for a spell, you'll understand how witnesses never tell tales that hang together worth shit. Folk ain't in the act of *re-membering* when they're scared out of their wits and more worried about staying alive. The memories come *later*, as they think back through the kaleidoscope and try to make *sense* of what they went through. Nobody remembers pissing down a leg, out loud, as they try to tell you whether the rooting-tooting-shooting terror was a white man, a colored woman or an armed and dangerous giraffe! I can read signs as good as you. I make it Miss Herta came out, gun in hand, making it here to the barn to shoot this bull, and catching that fatal round to stagger back for the house and drop where we found her. If her sister was just coming out at the time, it's no wonder she was con-founded!"

Longarm allowed he reckoned so. Not wanting to seem too wiseass, he kept his mouth shut with his eyes and ears open as Pink Armstrong ran the show. Professional enough, as he had his deputies herd the Double H help together so's he could question them thorough. Longarm couldn't think of any more important questions he'd have wanted to ask. Unless Hilda Zimmer had just murdered her own twin, butchered their prize bull and driven all that Cherokee seed stock off to parts unknown, all by herself, they had to buy her tale of woe the way she'd told it.

A cowboy off the Lazy Diamond asked Longarm, see-ing he'd ridden in with the Zimmer twins, how tough it might be to spot those Cherokee longhorns at some dis-tance, up on the Staked Plains to north or south.

Longarm said, "Shouldn't be hard at all. For as far off

as you can see 'em they're black-cat-black with shorter horns than steers of the same persuasion on account they're she-males, every one. I can't see cow thieves driving such a herd far, or unloading them once they get 'em anywheres."

He saw other professional drovers were listening intent as he went on, "They got a night's lead. But how far can you drive nigh a hundred head of anything in the dark? And, come sunrise, it ought to be easy to cut their trail and follow it, faster than anyone can move beef on the hoof!"

Pink Armstrong declared that by jimmies that was just what he'd been fixing to say. So by jimmies they got the rattled-but-willing Chinee cook to rustle up a late feed for one and all, rubbed down and rested their ponies, and unrolled their bedding hither and yon to rest up for some more hard riding as they waited out the night after poor little Herta Zimmer was bound for town in one of her own buckboards, wrapped in her own bedroll tarp.

Next morning, before sunrise, they were up and raring to go as soon as the Chinee filled 'em with coffee and beans. They forged up atop the bluffs behind the Zimmer home spread and fanned out to scout for signs. Four riders driving around a hundred cows across overgrazed and summerkilt buffalom grama and bunch grass leave a swamping amount of sign.

So Armstrong led his posse after them, north-northeast across nigh flat high and dry prairie one could see across from the saddle for many a mile. Having ridden with Hood in the war, Pink Armstrong had his men advance in line of skirmish, stirrup to stirrup, instead of in column so's one buffalo round could drill through one man after the other, six bodies or more in a row.

A Lazy Diamond hand who knew where they were called out, "I 'spect I know where they're headed! Sulfur Draw runs southeast to northwest but there's a shallower unsettled draw off thataways they could hide a thousand head in! It's got some water and a little timber shade. Four men could keep a hell of a herd in such surroundings indefinite!"

Pink Armstrong objected, pointing ahead with his rawhide quirt, "The tracks ain't headed thataway, Luke. They're headed thisaway and that's the way we're riding."

But they hadn't ridden on three miles before the trail they'd been following made a sudden swing to the east and Armstrong called out, "I stand corrected. Luke's likely right. Let's fan farther apart and move in with rounds in our saddle guns because the sons of bitches may be desperate as well as crazy mean!"

But when they followed the stolen herd's sign to the out-of-the-way draw that Lazy Diamond hand had recalled, they found nobody lying in wait for them with drawn guns.

The night riders were long gone, having had most of the night to just keep riding. The herd of Cherokee longhorns were where they'd left it, along with some other longhorns, a hundred and fourty-six head in all, sprawled along both slopes of the draw with some carcasses damming the trickle down the center to form puddles of bloody water hither and yon. The first rider down to dismount hunkered low, stood back up and shouted, "Throat's cut! Didn't even have the decency to *shoot* 'em!"

A younger hand near Longarm almost sobbed, "Aw, who'd want to do a chickenshit thing like that? What whas their fucking *point*? Why did they shoot Miss Herta and run off all these cows of hers if they didn't mean to *keep* 'em?"

Longarm soberly suggested, "They never wanted them for themselves. They just didn't want the Double H to have 'em!"

Pink Armstrong glumly conceded, "They succeeded, the way wolverines tear up and shit on anything they're too full to eat. What'll you bet their hoofprints swing west-southwest to that wagon trace that'll carry us back down Sulfur Draw as we lose their fucking trail amidst all the others?"

Longarm said it was no bet and added, "By this time they'll have made it back to town or beyond ahead of us. That's why they struck at sundown, giving themselves all the time they needed to leave us a trail to nowheres in the dark."

They all rode across a scene that looked as if that charge of the light brigade had been made on cows. Some of the cow ponies spooked at the smell of death. More than one rider looked ready to puke. As they picked up the trail of four trotting ponies on the far side, headed just the way Armstrong had predicted, the reddish blond lawman asked Longarm, "What in blue blazes do you reckon they did that for, Wolf?"

Longarm shrugged and suggested, "Why don't you ask 'em when you catch 'em? We . . . I mean you might have been eliminating backwards in your search for *motives*. Trying to figure out why a dumb or loco son of a bitch has done something that makes no sense can lead you up too many box canyons, Pink. I can think up *crazy* reasons as fast as I can discard 'em as crazy. But now you know there's a gang of natural men, not a witch on a broom or a headless horseman. That could be the chink in the armor of the master sneak behind it all, see?"

Armstrong frowned thoughtfully and decided, "Not entire. How can you be sure they're *men*, and where does it say they have to have some mastermind directing all this bullshit?"

Longarm said, "If we agree they can move about to set things up in broad daylight. One or more total strangers riding past even one sharp-eyed nester or line rider would have been reported by now if any crimes had taken place within the same twenty-four hours. You don't get a gang of four or more without a leader, even when such a gang rides around acting mad-dog dumb. The master sneak may be *loco en la cabeza* but he has to have his *followers* convinced he has some logical motive. So all you have to do is catch just *one* of the sons of bitches and make him talk!"

Pink Armstrong asked, "What if the mastermind is a

237

she, and how do you catch even one of 'em, and what if he won't talk?"

Longarm patiently explained, "It won't matter whether they've been taking their orders from a man or a woman as long as you get a gang member to tell you who it is and what he or she *said* the objective was. When you catch one gang member alive, alone, he *always* talks unless he's been arrested by total assholes. I did hear of one bank robber who'd been spilling his guts until a natural bully with a badge sneered that he was fixing to die with a stiff prick and a busted neck. A professional with a badge can almost always cut a deal with the prosecution allowing the prisoner to save his own neck by turning state's evidence."

Pink Armstrong turned in the saddle to stare thoughtfully as he asked where Wolf Kruger of Val Verde County had learned so much about getting the goods on gangs.

Aware others were listening, Longarm said, "Hell, everybody who's ever read a dime detective knows *that* much, Pink. If you're still after me about that job offer, I'm ever willing to posse-up like this during an emergency. But as a steady job I'd as soon worry about *cows*."

Anyone could see those four ponies had forged on north-northwest as if making for the far bluffs of the Staked Plains, overlooking the wide Pecos bottomlands. But Pink Armstrong snorted, "Shit, don't try to teach this child to suck eggs or track night riders. They'll have hairpinned back along that wagon trace and we're just wasting time and the sweat of man and beast!"

Reining sharply to his left the sheriff shouted, "Southwest and let her buck! No sense sparking a frigid woman or following a trail to nowheres. The sons of bitches got away, this time!"

Nobody argued with such logic but as they turned their backs to the morning sun Armstrong muttered, "God damn it to hell, this sure hurts, even when I know there's nothing smarter to try out this way!"

Longarm soothed, "That's the way I see it, Pink. Riding in circles this far from town could be giving them more time than they deserve to plan more devilment."

Armstrong said, "That's the exact word I've been groping for. It was pure and unadulterated *devilment*! Evil for the sake of evil! A pretty gal murdered, a prize bull gutted, a whole herd of prime beef slaughtered and left to rot on the range!"

Longarm soberly suggested, "Miss Hilda might get some skinners to salvage all them hides before they spoil. Ought to net her enough for a handsome funeral for her twin."

Armstrong made a wry face and said, "Nothing's going to make up the loss of her sister and all that prize beef. The cows alone are one hell of a loss!"

Longarm said, "You won't get no argument on that from *this* child. I *druv* that fucking herd all the way west from Truscott!"

•

Chapter 31

The raid on the Double H left everyone along Sulfur Draw
feeling mighty discouraged. They said Hilda Zimmer was
in bed with the vapors under a doctor's care and *Onkel*
Klaus had sort of taken over the rest of her herd and the
running of her spread until she made up her mind whether
she aimed to start over or sell out.

Under the post-war Texas constitution of '78 their
druggist and ad hoc coroner filed his findings and death
certificate with the nearest ranger station in the bigger
town of Sulfur Springs in another draw entire to the south,
called Sulfur Springs Creek. Both draws joined up way
to the southeast with both their wagon traces leading on
to La Mesa. Such confusions in West Texas had led to
the rangers having the power to sort things out in unincorporated territory. They had their job cut out for them.
Texas had always been too big for its britches, with a
thin, widely scattered population and way too many hos-
tile Indians and Mex bandits. So the Texas Rangers had
been set up back in the twenties as a jack-of-all-trades
public safety organization to provide law and order off
the cuff as needed.

Billy Vail had told Longarm, bitterly, how his old
ranger pals had been drawn into the War Betwixt the
States with Sam Houston and other sensible old-timers
pissing and moaning they had no dog in that fight. But

the rangers had fought, and lost, and been replaced for years by a hated Texas state police, organized by vindictive winners, until good old Rutherford B. Hayes had shown the guts, and distinguished combat record as a Union officer, to end Reconstruction and allow the rangers to reorganize leaner and meaner than ever.

As if enticed by all the excitement, that circuit judge rode in to hold court in the big red *Tanzsaal*, with a swamping back load of pending litigation. Longarm moseyed over around noon to listen in as he pondered some excuse for riding over to La Mesa or Sulfur Springs on some innocent-sounding errand. He didn't care where he rode as long as he could use the facilities of Western Union without anyone from either faction reading over his shoulder.

The circuit judge, a scrawny old buzzard in a rusty black suit and high hat he'd doubtless stolen from the estate of Abe Lincoln, was hearing the case of the Lazy Seven versus the Lazy Diamond, accused of running brands.

The owner of the Lazy Seven, a sort of pop-eyed excitable cuss from Creole country and of the Papist persuasion, was accusing the surly Dutch owner of the Lazy Diamond of running his simple Lazy Seven, a crudely drawn numeral seven lying on its side, to the four-sided diamond of a playing card, lying on its side. The Dutch defendant insisted his Lazy Sevens were all, dammit, neatly stamped, not crudely drawn with a running iron. The Creole wanted to know, in that case, where in thunder a whole mess of his veal had gone. He said it stood to reason that when you found hardly any calves in the company of your herd, come the spring roundup, some *sacre bleu* had by far stolen them, and there came a mutter of agreement from all but the Lutheran Dutch assembled.

Pink Armstrong was called as a friend of the court. He testified he'd investigated the complaints of the Lazy Seven and agreed there should have been more increase out on open range where cows of more than one herd dropped their calves beyond human ken. Pink agreed the

Lazy Diamond's increase had been handsome, albeit within the bounds of possible for a herd that size. In sum, Pink Armstrong simply couldn't say for certain either way. Then he pointed at Longarm, seated toward the back of the cavernous hall, to suggest they call such an old cow hand as another friend of the court.

So the next thing Longarm knew, he'd been sworn in, shooting some murderous looks at Pink Armstrong as he wondered whether this was as likely to hurt him as to help him play his undercover role.

The circuit judge questioned direct, once Longarm had protested he knew nothing about either outfit. The judge said, "The court would like your considered opinion on the matter of running brands."

There came a round of chuckles when Longarm said he didn't run brands any more often than anyone else in the beef business.

The judge warned him to be serious, and Longarm confirmed the old buzzard's beliefs about earmarking, cutting and branding new steers for one's own range, trail branding them behind the ear to drive to market in a consolidated herd, or blotting, crossing out, and then rebranding stock purchased for breeding or feeding up to market size.

The judge handed Longarm a fistful of photographs entered in evidence by the Lazy Seven and asked his opinion on some fuzzy photos of shaggy hides. As he studied them, Longarm casually asked if the two herd grazed together on consolidated range. But the judge had thought of that already and that angle was up for grabs. The outfits both ran stock on high range north of the draw but not cheek-by-jowel. So the Lazy Diamond riders would have to ride through other cows to get at the Lazy Seven cows but, as the Lazy Seven said, nobody else had such an easy brand to run to a Lazy Diamond.

Longarm looked up from the sepia tone prints to declare, "I'd say these Lazy Diamond brands introduced in evidence appear to have been made with a stamp brand. Each one a neat lazy diamond, all the same size."

242

"What did I tell you!" crowed the Dutch owner of the Lazy Diamond.

The judge banged his gavel and told him to shut up and sit down.

Then Longarm added, "These lazy sevens are lazy in more ways than one, your honor. Did I miss something earlier or did someone say the owner of that herd, Mr. Laroche, yonder, was of the Creole French persuasion?"

The pop-eyed cuss popped up to brag on being related to the late King Louis on his momma's side. The judge sat him back down and told Longarm to get to the point.

Longarm said, "Far be it for me to low-rate another man's education, your honor. But if Mr. Laroche ever studied arithmetic in most any parish school in Louisiana, he'd have learned to draw number seven with a short cross-line through the longer leg of what might otherwise be taken for an upside-down *L* or a sloppy number one. I believe there's a Louisiana trade statute to that effect, Louisiana being the only state as follows the Napoleonic Code to this day."

His honor asked Longarm how he knew so much about the state laws of Louisiana. Longarm didn't want to go into the time he'd tangled with that New Orleans Black Hand Society as a federal lawman, so he said he'd asked in Galveston about some Louisiana bills of lading all covered with those Frenchified number sevens and it worked. The judge said, "You're right. Now that I think back, I've seen literate frogs cross their sevens like we cross our *T*s!"

He turned to point his gavel at the plaintiff to demand, "Which shall it be, Mr. Laroche? Are you too lazy to cross your lazy sevens or don't you know how to read and write?"

The Creole's Anglo lawyer jumped up to ask what in thunder such a question had to do with whether someone had run the brands of his client's cows, no matter how their brands might read.

The judge ponificated, "They read as no more than two sloppy lines at right angles to one another. Any fool with a running iron could change such a dumb brand to dozens

243

of other designs whether he could read or not. The court rules the plaintiff's charges are without any merit and that a lazy brander and his cattle are soon parted. So get thee hence, Mr. Laroche, and for Pete's sake register yourself a sensible brand!"

As some laughed and others groaned, the judge adjourned for the day.

As Longarm rose from the witness chair, His Honor said, "Stick around, Kruger. I want a few more words with you, off-the-record."

Longarm, as Wolf Kruger, didn't argue as the circuit judge led him to the bar cum refreshment counter along the back wall under the skulls of most everything you could hit with a plains rifle, from buffalo and elk down to mule deer and pronghorns.

One of *Onkel* Klaus Brenner's minions served them fancy-figured steins of mighty fine lager, and when Longarm said so, His Honor told him, "*Onkel* Klaus brews it himself, and this big ballroom would be a gold mine if he had to haul his suds in from La Mesa. What do you make of this bullshit, Wolf? I understand you're not riding for either faction."

Longarm modestly confessed he'd just come to town. He knew the older man had heard plenty of gossip about him already. He added he'd met the nominal leaders of both factions and added, "To tell the pure truth, your honor, both *Onkel* Klaus and *Vater* Paul struck me as men of common sense."

"Meaning what?" asked the circuit judge from other parts.

Longarm replied, "Since you seem to have noticed yourself, most everyone assumes the recent rash of malicious mischief and worse was ordered by one bunch of Dutchmen or the other. But the *victims* have been members of both Dutch factions and some neutral Anglo or Mex Texicans. After that, speaking merely as a naturally curious cuss, I fail to see how a go-getting mushroom grower like Klaus Brenner would stand to gain by running *anybody* out of Sulfur Draw. For he *built* Saint Joe's church and all the other frame construction from here to the wagon trace to the south, save for a few old 'dobes that were here when he came in with more ambition. So he's *collecting rent* from many a new Austrian Dutch Papist and his stores along Main Street sell everything from beans to barbwire and windmill kits to anyone new or old-timer with the means to *pāy* for the same, so unless *Onkel* Klaus is a mighty narrow-minded lunatic . . ."

"Narrow-minded lunatics happen," His Honor cut in, asking, "What do you think of that Jesuit priest, speaking of narrow-minded lunatics?"

Longarm shrugged and allowed, "I've been slickered by two-facers in my time. But it's my understanding the Jesuit Order's supposed to be well educated and trained in the art of diplomacy. The Vatican sends them in where delicacy may be needed, such as Lakota country when Mister Lo was still in charge, or recently settled parts of a mostly Protestant west. If *Vater* Paul ordered that raid on the Double H last night, he sure plays a crude game of chess!"

"Who does that leave?" asked His Honor, sipping some suds before he mused, half to himself, "In all my years since Harvard Law I have yet to hear of a range war where somebody didn't *gain* something by winning!"

Longarm suggested, "I wasn't there. But that Lincoln County War they just tidied up over in the Pecos bottomlands wiped out *both* sides, as I've been told."

His Honor made a wry face, a dreadful sight to see, and objected, "Romantic and partisan reporters told it too simple by half as they paid more attention to the blood and thunder than the bottom line!"

He sipped more suds and said, "As a jurist, I've kept abreast of the lawsuits and bank foreclosures that followed the deaths of Murphy and McSween. Neither of *them* got more than worry and ruination for the school yard fight they'd indulged in. But once the dust settled the fatherly John Chisum of the Jingle Bob was a bigger cattle baron than before, having bought up heaps of property, cheap, from neighbors ruined by the short but nasty running gunfight he'd encouraged from a safe distance."

Longarm cautiously said, "Like I said, I wasn't there, but down to Val Verde County we did hear Uncle John Chisum endowed the poor widow McSween with a seed herd and a grubstake to start over."

His Honor shrugged and said, "He could well afford to, since he now owns most everything west of the Pecos. Pedro or Pete Maxwell owns most everything *east* of the Pecos. Both cattle barons encouraged McSween to go on fighting long after he should have been running. But neither of them ever backed his play against the Murphy-Dolan riders backed by the Santa Fe Ring, War Department and Bureau of Indian Affairs. It's so easy to say 'Hit 'em again and I'll hold your coat!' Be it recorded no Chisum or Maxwell rider ever fired or ducked one shot in that short, sharp Lincoln County War, and now those two big outfits are even bigger, with nobody else big enough to bother them as they range most of the beer on the Pecos bottomlands!"

Longarm asked if His Honor was suggesting some big but modest cattle baron or land developer could be encouraging the two Dutch factions to fight, in hopes of ruining both and picking up all the pieces, cheap.

His Honor said he didn't know but felt it was worth thinking about. Longarm didn't ask him if they knew who he was, over in some bigger towns along his circuit. A man who volunteered information when he didn't really need to was a man who couldn't keep a secret for shit.

By that time it was too late in the day to ride over to the Western Union in Sulfur Springs, "looking for work," so Longarm went back to that restaurant with table linen to see if Eliza Davenport was sore at him.

She wasn't. She'd washed and henna-rinsed her originally light brown hair since last they'd spoken and wanted to hear all about the awful murder of Herta Zimmer and her cows as she served his steak, smothered in mushrooms, this time.

Telling the tale took some doing as she kept dashing back and forth to serve other customers. But they managed as she'd ask a question, run off, and come by later for the answer.

He was putting away the extra serving of peach cobbler he'd ordered for dessert before she coyly repeated that remark about getting off around nine-thirty. A man had to let the trout nibble at its own good time before he stuck the hook.

Figuring he'd better, unless he was up to a *third* helping of peach cobbler, Longarm said, "Too bad they're not holding a dance anywheres in town this evening. For I have to ride some more in the morning, and there's no saying when I'll be by this way again."

It worked. She bit, saying, "Maybe you'd like to walk me home and maybe then we could play checkers or something, seeing it'll still be so early and, I don't know about you, Wolf. But I find that after a hard day on my feet I somehow don't feel ready for bed, alone, before midnight."

He soberly assured her he'd expected to have a tough time falling to sleep that night, facing a hard day's ride in the morning. So she suggested he come back just after closing and meet her out front so's they could try to help one another through the night.

Chapter 32

Eliza Davenport didn't henna-rinse all over, and it didn't take him 'til midnight to find out. She never even suggested checkers once she had him alone in her own one-room cabin with a sleeping loft along the eastern limits of the tiny town. You had to admire a gal who knew what she wanted and didn't beat about the bush when what she wanted had told her he was riding out, come sunrise.

Longarm had learned the hard way that most waitress gals wanted love and marriage or some hot-and-heavy down-and-dirty after a long tedious day serving other people's pleasure. Few waitresses were in it for flowers, books and candy because any gal asking a man to pay for her favors would have been dumb as a plank serving *grub* for a living!

They'd started trading spit, romantic, as he'd walked her home in the moonlight and, as they'd both hoped, that had them warmed up to where they just naturally kept cuddling on her sofa for a couple of stiff drinks and then so to bed.

He found he could hang both gun-rigs on the post of her mail-order queen-sized bed. She didn't ask how come he packed an extra six-gun under his jacket until they'd been at it a spell. With her own duds off, Liza's remarks about needing to watch her weight made better sense. She was built mighty fine, but the sort of rubbery layer of lard under her smooth skin from head to toe threatened to thicken up from its present state of delight if she gained five pounds. She proved she was saddled with oral cravings by going down on him to blow it hard some more the minute he pulled it out of her throbbing ring-dang-doo.

So once she had, he begged her not to let him come in her mouth when she was so pretty betwixt her thighs. So she spread her thighs to invite him back in and she could suck like hell down yonder, too!

Later, as they cuddled against her headboard, panting like hounds who'd caught the fox at last, Liza asked about the guns.

He explained, "Had the Colt when I rode in. Bought the Harrington Richardson the other day to wear to the dance at the *Tanzsaal*. Heard they made you check visible hardware at the door, and I'd heard another cuss was looking for me."

She snuggled closer and replied, "I heard about you running Junior Brewster out of town, and everyone said he was awfully tough!"

He was glad she was one of those gals who admired men for being tough instead of rich. Gals with the latter taste were less rare.

He modestly but truthfully replied, "Never met the man, myself. So I never ran him out of nowheres."

She insisted, "Oh, come on, Wolf. It was the talk of the town. A man who'd gunned three other men in Truscott declared this town was off limits to you and threatened to shoot you on sight! But then they told him you'd shot as many men in Truscott and faced down a gang of road agents and a band of Quill Indians as you carried the Zimmer twins and all those cowgirls safely home!"

He said, "Aw, mush."

She reached down to fondle him some more as she purred, "I'm sure glad you're on my side. Would you like to put this *inside*, some more?"

He allowed he could try, having gotten his second wind as he ran his free hand over her shapely but pleasantly

249

padded curves, and she seemed to take it friendly when it took him much longer to come in her again, posting slow but steady in her love-saddle whilst she sucked his tongue for a change. She surely craved to have something in her mouth. But what the hell, she had a pretty mouth and didn't bite.

So a good time was had by all and despite what he'd said about an early start, they got to lay slugabed past seven because she didn't have to report for work before nine and said she liked to see what she was up to when she went down on a man she admired.

So in the end, Longarm wound up having breakfast at her restaurant after walking her to work, sort of stiff from all that admiration.

She seemed to get an extra boot out of calling him "Sir" in front of her boss as she served his eggs sunnyside up over a slab of ham.

Pink Armstrong stopped him as he was leading the chestnut out to Main Street around eleven. The sheriff wanted to know what Longarm and the circuit judge had been talking about the day before. When Longarm repeated their conversation, truthfully enough, Armstrong nodded and said, "I've considered some sneaky troublemaker egging on one side or the other. Ain't been able to spot any. Neither Brenner nor that priest seem men who'd take orders from anybody who wasn't ready to stand by them in a showdown. I heard how Big John Chisum made all that war talk and offered to pay those fool kid regulators McSween deputized. Only he never paid dime one and just sat on his front veranda over on the Jingle Bob, whistling innocent nursery tunes as the two sides slugged it out in and about the McSween spread in Lincoln town. But we don't seem to have anybody like that in these parts, Wolf. After that, I have another objection. I've talked to Banker Redfern and he tells me there's no way anyone could buy land titles or water rights this early in the game."

Longarm never said the banker had told him the same thing.

Armstrong continued, "Old Brenner just told me that should Hilda Zimmer decide to liquidize and go somewheres else for her health, he can get her a fair price on her remaining stock and portable property. But nobody's likely to bid on her hundred-and-sixty-acre claim and such improvements as they made. He says it's less fuss at the land office to start from scratch with a new claim and not fuck around with what a sod this and a fenced that might be worth to folk you can't talk to."

Longarm said, "It's like I told you, Pink. Find somebody who's been doing it and then make the son of a bitch *explain* the motive!"

The sheriff sighed, "I reckon. Where you headed, Wolf?"

As Wolf Kruger, Longarm said, "Off to the south, far as say Sulfur Springs if I don't find a job closer in."

The sheriff thought and said. "That's over twenty miles and you'll never get back tonight, starting at this hour!"

Longarm shrugged and said, "Got me a bedroll on this saddle if they don't have a hotel in Sulfur Springs. Ain't in no hurry to get back. I haven't been able to *find* me a job around here."

Armstring said, "Bullshit! You know I want you as my senior deputy and I stand ready to pay a hundred a month and expenses!"

Longarm whistled softly and said, "That's a tempting offer. I'll let you know when I get back. It ain't that I'm afraid of the work. I just don't want that much responsibilty. Don't ask me why. I ain't sure my own self. Some men like to be boss. I just want to live-and-let-live."

Pink Armstring sighed and said, "We had riders like you in Hood's Brigade. Good men we could count on who wouldn't wear a lance corporal's stripe on a dare. A lot of you fucking cowboys are like that!"

Longarm said, "Well, up yours, too, and *adios*, you responsible cuss!" as he swung up into the saddle and reined his chestnut away and down Main Street.

As he rode, folk were peering out at him from all sides. Rosalinda waved to him and Robin Slade née Jones

251

ducked inside the *Sulfur Star* with her broom as she spotted him. Others just stared, impassive, and even though he was riding, not walking, he felt like that old gal in that book by Mr. Hawthorne, who'd had to wear this scarlet A to show she'd been naughty, only nobody said much as they pretended not to notice as she strode past with her head held high, trying to pretend she didn't notice, neither.

But at last he was across the wagon trace, through the tanglewood and following a narrower trail up and over the south rim of the draw to the wide-open plains above. A queer steer charged him and his mare on sight—twice— as his experienced semi-retired cow pony easily sidestepped the queer steer and Longarm was able to ride on without having to shoot it.

A queer steer was usually the result of an unskilled cutting, or castration, intended to convert a young bullock to a bigger and more manageable steer. Longhorn bulls were inclined to charge anything from a rival bull to a railroad locomotive when they had a hard-on. No steer was supposed to *get* a hard-on but, sometimes, having been left with half a ball or more, an unskillfully cut steer grew up to be as long across the horns as a steer and as anxious to gore somebody with 'em as a bull. It was up to the owner to decide whether the poor mixed-up critter should be shot or cut some more. Longarm had no beeswax in the matter once he'd gotten around and past the queer steer.

Trotting some, walking some and resting some it took them nigh seven tedious hours under a hot autumn sun under a cloudless Texas sky before he spotted the haze you always saw above a town late in the day and rode into the larger town of Sulfur Springs just before sundown.

He'd timed it that way. Folk payed less attention to a strange rider when everyone was knocking off for the day and the streets were more crowded in tricky light. Nobody seemed to notice him until he reined in at the municipal corral and bet a surly-looking Indian kid two bits that he couldn't rub a pony down, give it plenty of water and a little cracked corn with plenty of hay, and then find a place for the pony and his old roping saddle.

The handsome offer brought a smile to the Indian kid's lips, and since Longarm had left his valuables locked away at the coaching inn he was still paying, he only had to take his saddle gun with him as the Indian kid made some little brothers store the saddle in the tack room.

Getting to first things first, Longarm stode to the Western Union to hand over the carefully block-lettered progress report he'd worked on all that afternoon in the saddle. Passersby could get nosey when they spotted a stranger writing a novel in a telegraph office. Longarm sent the report night-letter rates to Marshal Vail's home address. Then he went to see about supper, and this time the waitress was just plain ugly.

He left her a whole dime tip, anyway, because their blue plate that evening seemed tasty as hell after missing his noon dinner out on the open range.

He found he could hire a flop at the Sulfur Springs stop of another short line running across the Staked Plains to the bottomlands along the Pecos.

He carried his Winchester upstairs and put it to bed for the night in a corner. He hung the fool shoulder-holstered .32 on a bedpost as needless baggage for now. He'd accomplished the most important chore inspiring such a long, hot, dusty ride. After losing contact with his home office for a spell that might have even old Billy worried about him, he'd assure his boss he was still alive and on the job. He'd told the outside world he was still working on those missing rangers after someone had tried to gun him just for being a stranger, near as he could tell.

There was nothing open so late that a stranger in Sulfur Springs had any call to mess with. Come morning he meant to make a few discreet calls, but as night fell with everything still going his way he knew the smartest move would be early-to-bed and early-to-rise.

Then he thought of somebody else and went back down to ask at the desk if a left-handed Irishman called Boyle had stayed there his own first night in Sulfur Springs.

The desk clerk allowed he'd never heard of Lefty Boyle.

Longarm thanked him and asked directions to the most cowboy saloon around. The man who worked there allowed that sounded like the Dead Chinaman Porter House near the municipal corral. So Longarm went to see if they knew Lefty Boyle around the corral and livery complex.

They didn't. Longarm failed to sense any reluctance on the part of the gray-haired barkeep, who decided in a noticeable brogue that Boyle did sound like an Irish name. From County Sligo unless a Paddy Boyle he'd served with in the army had been lying about that.

An Anglo rider bellied up to one side and a Mex dressed charro to the other seemed as anxious to help, but couldn't come up with a Lefty Boyle or even a left-handed Irishman who'd ridden in recent.

The Tex-Mexican seemed more interested. You called a rider a *charro* instead of a vaquero when he dressed that expensive in bell bottoms with silver *conchas* down the outside seams and a matching jacket cut short at the waist to clear his ivory gun grips. Vaquero, pronounced "buckaroo" by some Texicans, meant cowboy. A *charro*, short for *ranchero* or range rider was what a vaquero wanted to be when he won the lottery. The *charro* asked Longarm who he worked for, and why they were so anxious to find Lefty Boyle. So Longarm said he'd just been laid off, Lefty was an old pal, and hauled ass before he had to tell any more lies.

Giving up on Lefty Boyle, Longarm went back to the stage stop to turn in whilst the turning in was good. He knew it had been unwise to risk letting anyone know he'd ever heard of that deputy who'd left Sulfur Draw after they'd started to play rough over yonder.

He sauntered into the stage stop in the gathering dusk, just as someone lit an oil lamp in the lobby. Longarm had his key in his jeans and only needed to nod to the night man in passing.

Then, as he got to the foot of the stairs, somebody

coming down the same in seersucker skirts let out a startled laugh and before he could duck back outside she'd yelled, "Custis Long! I might have known I'd find *you* down here in Texas, you mean, cold-hearted thing! You're down here helping out the Texas Rangers with that range war I'm here to cover for my paper, aren't you?"

Chapter 33

The wasp-waisted dishwater blond in a seersucker riding habit and perky straw boater who'd nearly got him killed before with her big mouth and tendency to top Ned Buntline when it came to Wild West yarns joined him at the foot of the stairs to give him a hug as she thrust her high cheekbone up at him for a peck, insisting, "Fess up, Custis! They sent the famous Longarm down here to break up that blood feud here in Sulfur Springs, didn't they?"

To which he could only reply, with a brotherly peck. "I reckon I know better than to try to pull the wool over *your* eyes, Miss Sparky."

She said, "I'm not using that pen name, these days. I quit my uncle's paper when he wouldn't let me run stories *my* way. These days I write for Boston quarterly as Miss *Weyawitko*, little sister to the Sioux and guardian of the Pawnee. Who's ahead in this Silver Springs War, Custis? I can't get anyone out this way to tell me. They must know I want to write the story up. They keep trying to tell me there *isn't* any Sulfur Springs War!"

Longarm managed not to laugh. It wasn't easy. Aside from having the towns of Sulfur Springs and Sulfur Draw mixed up by more than twenty miles, she seemed mercifully unaware of what *weyawitko* meant in Lakota, as the folk she called Sioux, or snakes in the grass, preferred to be known. *Weyawitko* translated as "crazy woman" and one got the feeling the Indians who'd suggested her new pen name had known what they were talking about. It wasn't true Indians had no sense of humor. They got off some good ones, poker-faced, at *wasichu* who considered 'em noble savages or worse. He said, "It's likely to take some getting used to, Ma'am. I've thought of you so often as Miss Sparky, the light of Omaha. How did you get so thick with both Lakota and the Pawnee you're protecting, seeing the two nations have been at feud since Columbus was a pup?"

She demurely explained she'd ordered her Sioux brothers not to pick on the poor Pawnee, whom she'd found to be simple farmers who meant no harm.

That, he had to allow, was the simple truth from the Pawnee point of view. They told everyone who'd listen how they'd been growing corn, squash and tobacco along the bottomlands of the Platte and such for many a year when the Lakota, Dakota or Nakota everyone else called snakes in the grass had come west from the Great Lakes to kill women and rape buffalo right and left. The Pawnee and even the Sioux-Hokan-speaking Crows had sided with one another, the white settlers or anybody else who'd stand up to a self-proclaimed death singer. So he didn't argue with Miss Sparky, as she'd ever be to him until she'd come up with a better pen name than crazy woman.

Noting that the night man seemed interested in their conversation, Longarm suggested they split a fifth of Maryland rye he had hand, and so, seeing they'd know one another in the biblical sense a spell, Sparky turned around and marched right back up the stairs ahead of him as, down below, the night man called out, "See that you leave the door open, or hold it down to a roar if you can't!"

They wound up in her room instead because she said she found rye whiskey too savage for a little sister of the Sioux and guardian of the Pawnee.

So once she'd built them gin and tonics from her own carpetbag and Longarm had gotten his hat, gun belt and such out of their way to take her matters in hand, Sparky stared up adoringly to declare, "Oh, my, you *have* missed me, haven't you? But why did you ditch me that time in Omaha if you still felt *this* way about us, darling?"

He kissed her hard as he ran two fingers into her gently as she got to work on the buttons of her summerweight riding habit. He hadn't been surprised to find her wearing nothing under it. Autumn weather was hot in West Texas when the Blue Norther wasn't blowing.

He was more worried about shutting her up than her state of undress, albeit once you got her undressed, old Sparky wasn't bad, in her high-strung, lean, hungry and big-titted way.

Unlike Liza the night before, the little sister of the Sioux and guardian of the Pawnee didn't have an ounce of padding on her whipcord-and-whalebone slender being, save for her pelvic and pectoral regions, where her she-meat kept her from seeming too boyish. So in spite of the ride the softer Liza had given him and in spite of how pestiferous this writer-gal could be, Longarm found himself rising to the occasion by they time they'd wriggled out of their duds to get back to familiar fundamentals. For he'd almost forgotten what a great little groin she had to offer a man when she wasn't trying to get the both of them killed.

She moaned, "Oooh, yesss, I'd forgotten how swell this feels with you, darling!" as he mounted her once more to probe her warm depths with his homing pecker. That made two of them. There wasn't a thing wrong with the way old Sparky fornicated. She was simply unable to keep a secret no matter who might be listening. As he proceeded to hump her and she began to tell all four walls what each and every stroke felt like, Longarm felt sure that had she been presented at court to Queen Victoria that evening, she'd have been unable to keep from bragging that she'd just been fucked and, had they been sneaking off a quickie in the center of an Apache encampment, she'd have yelled out she was coming, even before she came.

She'd come close to getting him shot one time by yell-ing his name in unfriendly surroundings, and he knew that if he told her he was trying to work undercover down this way, she'd splash it all over in banner headlines that she'd just interviewed the famous lawman, Longarm, who was working undercover betwixt opposing sides of the famous Sulfur Springs War. So once they'd calmed enough to share a smoke and some pillow talk he commenced to lead her down the garden path she'd taken out of La Mesa by boarding the wrong coach, one town starting with Sulfur sounding much the same as another.

He didn't tell her he was pretending to be Wolf Kruger. He didn't want to see Wolf Kruger in banner headlines whilst he was still using the name an easy day's ride away. He'd learned in the past, the hard way, not to count on any publication dates this excitable writer of tall tales told him about. He knew that like other wandering reporter-gals she often acted as a "stringer," filing news items with the nationwide news services, and, when she wasn't screwing him madly, she was inclined to file mad tales of derring-do with himself as the hero whether he'd been there or not.

So he screwed her some more, madly, as he tried to sell her a story nobody might see fit to print. He told her that, like her, he'd heard-tell of trouble brewing over here by Sulfur Springs but, like her, he hadn't been able to get anyone to tell him anything. He said, "They're either afraid to talk or it's possible the whole thing was just one of them things, like the great diamond strike in Montana or the Baron of Arizona. Folk are always dreaming up western wonders in small towns where they don't have any opera house."

She hugged him with her almost skinny but well-muscled legs as she purred, "Maybe this time you'll listen to me and we can work on the story together, darling! You know what they say about two heads being better than one!"

He suggested two pubic bones banged together better than either might bang alone, and they lost the thread of the conversation for an all too short delightful spell.

Then she was at him again about the range war she'd come west to cover up the wrong draw. She asked him why they called this one Sulfur Springs. He said it seemed likely there were some springs up the draw as smelled of brimstone. Groundwater seeping out of cliffs could wind up smelling of most anything from tonic soda water to undrinkable alum, brine or borax to corrosive lye or deadly metallic salts. When she asked if he'd heard there were other Sulfur Springs in these parts Longarm was able to assure her truthfully he hadn't heard tell of any other sulfur water springing from below the Staked Plains. Then he kissed her tit to change the subject.

Of course, as most men learn by the time they get to kissing tits all that regular, it was impossible to stop a woman's train of thought entire, and so he tried to switch hers to another track as he confided he was looking for a suspect there in Sulfur Springs. When he told her true he'd just come in from hunting for the rascal when they'd met at the foot of the stairs, Sparky lost interest in local geography to nag him about the identity of his secret witness. So he let her suck him off before she got it out of him that he'd been hunting high and low in Sulfur Springs, Texas, for Billy the Kid.

He saw he might have underestimated the little sister of the Sioux and guardian of the Pawnee when she protested, thoughtfully twisting his dick, "Are you sure you know what you're doing, darling? The last I heard, Billy Bonney was hiding out in Shakespeare, New Mexico, down near the border."

He easily lied, "He ain't there. We looked. The boy answering to his description, washing dishes in that Shakespeare beanery, was just an unemployed cowboy, washing dishes for his beans. That new Governor Wallace has revoked the amnesty he offered the Kid since the sore loser gunned that Indian agent on the Mescallero Reserve. With that five-hundred-dollar bounty on him in New Mexico, and nobody yonder who wants to hire his gun, what some say about him being here in Texas makes a certain amount of sense."

She got too excited to twist his dick as she gasped, "Ooh, I see what you mean, darling! Who do you see as Sulfur Springs's answer to Tunstall and McSween?"

He was trying not to enjoy himself too much as he soberly told her, "I've been wondering about that myself. Try as I can, I haven't been able to fathom who stands to benefit most by running whomsoever off these Staked Plains. A banker I talked to tells me you can't transfer a homestead claim. Another old-timer who's been out this way all of a year or more says it's as easy to file from scratch on land and water whilst anything else can move away with you, once somebody scares you off."

She suggested, "But wouldn't the run-off cattlemen leave much more open range for the ones left behind?"

He kissed the part of her dishwater hair and murmured, "I see you've learned a little more about the West, since first you wrote me up as a half brother to Crazy Horse."

She innocently replied, "Well, it's *possible* the two of you could be at least *distantly* related. It was you who told me Crazy Horse had blue eyes and might have had white blood, you know."

"Me and my big mouth," he sighed, patiently adding, "I said that could have accounted for his blind hatred of our kind and his unique habit of avoiding photographers and sketch artists. Most Indians *like* to see themselves immortalized on a glass plate or paper print, even if that one chief did threaten a sketch artist with bodily harm for drawing him in profile, missing half his face, to the Indian's way of thinking."

"What has that to do with Billy the Kid? Are you trying to change the suject, Custis Long?"

He said, "I'm just trying to impress you with how much trouble you can cause by jumping to conclusions in shorthand, honey. I had a hell of a time convincing the *Rocky Mountain News* I had no intention of 'tending my half brother's funeral when Crazy Horse got himself killed up to Fort Robinson. So if you really want to work with me on this case, you have to agree to do so on my terms. Can I trust you to do that, honey?"

She husked, "Oh, Lordy, yes, yes, yes, and I'll take it up my ass for a scoop like that, darling!"

He said, "I just want you to wait for me in La Mesa for . . . oh, no more than a week at the most. I don't want you this far west, exposed to so much danger as my sidekick, see?"

She wriggled against him like a skinny naked kitten as she purred, "Are we really going to work as sidekicks, this time, Custis? Are you really going to let me be there at the kill? You're not fixing to duck out on me again, like you've ducked out more than once before, you mean thing?"

He snuggled her closer and promised, "If you'll be a good girl and wait for me in La Mesa just a few more days, I'll join you there on my way back to Denver, and I'll tell you all I've found out before I file my officious report to anyone else."

She repeated that she wanted to be in on the kill.

He said, "You can't be. You're a girl. Even if you weren't, I like to work alone so's I don't have to watch anybody's back but my own. But you have my word as an enlisted man who was raised gentle enough that I will look you up in La Mesa when it's over, and I will tell you the whole tangled tale to file as you see fit. Lord knows I've given up trying to get you to get your facts straight!"

She pouted, "My readers back East don't *want* the straight facts and can't you tell me just a little more of your tangled tale? For up until tonight I haven't been able to find out a blessed thing!"

He chuckled and said, "Welcome to the club. I've been running myself ragged in circles longer than you have."

"But you must know something?" she insisted.

He sighed and said, "I've made some educated guesses, based on what my boss calls the process of eliminating and forget I just mentioned any other lawmen. I'm only willing to go along with you this far on account you fornicate so fine, and I'd as soon have you working with me as against me."

She rolled atop him, reaching down between them as she suggested they work together some more. But taking advantage of her warm nature, Longarm insisted, "You promise you'll take the morning coach back to La Mesa and wait for me at their coaching inn there?"

She beat his meat betwixt her spread thighs as she pleaded, "I promise, I promise, and I swear I'll track you down and poison you, Custis Long, if you don't fuck me this very minute and meet me in La Mesa in less than one fucking week!"

Chapter 34

The bottomlands and higher range along the bigger and wetter Sulfur Springs Creek had been settled sooner and denser than Sulfur Draw to the northeast, so the folk down this way were closer to having themselves a fully incorporated county. So things were more organized, and Longarm saved himself a ride up the creek to the provisional county seat when he found their local Democrat party headquarters set up to run its own candidates in the next election.

To save time, and seeing neither the little sister of the Sioux nor anyone from Sulfur Draw was listening, Longarm introduced himself by name when he found himself alone in a back room with the local party boss. He explained he couldn't flash his badge or warrant because he was there unofficious. The party boss, a jovial gray-haired giant who quietly bragged on riding with the U.S. Army down Mexico way in '46 and against the same in '64 said he'd heard of Longarm and asked what they could do for him.

Longarm knew better than to swear him to secrecy. He said he'd heard-tell of irregular voter registration down this way and, seeing Texas got to vote on federal matters again, these days . . .

"Them Black Republicans would cheat their own mothers out of titty milk!" the West Texas Democrat allowed as he reached in a file drawer marked *B* for some bourbon, adding, "Feel free to double-check each and every name we've registered as our own. We don't have to cheat out here in West Texas. Texicans have long memories and we'll never forgive them damnyankee Republican carpet-baggers!"

Longarm said, "Ain't here to examine your books. I could lie and say I trusted you, but I'm a peace officer, not a bookkeeper, and your creative bookkeeping is doubtless designed to stand up to sharper eyes than mine."

The machine politician chuckled and poured heroic drinks for the two of them as he said, "You're too easy by half. What do you want to know, Longarm?"

His laconic visitor accepted a tumbler, sipped to be polite, and wheezed, "Good stuff. Couldn't have 'stilled it better my own self. I was wondering how easy it might be for either side to know in advance how newcomers to a voting district were most likely to vote in the next election."

The party boss sipped his own drink before he replied, "I'll have you know this is store-bought bourbon, all the way from Galveston, and in theory Texicans vote by secret ballot."

"That ain't what I asked." said Longarm.

The old pro grinned and said, "Now you're starting to make the game more interesting. To a certain point, the party a voter registers with is allowed to twist his arm. But the unsigned ballot he marks and stuffs in the box is tallied pure, with no way to say for certain, just who voted for whom and Texicans have been known to go crazy and vote Republican after signing up as a Democrat with all the other decent folk. It don't happen often, though."

"How do you know? How can you be sure?" Longarm insisted.

The machine boss shrugged and said, "Nothing is certain but death, taxes and the perfidity of women. But to begin with, Republicans hardly ever win in West Texas, and when and if they did, we'd know a heap of nominally registered Democrats had voted Republican on the sneak."

"Then you can usually guess the coming election results by tallying the qualified voters registered with each party?"

The Texas Democrat nodded curtly and said, "Damned A. Most decent men vote the way they register to vote. Wouldn't be much use for us to bust our balls getting out our registered voters on election day if none of 'em could be trusted to do the right thing!"

Longarm thanked him, finished the drink and offered him a three-for-a-nickel cheroot the politico allowed he might smoke later.

As the older man was seeing him out, Longarm asked in an offhand way whether he knew the Democrat and Republican bosses up to Sulfur Draw. The boss he was talking to answered easily, "Ain't no Republican boss up yonder. My opposite number there would be a gent called Klaus Brenner. Dutchman who owns a big dance hall and collects rent on most everything else. Met him at a party strategy meeting over to La Mesa. What about him?"

"What about him indeed?" Longarm answered, half to himself, as they shook and parted friendly out front.

Then Longarm and his Winchester checked out and went over to the municipal corral to ride out of town around nine A.M.

Longarm was out of sight from the municipal corral before another tall figure in faded denim dropped off the corral rail he'd been perching on with a Springield .45-70 across his thighs and a Schofield .45-Short on each hip. He stepped inside where his own buckskin gelding was waiting in a handy stall, already saddled. He'd settled up ahead of time. So he only had to lead his pony out, mount up, and mosey out of town at a walk. He knew where his target was headed. He didn't want to catch up until the both of them were way out yonder, where gunshots attracted less attention.

He knew who Longarm really was. The mastermind he rode for had known for some time. Just as he'd known who those other undercover lawmen had been. But this

266

particular lawman was proving to be a tougher nut to crack. They called him Longarm. That rep he bragged on as Wolf Kruger was nothing to the tally of gunslicks, some of them famous, he'd shot it out with in his time and won. So the killer they'd sent to stop Longarm's clock meant to take no chances as he stopped it for keeps with a long-range round of .44-70, as close as he could fire it from.

So the killer on Longarm's trail never tried to overtake him for the first couple of hours as the sun rose higher on another cloudless sunny day. An hour later, mayhaps nine miles out of Sulfur Springs, the man on Longarm's trail spurred his buckskin a tad faster and just as he'd started to worry he spied Longarm topping a far rise and dropped back to trail him slick, just fast enough to catch an occasional glimpse of that flat-crowned coffee-brown Stetson worn at a cavalry tilt.

The would-be killer told himself it was safer to wait until they were closer to Sulfur Draw than Sulfur Springs. His face was known, and he'd know what to say if anyone from Sulfur Springs saw him on range he rode regular. It never occured to him to ask himself whether he was just a tad scared as the moment of truth drew nearer. All things being equal, they figured to make it to Sulfur Draw by four. The mastermind he rode for wasn't expecting Longarm to ride in at four or any other time. It was well after noon and time to gun the son of a bitch. But how might one ride close enough to a son of a bitch that mean without getting shot, one's own self?

Gingerly topping a rise for another look-see, the would-be killer saw Longarm's chestnut a tad to the left of where she might have been. She was grazing under an empty saddle in the shade of a boxelder clump half a furlong off the pony trail Longarm had been following north.

The would-be killer wheeled south out of sight as he grinned like a mean little kid and said, "I just love a stationary target! The son of a bitch is taking a lay-down trail break in that grove of box elder! So we'd best just see he never gets up no more!"

Riding west on the far side of the gentle rise as he judged their position as regarded that shady grove, he dismounted when he knew he was well west of the same, grounded his reins, and eased upslope with the high-powered army rifle at port arms. Sneaking a peek over the grassy crest, he decided, "If I can't make him out through all them autumn leaves, he can't make me out and won't be expecting me from this direction."

Then he put his powerful but single-shot rifle down and drew both six-guns as he told it, "No offense, Mr. Springfield, but this is no time for precision! Me and these Schofields mean to pussyfoot close as we can and tear into them trees disturbing his shady repose with rapid fire!"

He would have done it, too, had things gone that way. But as he worked his way close enough for a final charge, took a deep breath and raised both gun muzzles to waist level, a laconic voice off to one side said, "Afternoon, fellow traveler. Would you like to drop them guns or would you rather die?"

The startled would-be killer spun, hairs atingle under his high-crowned ten gallon to throw down on Longarm, up on one knee behind the clump of knee-high rabbit bush he'd been waiting behind, prone. But of course Longarm fired first and, having the drop on the simp, they both found his one six-gun was more than enough.

The man who'd been sent to kill Longarm landed on his own ass in the grass, parting company with his hat and both guns as the sky above went from bright blue to dull red.

Then Longarm was hunkered over him to observe, "Aw, shit, I wanted to take you alive. Didn't I see you, or at least that buckskin, out to the Double H with me and that posse the other night?"

The man he'd hulled just under the heart blew some bloody froth and managed, "Fuck you, Longarm!"

His chosen target, having turned the tables on him, nodded and said, "I figured they were on to me once I could see that couldn't have been Herta Zimmer shooting at me near the Clover Bar, so far from home. Is there any message you'd care for me to deliver to your loved ones, old son?"

The internally bleeding as well as mighty disappointed *buscadero* didn't answer. Seeing he couldn't, Longarm closed his eyes for him and patted him down for ID.

He decided he could use the eighteen dollars and change he found on the body, but seriously doubted a library card made out to a Willy Purvis of Sulfur Draw. They didn't have a library yet in Sulfur Draw.

He reloaded and holstered his six-gun, gathered up the two Schofields to stuff under his belt, then bent to take the dead man by the heels and drag him in under the trees, explaining, "Don't want the carrion crows at your handsome face before I can find someone who might own up to recognizing it!"

Then he strode through the small grove to his chestnut, put the two Schofields and the dead man's wallet in a saddlebag, and mounted up to ride back over that other rise and gather the reins of the wary-eyed buckskin, soothing, "Sure you want to come along with us, old hoss. What in thunder would you do out here alone with that sun in the west sinking ever lower as we speak?"

Seeing he put things that way, the buckskin proved willing to be led by its reins. Trying to retrace old Willy's pussyfooting through the dry grass, Longarm found and retrieved the army rifle along the way.

Back at the grove, both ponies gave him a little trouble about the the smell of blood, or death, it was hard to tell which unsettled the species most, but he managed to get his would-be killer lashed facedown across his own centerfire dally roper. Cheerfully telling the cadaver as he did so, "You were mighty sneaky, old son, but I figured someone sweet as you might be out to get me. So I borrowed a bitty mirror from a lady's pocketbook and that's how come you never saw me turning in the saddle to look back toward you, see?"

Willy Purvis didn't answer.

Longarm rode on, resting both ponies from time to time but taking no trail breaks half so long until later that afternoon they were riding up Main Street in Sulfur Draw, occasioning quite a sensation.

As Longarm reined in near the sheriff's office, Ike Cooper came out to demand, "What are you doing with Wes Wade's pony and . . . Jesus H. Christ! Is that Willy Purvis I see you brought in as well?"

Longarm said, "Had to. He was out to kill me and, as you can see, he wasn't able to bring his fool *self* back. Who was Willy Purvis, Ike?"

The deputy gasped, "The son of a bitch who gunned Wes Wade and rode off on his horse, that very buckskin! You say he tried to gun you, too? He must have gone crazy as hell!"

Sheriff Armstrong and Duke Winters came out to join the growing crowd as Ike Cooper continued, "Wes caught the crazy son of a bitch trying to steal that buckskin and Willy shot him!"

Pink Armstrong elaborated, "Happened out back not long after you rode out, yesterday, Wolf. Wes wasn't able to offer many details but as near as we read the sign and canvassed the back alley for others who heard the same gunshots, Willy, there, was helping hisself to that buckskin out back when Wes stepped out the shithouse door to catch him in the act! Like I said, nobody witnessed the short tense results, but you could hear the shots all over town!"

Duke Winters opined, "Yon Willy must have fanned one of them army pistols like a dime-novel pistolero! Got off all five he was packing in the wheel but only hit Wes once!"

Armstrong grimaced and said, "Once was enough. The poor boy was hulled through the chest and fading fast by the time we could get to him. The druggist says the slug clipped more than one artery, tearing through him like so. But he managed to tell us who shot him and more than one witness saw Willy shortly thereafter, skulking down the back alley aboard my poor dead deputy's horse!"

"Who was this Will Purvis, then?" asked Longarm, regarding the now stiff nearby cadaver with renewed interest.

The sheriff said, "Part-time cowboy or saddle-bum, depending on the time of the year. Never figured him for dangerous, though. His last visible means of support was . . . where, Ike? You were the one who made him pay his bar tab at *Der Rinderhirt* before he bought another satin shirt on a payday."

Ike said, "He said he'd just been laid off. Made him pay anyhow. Old Otto at *Der Rinderhirt* was fixing to press charges for theft of services."

Pink Armstrong said, "That's not what I asked, Ike. Where was this son of a bitch working, the last time he was gainfully employed?"

Ike said, "Rode with the Slash VW as extra help with the fall roundup. Or so he said. Old Werner Von Waldorf druv his beef over to the Pecos to head 'em up the Goodnight trail and never bothered to come back. He was one of them Cat Licking Dutchmen who decided to quit whilst he was ahead. There's been a lot of that going around, lately."

Chapter 35

Longarm said he'd be obliged if they'd take the dead horse thief and a horse from their own remuda off his hands so's he could lead his own spent chestnut back to its own stall behind the stage stop. Pink Armstrong said he needed a signed officious deposition, even if it did seem easy-as-pie self-defense against a known criminal.

Longarm said, "I ain't ready to leave town, yet, and this old pony I rode better than twenty miles on a hot day deserves some damned consideration. Couldn't I come back later, say, after supper?"

Armstrong said, "I mean to go *home* for supper. But what say I stop by your quarters at the stage stop along the way? That'll give you time to write down what happened this afternoon and if it reads halfway sensible you can sign it and we'll shake on it."

Longarm nodded but said, "As long as you'll be by later, do you reckon you could furnish me with an alphabetical list of each and every victim of your mysterious night-riding vandals and killers out this way?"

Armstrong frowned to reply, "I could. But why should I? You keep telling us you don't want to be a lawman?"

Longarm considered the curious faces all around, shrugged and let fly, "I lied. Seeing the other side surely knows who I really am, I've no call to hide it from the rest of you. My name ain't Wolf Kruger. I am Deputy

272

U.S. Marshal Custis Long of the Denver District Court, down this way on special assignment to help your Texas Rangers out."

Someone in the crowd marveled, "Holy sweet Jesus! He's the hardass rider they call Longarm!"

Pink Armstrong swore softly and then smiled boyishly to declare, "You sure had this child fooled. But what makes you say that boy on that buckskin with his ass in the air had seen through your charade?"

Longarm said, "He had a horse to ride. He wasn't trying to steal mine. The way your reconstruction might read, he'd been told to tail me and gun at the first opportunity. When he saw me riding out of town unexpected, he needed a mount of his own, sudden, to follow me."

Someone in the crowd opined, "That's how come he tried to steal poor Deputy Wade's horse out back! That buckskin's famous for moving fast!"

Longarm said, "Whatever. I can't say why he failed to move in on me yesterday. They might have wanted him to see if he could tell what I was doing in Sulfur Springs. If so he might have seen me going in and coming out of their Western Union. I mean to check with your own telegraph office about wires whipping to and fro betwixt here and Sulfur Springs last evening. If none did, he was following standing orders to tail me, find out where I'd headed and who I'd talked to, and then gun me at his earliest convenience. The rest you know."

The sheriff said, "Hot damn! Duke, lead this buckskin and its load around to the celler door of the drugstore whilst Longarm tells us all who he means to let me charge with the murder of Wes Wade!"

As Duke gathered up the reins, Pink Armstrong explained, "Don't cut no ice who pulled the trigger when the bastard who hires the gun can be hung for the crime, right, Longarm?"

The federal lawman said, "That's about the size of it. Why don't we talk about it later, up to my hired room where it'll be less . . . public. I got to put this pony away, and then I have some other calls to make before it gets too late. Mind you bring along that list of known victims, Pink. We'll figure out what happened to some *missing* victims farther along, like the song goes."

Armstrong said he'd have it typed up on bond paper. They shook on it and parted friendly. Longarm led the spent chestnut afoot to the stage stop, led it back to the stable and told the colored stable hand he'd give him two bits to treat the poor critter right, explaining he had a whole lot of errands ahead before suppertime and couldn't see to his own mount like a gentleman.

The colored boy allowed he knew how to treat a lady right. So Longarm carried his saddlebags and Winchester inside, having left the dead man's guns with the rest of him as material evidence. The less said about the contents of that wallet the better.

Inside, he asked at the desk if they had a writing table he could take up to his hired room. The clerk said he'd send one up but seemed curious to know why. Longarm explained he had some homework to do.

So it was going on five P.M. and he was pushing his luck by the time he had his room fixed up to his liking, with the extra writing table set up so's he could work at it sitting on the bed whilst facing the door. He hung his saddlebags over the foot of the bed and stood his Winchester on its stock near the head of the same. Then he locked up, stuck that usual match steam in place, and got cracking.

He found *Onkel* Klaus in his office over the ballroom below. As he entered, the burly Dutchman said, "I heard. You're the law and you must feel so smart you could hug yourself. So what can we do for you, *Onkel* Sam?"

Longarm said, "I need some information you may be able to give me, Sir. Is it safe to say you have most everybody in these parts registered Democrat, seeing you run that as well as everything else around here?"

Onkel Klaus shook his bullet head and said, "If only. Try as I might I can't get half my stubborn Dutchmen to register as *anything*! Being so many are first- or second-generation Texicans more interested in proving their

274

claims than reading papers printed in English, few take as much interest in politics as me."

"But you surely have some machine votes to deliver, come the next elections, for court, state and federal offices?" Longarm insisted.

The local boss snapped, "Watch that guff about *machines*, Longarm! I know sassy reporters like to describe what I do here for my party by that sinister term. But every damned thing I may or may not do as the local party chairman is honest and above board and I'll be glad to give you a complete list of registered Democrats and you can shove it up your ass!"

Longarm allowed comparing such a list with the names of those run out of Sulfur Draw or worse would do him well enough.

Onkel Klaus looked startled as well as somewhat mollified as he reached down in a desk drawer, saying, "I have my typewriting clerks make plenty of carbon copies. Are you saying all this raiding and drygulching has been designed to scare off our few registered voters? I have dozens left to vote the straight ticket, come November! Don't need the votes of those who left and . . . thinking back, more than one of 'em I knew well enough to ask never registered with me to vote in any fool election!"

As he handed over the single sheet of single-spaced onionskin, Longarm observed, "That in itself could be worth something. Like everyone else before me, I've been dazzled some by red herrings and my own wild notions. But as you slice away ever more with Ockham's razor there ain't as much left to dazzle you."

As he rose, *Onkel* Klaus asked if he knew what he was talking about.

Longarm modestly replied, "Yep, and that's all that matters when you get to the bottom line."

Stuffing the list in a breast pocket, Longarm left, strode down Main Street as some were already knocking off for supper, and took a deep breath before he opened the door and strode into the ground-floor office of the *Sulfur Star*.

An older overweight gent with a drinker's nose came

out from their pressroom in shirtsleeves with a typestick in one hand to see what Longarm wanted. He introduced himself as Wilbur Slade.

Longarm gave his right name and said, "You'll never know how much I hate to bother you like this, Mr. Slade. But I need some information on local political machines."

Slade said, "There's only one. Klaus Brenner runs it. No mystery to that, in West Texas. Since Reconstruction ended in '78, you'd find a strange man under your bed before you'd find a registered Republican around here!"

Robin Slade née Jones came out from the back, smiling as if she'd never laid eyes on Longarm before. He nodded as innocently when old Wilbur introduced her as his little woman and boss printer. She asked why Longarm cared so much about the coming election. She told him, "Nobody will be running for local office here in Sulfur Draw. We've not been incorporated as a county yet. Those who might bother to vote this November can only cast a ballot in the state and federal elections this year. Are you suggesting some mastermind in Austin or back in Washington, D.C., is up to something sneaky with *Onkel* Klaus?"

Longarm truthfully replied, "I ain't certain, yet. Is it safe to say anyone aiming to vote as a Republican or Independent would hardly appear on a list of registered Democrats?"

The newspaper man and his obviously amused young wife both agreed to that. So Longarm thanked them and left, waiting until he got outside before he muttered, "Have fun, you round-heeled little sass. And don't come crying to me when someday he catches you, as they always do, sooner or later!"

He went next to see Father Paul in his rectory. The beetle-browed Jesuit had already heard as well, and mockingly asked, "Have you come to confession, my son?"

Longarm soberly replied, "Forgive me, Father, for I have sinned," since he knew some gals who went to confess every Saturday for what they'd done Friday night. As the priest offered him a seat, Longarm explained about voter registration lists. Father Paul nodded, but told him,

"I'm afraid that's nothing people confess to their priest, as shocking as voting Republican in Texas cattle country might appear to some. I just don't know whether any of my parishioners those mystery riders have killed or driven away may have voted Republican or Independent in that one pro tem provisional election we've held so far out our way. I'm ashamed to say so. But I don't take much interest in politics. I wasn't here yet when they organized this town to such an extent as you might call it organized. I haven't registered for the coming general elections. If I had, I couldn't vote for or against any of the powers that be around here, yet."

Longarm shrugged and replied, not unkindly, "Most immigrants and all too many native sons tend to ignore elections entire or vote the way a machine offering partonage tells 'em to, Father. I ain't saying that's good or bad. But it sure makes it easier for a crook or a fool to get elected in this land of opportunity!"

They shook on that, and Longarm went next to that gun shop he'd been to before. He asked the owner about that Springfield .44-70.

The man who sold or fixed firearms for a living nodded and pontificated, "Model 1873, superseding the trapdoor 1870 .50-70 single but sure shot. Fine rifle, does a man have time to reload when, not if, he misses a charging Comanche. Heaps have been sold slighty worn and cheap as dirt by the War Department. I don't stock the Springfield trap, myself. Ain't got store space for such cheap wares."

Longarm asked, "What about ammunition? Man could pick up a cheap but accurate hunting rifle lots of places. He'd still need ammunition for it, right?"

The shopkeeper said, "He would, and I sell a lot of .45-70 rounds. Like I said, it's a cheap hunting rifle that shoots far and accurate."

Longarm asked if by any chance he'd have a list of such customers. When the older man told him not to be silly, Longarm asked if the shopkeeper had ever served Willy Purvis, to his knowledge.

The older man brightened and said, "Oh, him? Heard he just got shot by the law after gunning a deputy yesterday! Sure, I've sold Purvis and other saddle-bums plenty of brass. They will shoot at bottles day after day. But that kid shot bottles and that deputy with a Schofield .45-Short. Twentyeight grains of powder, not seventy. Didn't know he owned a Springfield trap."

Longarm said, "He was likely issued one for a special chore and I thank you for telling me that, Sir."

He pressed a three-for-a-nickel cheroot on the shopkeeper, and on the walk outside he saw he didn't have time for supper before old Pink Armstrong dropped by his room on the way home for his own.

But Longarm went to that restaurant Liza worked at, anyhow. He went in, took a table in the back, and when Liza came over, smiling down at him radiantly, Longarm told her, "Ain't got time to order nothing, honey. Got to meet somebody else in a minute. Just wanted to let you know I'm back in town, but you'd best not wait out front nor light any candles in your window for me tonight."

The softly-padded but shapely waitress stiffly replied, "Oh, is she pretty, Wolf?"

He assured her, "You have my word I don't mean to meet any other gal in this town this evening," which was the simple truth. Then he told her, "My name's not Wolf Kruger. I'm a federal lawman working undercover in these parts. Or I was until the other side figured out who I was, so why not tell my pals?"

She gasped, "You're joshing me! I'm a big girl, Wolf. You don't have to make up fairy-tales if you want to go back to that old Hilda Zimmer!"

That struck him dumb. So she added, knowingly, "Of course I know you had both those Zimmer twins, all the way in from Truscott. It was the talk of the drive and lots of cowgirls like to dine here, properly dressed, of course."

He said, "Anything I done herding them cows out this way was in the line of duty. I was trying to be accepted as a harmless cowboy and not another lawman they could dry-gulch and bury somewhere sneaky out under all that grass. But what's done is done and the point is that I don't think we should be seen together anymore until I get me a better grip on this situation, see?"

She demanded, "If you're not the Wolf Kruger I've been fucking, who in hell *are* you?"

He gave his handle as Deputy U.S. Marshal Custis Long, hoping she hadn't read any of that shit reporters like old Sparky kept writing about him.

But Miss Eliza Davenport had, and it seemed to cheer her immense to be able to chortle, "Well, tan my hide if I haven't finally been fucked by somebody famous!"

Chapter 36

The sun was setting outside and Longarm's insides were growling as it got later than he'd expected whilst he sat on his bed, going over that list of registered Democrats and his own notes on that writing table from down below. Pink Armstrong had said he'd stop by on his way home to supper. It was commencing to look as if he dined late as a fashionable Mexican, and Longarm sincerely regretted turning down at least the coffee and donuts Liza had suggested.

Then, at last, there came a knock on the door of his hired room. Longarm slid his legs out from under the table, rose and drew his .44-40 from its holster hanging from the nearest bedpost before he went to open up.

When he saw it was Pink Armstrong with Ike Cooper he invited them in and moved to the head of his bed to reholster his six-gun before he sat down and swung his legs back where they'd been, saying, "That bentwood chair by the door's for you, Pink. Wasn't expecting a posse."

The sheriff waved his deputy to the chair, saying, "I've got a kink in my desk-bound leg to work out. What sort of company *were* you expecting with that double-action Colt in hand, old son?"

Longarm replied, "The late Willy Purvis was the tip of the iceberg. The son of a bitch who sent him after me is still at large, along with three others at the very least, if we assume Willy rode with the gang who raided the Double H the other night. Did you bring that list I asked for, Pink?"

As his deputy sat down, the sheriff moved forward to hand Longarm another typewritten list on thicker paper, saying, "In alphabetical order with the dates in question appended, like you asked. Can you read in this light, pard?"

Longarm said, "There's a wall lamp right behind you, Pink, could you get it before we all wind up bumping noses in the dark?"

Armstrong struck a match to raise the chimney and light the wick of the wall fixture, muttering, "Needs trimming to burn bright enough to read by. But they're your eyes. What do you expect to find on that list, Longarm? I know you're supposed to know more about motives and such than the rest of us, but I'll be whupped with snakes if I can find any common feature tying all those drygulched or run-out claim holders. Some were from *Onkel* Klaus Brenner's faction, some were with Father Paul Hauser's congregation and others, like us, were just good old boys who didn't give a shit about praying in High Dutch!"

Longarm nodded soberly and said, "I noticed. It made me wonder. I wasted time wondering more about *motives* than the nuts and bolts of who and how instead of *why*. I'd be out of a job if crooks limited themselves to what I'd call justifiable reasons. The poor scared master sneaktipped his mitt when he sent someone to ambush me down by the Clover Bar. I hadn't guessed, until then, they were *on* to me."

He glanced down at the papers atop the writing table and decided, "You're right. I'll compare 'em later in better light. It hardly matters, now, what the motive was, now that I've whittled down close to the core by the process of eliminating!"

"You told us you didn't *know* who pegged a shot at you as you were fording that still water near the Fitzgerald spread."

Longarm said, "I didn't. For a time I'm ashamed to admit I thought it could be a lady I knew. That's why you got to keep whittling down to what's possible, peeling away all the could-be fancies. I knew I'd winged him. I knew it couldn't have been me, the Gentle Geraldine or the crew and passenger of a coach coming up the road."

Ike Cooper laughed and said, "I was there and that lets me off, too. I'd have surely noticed if you'd just shot me, Longarm."

Pink Armstrong said, "Shut up and listen tight, you asshole. The man is talking about attempted murder."

Longarm nodded and said, "That's where we can eliminate more *fancy* in favor of *fact*. It's a fact I rid over to Sulfur Springs, alone, to pull a fast one on you, Pink. I fibbed when I said I was looking for a job. I had a job riding for Marshal Billy Vail and I wanted to wire him I was still on the job after dropping out of sight so long."

Armstrong grimaced impatiently and said, "I'd have done the same in your place. So you rode to Sulfur Springs and wired home. Then what?"

"Like I told you earlier this afternoon, I spotted a familiar pony in another stall as they were saddling my chestnut. I had this bitty pocketbook mirror in my hand as I had to mop my brow from time to time. So once I was sure someone on that same buckskin was following me, I set out to ask him why. I tethered my own bronc visible in a shady grove and let the sun bake the back of by denim jacket a million years as I waited for the bastard to sneak up on me. When he did, I got the drop on him and he acted like an asshole. Don't never try to throw down on a man when he's training a gun on you, from close."

Armstrong said, "I'll try not to. Tell me something I didn't know already. You shot Willy Purvis fair and brought him back on poor Wes Wade's favorite pony. Then what?"

Longarm said, "Let's not get ahead of Ockham's razor, Pink. Return with me to the middle of nowhere, with me standing over that dead son of a bitch, wondering what the two of us were doing out yonder. Try as one might, there's just no way to suspect anybody I talked to in Sulfur Springs sent a rider on a Sulfur Draw horse with a Sulfur Draw library card after me. Nobody I met up with in Sulfur Springs knew I would be headed back here to Sulfur Draw. I didn't have to lie. Nobody asked and I just never *told* 'em, see?"

Armstrong nodded and replied, "We've agreed Purvis followed you to Sulfur Springs from here. He murdered one of my deputies to steal a mount from my remuda, the son of a bitch. Of course he never had to ask you if you'd be coming back. You said yourself you spotted that stolen buckskin loitering around your own mare. He caught up with you too close to town to shoot, waited for you to head back, and made a mistake that ended his short but nasty criminal career. Is it safe to assume he forgot to tell you who he was riding for as you were shooting him dead?"

Longarm smiled up wistfully to confess, "I told you I tried to take him alive. He did manage to tell me one important thing as he lay dying. He told me *by name* to fuck myself. So that eliminated a road agent out to steal my purse or this hot-tempered lady I know in the biblical sense who's called me everything but Longarm in her time. I decided to stop pretending to be Wolf Kruger before I got back to town, seeing nobody but my *friends* in these parts seemed to be fooled. When they asked me to try to ride in undercover, I warned them too many folk down Texas way knew too much about me. The other lawmen who'd been sent in earlier had doubtless been recognized or just suspected by one mean, scared son of a bitch. There's a heap of wide-open range to bury all the men you might ever want to for miles and miles around."

"I told those rangers to be careful when they paid courtesy calls on us. So who in blue blazes have you narrowed it down to, damn it?"

Longarm said, "Educated suspicions are one thing. Evidence that can stand up in court can be another. Did you know that try as I might, over to Sulfur Springs, I couldn't find anyone who recalled a left-handed agitated Irishman named Boyle, Pink? I thought you told me he'd gone over yonder."

Armstrong shrugged and said, "We got a wire from there saying Lefty had quit. Maybe he went somewhere else from Sulfur Springs. How would I know? He quit from over twenty miles away!"

"A letter or a telegraph wire, Pink?" Longarm quietly asked.

The sheriff flustered, "Did I say wire, before? It might have been a wire, it might have been a letter. Lefty might have put a note in a bottle and cast in the sea! Are you accusing me of something, damn your smug smile?"

Longarm easily replied, "Letting you accuse yourself, as you've done before, Pink. I forget who the Frenchman was who wrote it was, but he advised good liars need good memories and I fear my memory's just way better than your own."

"Get down to it, goddamn it!" the sheriff thundered, all red in the face as he demanded, "What's the charge, your honor? I forgot if a scared deputy resigned by mail or telegraph? What does that prove?"

Longarm wearily replied, "Nothing, for certain. I've no idea where you and your boys buried Lefty Boyle when he refused to go along with a dead Navajo writing the name of his killer in the dust, in High Dutch."

From his seat near the door, Ike Cooper protested, "Just one old fucking minute, pilgrim! I was there, with Wes Wade and Lefty Boyle. Are you trying to say we just made up that shit about the Twisted Sister?"

Longarm pleasantly replied, "You had to make up *something*, once you or Wes shot him. You wouldn't have done so in front of Lefty Boyle if he hadn't gone along with a little earlier night riding. So he must have disappointed you considerable when he declared murder in cold blood was too rich for his blood. Who shot Lefty, you or Wes?"

Before Ike could answer, Pink Armstrong snapped, "Be

still and don't say or do shit until I say so, Ike. Let's hear what the man has to say."

He turned back to Longarm to sort of purr, "Who do you like best for shooting a fellow deputy, Mr. Know-It-All?"

Longarm said, "Don't know half but I reckon I know enough, Pink. Wes was likely the one who killed Pete Navajo as well as Lefty Boyle because he was in the lead, over by the Clover Bar, when I put a round in him through the tanglewood. Ike, yonder, covered for his wounded get-away by riding to meet me, helpful, on the road. He might have meant to cozy up close and kill me, too. But that coach came along. Your other riders had raided the Double H, off the other way, before you could work out another plan of execution. Ike, yonder, rode with me and Duke Winters that night, along with you and somebody mounted on that same buck in gelding from your remuda. So after Wes Wade died on you-all, you kept him on ice as Ike, there, suggested in another context whilst you considered all your options."

"Are you going to take that, Pink?" Ike protested.

Armstrong glanced at the six-gun a good arm's length from Longarm on his wrong side as he growled, "Shut up and let the man brag. Do you have any other grand notions to get off your chest, you chump?"

Longarm said, "Hell, you were there, Pink. You must have heard me tell you and *you alone* I'd be riding for Sulfur Springs the other afternoon. Who else would have issued the late Willy Purvis an army rifle and a bronc from the sheriff's remuda to follow me, find out as much as he could, and then kill me?"

He shook his head sadly to add, "I was hoping I was wrong, Pink. You can be likeable when you ain't acting crazy-mean, and I do admire a man who thinks on his feet. But you sort of overdid the dramatics when you tried to dispose of two corpses with one whopper about one member of your gang killing another member of your gang, accounting for the one corpse coming in aboard a bronc from your own remuda!"

He might have offered more, but that was when Pink Armstrong slapped leather and had his sidearm halfway clear of its holster when Longarm fired from under the table to drill him through the bladder and double him over so's the second double-action round of .32-20 busted a collar bone and drilled deeper for something more important.

As Longarm kicked the light table away and rose to throw down on Ike Cooper, the bewildered two-faced lawman whimpered, "Don't shoot. I give! I *told* them to leave you the fuck alone, Longarm!"

Doubled up in a ball at Longarm's feet, Pink Armstrong was making those *nnnnnnngh* noises a man makes in a dentist's chair whenever he's trying not to scream. Longarm doubted they'd get much more than hurt noises out of him as he went on bleeding inside.

Covering Ike Cooper, Longarm said, "There's something to be said for bitty whore-pistol rounds heard from parts uncertain. So listen tight and tell me true, Cooper. How many others are there and how many might Pink have told about this meeting? Don't lie to me, or I'll take you with me, gut-shot, if it's the last thing I do!"

Ike blubbered, "None of this bullshit was my notion, Marshal! I was roped in by bad company and had to go along after they killed Lefty Boyle for trying to back out!"

Longarm said, "Save it for the judge and, like I said, listen to me tight and shit me no bull. A bird in the hand can hang for two in the bush unless he'd like to turn state's evidence, this minute, and get us both out of here alive!"

He saw the flicker of low cunning on Cooper's face and quickly told him, "They ain't going to *try* to save you, Ike. Why should they? Pink is dying. You've been taken alive but nobody knows for certain who *they* are unless you talk, so why should they let you live?"

"What the fuck do you *want* from me?" Ike pleaded.

Longarm said, "That's better. I repeat. How many and what were they told about that gunplay they may have just heard?"

Ike said, "Pink told the others him and me were about to find you here shot dead, like all the others. So those who heard won't want to come running. Pink gave 'em all instructions to make sure they'd be seen in a public place at the time Pink and me heard gunshots, coming to deliver that list, and burst in to find that Twisted Sister or some other fiend had beaten us to you!"

Longarm said, "*Bueno*. Here's what we're fixing to do. First you rise slow to drop that gun belt fast around your boots. Then you step out of it, and I mean to cuff you with some jewelry from deep in my saddlebag. In front so's you can ride with me, despite a minor risk of slickery that I strongly advise against."

"I won't try nothing, Marshal! I'm too young to die!" sighed a cowardly sadist who'd just seen a far deadlier leader swatted like a fly.

Longarm moved to strap on the more serious shooting iron he'd just used as a decoy, saying, "Be with you in a minute with them handcuffs. Have to make sure this other cocksucker dosen't shoot me in the back as we're leaving. From here we go down to the stable. I got four fresh ponies snuffy to carry us alternate to La Mesa by tomorrow noon. So we'll have plenty of time for talking along the trail, and you did mean to do some talking along the trail, didn't you, you murderous son of a bitch?"

Chapter 37

Ike Cooper talked along the trail a heap. Longarm had long since learned suspects facing trial for murder in the first were inclined to clam up sullen or, hoping for friends in court, sing like birds.

So though he didn't claim a drop of Dutch blood, Ike Cooper trilled along the trail like one of those famous Harz Mountain canaries and it took them over eighteen hours to get to La Mesa!

The way more than one road was said to lead to Rome, the wagon ruts and drainage of Sulfur Draw and the bigger Sulfur Creek ran together to continue as one, southeast, long before they reached the seat of Dawson County. Long before *that* they were weary and saddle sore. None of the fresh ponies Longarm had bought from Wendy Delgado at the nearby livery were feeling all that frisky either, even though, as Longarm had promised the coldly polite she-male wrangler, he and his prisoner had switched from saddle to bareback once an hour as they rode mostly though the cool of an autumn night.

Longarm had never directly promised to appear in any court as Ike's character witness. The fool faced charges of mayhem and murder under the jurisdiction of the state of Texas. So once he'd turned his trail-worn half-unconscious prisoner over to the ranger station in La Mesa with a signed deposition, Texas could use as Texas saw fit. Longarm took his lathered half-dead ponies to a vet, not trusting your run-of-the-mill stable hand, and then dragged his trail-worn half-unconscious self to bed, alone, above the stage terminal in the larger cow town.

He was asleep before his head had sunk all the way into the pillow around noon, not worrying about dinner. They'd consumed canned beans and tomato preserves along the long, weary trail and had breakfast with some friendly Mex nesters at dawn. So he never wanted to eat, or even wake up again. But the little sister to the Sioux and guardian of the Pawnee had been out window shopping as he'd checked in, and she'd taken some time to ask once again at the desk whether they'd seen the famous Longarm she meant to interview for her readers. So Longarm got to sleep better than four hours before he awoke with a start to find his cock in someone's mouth.

When she saw she had his undivided interest, the dishwater blond confessed, "I got the upstairs maid to let me use her passkey. She's a woman. So she understands. We were both so worried about you and what took you so long, darling?"

He said, "Miles and miles of miles and miles, stopping now and then to make sure we hadn't been followed. A deal is a deal, and I told you I'd join you here if you'd get out of my way a spell. So here I am, and before I tell you and your readers the story, could I get on top and discharge this weapon, first?"

She must have wanted the story bad. She offered to suck him off all the way. But Longarm was considerate, and she was tight as a drum down yonder. So he insisted on finishing his own way, and by that time, she didn't seem to care, for the moment, what he'd been up to since last they'd been in such friendly position.

Sparky waited until they were in the more conversational dog-style position before she smiled smugly over a bare shoulder to ask if she'd been right about Billy the Kid playing the part of that Twisted Sister back in Sulfur Springs.

As he assumed the position above and behind her by

broad daylight her pale, wasp-waisted and bare-assed figure reminded him of a fine violin carved from ivory.

As he played it more like a slide trombone than a fiddle, Longarm told her, "We both made the mistake of assuming history repeats in detail. I don't know where the Kid and those other Lincoln County guns might be, this afternoon. None of them were anywhere near the troubles along Sulfur Draw."

She arched her spine to thrust her rump up to him as she pondered, "Sulfur *Draw*, Custis? I thought they called the place Sulfur *Springs*!"

He got a better grip on her hip bones to take advantage of the new angle she'd offered as he replied, "You were in the wrong place. I was sent to the right place but had things all wrong. For, like you, I was led astray by memories of that other range war not too long ago or far away. But this time it wasn't a case of rival cliques of new settlers squabbling over local trade and government beef contracts. I sure took too long making sure, but them two breeds of Dutch folk just felt *cool* to one another. They didn't socialize or marry one another's sisters. But left to their druthers, they weren't engaged in armed conflict. No big business or stockman was pulling puppet strings in hopes of grabbing land or water nobody for miles had proven title to. There was more open range north and south than twice as many herds really needed. Try as I might, I couldn't get anybody to come out ahead by the murder, ruination or withdrawal of anybody I suspected and, for a spell, I suspected everybody but me, and I wasn't so sure of myself!

She lowered her dishwater blond head to the mattress to sort of suck on sheeting as she murmured, "Oh, you're hitting bottom at this angle and I *love* it! Who was the puppet master if it wasn't someone like Uncle John Chisum west of the Pecos or Pete Maxwell just up the Goodnight-Loving trail, darling?"

He said, "Pink Armstrong, playing the part of that other Sheriff Henry Plummer, up Montana way in '63."

He tried to hold back as he sort of groaned, "Like I

said, you got to be careful about expecting the historic details to mesh like clockwork. After old Hank Plummer got hisself elected during the Montana gold rush, his way-bigger gang, called the Innocents in mockery, took advantage of the voter's trust to rob the stage lines of gold shipments with monotonous regularity. Do you want to turn over and kiss me whilst I come in you, Miss Sparky?"

She did, and they lost interest in Sulfur Draw for a spell. But as they shared a smoke against the headboard Longarm explained to her, "We look for means, motive and opportunity. It didn't take that Montana vigilante committee as long to see Sheriff Henry Plummer had the means, motive and opportunity to mark those coaches bearing gold with chalk marks for his Innocents to read, out on open range. Us less dishonest lawmen think about Sheriff Henry Plummer often. But whilst the informally elected Pink Armstrong had the means and opportunity the minute you studied on it, I wasted time searching for a *motive* that might tempt somebody as logical as me."

She snuggled closer and draped a slim leg over his muscular thigh to ask, "You mean this crooked sheriff and his deputies were out to stir up trouble between those Dutch factions just to be mean?"

He said, "Pink Armstrong didn't care about either side. He wasn't out to rob the bank or stage line. He didn't want anybody's stock. He did his sworn duty as the local sheriff, most of the time. All he felt desperate about was *keeping* the best job he'd ever had. In spite of his fibs, he was a buck-ass private during the war and a drover who never learned to rope 'til he got old and gruff enough to pass for a man of experience, according to his sidekick, Ike Cooper, speaking of big talkers. Armstrong was elected with no opposition in that ad hoc election before many others had filed claims along Sulfur Draw. He knew that once they had an incorporated county, they'd be holding regular elections for county offices. That was his hidden motive. I had to dig some for it, once I'd narrowed down the means and opportunity to nobody else but him and his riders, deputized or informal."

Sparky said, "I can see how a sheriff running loose without any adult supervision could literally get away with murder, dear, but why did he need to slaughter all those men and beasts?"

Longarm said, "He didn't. He thought he did. Most of the time he was a popular lawman, doing his duty with the approval of most of the folk of the various factions."

She reached down to fondle him some more as she demurely asked what all the fuss had been about, in that case.

Longarm said, "He was too scared to think straight. He was as fond of surprises as Miss Muffet was fond of spiders. He knew most every voter registered with the Brenner machine was likely to vote for him. He knew heaps of immigrants that hadn't registered weren't likely to vote for him, or *against* him, which he worried more about. He worried more than he needed to about old or new Texans of any faction who'd made him mighty proddy by registering as *Independents*. He thought of them as loose cannons on his ship of state and, like I said, old Pink just couldn't stand surprises!"

She began to stroke him, gently but firmly, as she absently asked if there'd been all that many loose cannons an insecure politcal hack had to worry about. Reporters used words like *insecure*.

Longarm grimaced and said, "That was the word I was groping for. Comparing lists, I saw none of the folk they'd killed or run off had registered with *Onkel* Klaus to vote the straight party ticket. Two sisters in thick with *Onkel* Klaus threw me off stride at first. But then I recalled they were both women, however contrary, who wouldn't have been *allowed* to register with *any* party in Texas. They were raided and one was murdered to cover the killing of their foreman, Elroy Brewster Junior, according to Ike Cooper.

"I never would have figured that out, myself. I thought *I'd* run old Junior out of town. We're all suckers for flattery. Junior never announced he was at feud with me. He had more important questions on his mind. He'd done some thinking about the troubles Armstrong and his confederates had stirred up. He made the mistake of taking his thoughts to the man he knew as the local law. They killed him, hid his body and conned us all into thinking I'd run him out of town.

"Riding in with Ike Cooper, I wrote down where he said *heaps* of bodies are buried. They vanished most men that they murdered, making it appear folk were pulling out to avoid the cross fire of a senseless range war. The pattern was so tough to make out because the worried provisional sheriff *had* the votes to win fair and square, had he been fair and square by nature. But like many a rider of the owlhoot trail before him, Pink Armstrong wasn't willing to take his chances, playing by the rules. He wanted to make sure. He aimed to rid Sulfur Draw of most all its independent voters and, of course, once he got started, he had to rid himself of outside lawman attracted by the smell of death. It was like that Scotch poet wrote about the tangled webs we weave once we get to lying. Ike tells me Lefty Boyle wasn't the only gang member they had to vanish as the game got too rough for any natural thief with common sense.

"So there you have it. In the end it was just a case of a desperate bullfrog in a little puddle, suffering delusions of intelligence. But the prisons of this great land of ours would be less crowded if nobody committed stupid crimes."

Sparky didn't answer. She couldn't talk when her mouth was full. So later on, they got up to have supper, went to bed early that night and even managed to catch some sleep before the next sunrise.

When that happened Longarm had a hell of a time persuading her she couldn't tag along with him and the ranger company he was leading back to Sulfur Draw to round up Pink Armstrong's gang with the aid of a list compiled from Ike's signed confession.

He left the little sister to the Sioux and guardian of the Pawnee a transcript of the same in hopes, this time, she'd get the damned story right, or at least possible.

It took Longarm and his ranger pals longer, getting back to Sulfur Draw, than the time he'd made riding for his life with a prisoner. Nobody was about to try and ambush a dozen serious lawmen on the prod. Some of the names on Ike's list had lit out for Apacheria, the border, or other safer parts before Longarm and his fellow lawmen swept up the draw and fanned out. Duke Winters was the only one killed in a running gunfight Longarm didn't take part in. The ones he threw down in *Der Rinderhirt* gave up without a fight, insisting they'd only been taking orders from a virtual Fagan who'd led young cowboys astray.

The roundup took less than forty-eight hours, and Liza Davenport allowed it was cruel and unusual for him to accomplish so much in so little time.

He sort of regretted the lack of resistance as well. For it sure beat all how two women could be so different in bed without either of them being ugly.

The more maturely padded waitress was less interested than the sort of boney newpaper gal in the motives of the late Pink Armstrong. But she allowed she was sure proud of Longarm for killing the mean thing. So he let her keep a lock of his hair and asked for one of her own before he had to ride off with the rangers and all those prisoners.

Back in La Mesa, the state of Texas tried to hold Longarm as a material witness for the trials, with Ike facing his own judge and jury on lesser charges after copping a plea in exchange for turning state's evidence against all his pals.

But by then, Sparky had left town and so Longarm and Western Union got busy until the right strings were pulled in Austin from Denver, and Texas decided they could hang the ones who'd taken part in more than malicious mischief on the strength of Longarm's signed deposition and the sworn testimony of Ike Cooper.

So in no time at all, except to Billy Vail, Longarm was back up to Denver, seated in the back office feeding tobacco ash to the rug mites as old Billy scanned his final report, tossed it aside atop his cluttered desk and grumbled, "I can't say as you did anything *wrong,* down yonder, but you sure took forever getting things *done*! I sent you to see if you could sort of blend in, not to engage in that long tedious cattle drive with all them contrary cowgirls!"

Longarm shrugged and said, "I never asked to go. I wired as soon as it seemed safe to risk it. I got in and got out of the game as best and as fast as I could, boss."

Vail shot him a thoughtful look and slyly suggested, "I'll just bet you did. I'll just bet you took time to lay every single woman in or about Sulfur Draw!"

Longarm innocently replied, "Not *every* one, boss," and this was the simple truth. For Robin Slade née Jones hadn't been single and he'd never even kissed old Rosalinda!

**Explore the exciting Old West with one
of the men who made it wild!**